Praise for th

VIRGIN

"An amazing read… hot and explicit."

—*Night Owl Reviews*

"This one is all about the heat."

—*Publishers Weekly*

"*Virgin* is proof that with each Cat Star Chronicles book they get better. I loved *Virgin*, and Dax—oh, what a great hero he was."

—*Sizzling Hot Reads*

"Brooks explores a new avenue with her version of the ultimate male, and readers will be happily swept along for the ride!"

—*Debbie's Book Bag*

"Interesting, full of humor and love… Almost too hot to hold."

—*BookLoons*

"*Virgin* is high caliber entertainment from beginning to end—it hit all my happy buttons and I couldn't put it down."

—*Whipped Cream Erotic Reviews*

HERO

STUD

"Another stellar book in this phenomenal series that just gets better and better. Awe inspiring… It's sexy space travel at its finest."
—*Night Owl Romance*

"A steamy, action-filled ride. Ms. Brooks's world-building is impressive as well as creative."
—*Anna's Book Blog*

"Cat Star Chronicles has become one of my favorite futuristic series… There's plenty of kick-butt action as well as laugh-out-loud moments."
—*Romance Junkies*

OUTCAST

"Cheryl Brooks is at the top of her game with this excellent entry that will have her fans purring for more."
—*Genre-Go-Round Reviews*

"Ms. Brooks has a way of carrying the reader off into the stars where they discover worlds with amazing creatures and unique, exciting landscapes."
—*The Romance Studio*

ROGUE

WARRIOR

SLAVE

"Cheryl Brooks brought the scents and smells of a far off galaxy to life… If you are seeking something different, where your imagination can soar, then check out *Slave*."

—*Night Owl Romance*

"A hugely remarkable first foray into the written word, *Slave* will enthrall and entice."

—*Romance Junkies*

"If you're looking for a different sort of paranormal romance with plenty of heat, you may want to pick this one up and check it out further. It was an intriguing read… you will fall quickly in love with Cat and even be sorry to see the end of their story."

—*Bella Online*

"If you like a rollicking good time, pick this up and prepare yourself for a great ride."

—*Fresh Fiction*

**Other books in
The Cat Star Chronicles series:**

THE CAT STAR CHRONICLES

STUD

CHERYL BROOKS

sourcebooks
casablanca

Published by Sourcebooks Casablanca, an imprint of Sourcebooks, Inc.
P.O. Box 4410, Naperville, Illinois 60567-4410
(630) 961-3900
FAX: (630) 961-2168
www.sourcebooks.com

Printed and bound in the United States of America
VP 10 9 8 7 6 5 4 3 2 1

*For my son Sam who, in spite of the naysayers
who maintained that because of his
language-based learning disability and autism
he would never drive a car or graduate high school,
somehow managed to do just that.
Way to go, Sam!*

Chapter 1

There was only one thing he was good at…

—⁓—

TARQ SMELLED HER BEFORE HE EVER LAID EYES ON her—a glorious, delectable aroma that curled through his head and shot straight into his bloodstream. Closing his eyes, he inhaled deeply as the effect of her fragrance hit his cock like a pulse blast, obliterating his every thought with the instantaneous ecstasy of an erection so hard it made his head swim.

He glanced away from his menu, taking in the shape of her legs out of the corner of his eye—what he could see of them, that is. Her baggy trousers and apron concealed everything about her legs except the fact that she had two of them.

"Hi, my name is Lucy, and I'll be your server," she said. "Do you already know what you'd like, or do you need more time?"

Tarq smiled to himself as he shook his head. No, he didn't need more time. He knew exactly what he wanted. "You," he replied. "I'd like a full order of *you*."

"I-I beg your pardon?" she stammered.

He could hear the words catch in her throat and hoped he'd just done the same thing to her that she'd done to him. She was human—he could tell that much from her voice—but a human female who didn't mask her natural scent with heavy perfumes was rare. Tarq could never understand why they did that, but then, humans weren't the dedicated scent breeders that Zetithians were. It didn't matter what a woman looked like; if she didn't smell right, his cock was going nowhere.

This woman, however, wasn't hiding her scent and it assailed him full force. His mouth filled with saliva at the thought of tasting her—to the point that Tarq had to swallow before he could speak. With one more deep, satisfying breath, he looked up at her.

No, she wasn't beautiful, but the way she stared down at him, round-eyed and speechless, was enough to make him want to purr. She was young, but not too young to mate with a man of his age. Her dark hair was pulled back from her face, though a few soft tendrils had escaped near her temples, accentuating fair skin and round cheeks that needed no artificial enhancements to put a rosy blush on them—though his words might have been responsible.

The expression in her deep brown eyes intrigued him. It was as if she wasn't sure if she'd heard him correctly and was somewhere between laughter and astonishment. Tarq drank in her appearance just as he had done with her scent. Her nose was dusted with freckles, her dark eyelashes curled enticingly, and, as he watched, her generous mouth finally smiled.

Actually, it was more of a grin. Then, all at once, her face went blank and she recoiled slightly. Her eyes swept from his chest to the roots of his hair, with a darted glance at his features. He knew what she was seeing—blue eyes with catlike pupils, ears that curved to a pointed tip, eyebrows that slanted upward toward his temples, and blond hair that hung in spiral curls to his waist. She wasn't going to say it out loud, but the shock of recognition was clear; she knew *precisely* who he was and why he was there.

A nervous giggle escaped her. "Do you want to hear today's specials?"

Tarq shook his head and smiled, drawing her attention to his fangs as he slowly licked his lips. "What would you recommend?"

Swallowing hard, she blurted out, "The fish."

Nodding, Tarq exhaled with a loud purr. "Then I'll have the fish." Shifting his weight, he leaned back, shaking the hair back from his face. His dick was starting to hurt and his balls were tingling like crazy. It had been three days since he'd had a woman. One more whiff of her and he'd probably lose all control.

She tapped his order into her notepad. Without looking up, she went on, "Baked, broiled, or grilled?"

"How do *you* like it, Lucy?" Tarq put as much seductive emphasis into those words as he possibly could—a question he'd asked countless women, but in a far different situation.

Still not taking her eyes off the pad, she said, "Um… grilled."

"Then I'll have it grilled." Tarq let his own eyes roam over her round hips, ample breasts, and capable hands. She looked every bit as luscious as she smelled. A woman like that had to be mated already. Then he remembered the human custom of wearing rings on their left hand. He could see both of her hands clearly; there were no rings on either of them, but they were shaking.

"You get two sides with that." There was a tremor in

her voice; Tarq knew he was making her nervous, which was the very last thing he wanted to do. He wanted her relaxed and receptive.

"Why don't you choose for me?" he suggested. "I don't recognize any of them."

"How about the Greek salad and eggplant with tomatoes and kalamata olives?"

"That sounds good."

"And to drink?"

Tarq couldn't say what he *really* wanted to drink; there were some things you didn't say to a woman you'd only met a few moments before—unless she was a client, of course. "Water."

"Anything else?"

Tarq had to bite his lip to keep from saying what was on the tip of his tongue, opting to reply with a shake of his head.

"I'll be right back with your drink."

Tarq smiled as he watched her go, her soft moccasins making no sound as she walked away. No wonder she had been able to sneak up on him like that. Tarq had excellent hearing—though his sense of smell was better—and there was nothing wrong with his eyesight, either. He'd lied when he said he didn't recognize the side dishes; the truth was he couldn't read the menu.

Not very well, anyway. If he sat and stared at it long enough, a few words would make sense eventually, but he couldn't just glance at a word and know what it meant—no matter what language it was written in. He had to figure it out every time, or use his pocket scanner. The device was useful and could translate almost any language, but, viewing its use as a sign of weakness, he only used it as a last resort. His memory was excellent when it came to remembering other things—images, faces, locations—just not printed words.

The navigation system on his speeder kept him from getting lost on the planets he visited; without that, he could never have left Rhylos. Dax had been a big help; not only did he shuttle Tarq from planet to planet on his starship, the *Valorcry*, but his navigator, Waroun, set up the speeder to tell him everything he needed to know. It was good to have smart friends; otherwise, Tarq wouldn't have been able to go anywhere—at least not by himself.

Places like this, he thought, glancing about the room. Like the rest of the town of Reltan, the decor of the café was more rustic than elegant. Patrons were served at tables made of rough-hewn wood, and the food arrived on handmade ceramic plates. Paintings of fishing boats from a bygone era hung on stuccoed walls above a floor of cobbled stone. According to the video history he'd watched while en route to Talus Five, this region had been settled by Terran immigrants of primarily Mediterranean descent who wanted to return to a simpler lifestyle than that found on present-day Earth. The style of architecture was based on old-world fishing villages, and though the buildings weren't without modern conveniences, the ambiance was decidedly historic.

Fortunately, they hadn't taken it a step further and revived an ancient language. The Standard Tongue—or Stantongue as it was often called—had been difficult enough for Tarq to learn. He would never have been able to communicate with people who spoke anything else, and Zetithian was, for all practical purposes, a dead language.

Waroun's information had also told him that the food at this café was quite good, which was something his nose confirmed. Though they served a variety of foods from Earth's North American and European regions, the emphasis was on Greek and Italian. Now that Lucy wasn't nearby, other aromas drifted back into his awareness and he picked up the pungent scent of garlic in the air, along with the essence of olive oil and herbs like fennel, oregano, basil, and sage… smells as clear to him as written words were to everyone else.

He was studying the head of a great beast mounted high up on the wall when Lucy returned with a tray. "What *is* that?" he asked, pointing a finger.

"It's a vrelnot," she replied as she set his salad in front of him. "At least that's what everyone around here calls them. They live in the Eradic Mountains. Very dangerous."

Nothing by that name was on his planned route, fortunately. Waroun obviously didn't know everything about every planet; this was one thing he hadn't mentioned. "Have you ever seen a live one?"

Lucy shook her head as she set out a small loaf of freshly baked bread on a cutting board. "Only sport hunters ever go there, and sometimes they don't come back." Placing a small dish of balsamic vinegar mixed with herbed olive oil beside his plate, she topped it with freshly ground pepper. "It's the one place everyone else learned to avoid when this region was settled."

Tarq nodded. "Stay out of the mountains."

"Right."

Despite the salad sitting right under his nose with its medley of aromas and the steam rising from the bread, he could still find the essence of Lucy tucked in along with the others. His penis, which had softened slightly while she was gone, sprang back to attention with that first whiff. Tarq was trying to figure out how to keep her there, short of pulling her onto his lap, when an irate male called out, "Lucy! Quit yakking and get your ass over here. The next order is up."

Tarq was looking right at her face, ignoring the food despite his growling stomach, and saw the spasm of embarrassment cross her features, followed closely by one of irritation. "Is that your mate?"

"No," she replied. "He's my father. I don't have a 'mate' and probably never will." Lucy set his glass of water on the table, knocking over the saltshaker in her haste, but righted it in an instant and was gone before Tarq could draw another breath. He watched as she collected the steaming plates from the kitchen and delivered them to another table, smiling at the customers as though nothing had happened.

Lucy was obviously used to being yelled at, but Tarq thought it was horrible. He didn't understand why she put up with it, nor could he imagine a father treating his daughter that way. *He* certainly never would, though he'd never actually met any of his daughters—or his sons, for that matter. At last count, he had over five hundred offspring, and though very few were female, he sincerely hoped that none of their surrogate fathers were as nasty as Lucy's, though he had no way of knowing for sure. Some things were best left unknown, but the not knowing bothered him at times. Where were they? Were they growing up strong and happy? He could get reports through the registry, but there was nothing quite like firsthand knowledge. He'd never been present at their births, only their conceptions.

Her father's outburst was completely forgotten as Loucinda Force cornered Jublansk by the stasis unit. "Oh, God," she exclaimed. "Did you see who that *is* sitting out there? It's *him*!"

"What do you mean, *him*?" Jublansk demanded as she pulled out a bag of onions. Shutting the door with her broad hip, she carried the onions over to the processor and dumped them in.

"It's the guy in the commercial," Lucy said, raising her voice enough to be heard over the noise from the processor. There were quieter models available, but Lucy's father considered it an unnecessary upgrade. "The Zetithian guy. You know, the one who says he'll give you joy unlike any you have ever known?"

"Girl, are you shittin' me?" Jublansk's colorful robes swirled as she spun around, nearly hitting Lucy in the head with her tusk. "It can't be."

"Why not? He's supposed to be around here for the next few weeks, and he's got to eat, doesn't he?"

"Well, yes, but why here?"

"Why not here?" Lucy shot back. "My father may be an asshole, but he can cook."

"But are you sure it's him?"

"Sure? Of course I'm sure. How could anyone possibly forget him?"

Lucy remembered the precise moment she'd first seen him. Passing through where her younger sister, Reba, had been lounging as she watched television, Lucy had spotted his face filling the screen and had been instantly mesmerized. Blond, blue-eyed, and very handsome—though definitely not human—his hair fell to his waist in thick, shining curls, and though his fang-like canines drew the eye, it was the seductive curl of his full lips and the purring note in his voice that was so arresting. A straight nose and strong square jaw spoke clearly of a man unwise to cross, but the twinkle in his feline eyes promised untold delights, pleasures, and secrets the likes of which Lucy had never even allowed herself to dream.

He had introduced himself as Tarquinian Zulveidinoe and reported that he would be in the Har-al-kaq region of Talus Five over the next several weeks.

"The planet Zetith was destroyed in the year twenty-nine eighty-four, and our species is nearly extinct, therefore it is up to those of us who are left to continue our race as best we can. We are genetically compatible with many species but seem to cross best with humans of Terran origin. Our children are nearly always born in litters of three, and our genes are dominant. Unfortunately, our females are less receptive to males of other species, and since I tend to sire male children, I am making myself available to any ladies wishing to conceive and bear my young. There is no charge for my services, but all offspring must be registered with the Zetithian Birth Registry." A soft smile played across his sensuous lips. "Call me, and I will give you joy unlike any you have ever known."

His name and call number were displayed at the bottom of the screen as the list of compatible species scrolled by. Lucy had glanced at it briefly, knowing she would be able to recall any of it effortlessly at any time. His face, however, was burned into her memory like a brand.

No, she couldn't forget him. Ever.

"Humph," Jublansk snorted. "You thinkin' of callin' him?"

"Well, no, but—"

"Your father would hang you up to dry if you went anywhere near that beast."

Lucy bit back a laugh. "You're calling *him* a beast?" Her father had more "beastly" qualifications than anyone she could think of. This "Tarquinian" was more like a house cat than a beast—he purred like one, anyway.

"You know what I mean," Jublansk said with a meaningful look. She picked up the bowl of freshly chopped onions and headed toward the grill.

Lucy felt her eyes stinging with tears but wasn't entirely sure the onions were to blame. "Yeah, I know."

Lucy knew her father needed her help, though he never put it that way. Getting involved with a man might mean she would leave home, and her father had done his best to discourage that—though Lucy wasn't sure just who he'd had to discourage. With plenty of other—and far more accessible—girls from which to choose, the boys she'd known in school hadn't considered her worth the trouble of dealing with her notoriously ill-tempered parent. As a result, at the age of twenty-nine, Lucy was as chaste as she had been on the day of her birth.

It rankled with her, however. She was no less attractive than many of her schoolmates, but, thanks to her father, the boys had given her a wide berth, despite the fact that she could have at least helped to improve their grades. None of that mattered, though; even if a boy had asked her out, her father would have seen to it that she didn't have the time to spare.

Natasha, one of Lucy's best friends, had married and moved to Yalka, a town that lay to the north of the Malturn wilderness, and had repeatedly urged Lucy to leave her home and stay with her until she found a job. Thus far, Lucy had seen no reason to do so. It had been drummed into her head that she was made for work, not romance, for so long that she didn't believe her life would be measurably improved by the change. She could always find work but no one to love, so why bother? Though her present situation wasn't paradise, at least it was familiar.

So what was it about the Zetithian that made her suddenly want to break the chains and habits of a lifetime? Was he like the Mordrials who could read minds and somehow control the elements? She'd never heard that Zetithians possessed magical powers beyond the occasional vision of the future, so why was he so compelling?

Lucy couldn't begin to imagine her father's reaction if she were to give birth to triplets who, if the rumors were to be believed, would come out looking more like pureblood Zetithians than half-breed humans. There would be no hiding their parentage from anyone. Aside from that, everyone would know she had been desperate enough to call him. Better to remain a spinster than to admit that she'd had to hire a man to be her lover. The fact that he didn't charge for his services wouldn't matter.

Even if she left her hometown of Reltan and took Natasha up on her offer, the stigma would remain—or would it? She didn't know anyone in Yalka besides her friend; if she kept a low profile until after they were born, she could say the children were adopted, or belonged to her sister who had died giving birth to them. No one had to know the truth…

Her father's voice snatched Lucy from her reverie. Would he ever stop hollering at her and just punch the order onto her notepad? Restaurants everywhere used that system; why did he have to be so old-fashioned? It probably made him feel more in control to simply yell "Order up, Lucy!" than to tap a screen, but *still*…

Lucy collected the Zetithian's order and carried it out to him. If anything, he appeared even more irresistible than he had before. Was it because he was Zetithian? Did they all have that effect on women, or was he the only one who could make her feel like that? He was just sitting there, picking at the remains of his salad with that curtain of blond hair hiding half of his face, and he still looked like her wildest dreams come to life. *It doesn't matter*, she told herself. *I'll never go through with it. By the time I'd get the nerve, I'd have forgotten his call number was 322-13738-477783-4. Why am I even thinking about it?*

She felt a blush rising to her cheeks that intensified with each step she took in his direction. Sighing deeply, Lucy was beginning to wish she'd never even heard of Tarquinian Zulveidinoe—ridiculous name, anyway—until he smiled at her.

He could be the answer to every dream she'd ever had. Children of her own. Independence. The only missing ingredient was love, something that might elude her for the rest of her life whether she took this chance or not. Oh, yes. If she didn't work up the nerve to ask him now, she would most *definitely* call him.

Chapter 2

TARQ STILL HADN'T FIGURED OUT WHAT HER SCENT was doing to him when he realized that just the sight of her had him salivating—and it had nothing to do with the plate she was carrying.

"That was the best bread I've ever tasted, and the salad was very good too," he said, hoping to get her talking again. Her father couldn't fuss if he was complimenting the food.

"Jublansk makes the bread—and the salad dressing," Lucy said as she replaced his empty salad bowl with the plate of fish and eggplant. "It makes my father so mad because he can't figure out what's in it and she won't tell him." With a giggle, she added, "But I've watched her, so I know."

"And you won't tell him either?"

Lucy smiled and shook her head. "We all have to have our little secrets."

Tarq wanted her secret to be the fact that she'd met him in some secluded spot, then made mad, passionate love with him until his dick gave out, but, of course, he didn't say that. It was odd having to watch what he said to a woman. In all the time he'd spent working in the brothel he and his friends shared, he'd never been with a lady who was the least bit shy. Usually they were all over him, begging him to do all sorts of inventive and erotic things—some that he hadn't particularly enjoyed.

But Lucy was different. She'd said she didn't have a mate, but whether she was innocent or experienced, the scent of her desire was so strong it was screaming at him. Tarq took a deep breath and tried again. "Would you like to have one more?"

"What? You mean another secret?" She seemed puzzled by this. Perhaps he was being too subtle. Then another blush crept up her neck and blossomed in her cheeks. "The salad dressing recipe isn't the only one I've got."

Tarq didn't know what to say next. This was getting too hard. Then he remembered his cards. He could barely read them himself, but he knew what they said. Lucy was obviously intelligent. She could read. Reaching into his pack, he pulled out one of his business cards and tucked it into the front of her apron. "I don't give those to just anyone," he said. He'd never had to ask this before, either—at least not in person. "Please. Call me."

"And you will give me joy unlike any I have ever known?" Her slow smile warmed his heart.

"So, you *do* know who I am."

"You're kinda hard to miss," she said dryly. "We don't get many guys like you in here."

"No, I don't suppose you do." Tarq waited for her to say something else, but she never did. "Would you at least think about it? I don't normally ask, but—"

Without missing a beat, but in a completely different tone of voice, she pointed to a small jar and said, "You've got aioli sauce there for the fish. Would you like anything else?"

Tarq ran a hand through his hair and shook his head, not bothering to look up. "No, nothing else. Thank you."

He glanced up as she walked away, catching her father scowling at her from behind the counter. She must've seen him too, which would explain her sudden change of mood. Tarq felt his own anger flare, along with a sudden urge to throw the plate across the room. But he knew that wouldn't do Lucy any good, so he just ate it.

It wasn't bad. Not as tasty as what he'd had on Rhylos, but then, few things were. He sometimes wondered if his decision to leave that world had been a good one. He'd been to a lot of different planets—some, like this one, had breathtaking scenery—but people, or beings or whatever they called themselves, were pretty much the same throughout the galaxy. There were good and bad wherever you went, and love was as elusive as ever.

When Lucy stopped by his table again to refill his glass, Tarq took advantage of the opportunity to try again.

"Jublansk must be Twilanan."

She nodded. "Your point?"

"Powdered *lycaque* root," he said. "The secret salad dressing ingredient. It's the sort of thing a Twilanan would add—that and the fact that Twilanans are among the best bakers in the galaxy."

"Yes, but how did you—?"

Tarq smiled ruefully. "My one other talent: excellent taste buds."

"Don't tell my father."

"I wouldn't dream of it." Tarq took a deep breath. It was now or never.

He opened his mouth to speak, but Lucy beat him to the punch. "Busy tonight?"

Relief, hope, and just plain lust swept over him like a wave. "Not unless you want me to be."

"I do. And not just for the fun and games. I want to have your babies. Okay?"

His reply was barely a sigh. "Oh, yeah."

"We close at nine. Follow me home, but don't let anyone see you. I live with my parents and sister, so I'll have to let you in through my window. This is the kind of thing I should have done a long time ago. Not sure why I didn't." She laid the bill on the table. "You can pay me whenever you're ready."

Tarq grinned. "What? No dessert?"

"I was *trying* to get you out of here before my father says anything else."

"Don't worry, I can take it," he said. "Now, about that dessert. What would you recommend?"

Rolling her eyes, she said, "Chocolate pie. That's *my* one other talent."

"Your 'other' talent? What was the first one?"

"Patience," she replied. "Limitless patience."

Lucy wasn't kidding. She'd wanted children her entire life, and though Tarq's advertisement might have renewed her interest, the seed had been sown long ago, and it now seemed that her patience was about to pay off. So what if he was only passing through? He was still a cut above any of the men in Reltan, and perhaps the entire planet of Talus Five. Granted, most were at least human, but that didn't matter to Lucy. Humans and Zetithians were genetically compatible, so there was nothing stopping her.

Except her father. Why he had gotten it in his head to keep her from ever marrying—or even dating—was a mystery. Lucy liked to think it was simply a control issue, but though there might have been more to it than that, the actual reason eluded her. And heaven forbid she should ever ask because it simply wouldn't be worth all the drama. She'd never hear the end of it.

If there had ever been a man she fell for like a ton of bricks, it might have been different, but she never had and so had allowed things to continue on as they were. Not that her life had ever been perfectly smooth, but she was beginning to realize that some things were worth a little turbulence. If her father didn't like the idea of her having Zetithian triplets, he would just have to get over it. Murder was, after all, illegal, and abortions simply weren't done on Talus. He might try to pressure her into putting the children up for adoption, but Lucy could be very determined when it suited her, and this was something she felt very strongly about. Even if he kicked her out of the house, she suspected that this would be more of a blessing than a curse because then she might actually be able to have a home of her own.

The sheer bliss of that possibility swept over Lucy the same way Tarq's eyes had. *Her own home.* Not her father's or her mother's, but her very own. The more she pondered the idea, the more appealing it became. She had a reason to leave now—children of her own whose lives she didn't want contaminated by her parents' attitudes. Nodding firmly, her mind was made up. She would conceive Tarq's babies and then she would get out of Reltan even if she had to walk all the way to Yalka.

With that happy thought in mind, she cut Tarq an extra-large piece of pie. The hell with what her father would say; his opinions couldn't affect her anymore. She was already on her way.

"You trying to fatten him up?" Jublansk asked, glancing up from her task. She was making bread, kneading it with her big hands.

"Maybe," Lucy replied.

"I don't think he needs any improvements, myself," Jublansk said with a sniff. "He looks damn near perfect."

"Don't be silly, nobody's perfect. I'm sure we could find *something* wrong with him if we looked hard enough." Lucy nearly choked as she realized that before the next day dawned, she would know the answer to that. She would have seen and touched every bit of him by then—at least that was her intention.

Jublansk must've been reading her mind. Grabbing a dish towel, she wiped the sticky dough from between her fingers. "Let's go strip him down and find out."

"No way!" Lucy exclaimed.

Jublansk shrugged and went back to kneading the dough. "Bet he's hung like a donkey," she went on. "And with thighs like that, he could probably ram it through a wall. Got a fine ass on him too." As though she'd like to do the same thing to Tarq's bottom, she gave the dough a firm slap.

"When did you—?"

"I watched him walk in here," Jublansk said with a slow, superior smile. "You were busy."

"Ha! You've been holding out on me." She paused as another thought occurred to her. "You're not thinking of calling him yourself, are you?"

"Me? Twelk would kill me for even thinking about it." She paused, tapping her tusk with a contemplative finger. "Might be worth it, though—getting killed, I mean. At least I'd die happy."

"What makes you so sure about that?"

"Oh, I've heard about those cat boys. They've got a ruffle around the head of their dick that secretes a fluid that will give you an orgasm if you so much as taste it. Big cocks, too, and they can point them in any direction—some of them can move it so fast it vibrates. Hell, they even *taste* good. It's no wonder some jealous asshole decided to disintegrate their planet."

Lucy felt her scalp tingle as she blushed to the roots of her hair. The other sensation was much lower—like her uterus had blushed as well.

"I'm surprised some of the assholes around here haven't tried to kill him," Jublansk went on. "He's taking a big risk advertising himself like that."

The thought of Tarq being in danger sent a rush of adrenaline coursing through Lucy's blood. Her hands were shaking as she scooped the wedge of pie onto a plate. "But he's not doing it for the sex," she protested. "He's trying to produce more Zetithians."

Jublansk shook her head. "He could do that artificially. He doesn't have to be here; he could have sent his semen to the local clinics. No, make no mistake, Lucy. He likes spreading it around and he likes women. He was eyeing you as a potential customer—though you probably didn't realize it."

"C-customer?" Lucy stammered. "That makes it sound like I'd have to pay him. He didn't say anything about money, and he does it for free—he said so on the commercial."

"Didn't when he was on Rhylos." Dipping her fingers

in a lump of soft butter, she greased the dough and then covered it with a large bowl. "From what I hear, to spend time with him, you had to book him a year in advance—*and* pay a thousand credits."

Lucy's jaw dropped. "A *thousand* credits?"

Jublansk nodded. "Friend of mine said her cousin went there once—place called the Zetithian Palace. Didn't do this guy, but the one she had was a redhead who could fuck the tusk off a Twilanan—damn near did, seeing as how she *is* Twilanan," Jublansk added reflectively. "Anyway, if he's not charging for it now, it's because he's already made a fortune."

"But if he's rich, then why would he—?"

"Because he *likes* it," Jublansk said firmly. "He's the kind of man who could never be satisfied with just one woman. The kind who could seriously break your heart."

Lucy wasn't deterred by this since she never intended to give him her heart anyway. She could never hold on to a man like that; she only wanted his children. Not having to pay the thousand credits made it a win/ win proposition.

But there was a tiny little spark inside her that wanted just a little more. Granted, she'd seen very few examples of lasting love—her own parents barely spoke to one another—but never having had the opportunity to give it a shot bothered her a bit. It would have been nice to think that her father's attitude had kept her from heartbreak, but what good was a heart if you never used it? Having children to love would be better than nothing. But loving one's children wasn't the same as loving a spouse—something she would probably never experience unless she left town, and there was no guarantee even then. No, if Tarq didn't want a lasting relationship, so much the better. She would go into the arrangement knowing that her heart would remain intact and she would emerge with three beautiful children. Jublansk's warnings didn't deter her in the slightest. In fact, they only strengthened her resolve.

Lucy yawned, feigning boredom. "I don't know why anyone would want to have triplets anyway. One at a time is bad enough."

Jublansk shrugged. "Good thing if you're trying to bring back an endangered species, though. Just imagine how many descendants he'll have. It boggles the mind."

Lucy couldn't argue with that; her babies would have half siblings out the wazoo.

"How many descendants will who have?" Neris asked as she came bouncing in to pick up a loaf of fresh bread.

Not wanting to seem too anxious or interested in him, Lucy didn't bother to answer, knowing that Jublansk would say it for her. Then again, Neris wasn't what you'd call incisive; she might not draw the obvious conclusion even if Lucy were to state her intentions out loud. Jublansk explained while pulling a tray of loaves from the oven. Lucy took a deep breath, inhaling the heavenly aroma of Jublansk's bread. She could bake like no one else and was one of the restaurant's biggest draws, no matter how good the fish was.

"Oh, yeah. I've seen him," Neris said, brushing off the idea like a crumb from her sleeve. "Not my type."

Lucy, for one, couldn't imagine any woman saying such a thing, but then, Neris wasn't your typical female. Lucy had always thought of her as a woman—and with her perky blond ponytail and earrings, she certainly looked like one—but being a hermaphrodite from Tryos, Neris had never claimed to belong to either gender. Her clothing tended to be more masculine, and there was something in the line of her jaw as well as the corded muscles in her arms that suggested the male, but she had a softness in her eyes that was quite feminine.

"I wonder if he's ever done a Tryosian," Jublansk mused.

Neris laughed. "He might just as easily wind up with a Tryosian doing *him*."

Lucy choked. The thought of some guy nailing Tarq was all wrong. He was a ladies' man if she'd ever seen one—and he must not be too choosy if he had, indeed, been eyeing her as a potential customer. The "I'd like a full order of *you*" line was probably the sort of thing he said to every woman he met—he'd even said it before ever laying eyes on her.

She delivered the pie to him, once again feeling a strange presence surrounding him—as though the air in his immediate vicinity was filled with some sort of sexual stimulant. His smile was like an intoxicant and she was even fascinated by the way he picked up his fork and ate a bite of the pie. His blissful expression as he tasted it was rewarding—though Lucy had seldom seen anyone who didn't go into raptures over it. Her coconut pie was just as appealing to the rare being who didn't like chocolate.

"You made this?" he asked.

Lucy nodded dumbly, the look on his face robbing her of speech.

He chuckled. "Would you be my mate and feed this to me for the rest of my life?"

Having fielded similar comments in the past, Lucy

rediscovered her voice. "Oh, no problem. I'll be sure to put you on my list." He'd have been at the top of her list, if she'd actually had one. Then it struck her that he really *would* be at the top—was coming to her room that very night—and she began trembling uncontrollably. "Glad you like it," she added before retreating to the kitchen as quickly as her wobbly knees would allow.

She stayed away from his table after that, doing her best to appear unaffected, but it was difficult. Eventually, he paid his bill and left, but the smoldering glance he gave her promised that he hadn't forgotten their assignation, and might even have been looking forward to it.

When Lucy finally got the nerve to approach the now empty table to clear it, she bit back a cry and gripped the back of his chair with palms that were suddenly clammy with sweat. *What have I gotten myself into?*

He'd left her a five-hundred-credit tip.

―――᳘―――

Tarq couldn't have said why he'd left her such a huge tip, but he'd had to restrain himself from emptying his wallet onto the table. And he wasn't paying her for sex, either. He felt an overwhelming desire to give her everything he possessed. He knew she hadn't taken his proposal seriously, but he almost wished she had. The situation had rendered it harmless enough—her response proved that much—but the thought of being with her forever went through him like a blade. It was ridiculous, though. You didn't make decisions like that based on chocolate pie, or even how good a woman smelled. There was more to it than that, at least he thought there must be.

With a couple of hours to kill before he could go to her, Tarq returned to his room at the hotel. He already liked the town; it was a pleasant seaside fishing village composed of whitewashed buildings with terra-cotta tiled roofs and brightly colored awnings above the windows. Narrow cobblestone streets fanned out from a tiny harbor where quaint boats bobbed at their moorings. Tarq had never been to Earth's Mediterranean region, but he'd seen photographs, and though there were obvious similarities, he doubted that vrelnots lived in the Grecian mountains. He'd seen the Eradic mountain range in the distance as he'd traveled up the coast, and it was every bit as forbidding as Lucy had painted it.

Selecting a bottle of the local wine from the stasis unit, he recalled the hillside vineyards and groves of olive trees he'd passed along his route. The dry, reddish soil didn't look as though anything would grow in it, but apparently these crops weren't fussy about where they grew as long as it was hot enough. Taking a seat on the balcony, he sipped the wine while seabirds soared above the waves until the sun slid beneath the horizon.

Chapter 3

LUCY WAITED BREATHLESSLY AS TARQ CLIMBED through the open window. She'd showered and dressed in the nicest nightgown she possessed, but that wasn't saying much. Shivering, she wondered if he would let her keep it on, at least for a little while. No man had ever seen her nude body, let alone touched it.

He landed on his feet, already purring, his eyes glowing as he came toward her with the fluid grace of a mountain cat. Lucy had no idea what he would do. Would he speak to her, kiss her, or just throw her down on the bed and take her? Any of those would have been exciting, though he could have simply recited the names of all of his conquests and she wouldn't have felt cheated.

Her questions were soon answered. Though there was only a short distance between them, Tarq somehow managed to shed all of his clothing before he closed the gap.

Lucy hadn't expected him to be quite so forward or blatant, but when she spotted his cock, she understood why. It was already fully erect and dripping with moisture—was this the stuff that triggered orgasms? Never having seen anyone's penis firsthand, she might have expected it to be straight, but it wasn't. Arising from its nest of blond curls in a sinuous arch, it took a slight dip before rising up again at the apex of the scalloped head. It was thick and meaty, just begging to be touched, and his balls hung low, brushing against his heavily muscled thighs as he walked. Lucy was already beginning to wish she'd at least had sex with someone a bit less well-endowed; the thought of starting off with something that size was rather daunting.

If Tarq had noticed her reticence, he gave no sign, but took her in his arms and kissed her without preamble. His lips were soft, warm, and though not precisely demanding, they were nonetheless insistent—the way Lucy had always dreamed of being kissed. His purring filled her ears, blocking out every other sound or thought. He tasted like wine yet didn't act as though he'd needed it for courage, but rather as a source of solace during the hours they'd been apart. Unable to explain how she knew this, Lucy returned his kiss, opening herself to him completely. He could have sucked out her soul and she wouldn't have cared. As his hand slid through her hair to cup the back of her head, his tongue slipped past her lips, making her feel not so much invaded or plundered as savored. Groaning as his hands slid to the small of her back, he pulled her tightly against his hard cock.

Lucy's knees threatened to give way beneath her. Noting the smoothness of his skin, she recalled having heard that Zetithian men didn't grow beards. Some women might have preferred the roughness, but Lucy wasn't one of them; she liked Tarq just the way he was. She raised a tentative hand to his silky hair. As her fingers threaded through his thick curls, she felt herself becoming lost, forgetting herself, her family—everything but the way he made her feel.

"I'm sure this is beautiful," he said, tugging at her gown. "But I don't want anything between us."

Lucy nodded and he pulled it off over her head with practiced ease. Knowing herself to be generously built, Lucy held her breath as she waited for his reaction.

She needn't have worried; if he didn't like her body, it certainly didn't show. With a low growl he scooped her up in his arms and propelled her backward onto her bed with a speed that made it feel like an attack, but it was softened by his purring and the hot swipe of his tongue across her nipple. Breathing hard, he nipped at her with his fangs until she finally got the nerve to touch him again. With a tentative hand, she smoothed the hair back from his face, combing her fingers through his long blond locks. Her passion overcame her then and her hands knotted into fists as she pulled his head toward her mouth.

As if this was the signal he'd been waiting for, Tarq let out a snarl and pounced. Their lips fused, and Lucy felt his hands everywhere—seeking, delving, caressing. If Lucy had been afraid he would find her unappealing, that fear evaporated. Whether he was giving it away or whether he was paid, he was certainly convincing. Lucy would come away from this night feeling that she'd had his undivided attention and had aroused his passions like no other before her.

He teased the tip of her tongue with his own, and, following his lead, she gave it right back to him. A slick gush wet her thighs; Lucy would never have guessed that the mere mating of tongues could cause such a reaction, but it did something even more remarkable to Tarq.

He must have felt it or smelled it because he wrestled free of her grip on his hair and dove headfirst into her core. She could feel the roughness of his tongue, the softness of his lips, and his hot breath stoking the fire that sizzled between her thighs. He seemed to have gone insane with need—growling, purring, and snarling as he licked her vaginal lips and then thrust inside. His body tightened and his movements became increasingly erratic—like a starving man licking the remnants of pudding from a bowl or a shark in the midst of a feeding frenzy. When he pulled out to suckle her clit, Lucy stifled a scream as the pressure building there reached a terrifying peak before crashing all around her. Her eyes flew open in amazement as he teased her to yet another summit.

"Lucy," he panted. "I can't wait anymore…"

Not even pausing for her response, Tarq took aim and pierced her with his hard, hot cock in one swift thrust. Letting out an involuntary yelp from the sharp sting of pain as he broke through, she took the full length of him inside as the pain was instantly replaced by the incredible pleasure of being filled by him.

A fist hammered on her door and tried the knob, which Lucy had thankfully thought to lock. "What the hell is going on in there?" her father demanded.

"Nothing," Lucy gasped. "Just stubbed my toe in the dark."

She heard him muttering something about her being stupid and clumsy, but nothing mattered as long as the door remained shut. Tarq had frozen for a moment but, hearing the sound of retreating footsteps, took up a steady rhythm, pushing as hard as he could without making the bed squeak. Afraid to make another sound, Lucy clapped one hand over her mouth, but Tarq pushed her hand away, and as his mouth came down on hers, he whispered, "My hair. Pull it again—hard."

When she complied, he backed out completely and then drilled into her again, beginning a sweeping, rotating movement that nearly had Lucy screaming. She'd never felt anything like the sensations he elicited and was sure it could never be better, until an orgasm even stronger than the one he'd given her with his tongue detonated.

Glad that her ecstatic moans were muffled by his kisses, Lucy spread her legs as wide as she could, still not quite believing that his massive organ had some-how managed to fit inside her virgin body. She should have been writhing in agony rather than ecstasy, but there was no more pain, only an overwhelming need to take everything he had to give. That orgasm was the first of many as he rocked into her, pausing at intervals to swivel his cock, its curved shape stimulating every possible surface.

Lucy's mind and body both dissolved into an orgas-mic blur. No longer able to tell where she ended and he began, she recalled hearing sexual union being referred to as "becoming one," but had never believed it until now. Tarq had all but stopped purring, his breath now coming in short, hard gasps. Tearing his mouth away from hers, he sank his fangs into her shoulder, but even that didn't hurt as she felt his cock spurting his creamy semen into her.

Moments later, her womb contracted and then burst into flower as warmth raced from her core to the outer reaches of her being. Lucy felt like she was floating, as opposed to being pinned beneath the weight of his body, and was only dimly aware that he was speaking. He must've whispered "I'm sorry" a dozen times before she realized that he was actually apologizing.

Tarq couldn't believe what he'd just done; he'd completely lost control—and with a virgin, no less. She was even bleeding from where he'd bitten her. He'd never drawn blood before—had never felt the need to—but Lucy's effect on him had changed everything. He would have liked to blame the wine, but knew that to be unlikely. He'd hurt her with his cock, too—but hadn't been able to stop what he was doing or even slow down. Her scent had hit him the instant she opened her window and, as before, had gone far beyond eliciting simple arousal to obliterate everything he'd ever learned about making a woman feel cherished. And then, when she'd responded to him in kind, yanking on his hair, demanding to be kissed, he'd just plain lost it. Even now, he wanted her again; he could feel blood surging through his groin, filling him with desire when he should have been feeling remorse.

"Holy cow!" she whispered fervently. "Is it always like that?"

"Well, no," he admitted. "Not usually."

"Bummer," she said with apparent regret. "I guess it's just the 'first time' thing then, huh?"

Tarq wasn't sure what to make of that, focusing on only part of it. "You should have told me you were a virgin."

"That's funny, I thought I had. I mean, the whole *No, I don't have a mate and probably never will* comment. What did you think I meant?"

"Just that you had no mate, not that you'd never been with a man."

"Well, it meant both," she said firmly. With a frown, she added, "Do you mean you wouldn't have come here if you'd known?"

It was on the tip of his tongue to say that he would have been there even if she hadn't invited him, but he caught himself at the last second. "N-no," he replied. "But I would have tried harder."

Lucy stared up at him with huge, disbelieving brown eyes.

"To be careful, I mean. I wouldn't have been so rough."

"Glad I didn't say anything then."

"But I *bit* you," he protested. "And you're bleeding. I can't believe I did that."

In an innocent tone completely at odds with her wicked grin, she said, "I guess I'll just have to bite you back."

Tarq's balls clenched in anticipation. "I should lick it," he said, doing his best to ignore his body's response to her words, "to make it heal faster."

"Does that really help?"

"It's supposed to," he replied. "I've never tried it, though." Had never *needed* to, he reminded himself. Dipping his head, he realized he was still lying on top of her. He made a move to disengage himself, but she stopped him.

"Don't get up just yet," she said. "I want to enjoy this as long as I can." With a short laugh, she added, "After all, this may be my one and only chance."

Tarq couldn't believe his ears. She truly didn't know he could keep on all night if she liked. In the brothel, he'd fucked a different woman every three hours—only taking that long between clients because he always showered after each session. Now that he was traveling, the trips between planets were usually lacking in sex and sometimes took up to a month, but still, three days was a long time for Tarq—bordering on celibacy. "I can go again," he said. "I sometimes do—to ensure conception—and I've got a medscanner—"

He broke off there, realizing he'd done something else wrong. He'd forgotten to scan her first, to determine not only her fertility but her lack of communicable disease. Still, a virgin couldn't have been carrying much in the way of venereal disease, which was what he was most anxious to avoid. Most were curable, but some could affect his sperm production, and without that, he knew he was, well... useless. The fact that he had plenty of money banked away didn't mean a damn thing. A man had to have *some* useful occupation.

She laughed again. "So scan me."

Tarq didn't want to break the connection either. "I'll have to get up."

"Okay, I'll let you."

Tarq thought it best to lick her wound first. "In a minute." Leaning down, he began licking the blood from her shoulder, noting the two puncture wounds. She looked like she'd been bitten by a vampire with bad aim.

"I'm sure it'll heal up just fine by itself," she said after her initial gasp—a gasp that was quickly replaced with a sigh. "Wow. Even *that* feels good. What *is* it with you Zetithian guys?"

Tarq shrugged. "I don't know. It's just the way we are—but we're only interesting to alien women. Zetithian girls think we're boring."

"I find that *very* hard to believe."

"Well, that's what they always say. Maybe they're

lying. I wouldn't know. I've only done one, and that was years ago." Dismissing the vagaries of the Zetithian female libido, he went back to licking her shoulder. The bleeding had already stopped, but he kept on anyway. If nothing else, it gave him an excuse to stay right where he was.

"Is that why you're traveling around like this? You're hoping to find one who *doesn't* think it's boring?"

"No, I'm doing it because—" He stopped there, not wanting to admit he was too stupid to do anything else. "It just seemed like the right thing to do."

With a reluctant sigh, he backed out and got up. He missed her warmth immediately, and it was all he could do to keep from diving back into her. Crossing the room to where he'd stripped off his clothes, he found the med-scanner in the pocket of his jeans and activated it. A soft moan from Lucy made him hurry back to her.

"Are you all right?"

"Yeah," she replied. "I think so. I've never seen—" She paused, blowing out a pent-up breath. "It's just that, well…" She finished her sentence in a rush as another orgasm seized her. "…you've got a *really* nice, um, backside."

It wasn't anything Tarq hadn't heard before, but somehow coming from her it was different. He felt the flush of heat rising in his face and avoided her eyes. "So I've been told," he muttered.

Sweeping the beam over her, he checked the results. He'd looked at this thing enough times to know what the words meant, even without using the audio feature: She was free of disease and a day or two short of her fertile period. A satisfied smile crept across his lips.

"You are healthy but haven't conceived. I'll have to come back."

"When?"

"Tomorrow and every day until you are with child."

With anyone else, he would've waited until closer to the time of ovulation, but Lucy didn't have to know that. Tarq was very truthful as a rule, but he wasn't about to give up the opportunity to be with her as many times as he possibly could. A quick glance confirmed that she was pleased with the idea, but he figured it was best to ask. "Is that okay with you?"

Pensively chewing on a fingernail, she didn't reply immediately.

"Is it because of your father?"

Nodding, she said, "I just don't want him to find out until it's too late to stop me."

Tarq hadn't forgotten how hateful her father was to her. The last thing he wanted to do was to talk her out of it, but he didn't want her taking unnecessary risks either. "Are you sure about this?"

"Oh, yes," she replied. "Very sure."

"What about the children? Will he allow you to keep them?"

"Don't worry about that," she said. "I've got it all figured out. He won't know anything about any of this until you're long gone." She didn't elaborate, but from the firm set of her jaw, Tarq got the message: She wasn't going to tell him or anyone else about her plans.

He couldn't argue with her because he knew she was right not to tell him. If questioned, he wouldn't be able to answer. "Do you want to meet somewhere else?"

"Maybe, but I don't know where it would be or what excuse I could give."

Tarq wanted to lock himself in with her for the next week and never leave, but he doubted that was an option. Setting the scanner on the rickety little nightstand, he climbed back in bed with her. He knew he shouldn't stay all night, but it was early yet and there was no point in wasting what little time they might have together. He could stay a while longer.

She seemed surprised. "I-I thought you were leaving."

His heart plummeted painfully. "Do you want me to go?"

"No, not really. I just figured you'd do your thing and head out."

It was what he should have done—what he usually did when he knew the timing wasn't right—but every fiber of his being rebelled at the idea. Tarq was getting confused. He knew he was no good at deception. She was too smart; she'd catch him if he lied. "We could try again."

"I doubt if a couple of hours would make any difference," she said. "Not that I've ever made a study of it, but—"

"I don't want to leave until I'm sure you're all right," he blurted out.

"I'm fine, really. I may never be the same, but—" she paused, smiling at him, "that probably goes without saying." Shifting sideways, she turned over to face him. The moon shining in behind thin white curtains outlined the contours of her shoulder, the line of her neck, the curve of her cheek. Tarq started to say something else but had already forgotten what it was. Unable to stop himself, he leaned closer and kissed her. She couldn't make him leave in the middle of a kiss, and if he kept it up long enough, she might forget all about it.

She still tasted good—almost *too* good. He only wished he understood why.

Chapter 4

LUCY COULDN'T FIGURE OUT WHY HE WAS LINGERING when he should have already been gone. He was treating her more like a lover than a client, something she hadn't expected. Remembering what Jublansk had said about him—that he liked women and liked "spreading it around"—perhaps he did this with everyone he impregnated—made them feel singled out and special rather than random females to be serviced. It would make it that much harder when he left, however—which he would do in the end. Lucy had no illusions about her ability to hold onto a man like Tarq, but she was already becoming attached to him, and it wasn't only because of the sex. He was acting differently, more innocent and uncertain than seductive. More appealing—or was it endearing?

Another round with him would have been fabulous, but she hadn't completely recovered from the first. It was no wonder someone disintegrated their planet; sex with human males was probably very nice—might even be wonderful at times—but if anyone could top Tarq, well, it would have to be another Zetithian or Tarq himself.

His kisses shouldn't have been more intoxicating than a human's, but she suspected they were. It bothered her that she had no human male to use as a comparison, but no one had ever kissed her like that, nor had anyone ever crawled naked into her bed as though he belonged there. She had tried to distance herself slightly—keeping her sense of humor close at hand—but as he deepened the kiss, she began to wish that she had conceived and that he wouldn't need to come back. She already felt as though he was becoming imprinted on her psyche. How would she feel if it took a week or more?

She tried to put it out of her mind—tried not think about the future and only focus on the present moment, the fact that she was being kissed by the sexiest man in the quadrant. Sighing against his lips, she succumbed to temptation and enfolded him in her arms, touching him, stroking his muscular arms and back, delighting in the silken texture of his hair and the smooth heat of his skin. Out of so many other moments she had done her best to forget, this was a moment to remember.

He had done this many times before; she would let him take the lead. He knew what he was doing, and if he wanted to go or stay or come back a hundred times, it was up to him. She wouldn't say no to him, ever, not even when he left her.

His kiss became more of a purr as she surrendered, focusing on the blissful feel of his lips on hers, his skin against her skin, his arms surrounding her, keeping her safe. Releasing her from the kiss so slowly she wasn't even aware it had ended, he held her close to his chest while his purring soothed her, lulling her to sleep.

When she awoke the next morning, he was gone.

Tarq spent the rest of the night caught up in dreams that tormented him. Huge beasts with heads like the vrelnot. Birds with razor sharp beaks that preyed on animals as large as himself. Fierce storms with lightning crackling all around him. Treacherous, rocky terrain, but through it all, there was a path that led… somewhere.

He awoke with the dawn, thankful that the night had ended. Sunlight reflected off the ocean waves streamed through the narrow window above his bed. Even from his room, he could hear the hoarse cry of the seabirds, and the sound helped him forget the fear that had gripped him.

It was just a dream, he told himself, though he knew that his kind sometimes had visions of the future. Not everyone did; he himself had never glimpsed anything that couldn't be explained in another way. There were no such terrors here, however—the soft quilted mattress he slept on, the colorful braided rug on the floor, scenes of the seashore in paintings on the walls—it was cheery but impersonal, giving no hint of the thoughts and dreams of anyone who had been there before, just as he would leave no trace of himself behind.

Rising from the bed, he crossed the uneven wooden floor to the balcony. The sea looked the same as it had on the previous morning—the waves swept in to crash on the sandy beach as they had probably done forever—only he had changed.

There was another woman living on the other side of town who had requested his services. He had scanned her and knew she was a good two weeks away from her fertile period. Normally, Tarq wouldn't mind, and if the woman was willing, he wouldn't wait, but something had made him tell her he would return later, when the time was right. Going back to her now was the farthest thing from his mind. The only woman he could think about was Lucy.

Leaving her room had been one of the toughest things he'd ever done. He had to respect her wishes, but what he really wanted to do was to go pound on her father's door and demand that he be kinder to Lucy, and if not, well, he would... do what? Kill him? Carry her off?

No, Tarq wouldn't do either of those things. Not that he was lacking in courage, but he didn't think Lucy would appreciate the interference. Speaking to her father would only make matters worse, and she hadn't acted like she wanted him to carry her off. She had it all figured out, she'd said, and her solution obviously didn't include him. She might be attracted to him, but she didn't want to be his mate; she only wanted his children.

After pulling on a pair of shorts, he opened the glass door and stepped out onto the balcony, only then noticing the stairway that went down to the beach. Descending quickly, he paused for a moment, delighting in the feel of warm sand between his toes before he took off running. The day would be hot; he could feel it building in the air, and soon the sand would be too hot for bare feet, but that didn't matter now. He needed to run and then swim to wash away the dregs of his dreams in the sea.

Dax, his friend and fellow refugee, didn't like water, but Tarq had learned to swim as a child on Zetith and he'd spent hours at the beach on Rhylos, loving the way the waves buffeted him about. Tarq enjoyed the freedom of the outdoors and had felt cramped aboard Amelyana's ship full of refugees. Having to spend his days studying only compounded the misery. He could understand most things if they were explained to him verbally, but reading was pure torture. When Rutger Grekkor—Amelyana's husband and the man responsible for the destruction of

Zetith—had been killed and his considerable assets divided among the remaining few Zetithians, Jerden and Onca had come to him with their idea for a brothel on Rhylos. With money to invest, Tarq had jumped at the chance. At last he could do something he was good at that didn't require much in the way of brains.

He'd been told repeatedly that his reading disability wasn't due to a lack of intelligence, but he still felt stupid most of the time. Even on Rhylos, there had been signs to read and menus to decipher. His seductive attitude with waitresses got him through that most of the time, but waiters generally weren't as responsive and some of them were downright snooty about it.

Smiling as he ran, he remembered Lucy. It had been so easy with her—all of it. Not just suggesting a meal, but making love with her had been a dream come true. She had no expectations, no special requests. She had just gone with it, letting him discover the best ways to pleasure her. He was anxious to return to her, knowing he could do even better the next time.

Sweat was soon pouring from his overheated body and, on impulse, he veered off course, running straight into the sea until the water reached his waist. He loved swimming in the ocean, loved feeling the power of the waves and the way the water swirled between his legs, teasing his genitals. He would have preferred to swim in the nude, but this wasn't Rhylos and there were children playing nearby, so Tarq kept his pants on. If Lucy had been with him it wouldn't have mattered; with or without clothing, his penis would have been fully erect, withstanding the force of the water to plunge inside her...

Diving into the waves, he swam the length of the beach and back again, then let himself drift, floating on the waves until he washed up on the sand. He lay at the water's edge with his eyes closed, letting the waves crash over him and then recede. It was humbling in a way—reminding him that there were forces of nature far stronger than he was.

"You haven't drowned, have you?"

Tarq opened his eyes to see a Terran child frowning down at him. Her concern was obvious, but her face lit up when he smiled at her. "No, I haven't drowned."

"I'm glad," she said, giggling. "You're very pretty."

"So are you."

Laughing again, she held up a toy shovel. "I'm going to build a sand castle. Would you like to be the king?"

Tarq grinned. He knew the old stories of castles and kings, knights and dragons, having heard them from Amelyana as a child. "I'm not cut out to be a king. I think I'd make a better knight."

"In shining armor?"

"Absolutely."

"Good. You can be my knight and I'll be the princess."

With her auburn curls and bright green eyes, she would make a beautiful princess, Tarq decided. He glanced at her mother, a lovely woman with bright red hair and a shapely body, who nodded her permission. "Climb on my back and we'll go slay some dragons."

Rolling over and getting up on his hands and knees, he lowered his head while she straddled his neck. Tarq stood up effortlessly under her light weight and began running through the waves, holding tightly to her ankles while she shouted with laughter. Her delight was infectious, and Tarq felt a freedom of spirit he hadn't felt since his days in the forests of Zetith.

Unfortunately, this triggered another memory. This child wasn't much older than Dax had been when Tarq found him wandering alone through the deserted streets of Waynochthia.

Tarq had been up in a tree when the marauders came, leaving death and destruction in their wake. When all was silent at last, Tarq hadn't needed to enter the wreck of their home to know his family was all dead. He'd turned and walked straight into the forest, always heading in the same direction as if he knew exactly where he was going.

For days he travelled without seeing another living soul. Adept at hunting and fishing and knowing which plants were good to eat, he'd had no trouble keeping himself fed. However, upon his arrival in Waynochthia, a city that was a ghost of its former self, he'd found Dax, starving and terrified, his tears carving a path down his dirty cheeks. Taking the child by the hand, he kept on until they reached the hidden place where Amelyana's ship was about to depart.

The hatch had opened and he led Dax aboard without question, somehow knowing that this had been his destination from the very beginning. He hadn't understood why the city was deserted until they reached the outer limits of the solar system and Zetith exploded. He hadn't seen the asteroid approaching, nor had he known that it was no natural phenomenon, but an act of war.

He knew differently now. He considered the peril that this small child might be in had she been Zetithian. The thought of his own children being murdered brought him up short. Zetith had been destroyed by Amelyana's insanely jealous husband—a man rich enough to stage a war against an entire world and win.

Almost. He hadn't succeeded in killing all of them, and Tarq knew he couldn't let those fears deter him. He had a mission to accomplish.

But he'd forgotten about most of that when he first met Lucy and inhaled her scent. He couldn't explain why, but his reasons for traveling deserted him, and he wanted nothing more than to stay with her and watch as their children were born and grew up—children that would have her deep brown eyes...

The child's mother waved and called out. "Saree! You're going to wear that man out!"

"Are you worn out?" Saree asked.

"Not really. Ready to get down now?"

Saree giggled. "I'd like to keep going, but we do need to build the castle."

Tarq knelt down and set her on her feet. Saree took him by the hand and led him over to a partially built structure that looked more like hills than a castle. "Your sand needs to be wet, princess," he observed. "Here, let me show you."

Spending the next hour or so with Saree had an unexpected effect on Tarq; he was enjoying himself enormously until he realized he'd never played with a child since becoming an adult himself. He had fathered hundreds of children and had never played with any of them. Not one.

His mind had been diverted from thoughts of Lucy by the child's antics, but this realization brought her back to the forefront with a palpable jolt. She wasn't even pregnant yet and he was already thinking about playing with their children—except that they probably wouldn't be girls. Tarq's tendency to sire males suddenly became a flaw rather than a desirable attribute. To have daughters with eyes like Lucy's—daughters that he would gladly give his life to protect—would be worth more to him than a thousand males conceived with other women.

This notion hit Tarq with the force of a stun blast as a sense of loss, of utter and complete futility, flooded through him. Lucy would never want him as her mate—he was too stupid and... *used*. No woman would want a man who had been so unselective in the past, would she? Tarq had been with hundreds of women, but he still didn't completely understand the way their minds worked, with the result that he probably couldn't predict what she would do or say. Of course, this was assuming that he could ever bring himself to ask the question—if he even knew what the question was.

Saree must have sensed his distress with all the intuition of womanhood, for she paused at her task, gazing at him curiously. "Do you need a nap?" As if suddenly overcome by weariness herself, she yawned.

Tarq chuckled. "I think *you* might be the one who needs a nap." Glancing up, he saw her mother approaching. "Your mother probably thinks so too."

Frowning as her mother held out her hand, Saree shook her head but was unable to stifle another huge yawn. "But the castle isn't finished," she protested.

"I'll finish it, princess," Tarq promised. "It will be waiting for you when you come back."

Her expression changed to a pout, but there was real fear mixed in. "If the bad king's soldiers don't knock it down."

Tarq thought it sad that even a small child expected the worst, but then he had seen enough horrors to know children were not immune to danger—even in a peaceful village like this. His own home had been very peaceful, until it was invaded.

Tarq didn't know what to say. "I can't promise they won't," he said finally, "but I'll finish it anyway."

"You don't have to do that," Saree's mother said. "She can work on it later."

Tarq shook his head. "It's not like I have anything better to do."

What the woman made of that, Tarq never knew, but Saree seemed pleased, which was the only thing that mattered. They lingered for a short time while Tarq went right on building turrets and towers until the castle was waist high—a strong fortress to protect Princess Saree.

In truth, he knew quite well that walls of sand wouldn't protect anyone, but he hoped Saree had a dad who loved and protected her, not like Lucy's who made her life miserable—or at least not as happy as it could have been. He desperately wanted to see Lucy again, but he didn't want to arouse any suspicions, and showing up at their restaurant for every meal would probably do just that.

So wrapped up in thoughts of Lucy and the task at hand, Tarq almost didn't notice when they left him, or how Saree's mother had affected him—or, rather, how she *hadn't* affected him. The scent of her desire was there, but it hadn't aroused him at all.

Lucy got through the day somehow, though her moods swung wildly from elation to irritation to regret to breathless anticipation and back again. The day before had passed slowly, but this one was pure torture. She'd made several blunders but couldn't explain that she'd been a brainless klutz because all she could think about was seeing Tarq again. Her disappointment that he hadn't come in for a meal was profound, but she understood why he hadn't.

Jublansk wasn't blind, however, and noticed her eager glances toward the door anytime a customer arrived. "Haven't seen him today, have we?"

Lucy blushed. "Have I been that obvious?"

Jublansk nodded. "You're about as subtle as a Twilanan's tusk. Don't blame you for looking, of course. He's a mighty fine man. But you might want to consider doing more than just mooning over him."

"I'm not mooning!" Lucy knew her protest was feeble, and Jublansk's skeptical expression proved it.

"Seems like a golden opportunity for you to have a little fun," Jublansk said briskly. *"I'd* certainly never tell."

"You've been giving this some thought."

"I have," she said with a nod. "And I think you'd have fun and be doing a good deed in the process. Plus, the kids would be adorable."

Lucy couldn't believe her ears. "So you're saying I should call him?"

Jublansk waved her floury hands in protest. "I'm not saying anything of the kind, but if I were you and *didn't* call him, I'd be kicking myself in the ass for the rest of my life."

Since this was in complete accord with Lucy's own thoughts on the subject, she started to nod, but shook her head instead. No. There should be no clues, no inkling, no hints. She didn't want Jublansk to get into any trouble over this—perhaps even losing her job if her father was angry enough. The less she knew the better. "I'd be too chicken. He's too much… *man* for me."

Jublansk rolled her eyes. "That's like saying the ocean is too big for this planet, or the sun isn't the right size for the solar system." She shook her head. "No, Lucy. He is what he is and you are what you are. Don't sell yourself short."

"Yeah, right," Lucy grumbled. "Whatever *that* means."

At long last, she was home for the night. Closing her bedroom door and locking it, she took a deep breath, shivering with anticipation, but couldn't help bowing her head in sadness as she whispered a fervent prayer. If only she could have had Tarq for real—in broad daylight and with full knowledge of everyone—not clandestine meetings in a locked room after dark. She wanted her fertile period to come quickly so that he could move on and she could forget him—forget the way he made her feel, the things he made her want…

Quickly changing into her nightgown, she doused the light and opened the window. It might have made her feel better to know that Tarq was already waiting for her, but his prompt entry was such a welcome event that she never gave it a thought; she only felt intense relief at the sight of him.

He swept her up in his arms in a manner that spoke of

his own impatience, but the tears in Lucy's eyes kept her from seeing it. She only felt the heat of his body, the soft warmth of his kisses, and the security of his embrace. As he lay her on the bed, he whispered words she didn't understand, which made her feel even more fulfilled, for she was free to imagine that he was telling her how he'd missed her, that he'd counted the seconds until they could be together again, and that the day had been every bit as interminable for him as it had been for her.

She should have known how anxious he was when he didn't bother to remove her gown, nor did he disrobe completely—only exposing his sex enough to penetrate her with it—but all she felt was relief that they were finally together again. She did her best to keep from begging him to stay with her forever, but the words crashed through her mind over and over until she had to bite her tongue to keep from saying them aloud.

Even when her orgasms began, she ignored the feelings, wanting only to feel him inside her and to bask in the warm glow of his eyes. Was this how it felt to be in love, or was this merely lust? Never having experienced either of those emotions before, she could only speculate, but surely lust wouldn't be so painful.

Mental pain, that is. There was no physical discomfort this time—what little she'd felt the night before was already forgotten—but the pain of anticipated loss, of knowing that she had only a short time to be with him overrode a great deal of the pleasure. She tried to put it out of her mind, but it wouldn't stop, nor would it listen to her wishes, but kept right on tormenting her.

"Don't leave me," she gasped at last.

"It isn't safe for me to stay," he groaned. "Your father—"

"Can go hang for all I care," she shot back at him.
"He doesn't own me. I know I've put up with it for a
long time, but—" She broke off there. Tarq didn't know
her plans, and she reminded herself that it would be best
if he never did. "It's okay," she whispered. "I'm just…
it's been a long day, that's all."

"I know the feeling."

His tone made her wonder how he'd spent the time,
but when his thrusts altered subtly, her thoughts were
once again riveted on the present. *Don't think, just feel,*
she told herself silently. *Remember this moment forever.*

The blessed moon was still full and bright, sending
tiny sparks flickering over the soft spirals of his hair. The
scent of his body, so seductive and compelling, swirled
through her head while the sound of his breathing filled
her ears and his strong shaft filled her core. She reached
up and touched his face, thinking that surely he couldn't
be real. How could anything be so perfect and still be
real? He had to be a dream.

"I missed you today." The words were out of her
mouth before she could stop them.

He smiled down at her, his sharp fangs gleaming in
the moonlight. "I know that feeling too."

Her heart nearly leapt out of her chest. Was *she*
the one he'd missed? It was too much to hope for, but
whether he meant it or not didn't matter. He was here
now, making love to her like the dream lover he was.
Perhaps it was best not to discuss it.

Tarq, however, seemed to think that further conversation was indicated. "Mmm… Lucy," he purred as he
rocked her slowly and gently. "You feel *so* good."

Just the way he said her name made her shiver with

delight, but what he was doing with his penis was even better. She could feel that arch pressing against... something—something wonderfully sensitive. Licking his lips, he reached beneath her to pull up her gown. "I was in too much of a hurry before," he said. "Sorry about that."

She didn't reply immediately since her gown was covering her face, but in another second it was fluttering, whisper soft, to the floor. His shirt followed and then he eased out of his jeans after toeing off his sandals.

"That's better." His lips found her breast as his hair brushed lightly over her arms. "Wouldn't want my Lucy to miss out on anything."

The "my Lucy" sent her rocketing straight back to dreamland—a place where they were not only lovers but lifelong mates—and prompted her to consider his needs, desires, and preferences even more than her own. Gasping as he teased her nipple, she whispered, "Is there anything you want me to do for you? Something you like better than anything else?"

She thought he hesitated. "Lucy," he murmured against her skin, "I can't think of anything that wouldn't be better because you were the one doing it. You can do whatever you wish. I promise to love every second of it."

Recalling what Jublansk had said about Zetithians tasting good had set Lucy's thoughts on a wicked path, but how did you ask a man if he would like to be tasted? Did you just blurt it out, or was there a more graceful way of putting it? "I-I want to... Jublansk said you would taste good, and I thought you might like—"

His purr was loud and rough. "I would like that very much." Withdrawing slowly, he crawled up to kneel beside her shoulder with his muscular thighs spread wide, offering her his glistening cock.

She gave the glans a tentative lick, just as she would have done with an ice cream cone that needed to be whittled down in size. But as the clear fluid began to flow freely from the points of the ruffled corona, she lost all inhibitions and sucked it deeply into her mouth.

There was a sharp tang to it at first, but she decided that that part must have come from her, because after a few moments, the flavor settled into something warm, seductive, explosively orgasmic but at the same time oddly familiar. Letting go of him, she exclaimed, "You—you taste like chocolate—well, not *exactly*, but it's the same sort of effect, only a lot stronger."

"Good?" Still purring, he slid the blunt head across her cheek.

"*Very* good." She was still fascinated by the control he had of it, the way he could move it without touching it at all.

Circling her lips with the glans, he added, "My *snard* tastes even better—or so I've been told."

"*Snard?*"

"That's the Zetithian word for semen."

"Oh." Somehow she hadn't thought about tasting *that* part of him.

"It's sweet and creamy—a Terran lady once said it tasted like whipped cream."

Giggling, she traced a finger over his scrotum. "And what do *these* taste like? Nuts?"

Tarq let out a soft chuckle. "I believe they do."

"Well, obviously I'm going to have to try all of you— just to form my own opinion, you understand."

Tarq nodded solemnly, but his grin was infectious. Again, without having to use his hand, he pointed his cock up toward his chest, allowing better access to his balls. "Help yourself, Lucy. I'm all yours."

His egg-shaped testicles were big and smooth beneath the rough-looking skin, and a light dusting of curly blond hair tickled her nose as Lucy leaned closer to lick him. With that first touch, something deep inside her pelvis curled into a knot and squeezed, sending moisture running down between her legs. She retained enough of her wits to note that he did taste sort of nutty, but even more amazing was the way his sac turned buttery soft beneath her tongue. The need to know what it would be like to hold his balls in her mouth overcame her and when she sucked one of them in, her whole body contracted, drawing her knees up to her chest. The feeling was indescribable, but the sound Tarq made—a groan mixed with a sigh and a purr—was like music to her ears. She was giving him pleasure, and it filled her with a sense of total fulfillment—even more so than the orgasms he elicited from her.

The joy of giving—something she'd seldom experienced—held her in thrall, and she reached up, filling her hands with his heavy cock. Glittering like a diamond in the moonlight and almost as hard, it quivered in her grasp as Tarq thrust his hips forward, begging for more. It might not have been something Lucy had ever considered doing before, but Tarq obviously liked it—a lot.

Lubrication might have been a problem with any other man, but Tarq was pouring it out faster than it could evaporate, and Lucy's hands slid up and down his shaft in a smooth, effortless, erotic glide. Within moments, his breaths grew short while, unbelievably, his cock became even more engorged. She had just reached the apex of a stroke when Tarq sucked in a ragged breath as his head snapped back. He held it for a moment, then exhaled with a loud purr.

When the first drops of semen landed on her face, Lucy let go of his scrotum and pulled his cock down, aiming the head toward her waiting tongue.

The whipped cream analogy was close, but it didn't adequately describe the sweetness, nor did it address the blissful warmth that settled in the small of her back before flowing outward to the periphery of her body. True, she'd never conceive a child in that manner, but a man who could elicit such feelings without even trying? It went beyond sex, beyond mere procreation, to something deeper, more powerful, more *binding* than anything she could imagine.

How had all of those other women ever been able to let him go? Did conception stop these feelings in their tracks? Once impregnated, were they able to forget what he could do to them?

Lucy certainly hoped so. Otherwise, she was in for the heartbreak of her life.

Chapter 5

TARQ STILL COULDN'T FIGURE OUT WHY LUCY WAS able to hold his thoughts even when she was nowhere around, and, never having had this problem before, it concerned him greatly. He'd always heard that women longed to be missed, but this was the first time he'd felt it. It was also the first time he'd come in the mouth of a lady he was trying to impregnate.

Not that he hadn't done it many times in the brothel, but those encounters were purely for the lady's pleasure, and there had been several who didn't want to do anything else. Lucy, on the other hand, wanted to conceive. Granted, she probably hadn't ovulated yet—Tarq chastised himself once again for forgetting to scan her first—but there was a purpose to his wanderings. He wasn't doing it for entertainment.

Or for demonstrating his love. The idea crept into his thoughts like a stealthy predator bent on destroying any other feelings he might have had on the subject. Love? It couldn't be that. He'd only met her the day before. How could he possibly feel love for her? Even so, he couldn't put another label on the feeling. Not that he'd tried to avoid falling in love; it had simply never happened to him before.

Easing down onto the bed beside her, he began purring again. It was natural and had a calming effect on his mind, but he still wanted to know her thoughts. "So, do you like the way I taste?"

Lucy cleared her throat as though about to say something unpleasant. Tarq held his breath, waiting. "I— um..." She stopped there, shaking her head.

This was *not* going to be good. "It... doesn't matter," he said quickly. "Not everyone likes it—well, most ladies do, but it won't hurt my feelings if you don't."

Lucy laughed softly. "That isn't what I was going to say, Tarq. It's just that I've never had to tell a man that he tastes like a hot fudge sundae—with nuts—before. It sounds sort of... silly."

Tarq smiled. "And do you *like* hot fudge sundaes with nuts?"

"Oh, yeah," she whispered. "But they make me gain weight, so I don't ever eat them."

"How sad—but you can eat as much of me as you like. I don't think anyone has ever gotten fat on Zetithian *snard*—though I could be wrong about that."

"Sundaes never made me feel like this, either," she went on. "I feel sort of... floaty. Does that make sense? I felt it last night too."

Tarq nodded. This much he understood. "It's called *laetralance* in my language," he said, and went on to quote the definition he'd learned as a child. "'A blissful sense of peace and tranquility of the mind, body, and soul.'"

"I like that word," she said. "But I like the feeling even more."

"So do I."

She rose up, propping herself on one elbow to study him curiously. "You feel it too?"

Tarq smiled. "Sometimes."

"Do you feel it now?"

Thus far, Tarq had felt it every time he'd been in Lucy's presence but rarely prior to his visit to Talus Five. "Yes, but I would still like to mate with you again. Usually I feel sated, but right now I only want more of you."

Tarq knew it sounded like a line, but Lucy seemed puzzled more than annoyed. "You can, um, do it again—even when you feel *laetralance*? I wouldn't have thought—"

"With a woman like you? Always."

Her expression changed slightly. She seemed pleased that their interlude could continue, but there was something wistful about her smile. Then Tarq realized what he'd said. It made her sound like one of many, a "type" that could always be counted on to arouse him. He frowned, trying to think of a better way to put it. "You still want me, don't you?"

Lucy nodded. "I'd be lying if I said I didn't."

"Well, you see, it takes the scent of a woman's desire to arouse a Zetithian man. If I can smell your desire, I can keep going."

Her eyes widened. "Right away?"

Tarq smiled sheepishly. "Try me."

Reaching toward his groin, she curled her hand around his shaft and then ran her fingertips over the head. Letting out a startled gasp, she sat up and bent her head down so close to his cock he could feel her breath tickling his skin. "That ruffle on your dick... it's—it's *moving*."

For a fleeting moment, he'd thought she was going down on him again, and Tarq had to swallow his disappointment before he spoke. "Don't worry, it, um, does that. Women like the way it feels and it pushes the *snard* in the right direction. Sorry, I-I guess I should have warned you."

Lucy chuckled merrily. "Obviously I should have read the directions first so I'd know what to expect. I mean, I haven't even been with a human male before, but I'm pretty sure they don't do that."

"No, they don't—actually, there are several things about us that are different." Differences which were significant enough to send a genocidal maniac rampaging after them. "Zetithian women need lots of… encouragement."

Lucy laughed even harder. "So, you're saying that Terran girls are easy?"

Tarq had yet to encounter a human female that wasn't, but he was pretty sure it would be unwise to admit it at this point. "I wouldn't say that," he replied cautiously, "but they *are* more enthusiastic."

"And do you *like* enthusiasm in a woman?" She sounded almost coy, and her crooked little smile intrigued him, prompting him to grin back at her.

"I *love* enthusiasm."

"Ah, then that explains it."

"Explains what?"

"Why you want to go again. You can smell my enthusiasm."

"Yes, but I also want to be sure you get your money's worth."

Her face fell and her voice went flat. "I thought you did this for free."

"Sorry," he said quickly. "Force of habit. I *used* to do it for money, but not anymore. What I meant was that I want you to…" Tarq stopped. He'd done okay up to now, but she was too smart for him and had backed him right into a corner. There was no way he could finish that sentence without sounding cocky or callous. There was nothing to do but admit it. "Look, Lucy, I'm not very smart. I say stupid things all the time. Please don't hold it against me."

"I won't," she said, "but I—oh, never mind. Just forget it."

Tarq had no idea what it was he was supposed to forget, but he knew that fucking her into a *laetralance* stupor was probably the best way out of this predicament—just as it was with most awkward situations that involved women. *When in doubt, just shut up and purr.* Tarq couldn't recall who had given him that piece of advice, but it had always served him well, and sex was the one thing he was good at.

He took her hand—the hand that still lingered on his penis—and kissed it, threading his fingers through hers. A lock of her hair hid her face from him, and, purring softly, he tucked it behind her ear. "Kiss me and tell me I'm forgiven."

"There's nothing to forgive." Sighing, she sank down onto his chest as he let go of her hand to wrap her in his arms. "And you're a lot smarter than you think." Her lips were warm and welcoming as she pressed them to his mouth, her tongue seeking entrance.

Tarq had sense enough not to argue. She could think whatever she liked as long as she kissed him like that—like he was worthy of her, like she truly loved him, and would be with him always. Her body covered him, enveloping him with desire as her legs slid down on either side of his own. Curling his hips up, his cock found her entrance, and the heat of her core drew him in. He rocked against her slowly, blissfully, as his hands lost themselves in her hair and his lips bathed her with kisses. Her soft moans of pleasure lured him on, and he could feel her complete surrender. When she reached her first climax, he stopped all movement, delighting in the firm squeeze of her inner muscles on his rigid cock. Then, as her body relaxed, he swept his hands down her back, cupping her bottom as he rolled over with her.

Still ensconced in her liquid core, he picked up the rhythm again, feeling closer to heaven with each slow, deliberate thrust and withdrawal. Her hair was fanned out in dark waves, providing a sharp contrast to the white of the sheets and the fairness of her skin. With her eyes half-closed and lips softly parted, he let the sounds she made with each pinnacle she reached wash over him, pulling him under and drowning him in ecstasy.

When his own release came at last, he not only felt the joy rushing through his body, but saw it in her eyes, eyes that were looking at him and *only* him— nothing else.

Lucy had a feeling that if she woke up the next morning without him, she wouldn't live through the day. Why, why, *why* had she done this? It was hopeless. She could have his children, but she could never have some-one like Tarq. It was a complete and utter impossibility. She wasn't meant for the kind of happiness he could give her—whether he was stupid or not—and she didn't believe that he was, not for one moment. She needed to strengthen her resolve to get through this—as she had done with so many rough times in her life.

Strengthen her resolve? That wasn't how she'd coped in the past. She coped with it all by putting it firmly out of her mind. The loneliness and despair of her school days. The knowledge that her life had never changed. The fear that it would go on as before. Tarq was her salvation but not her reward. Having his *children* would be her reward. She needed to remember that.

But as he lay with his head pillowed on her breast—just this once—Lucy allowed herself to dream of a neat, spacious house with gaily striped awnings, sitting beneath a brilliant blue sky on the edge of town, kept fresh by the ocean breeze. Children playing in the yard; the boys climbing olive trees; and the girls laughing as they sat whispering in the shade. A sun-drenched porch with potted flowers blooming in profusion. Braided rugs on the floor, fragrant herbs drying above the kitchen window, dinner cooking on the stove, and Tarq coming home. Home to the one who loved him and would show him how much in the bed they shared—and in everything they did together, everything she did for him and he for her.

Caught up in her fantasy, Lucy didn't notice her tears until they trickled toward her ears. With an aching heart, she inclined her head to kiss his golden hair and inhale his scent. Memories had a tendency to fade with time; would she remember this in the years to come? Suddenly, a reprieve came to her in the form of another memory. Tarq tended to father sons—he'd said as much in his advertisement—and those sons would undoubtedly resemble him in many ways. She would always have them to keep Tarq's memory from fading completely. Perhaps she could also have a photograph, or a lock of his hair, to keep for herself.

This ache in her heart wouldn't last forever.

Eventually the pain would ease and she would only remember the good things, not the fact that she would never see him again. Yes, that was the way to view it — the way that wouldn't hurt.

Tarq shifted, purring in his sleep. He seemed content to be with her now, but it wouldn't last. He was a drifter, the type who would move on to the next woman without a backward glance. And she would let him do it. She wouldn't beg, wouldn't weep, wouldn't cling to him beseechingly. She would be strong. Other women had done it before her, and she was no different from any of them. He would forget her more quickly than some, or perhaps remember her longer than others. But she would never be more than a brief stop in a tiny fishing village on Talus Five. On distant worlds other women would call him, would conceive his offspring, and be satisfied. She would do the same.

As she'd anticipated, Tarq's presence was no more permanent than a dream. Dawn came and Lucy arose from her bed — alone. He was right to do it, but waking up with him would have been such a treat. Perhaps on the last night… but, no. She couldn't risk his safety in that manner. Her father's fury at finding Tarq in her bed, along with the knowledge that she was actually trying to conceive his children, would be intense. No, this whole thing had to be kept a secret — hopefully until Tarq had left Talus Five. She wanted there to be no possibility of repercussions against Tarq. Ever. Pregnancies weren't obvious for months, even when a woman was carrying triplets. Morning sickness would be easy enough to explain away—or hidden. Her clothing wasn't revealing and could be altered. Yes, she could keep it a secret for a very long time.

Then there was the other part of her plan. She could leave Reltan and head to Yalka long before any symptoms appeared, and if she left ahead of Tarq, that would divert suspicion from him even more. That way, it wouldn't seem as though she had followed him, if anyone ever made the connection to begin with. She wouldn't put it past Jublansk to arrive at the truth, but doubted that she would ever pass that information on to Lucy's father. The satisfaction of knowing that her salad dressing recipe was a mystery to him would be nothing in comparison to keeping Lucy's whereabouts a secret.

Dressing quickly, she went into the kitchen with a smile on her face.

A smile that caught her sister's immediate attention. "What are you so happy about?" Reba grumbled.

"It's a-a beautiful day," Lucy improvised.

Reba let out a derisive snort. "Just like every other day. The weather never changes around here. Always the same, unless it rains."

Lucy felt that there was a lot to be said for clear blue skies and puffy clouds, but didn't bother to argue. Reba was obviously waiting for her breakfast. Lucy began pulling out eggs, milk, and cheese, and was mixing up an omelet when it hit her that soon she wouldn't be catering to Reba's every whim—or her father's—nor would she be listening to her mother's incessant whining. This realization cheered her even more, and she went so far as to hum a happy little tune while she worked.

Her father came in, brusque and snarling as usual,

and her mother followed, already complaining. "That table is perfectly hideous, Uther. We should replace it."

Lucy kept smiling but was mentally rolling her eyes. Her mother had been saying the same thing every morning for the past month.

Today, however, her father growled a different response. "Go buy a new one, then, Tourelda! I'm sick of hearing about it."

"Don't take that tone with me," Tourelda said piteously. "My poor nerves!"

Then leave him, Lucy thought. *Go someplace quiet where we won't have to listen to you.* Why her mother had never done such a thing was beyond Lucy, though she knew Tourelda to be incapable of looking after herself, nor could she possibly earn a living. She was about as useless as an umbrella in a hurricane. Just why this trait had emerged, Lucy wasn't sure, but not long after Reba was out of diapers, Tourelda had decided to take to her bed—or the sofa, or her velvet chaise—and rarely budged from them except for meals, leaving Lucy in charge of the household.

Though Tourelda often complained, she rarely interfered except to ensure that Reba was treated like the little princess she was and gave Lucy no assistance whatsoever. Lucy had never understood why, but thought it might be due to the fact that Reba was beautiful while Lucy was not. On the other hand, it might have been because Reba was worse than no help at all. If Tarq was stupid, then Reba was downright imbecilic—particularly when it came to anything that didn't affect her directly.

But today, none of that bothered Lucy. It was as

though she'd been given a sword and shield that made her impervious to their peevish anger, unwarranted pride, and blatant hedonism. She was free to laugh inwardly rather than wince, and it felt marvelous.

Glancing out the window, she noted that the sky was a clearer, more vibrant blue, the olive trees sparkled and danced in the morning sun, and the breeze stirring the crisp curtains felt particularly pleasant. In short, it was a perfect day to be alive. All the things that had been weighing her down simply didn't matter anymore. She had yielded to the misery of the night before—the realization that her relationship with Tarq could only be temporary—and she now knew she could deal with it, along with any other obstacles in her path. The notion that the joy he had given her could carry over into the rest of her life had never occurred to her, but in addition to the promise of children, he had given her a precious gift—one she would cherish forever—whether she had a lock of his hair to carry with her or not.

Pouring a glass of the tea she'd brewed the night before, Lucy took a long drink, noting that even it seemed more refreshing than usual, and began buttering the toast and plating up the omelets with renewed efficiency. She enjoyed cooking—far more than waiting tables—and knew herself to be every bit as capable of running a restaurant kitchen as her father, perhaps even more so because she knew she could do it without screaming at the help. If her plans for independence had actually included the wherewithal to start her own establishment, she would have done it in a heartbeat; she might even provide her father with a bit of competition. Luring Jublansk away from him would probably put him out of business; her delectable bread was largely responsible for the loyalty of his clientele and was the one thing Lucy knew she would miss—though eating less of it would undoubtedly improve her figure.

With this heartening thought in mind, she sat down to breakfast, shielded from her family by an impenetrable aura of serenity. Was this what being the recipient of Tarq's lovemaking did to a woman? Did he impart the same to every lady he consorted with? If so, then he had left more than children in his wake; he had left behind legions of highly contented women now empowered by the knowledge that they had been part of a truly remarkable event. An elite club, perhaps. One whose members shared more than the satisfaction of helping an endangered species to recover, but knew something that others didn't—that making love with Tarq could, and would, change their lives for the better.

She wondered if it was possible to find others and discuss it with them. After all, if there was a Zetithian Birth Registry, then there might be a mothers' group too—and if there wasn't, she might start one herself. As it was, she would have loved to share her experiences with others—and she was fairly certain it would have to be with women who had the pleasure of the company of a Zetithian rather than that of mere humans. Though she was certain there were exceptions, women like her mother, for example, would have no similar frame of reference; it would be like comparing vrelnots to purring kittens.

On the other hand, Natasha might be a good confidant. Her husband was a Mordrial, and their ability to read minds and control the elements probably made them remarkable lovers. Nat had certainly seemed to be happy in her marriage, though sexual matters had never been mentioned—perhaps because Lucy, being a virgin, had no comparable experiences.

Not having heard from her friend for several months hadn't concerned her overly; Nat was undoubtedly enmeshed in her own life and had little in common with the pitfalls of Lucy's sad existence. But, thanks to Tarq's arrival, things were different now and she and Nat would have even more to discuss once her babies were born. Natasha had put off having children until their farm was more established, but had hinted that she might be nearing a point where it would become practical.

Even so, not wanting her father to know where she'd gone—at least, not until she'd found work and her own place—made her reluctant to contact Nat. The more obscure the trail, the better, she decided, and if she took Nat and her husband Traldeck by surprise, they would either welcome her into their home or at least aid her in finding one of her own, and there would be no inkling of where she had gone.

Yalka was simply the nearest town, after all—she might have made her way to the spaceport city of Noklar instead, though it was on the other side of the mountains and would require a circuitous route to reach it safely. She could even call herself by a different name—she had every intention of giving her children Tarq's surname— though the idea that she might change her own by marrying never occurred to her.

The simple truth was that she had no intention of sharing her children with anyone. She'd heard enough tales of stepfathers and boyfriends abusing the children of their women's previous liaisons that she didn't want to risk it. Her father's treatment of his own daughter was warning enough.

As her family left the table, Lucy gathered up the dirty dishes, realizing that she had completely tuned out their conversation, which was a blessing in itself and made the task of cleaning up after them quite enjoyable as opposed to the usual drudgery. She would have to make a point of thanking Tarq for this unexpected side effect of the time they'd spent together, and she barely acknowledged her father's brusque "Don't be late to work" admonition.

Work? "Yeah, right," she muttered when she had the kitchen to herself. "Most people who work actually get paid." Lucy had her tips, of course, but they didn't amount to much—though the tip Tarq had given her had been huge. She still wasn't sure why he'd done it—it was, after all, a ridiculous amount of money to tip a waitress—and the subject had never come up when they were together. If she'd had other customers who were as generous she probably would have left town a long time ago, with the result that their paths might never have crossed. Not having a life of her own was bad enough, but never meeting Tarq? Now *that* would have been a tragedy.

Chapter 6

HER FAMILY MIGHT NOT HAVE NOTICED LUCY'S newfound serenity, but Jublansk spotted it in short order. "You seem to be enjoying yourself today," she remarked as she threw a batch of dough onto her board.

Noting the emphasis on the "joy," Lucy stopped short, nearly spilling the contents of her tray. Was it *that* obvious what she'd been up to? She may have *felt* like she was glowing, but surely it didn't *show*... "It's... a beautiful day." Reba hadn't bought it either, but Lucy couldn't think of anything else.

"Uh-huh." The dry skepticism in her tone spoke volumes, but Lucy ignored it. She would have loved to confide in Jublansk, but also knew that the fewer people who knew of it, the better.

Nodding toward the door with her tusk, Jublansk added, "Don't suppose it could have anything to do with who just sat down at table ten, now, could it?"

Her tray bobbled dangerously, but Lucy managed to avert the disaster somehow. Drawing attention to Tarq or her reaction to him would be far more disastrous than spilled soda. "Hadn't noticed him," was Lucy's perfectly honest reply.

True, she hadn't seen him yet, but when she looked out at the tables, there he sat, studying the menu in all his stunning blond glory—hair that she knew adorned more than just his head. The light dusting of golden fur on his butt was the stuff of fantasy, and the nest of curls in his groin rivaled the beauty of his mane. Just realizing that she knew this from firsthand experience sent liquid fire racing to her core.

"Uh-huh," Jublansk said again. "*Sure* you didn't."

"Yeah, well, look who's talking," Lucy retorted, thankful that Jublansk couldn't smell the scent of her desire the way Tarq could.

Jublansk grinned. "He's not sitting at one of *my* tables, is he?"

"No, but he could just as easily have been Neris's customer."

A sly sidelong glance and a flick of her brow was Jublansk's only retort.

Shaking her head to hide her smile, Lucy delivered the drinks, somehow managing to maintain her composure enough to avoid dumping them in the lap of a surly Herpatronian. The ape-like humanoids always made her nervous—and this one was nastier than most—but her new serenity served her well, enabling her to deflect his taunts with genuine grace.

A grace which deserted her the moment she approached Tarq's table. The mere sight of him was enough to have her tripping over her own feet. His killer smile nearly knocked her down. Giving herself a quick mental shake, she recovered quickly, whispering, "You shouldn't be here."

"Really? Why not?"

He looked so innocent, she wanted to smack him, but two could play that game. "Do you know what you want?"

She kept her expression neutral and her voice gave

nothing away, but Tarq obviously wasn't fooled. His glowing eyes began to smolder with undisguised interest, and Lucy could have sworn he was purring, albeit very softly. She didn't have to see the boner in his jeans to know he was picking up her scent.

Nodding, he opened his mouth to speak, but Lucy cut him off. "And don't say you want a full order of *me*," she whispered. "Someone might hear you." With the lunch crowd creating their usual din, this was unlikely, but it could also mean the difference between success and failure—a chance she didn't want to take.

"I do, of course," he said with a sultry smirk, "but I'll have the fish instead—broiled this time."

"Anything else?"

He shifted in his chair as though trying to draw attention to the fact that a specific part of him was extremely uncomfortable. "Surprise me."

"I'd like to," she muttered, tapping his order into the notepad with more vigor than necessary.

"I look forward to it."

Unable to stop herself, she finally met his gaze and let out a giggle. "You're gonna get me in *so* much trouble…"

"That's my plan." Moistening his lower lip with a sensuous swipe of his tongue, he then captured it with a fang, leaving her no doubts as to what he wanted to do with her.

"Damn, you're good," she whispered under her breath.

"And I taste good, too."

"Oh, hush up," she admonished him but went back to the kitchen with a smile on her face. At that point, she didn't care whether Jublansk saw it or not.

Which, of course, she did. Deciding to meet adversity head-on, Lucy took the offensive. "Wow! That is one incredibly sexy man!" she exclaimed when Jublansk glanced up as she came back to get Tarq's drink. "I don't know how anyone could resist him."

Jublansk nodded her agreement. "I don't know why anyone would want to try." She went on kneading her dough with a nonchalance that seemed a little too stud-ied to be natural. "You haven't, have you?"

"What? Tried to resist him? I haven't needed to so far." Which was perfectly true. Resistance would have been futile anyway, but a moment's reflection proved that she had, in fact, exercised incredible self-control just moments before when she stifled the urge to kiss him or, at the very least run her fingers through his hair.

"I dunno… a nice young woman like you and a man like that…" Jublansk let her sentence trail off with a shrug.

"Now, let me get this straight," Lucy began, planting her fists on her hips. "Two days ago you were warning me to stay away from him—at least, I think that's what you meant."

Jublansk looked up in surprise. "Did I say that?" Giving the dough a punch, she added, "I must've been out of my mind."

"So what are you telling me to do?"

"I'm not telling you to do anything, Lucy. I just think it's about time you did something for yourself—something nice."

Lucy didn't know what to make of that. Was Jublansk telling her to do exactly what she *was* doing, or did she mean something else?

"I mean, it's not like anyone around here is gonna do it for you."

Meaning her family, of course, and, more specifically, her father. Lucy knew this to be true, and though
she'd already taken the first step, she also knew there
was more to it than the joy of sleeping with a Zetithian.
She had to conceive.

Tarq simply refused to spend another day as he had
the previous one, particularly since there was a perfectly
valid reason for him to have lunch at Lucy's restaurant—
and dinner too, if he liked. Waroun had recommended it,
and with only two other cafés in the entire village, there
weren't a lot of choices anyway. Tarq had eaten meals
at each of them and concluded that the food wasn't anywhere near as good, therefore returning to this place was
what any sensible tourist would have done, whether he
was fucking the waitress on the sly or not.

Although the waitresses at the other cafés had flirted
with him blatantly, he simply wasn't interested in carrying it any further. One had hinted that she might call him,
but he had an idea it was purely for the sex rather than
for breeding purposes. He tended to avoid that sort on
principle. Besides, he was already working with a client,
though he hated to think of Lucy that coldly, and within
the confines of that relationship, he was monogamous.

These fine moral distinctions would have been
laughed at by some, but Tarq had his own set of rules.
He only serviced one woman at a time, doing his best to
make her feel special and unique, and then, once conception was confirmed, he moved on to the next. He
wasn't finished with Lucy, so the others would simply
have to wait their turn.

Perhaps it was the clandestine nature of their relationship that made him want to be with her in public. He'd

never had to be so secretive before. In fact, many of his clients had even invited him to stay in their homes until they conceived, but there was no chance of that happening this time, and Tarq had been perfectly miserable without her.

He could, in theory, spend the entire day sitting right where he was. It might seem a bit odd, but as long as he ordered a drink now and then, no one would kick him out. Of course, if he never left, he couldn't very well leave large tips for Lucy, which he fully intended to do.

For some inexplicable reason Tarq felt a deep-seated need to give something to Lucy, to provide for her in some way. And while there were many things Tarq didn't have, money wasn't one of them. The fact that Lucy had so little support might have been the stimulus, and if giving her huge tips meant that she could better provide for her children, he saw nothing wrong with it. He wasn't paying her for sex—hell, most women wanted to pay *him*—but there was something about Lucy that made him want to give her things. Perhaps that was what he should do with the day—go shopping and buy her something. But what?

Jewelry? The fact that she wasn't wearing any didn't necessarily mean she didn't like it. Her only accessory was the clip that held her hair twisted up in that funny, floppy style. Clothes? Men weren't supposed to give clothing to casual female acquaintances, though she wasn't precisely casual. Perfume he rejected outright. In his opinion, it was unnecessary, aside from the fact that it tended to make him feel queasy. Candy or flowers were common romantic gestures in most cultures, of course, but—

This train of thought halted abruptly as Tarq realized that he'd never gone out and bought anything for a lady before. Ever. The novelty of it should have given him a clue that Lucy was affecting him strangely, but deep down, he already knew that.

He told himself it was only because of her situation: the way her father treated her, the way she had to work so hard, both at the restaurant and at home. Tarq could be as stealthy as any Zetithian; he'd watched through the windows and had some idea of how things worked in Lucy's household—or rather, how *Lucy* worked—and on top of all that, he would be leaving her with not one but three children. She was an oddity among his clients; most were well-equipped to handle triplets—both in terms of money and the ability to house and care for them—but the more he saw of Lucy and her family, the more convinced he became that he was doing her a disservice. Her family wouldn't lift a finger or spend a single credit to help her.

She hadn't mentioned the tip he'd left her on the first day. Tarq was a generous tipper as a rule, but he'd never left one that big and still wasn't sure why he'd done it. But the more he considered the matter, the better it seemed. A tip was discreet. He wasn't making a big show of giving her some expensive bauble. She could tuck the money in her apron, just as she would do with any other gratuity, and never mention the amount to anyone. She could use the cash to buy things she truly needed, as opposed to useless flowers or jewels. Perhaps he'd known what he was doing after all.

Tarq watched as Lucy returned with his order, her expression neutral except for the dimple in one softly rounded cheek. Tarq was developing quite an attachment to that dimple, for it seemed to be the one thing she couldn't control—well, maybe not the *only* thing, but one that was at least obvious when she was out in public.

"This is fun," he said as she leaned closer to set the bowl in front of him.

"For you, maybe."

Tarq thought she sounded a little miffed and a deep breath confirmed it. Her scent was a blend of lust and irritation. "You aren't mad at me, are you?"

The shake of her head was barely perceptible. "No, it's not you. I just wish I could—oh, never mind." She hurried off to wait on another table, leaving just enough of her fragrance behind to send blood surging back into his groin. Tarq had never been up and down so often in his life. He felt like an inflatable toy in the hands of an indecisive child.

What was it she wished she could do? Tarq knew exactly what *he* wanted to do. He wanted to pull her into his lap and kiss her until she couldn't see straight, but was it the same for her? The sharp tang of her lust lingered, giving him at least one clue, but the irritation? What was its source?

Perhaps he'd made a mistake in coming here. He was feeling almost as miserable and frustrated as he had when he'd stayed away. Well, maybe not quite—at least this way he could see and talk to her and inhale her luscious fragrance—but not being able to touch her or taste her bordered on torture.

When Lucy picked up his salad plate and brought his entrée, Tarq fully intended to simply smile and say thank you, but the words came out anyhow. "I wanted to see you, Lucy. Is that so wrong?"

"No, of course not. It's just that I don't want anyone connecting us."

Tarq felt a pang strike somewhere near his heart. "Oh."

"I mean, I don't want to get you in trouble. I can handle anything that gets thrown at me, but this is... different from your other jobs, isn't it?"

"The having to keep it a secret, you mean?"

"Yeah, that."

"But I'm here as a customer. I'm not making trouble, and I'm a good tipper."

She winced. "A little too good."

"Is that bad?"

"Maybe." She hesitated, and then went on, keeping her voice down. "Feels like you're trying to pay me child support."

Tarq was about to say something—whether he would have agreed or protested, he wasn't sure—but she wasn't finished.

"I'm gonna do something really stupid if you're here all the time—something that might give us away, and I don't want to mess this up now. Timing is everything, you know."

"Yeah, I suppose so. But I'd still like some more of your chocolate pie."

That got a smile out of her—one that warmed his heart. "I can understand that." Giggling, she returned to the kitchen.

According to his scan, it was likely that she would conceive tonight. He'd forgotten that, but the fact that she remembered only reinforced what he already knew. Another pang stabbed his heart. His only purpose was to sire offspring and move on. Being anyone's lifelong mate was out of the question, and he knew he wasn't good enough for a woman like Lucy. There was no point in getting all worked up for nothing. He would have the night to fulfill his desires.

A few minutes later, Tarq heard an argument begin between Lucy and her father. He grimaced at the man's harsh voice. From the sound of things, her father had seen Lucy giggling as she left his table.

Tarq hadn't even finished his entrée when Lucy returned with his pie. "Got your scanner with you?"

"Yes," he replied.

"Do me a favor and scan me. My father is giving me hell for even talking to you. Tonight had better be the night or this may not work."

Tarq reached into his pocket and withdrew the device. After a quick check of the settings, he ran the scan.

The results nearly stopped his heart.

Tarq wanted to lie so badly it hurt, but he couldn't. "You're pregnant. With triplets."

Chapter 7

"Thank God," Lucy said fervently. "I'm not sure we could risk meeting again." Then she realized what it would mean. She would have three of his children, but she would never see Tarq again. Her stomach heaved with sickness unrelated to her pregnancy. Closing her eyes, she took a deep breath, forcing the nausea to subside. After today, it wouldn't matter if Tarq ate every meal in her father's establishment; Lucy would be long gone.

That ridiculous argument with her father had solidified her conviction. There was no point in waiting for the inevitable scene with her father when he discovered the news. She would leave for Yalka as soon as she was sure her family was asleep. The journey to Yalka would be hard enough, which meant that leaving before she began to feel any symptoms was best. In the meantime, she would play the part of the dutiful, repentant daughter to the very best of her ability. Being convincing wouldn't be difficult. After all, she'd had plenty of practice.

Tarq slipped the scanner back into his pocket. "Congratulations." His voice sounded flat, as though the news brought him no excitement, no joy. It was simply the acknowledgement that his obligation to her was now fulfilled and it was time to move on to the next client. He didn't feel any of the same things she was feeling. This was what he did, and she wasn't beautiful enough or special enough to change that. She was simply another client. There was no point in pleading with him.

"Thank you." She nearly choked on the words. "I'll take very good care of them."

"I'm sure you will. Don't forget the registry." His expression was as wooden as his voice.

"I won't." Lucy couldn't bring herself to say goodbye. She really *would* have choked on that one. Nodding slowly, she moved on to another table.

She took the next order with all the animation of a poorly programmed droid. *I should be happy*. Telling herself that didn't make it happen, however. Pain unlike any she'd ever felt blossomed in her heart, fanning out across her chest.

"Order up!" Her father's voice cut through her like a knife. Crossing the floor to the warming counter, Lucy picked up the plates, ignoring his scowl. Delivering the order to a trio of elderly ladies out to enjoy the day together, Lucy wished she was one of them with all her heart. They didn't have fathers who berated and belittled them. Someday she would be every bit as free. That day couldn't come soon enough.

Lucy avoided any painful glances in Tarq's direction on her return to the kitchen. Better to begin their separation now and not give her father any more fuel for his suspicions. Tarq obviously knew how to leave women behind. He'd done it hundreds of times. If only moving on hadn't been so new to Lucy.

Jublansk looked up from her kneading as Lucy passed but didn't comment as she went out the rear door, shutting it behind her. With her back against the wall, Lucy bent over with her hands braced on her knees as the pain hit her again. Her chest constricted with the effort to control her emotions, but they spilled out anyway. Muscles knotted on the back of her neck and her breath came in short gasps. She did her best to focus on the new life ahead of her, but for a little while, she had to mourn the one she was leaving behind. The one that included Tarq.

Natasha would be delighted to see her. Lucy had no doubt of that. She would be free at last. Once she was gone from here, her father couldn't make her return. He would have no means to coerce or bully her. If, indeed, he ever found her.

These thoughts strengthened her resolve and straightened her spine. Wiping her tears with a corner of her apron, she walked back inside.

"You all right?" Jublansk asked.

Lucy nodded. "Yeah, just needed some… air."

Jublansk obviously didn't believe her. "Uh-huh. Your father getting on your nerves?"

"Yeah." It was, after all, the perfect excuse. "So what else is new?"

"Not much—unless there's something you'd like to tell me."

Lucy would have welcomed the opportunity to unburden herself to Jublansk, but the less she knew, the better. As far as anyone knew, Lucy had never heard from Natasha once she had left Reltan. Knowing that her overbearing father would do his best to prevent her from even going on a brief visit, Lucy had kept that to herself. Unfortunately, her dissatisfaction was well known to Jublansk, who was the closest thing to a friend Lucy had left. In fact, she was more like a mother.

"No, nothing new. But thanks for asking—and for being here." Lucy felt more tears attempting to flow. She hadn't realized just how hard it would be to leave the stout Twilanan behind.

"I'll always be here. When you need me, you know where to find me."

Lucy nodded her reply, wondering if Jublansk knew more than she let on. Jublansk was very shrewd and could see though most lies. Fortunately, Lucy hadn't been forced into telling an outright lie—yet.

Gathering up salads and bread for a rough-looking group of Terran men from Madric, Lucy headed out.

The first thing she noticed was Tarq's empty table. Doing her best to ignore the ache it caused her, she went on to serve the salads without comment. Unfortunately, her customers weren't as considerate.

"I'm glad that filthy Zetithian is gone," one of them said. "Couldn't stand the smell."

Lucy frowned. "He doesn't smell bad." *But you do*.

"He ought to. The fuckin' man-whore. Sonofabitch has had his dick in more pussy than a studhorse."

Lucy was at a loss for words—and it wasn't only because of the man's nasty mouth. Should she defend Tarq and risk drawing attention to her feelings toward him? Or ignore the asshole? "I wouldn't know anything about that."

"We saw you talking to him," another man said. His hair was thinning, and unkempt stubble darkened his face. "Your father is right. You need to stay away from his kind. They're dangerous."

And you're ugly. Lucy's eyes began to twitch as she fought the urge to roll them at the man. "I'll keep that in mind."

Lucy carried her empty tray over to clear Tarq's table. He'd eaten every bite of the pie.

And left her a thousand-credit tip.

The twitch in her eye became more pronounced. Lucy blinked and looked again. Still there. Still a thousand credits. *Oh, my God.*

Lucy was torn between wanting to berate Tarq for his extravagance and offering him her profound gratitude, though the fact that she'd probably never see him again made it a moot point. A few more tips like that and she could buy her own house without having to bother Nat at all.

Lucy worked through the rest of the day feeling like she had a dozen trelinks chasing each other around in her stomach. It wasn't every day a girl found out she was pregnant with triplets and had to leave home. The money Tarq had given her would help enormously, but she had no intention of spending it anytime soon. She devoted considerable thought to how to conceal it from potential thieves, and then realized that no thief worth his salt would give her a second glance.

Still, it paid to be prepared. Her father had a pulse pistol in the drawer of his desk at home. Lucy knew it was there because she was the only one who ever cleaned anything. Her father wouldn't miss it—at least not immediately. Fortunately, the desk wasn't in her parents' bedroom. The thought of needing to arm herself was a little scary. Prior to this, she'd never felt the need for protection from anyone but her father—though those guys from Madric were a little unnerving. Lucy hoped Tarq never ran into them again. They were the sort who wouldn't feel any qualms about roughing him up a little. They'd probably see it as a public service.

———∿∿∿———

That evening, Lucy went through her things as silently as she knew how. She didn't have much—not even a suitcase—and most of the evening was spent sewing up a makeshift duffel bag out of an old sheet, cutting off the hemmed portion and doubling it over to use as a carrying strap. It was a long walk to Yalka and she would need the rest of her bedding to camp out along the way, along with extra clothes and a towel. She threw in her needle and thread just in case the bag needed repair along the way. Food wasn't a problem since she had a key to the restaurant and could stock up before she left. The fact that she'd never done anything of this sort before didn't deter her in the slightest. The only limiting factor was how much she could carry.

Not long after dinner, Lucy had tucked her mother into bed, wishing that the rest of the family would turn in as early. "Sleep well, Mom."

"I'll try. But it's so difficult." Tourelda's voice was pettish and weak. "What would I do without you, Lucy?"

Lucy was so stunned it took a moment for her to reply. "I-I'm sure Reba would take care of you."

Tourelda shifted uncomfortably in her bed. "No, I don't believe she would. She doesn't have your kindness."

Lucy's eyes widened. Was this really her *mother* speaking? She'd never said anything of the sort in her life—at least not that Lucy could recall. "She would if she had to. You've never needed her."

"True. You've always been here." Tourelda frowned. "Did you know that was why your father never let you marry? He needs you at the café, of course, but he also wants to make sure you're here to take care of me." Blinking, she went on, her voice even weaker. "I'm so useless. Have been for such a long time."

Lucy felt more used than ever. She owed her parents a lot, but her whole life? No parent had the right to ask that of a child, much less force it on them. Even so, she felt some compassion for her mother. Having to rely so heavily on others couldn't be easy. "Don't worry, Mom. I'm sure everything will work out eventually."

"When I die, perhaps."

"Which won't be anytime soon," Lucy said firmly. "At least not according to your doctor."

Tourelda's mouth formed a moue of distaste. "Doctors," she said contemptuously. "They don't know anything."

Lucy didn't see any point in arguing, but did wonder why her mother had seen fit to say all of this. It was the closest thing to a real conversation they'd had in a very long time. And today, of all days…

Lucy began to realize that her entire family would be better off without her to cater to their whims. Reba might actually get up and do something for a change, and Tourelda might find that she had more strength than she gave herself credit for. Of course, lying about for years would have weakened her muscles—including her heart—simply from disuse. Any sustained activity might actually be the death of Tourelda, though her doctor routinely recommended that she get more exercise. Lucy could see her mother dying from following the doctor's orders, just to prove him wrong. "I'm sure you'll be fine," Lucy said at last. "Just get some sleep. Maybe you could go for a short walk tomorrow."

"Not likely," Tourelda said as her eyes drifted shut. "Not likely."

As she left the room, Lucy heard her father call out from his study. "Get to bed, Lucy. You've been dragging around too much lately. Can't get anything done with you wandering around in a daze."

Lucy's response was automatic. "I'm sure you're right."

As it happened, he was right this time. Lucy *hadn't* been getting enough sleep, and she wouldn't be getting much tonight, either. Not that it would matter to him. When he woke up, she would be gone.

Lucy would've given a lot to be a fly on the wall when breakfast time rolled around. Her father could cook it himself, of course, but as angry as he was bound to be, he would probably burn the oatmeal.

———

Tarq had finished his pie and left the biggest tip he could. He was still having a hard time believing that Lucy was already pregnant. The scanner had misjudged fertile periods before, but usually it was a delay rather than an early ovulation. It figured. The one woman he never wanted to leave had to be the one who was early.

There was no point in hanging around any longer, especially after she'd thanked God she was already with child. It didn't fit with the way she'd acted toward him before, but, even so, her response had hurt. Knowing that he had no reason to visit her again hurt even more.

He wandered the streets wondering if he should try his next client, Rallene. Perhaps that would be best. Move on to the next and try to forget Lucy.

Tarq found the house again with no trouble; as long as he'd been somewhere before, his spatial orientation was excellent. He might not be able to tell you the name of the street, but he knew where it was located. When he knocked on the door, she opened it with a smile.

"I thought I should check and see if you were in your fertile period," he said. "My scanner hasn't been making very accurate predictions lately."

Rallene welcomed him inside. A Terran blonde, she was small but shapely, with a pleasant face. Tarq had done a hundred women just like her. He could tell by her strong scent that she was anxious to mate with him. A quick scan showed that ovulation was imminent, but Tarq felt no inkling of desire. Not one tiny flicker. He tried purring and noted when her scent altered. She offered him a glass of tea. He took it from her hand and inhaled deeply.

Nothing.

No response from his cock, no twitch of his balls.

Nothing.

Terrans usually smelled good enough to give him an erection even when they weren't interested, which was a rare occurrence in itself.

"You *are* Terran, aren't you?"

"Full-blooded," Rallene replied. "Is there a problem?"

"No, just wanted to verify that for my… records. I— you're not ready yet. Almost, but not quite."

Rallene smiled seductively. "Does it matter?"

Normally it wouldn't, but this time, apparently, it did. "I have another client tonight. I'll come back tomorrow."

Rallene didn't even attempt to hide her disappointment. Her face fell so quickly it was almost funny. Too bad Tarq didn't feel like laughing.

He didn't feel like fucking, either—another rare occurrence. Tarq thanked Rallene for her hospitality and left. With nowhere else to go, he went back to his hotel and lay down on the bed. The setting was serene enough to have calmed anyone—patterns of sunlight adorned the walls, a soothing ocean breeze wafted in through the open casement while rhythmic waves lapped the shore and sea birds called to their mates—but Tarq seemed to be immune.

There was a perfectly good explanation for his current state, but Tarq refused to acknowledge it because it would have meant the end of the only useful occupation he'd ever had. Others might have assumed he was only spreading his seed for the pleasure he derived from the females he serviced, but it was much more than that. It was his calling; it gave him purpose. Without the ability to sire offspring, Tarq would be completely lost.

He'd lied when he'd told Rallene about the "other client." He should have been with Lucy that night, but giving her time slot to someone else felt wrong. He didn't know why. Part of him wanted to go to her anyway, but she'd made it very clear that another night with him would have been too much of a risk. Tarq was willing to take that risk, but he wasn't the one who had to live with Lucy's father.

Of course, there was a way around all of that. Lucy was a grown woman. She didn't have to remain with her family. Tarq had already provided her with money, and he could just as easily give her a ride to any place she chose, which would give him even more time with her.

Or you could ask her to be your mate.

In Tarq's eyes, it was the perfect solution, though the possibility that Lucy might reject him because of his past was a genuine concern—aside from the fact that she'd only met him two days ago. She was a lot smarter than he was, too. She might not want to be stuck with a man who couldn't read. Still, he was already kicking himself for not thinking of it sooner—for not asking her, at least giving her the opportunity to choose. Her refusal would destroy his hopes on several fronts, but at least he wouldn't have that unanswered question plaguing him forever.

Lying there thinking about it wasn't going to solve anything. With a sigh, he got to his feet and changed into running shorts and went out on the beach. He ran until he was exhausted and completely out of sight of the town. Then he swam back. The tide was against him, delaying his return. When he finally crossed the beach to return to his room, the sun was setting. He hadn't eaten since lunchtime, but wasn't the slightest bit hungry. Thirsty, yes, but not for wine. He wanted Lucy.

Darkness fell, but sleep eluded him. Sitting out on the balcony gazing at the stars didn't help; he was too restless. A walk along the shore soon became a stroll through the dark streets of the town. When he reached Lucy's dark, uninviting window, he realized where he'd been headed all along. Tapping on the glass, he waited, but there was no response. Either she didn't want to see him, or she was sleeping too soundly to hear his knock. It didn't matter which was true; the end result was the same.

The last time Tarq had felt this alone, he'd been traveling through the forest after the massacre of his family. When had Lucy become as much a part of his life as his parents, his siblings? He'd only known her for two days. How was it possible?

Dawn was breaking when he returned to his room. He showered methodically and dressed. The café would be open soon and he would see Lucy again—whether she would talk to him or not.

—⁂—

Tarq heard Lucy's father shouting as soon as he walked through the doorway.

"What the devil do you mean, she's not here?"

"I mean she's not here, Uther," the Twilanan replied. "Had to unlock the door myself this morning. Good thing I've got a key."

Tarq had never seen a man so incensed. Uther's eyes were wide and bulging and his cheeks were the color of a Norludian plum. Then his gaze landed on Tarq, and all the color drained from his face.

"You!" he shouted. "You've, you've…" He stopped in mid-tirade, seemingly unable to find the right words. "My daughter!" he finally blurted out. "Where is she? Did you take her?"

Tarq's mouth fell open, but no words came out. He shook his head in reply.

"If he'd taken her, why would he be coming here now?" the Twilanan demanded. "Look at him. He doesn't have a clue. What you ought to be asking yourself is *why* she's gone, not *where*."

The Tryosian server was nodding in agreement. "I've

got a good idea about that myself. And if I can figure it out, it's pretty damned obvious."

Uther glared at the server. "Are you saying this is my fault?"

"If the shoe fits…" the Twilanan said.

"One more word out of you, Jublansk, and I'll—"

"You'll what, Uther? Fire me? I'd like to see you run this place without me."

"And if you fire Jublansk, I'm leaving too." The Tryosian crossed its arms and set its jaw in a firm line, displaying its more masculine side. Tarq had previously thought that this one seemed to be more female than male. Now he wasn't so sure.

"No need for that, Neris," Uther said. Scowling at Tarq, he snapped out, "If you haven't got my daughter, what the hell are you doing here?"

"Breakfast?" Tarq began. "The door was open…"

"Well, then, sit down and Neris will take your order," Uther snapped. "Otherwise, get your ass out of here."

"Nice way to talk to a customer," Jublansk muttered. She smiled at Tarq. "Don't mind him, honey. His daughter ran away last night, and if you ask me, it's about time she did!"

Tarq was already speechless, but this news nearly stopped his heart.

"Nobody asked you, Jublansk," Uther said. Turning away, he ran a hand through his short black hair. "When she gets hungry enough, she'll be back. She's barely got a credit to her name. Shouldn't take long."

Tarq knew for a fact that Lucy had at least fifteen hundred credits, which would enable her to go a long way on a planet like Talus. No, she wouldn't be back anytime soon. Tarq, however unwittingly, had made sure of that.

Uther stomped back to his grill, grumbling. Neris began picking up the chairs that Uther must've knocked over in his rage.

"Do you have any idea where she might have gone?" Tarq asked Jublansk.

"If I did, I certainly wouldn't tell *him*," she replied with a nod toward Uther. Gazing steadily at Tarq, her eyes narrowed. "Not sure I should tell you, either."

Tarq frowned. "Why not?"

"Because something tells me that just because you didn't take her doesn't mean you aren't part of the reason she left."

Tarq knew she was right, but *how* she knew it was a mystery. "Why do you say that?"

Jublansk rubbed the side of her tusk with a blunt fingertip, a sly expression in her eyes. *"Joy, unlike any she has ever known?"*

Tarq felt his face go numb. He didn't know whether to deny it or tell her everything.

Jublansk didn't wait for an answer. "Where are you headed after you leave here?"

"Yalka," Tarq replied. "I have some appointments there."

Jublansk chuckled. "Is that what you call them? Well, maybe you ought to head that way."

"You think that's where she'll go?"

"That'd be my guess, though she might have gone the other direction, towards Madric."

Tarq had already been to Madric and had no desire to return. He hadn't exactly been run out of town, but his reception had been… chilly. "But Yalka is more likely?"

STUD   93

Jublansk nodded. "She has a friend living there—at least the last I heard she did. Though I could be wrong about that."

Tarq didn't think so. Nodding, he turned to go, but Jublansk stopped him, motioning for him to follow.

"Come on into the kitchen," she said. "You need some breakfast."

"Don't I need to get going?" Tarq realized he was giving himself away completely. Not that it mattered. Jublansk seemed to have Lucy's best interests at heart. If she hadn't told Uther her suspicions before, he doubted she ever would.

Jublansk snickered. "You've got a speeder, don't you?"

"Well, yeah…"

"I'm betting she'll be on foot. Don't worry, you'll catch her."

Tarq still had a chance to make Lucy his mate. Even if Uther found her first, Tarq was sure he could convince her. After all, Lucy had left home, presumably to escape Uther.

Then it occurred to Tarq that she'd made sure he could never see her again either, whether he wanted to or not. In effect, she'd run away from him too.

Chapter 8

WITH NAT'S DIRECTIONS TO GUIDE HER, LUCY SET OUT for Yalka. Since the colonies on Talus Five had been established long after speeders made wheeled vehicles obsolete, there was no actual road to follow, only a trail with the occasional sign to mark the shortest distance across the Malturn Wilderness. By the time she passed the first one after an hour's walk, Lucy was beginning to wish the signs were a little closer together.

They would seem closer together if one was traveling in a speeder, of course. Nat had known Lucy would be on foot if she ever made the journey, and she had assured Lucy that the way was impossible to miss. She had only to keep the sea on her left and the mountains on her right and she would eventually reach Yalka. Even so, Lucy was thankful for a clear sky and a waning gibbous moon to light the way.

The land was relatively flat, the mountains sloping down from the east to become a rocky plain stretching to the sea. Twisted trees and tall grasses grew in clumps among the stones, the sea breeze rustling through them as she passed. From time to time, Lucy was startled by the scuttling of wildlife. Most, she knew, were harmless, but the occasional vrelnot had been known to come down from the mountains to prey on the smaller animals living on the plain. Lucy might have armed herself with thieves in mind, but running into a vrelnot would've been much worse. She kept her pistol in her hand.

Lucy had often walked home from the café at night, so she was no stranger to the darkness, but out on the open road, her feelings of vulnerability and freedom warred with each other. The sky seemed larger than it had above Reltan; the stars more brilliant and numerous; the mountains more ominous.

After a few hours of walking, hunger and thirst overcame her and Lucy stopped to rest. Thus far, she hadn't met a soul on the road, aside from the two dogs who had followed her out of town, and even they had turned back after a hundred meters or so.

Despite the ever-present wind, Lucy was sure she would hear a speeder approaching from a distance. She doubted anyone would be looking at anything but the trail ahead; after all, there wasn't much to see. Though the climate was temperate, the Malturn would have been more aptly called a desert. The land was simply too rocky for much of anything to grow, hence the lack of settlements.

Lucy ate some bread and cheese and took a few swallows of water. Though her water bottles were the heaviest thing she carried, they were also the most precious. Nat had assured her that there were several streams winding across the plain from the mountains to the sea, but she had yet to come across one.

A glance toward the east revealed that she'd been on the road longer than she thought; the stars above the mountains were already beginning to fade. Her absence had surely been noticed by now. Tourelda's words from the night before haunted Lucy, but they didn't alter her determination. Her family would adjust and learn to manage without her, just as they would have done if she had left home to marry. The realization that nothing she did would affect Tarq was much more difficult to bear. He would never miss her—wouldn't even know she was gone.

As the sun rose, it became apparent that anyone on the road would be able to spot her from a long way off. If her moccasins had been better suited to a trek across the rocky terrain, she might have considered moving away from the trail, but decided that bedding down during the day was her best option. Unfortunately, there wasn't much in the way of shelter, either from the sun or from prying eyes.

Gathering up several loose branches from beneath one of the stunted trees, Lucy was able to construct a bower behind one of the larger rock formations, which would provide some shade and conceal her from all but the most diligent search. Her blankets were the same dusty gray as the surrounding rocks. Snug beneath them, she would be practically invisible.

As the sun climbed higher, the wind died down, leaving a deafening silence in its wake. Even if she was able to sleep, which she very much doubted, Lucy would certainly hear anyone's approach. Placing her pistol where she could reach it quickly, she curled up in her blankets. It wasn't long before exhaustion and the warmth of the sun worked their magic on her and she drifted off to sleep.

The bestial growls of a vrelnot ripped through her dreams and Lucy screamed as she felt something grip her shoulder. She had her pistol in her hand and was

about to fire when she saw what—or rather who—
it was.

Lucy had been ridiculously easy to find—particularly
for a Zetithian who was already craving her scent. As
vulnerable as she was, alone and asleep, Tarq was very
glad he'd been the one to locate her—his dear, sweet
Lucy. Even with dead leaves clinging to her hair and a
smudge of dirt on her chin, she was still the most beautiful thing he could imagine.

"H… how did you find me?" she asked, lowering
her weapon.

"It wasn't hard," Tarq replied. "I've got sharp eyes
and an excellent nose—and I was on my way to Yalka,
just as you seem to be." He took a deep breath. She
smelled different, probably due to her pregnant state.
The subtle change affected him more profoundly than he
would've thought; the urge to pounce on her was overwhelming. Only the realization that she probably would
have shot him made him thankful he hadn't pounced
first and asked questions later.

Lucy frowned. "I thought you had another, um, *client*
in Reltan."

"I did, but she canceled on me at the last minute."
Actually, Tarq had been the one to back out—he'd
called Rallene before he left town—but Lucy didn't
need to know that.

Tired and dusty, Lucy brought out every protective
instinct Tarq possessed. The thought of what might have
happened to her alone in the wilderness completely un-
nerved him, and his hands were shaking as he reached out
to push back a lock of her hair. "You should have told me
you were leaving, Lucy. I wouldn't have let you go alone."

"Which is exactly why I didn't tell you. I didn't want my father blaming you for any of this."

"But I *am* to blame."

Lucy shook her head. "No. None of this is your fault. It was my decision to have your children and my decision to leave home. I have a friend in Yalka. She's been begging me to come and stay with her for a long time."

Which was exactly what Tarq wanted to do himself, but he had an idea that blurting it out would have been a mistake. "Is that what you're going to do?"

"Yes," she said firmly. "I'm going to stay with Natasha until I can find a job and a place of my own." She glanced at Tarq and then at his speeder. "Maybe you *are* to blame a little. I envy your freedom. Walking out of that town felt *so* good."

Tarq winced. So, she *had* run away from him. Now that she was with child, he couldn't judge her desire for him by her scent anymore. Pregnant women had an aroma all their own, even more intoxicating than lust. He'd heard that this was a physiological change that kept a male from deserting his mate in her time of need…

His *mate*. *That* was why Rallene hadn't excited him. He was already mated with Lucy—and she hadn't exactly welcomed him with open arms. She'd even pulled a gun on him.

"Were you really planning to walk the whole way?"

"Well… yeah."

Despite her apparent exhaustion, Lucy obviously didn't intend to beg him for a ride, nor would she fall into his arms and declare her undying love for him. That would have been too easy. "Lucy, it's a two-day journey to Yalka in a *speeder*."

"So?"

Even if he had to force her to accept a ride from him—though he wasn't sure how he'd do it—Tarq wasn't about to let her continue on alone. "If I promise not to tell your father, will you at least let me give you a ride?"

"I probably shouldn't," she said, frowning. "I don't want to put you to any trouble—or *get* you in trouble."

"I'd be in more trouble if I left you out here alone. You could be attacked by wild animals, or break your leg on these rocks." He shook his head. "I can't do it, Lucy. If anything bad ever happened to you I'd—"

"Never know," she finished for him. "You'd be gone and…" She paused, narrowing her eyes. "Wait a minute—you wouldn't have found me if you hadn't been looking. How did you know I'd left Reltan?"

"I went to the café for breakfast this morning." Tarq gave her a sheepish grin. "Your father was really pissed."

Lucy giggled. "I'll just bet he was. And I'll bet Jublansk had some choice words for him too."

"Oh, yeah. Told him it was his fault you left. You should have heard her."

"I wish I had." She paused, shaking her head. "I should've stood up to him years ago. It wasn't until I thought about my kids having to listen to him rant that I decided to leave." She looked up, seeming suddenly shy. "Your, um, tips helped me decide too. That last one was really something. You shouldn't have done it, of course, but thank you."

Tarq shrugged, feeling a little embarrassed. "Like I said before, your situation is different from the other mothers. I thought it might help."

"It will."

"I still wish you hadn't run away like that. I would have helped you—"

"I didn't want to drag you into it, Tarq. The less you knew, the better."

Tarq chuckled. "I wound up in the middle of it anyway. Your father accused me of kidnapping you as soon as I walked into the café."

"That was pretty stupid of him."

Tarq couldn't argue with that. Uther had said and done a lot of stupid things.

Lucy fell silent for a few moments, frowning. "You didn't just happen to find me on your way to Yalka, did you?"

Tarq shook his head. "Jublansk thought you might head this way."

Lucy grimaced. "I'm glad you found me before my father did."

"I don't think he intends to look. He figures you'll come home when you get hungry. He doesn't know about the money I gave you. Besides, Jublansk didn't tell him anything. She told me."

Lucy glanced up at him with dismay. "Why you?"

"Jublansk knows—or at least suspects—more than you might think, Lucy."

Her expression changed, becoming more thoughtful. It was a long moment before she spoke again. "I probably should have told her everything, but I thought it would be better if she didn't know. That way she wouldn't have to lie."

Tarq smiled. "And I wouldn't either?"

"I never dreamed you'd have to," Lucy replied.

Tarq wrestled with his conscience, trying to come up with the best plan of action. A two-day trip in his speeder, plus camping out together at night. Surely he could convince her to stay with him during that time. The hard part would be getting her to understand that his past didn't matter anymore. He'd never be able to keep on with his current project with a limp dick, anyway— though it was perfectly hard at the moment. The need to mate with her was so strong he was surprised he could still think rationally.

"If you don't mind, I'd like to take you to Yalka," he said at last. "That way I'll at least know you got there safely."

When she began to protest, he cut her off. "It's not just your safety that's at stake, Lucy. You have to think about the children."

Her resistance crumbled. "You're right." She was agreeing with him, but she sounded so small, so defeated.

"Come on, Lucy, it'll be fun. I've never been on a road trip with anyone before; have you?"

She took a long time to reply. Tarq was beginning to believe she actually disliked him—and the idea of spending time with him. It hurt.

"No, I never have." She paused, smiling. "I've never been anywhere with anybody."

Tarq felt a faint glimmer of hope.

"But I really liked traveling by myself," she went on. "Someone has been telling me what to do for as long as I can remember. It was nice only having to consider my own wishes for a change. Is that selfish?"

"No," Tarq replied. "I know exactly how you feel. I enjoy the freedom too. But just this once, it would be nice to have someone along for the ride." *Someone like you*. Much as he wanted to, he couldn't just demand that she be his mate. They needed to spend this time together. Then she would see how he felt and maybe fall in love with him. If she didn't, Tarq didn't know what he was going to do.

She didn't say yes right away. In fact, she didn't say anything at all. Tarq had never dealt with a reluctant female before, and the suspense was killing him. Kidnapping was sounding better all the time. After all, she wasn't the only one with a pulse pistol. If he hadn't been afraid it would harm the babies, he would have stunned her and stuffed her in his speeder. But that would have made him just as bad as her father.

Despite the growing heat of the day, Tarq's hands felt like ice, and his heart was beating erratically. He knew she had to be the one to make the decision, but he simply couldn't wait any longer. He was already on his knees. Now he would have to beg.

"Lucy, please come with me. Freedom is a wonderful thing, but it gets lonely sometimes."

"You're *lonely*?" she asked, her disbelief quite plain.

He nodded. "All the time."

"But—but you have women everywhere!"

"*Had* women everywhere," he said grimly. "There's a difference."

Lucy frowned. "I don't get it."

"They're all strangers, Lucy. I can't remember any of their names, and I might not even recognize their faces. I've got hundreds of children too, but I've never held a single one of them in my arms. They'll learn how to swim and climb trees and pilot a speeder from someone else. I've seen pictures, of course, but it isn't the same as watching them grow up with my own eyes. Oh, yeah, Lucy. Believe me, there's a difference."

Her shoulders slumped visibly as she drew in a ragged breath. "Well... I guess it wouldn't hurt to ride to Yalka with you."

"Wouldn't *hurt*?" Tarq felt like she'd plunged a knife into his heart. "I-I thought you liked me."

"Oh, no, it isn't that I don't like you!" she said quickly. "I just... well, it's hard to explain."

Her frank dismay made him feel a little better, but this was obviously the best he was going to get for now. Tarq took a moment to collect his thoughts, knowing that if he said the wrong thing now, it was all over and he might lose her. Forever. "That's okay. You don't have to explain. Just as long as you come with me." Reaching out, he ran a fingertip down the side of her cheek, tilting her chin up to gaze into her warm brown eyes. He wanted to kiss her so badly he could hardly stand it. "I won't hurt you, Lucy. And I won't tell you what to do. I won't tell anyone who you are or where you came from. You can trust me."

Her voice was barely a whisper. "I know that. I'm sorry to put you to so much trouble. I never intended—"

Tarq put a finger to her lips. "You aren't causing me any trouble."

She swallowed with apparent difficulty. "Maybe not, but I did wind up costing you a lot of money."

"That was a gift, Lucy. You didn't ask for it. I *gave* it to you."

She nodded, but Tarq could see tears gathering in her eyes. "I don't understand why you're so nice to me. I'm not used to it."

Tarq knew kindness was unusual for her—at least with respect to her family. He couldn't understand why anyone would be hateful to such a kind and giving woman. It was like cursing a flower for being beautiful. "It's not hard to do. And I intend to go on being nice, so you'll just have to get over it."

"For a couple of days, anyway."

It took a moment before he realized what she meant. He only had the time it would take to reach Yalka. Then she would be with her friend and wouldn't need him anymore. Tarq didn't want to think about that.

Getting to his feet, he held out his hand. "Come on, then. You can sleep in the speeder if you like."

"I don't know if I'll be able to sleep or not," Lucy said as he pulled her upright. After dusting the dry leaves from her clothes, she picked up her blanket and shook it out.

Tarq slung her bag over his shoulder, taking note of the weight. She had to be completely exhausted from carrying it. "It's quiet and rides pretty smooth. The seat reclines too."

"I'm not worried about that. It's just that I've never ridden in a speeder before."

Tarq found this hard to believe, but it did explain why she'd been so willing to walk. A slow smile crept across his lips. "You're gonna love it."

Lucy approached Tarq's speeder with serious trepidation. It never ceased to amaze her that the pod-shaped vehicles could fly less than a meter off the ground without kicking up any dust. Dark green and streamlined, the speeder rested on three legs, each of which terminated in a wheel. The interior was covered with a clear dome that slowly parted in the middle in response to a tap from Tarq, revealing two upholstered seats at the front end and a rear cargo compartment.

Tarq tossed her bag in the back. There wasn't a whole lot there; just an assortment of boxes and what appeared to be a small, folded-up tent. He obviously believed in traveling light. Not that Lucy had much herself. Aside from a few clothes, most of what she carried was food and water, though probably not enough of either.

Tarq tapped the side and the passenger door folded out and down to form a step. He took her hand again and helped her to climb aboard. He was treating her like… a lady. Lucy didn't quite know what to make of it. No one had ever helped her do anything as simple as stepping into a speeder.

As she settled in, the seat instantly conformed to her shape and a belt arched over her, holding her snuggly in place. When Tarq closed the door, she spotted the controls on the side panel. With a touch of the recline icon, the seat back folded down while the underside rose up to form a footrest. *Yeah, I could get used to this.*

Tarq hopped into the driver's seat and started the engine. He hadn't been kidding about it being quiet. She barely heard a sound as the speeder lifted off and the supports retracted.

"Want the canopy open or closed?" he asked.

"Um, open," she replied, not completely sure what he meant.

Another touch of the controls and a cover slid over the cargo compartment, leaving the front seats open to the air. A windshield rose up out of the front panel. "You might want to sit up to start with."

Lucy readjusted her seat to the upright position and gave him a tentative smile.

"Ready?"

She nodded, doing her best to appear calm when she felt anything but.

With a wicked grin, Tarq slid his finger up the control bar.

The initial accelerative force hit Lucy in the middle of her chest, forcing her back against the seat. "Whoa, momma!"

Tarq was laughing, his hair flying out behind him. "Too fast?"

Lucy shook her head, feeling the thrill all the way to her toes. The wind rippled through her hair as the rocky landscape sped past. No, she didn't want him to slow down, not one tiny little bit. Hiking across the wilderness might have been liberating, but this was *fun*.

Lucy couldn't suppress her giggles, and soon she was laughing for the sheer joy of it. A feeling like this couldn't possibly be real. Surely she was still asleep and dreaming—which was the only possible explanation for the way Tarq had reappeared, seemingly out of nowhere. Her initial reluctance to travel with him was forgotten as she became swept up in the moment. Never mind the fact that she would have to go through the torture of giving him up all over again when they reached Yalka. For now, she and Tarq were free to be together, and the feeling was pure magic.

Whether he ever made love to her again or not was immaterial. *You've got two days, Lucy. Two whole days. Enjoy them, and never forget them.* She was giving herself excellent advice. Now all she had to do was follow it.

Chapter 9

THE EXCITEMENT OF THAT INITIAL BURST OF SPEED eventually settled into the tedious monotony of a long journey. Lucy's nap had been far too short, and the unchanging landscape and steady rush of the wind soon lulled her to sleep.

A full bladder woke her. She glanced at Tarq but was too embarrassed to say anything. True, she'd seen him naked—had been as intimate with him as a woman could be—but this was different. She shifted uncomfortably in her seat. Surely he'd have to go at some point himself. Then he would stop.

After several kilometers passed by, Lucy decided he wasn't going to stop anywhere near soon enough, if at all. She tried turning on her side, which only made matters worse. Why couldn't she just ask him? After all, she didn't have to say why…

"Do you need to take a break?"

His question startled her to the point that letting her out was nearly a moot point. "Um, yeah."

Tarq brought the speeder to a halt just off the trail near some tall jagged rocks that erupted from the ground like teeth.

Lucy raised her seat and twisted around, gazing back down the trail. "Nobody's following us, are they?"

"No. We've passed a few speeders coming from the other direction, though." He looked at her curiously.

"Do you really think your father could catch up with us now?"

Lucy shivered. "To tell you the truth, I wouldn't put it past him to be in Yalka waiting for me."

Tarq raised a skeptical eyebrow and patted her hand. "Not likely."

"I know, but I can't help feeling that way." She studied the control icons. "How do I open the door?"

Tarq stretched his arm across her and pointed. "That one."

Lucy winced. If she could keep him just a little further away, she might be able to get through the next two days without doing something stupid. Like grabbing him around the neck and kissing his lips off. She wondered if he would mind, or if he'd ever made love with one of his previous clients for old times' sake. Somehow she doubted it.

She tapped the icon and the side folded down. Climbing out, she noted how much cooler it was inside the speeder than out in the open air. She would've been getting very hot if she'd stayed where she was when he found her. The speeder must've had some sort of climate control feature even with the canopy open.

Tarq got out on the other side. "I'll be over this way," he said, gesturing toward a large rock formation.

She nodded, thinking he was being terribly considerate until she realized he probably needed to go too. Maybe he'd been waiting for her to ask. Picking her way through the rocks, she searched for a sheltered spot. This road trip together was proving to be more awkward than she would've expected. Still, though he wasn't human, he was bound to have some of the same needs. On the other hand, he wasn't pregnant.

Lucy wasn't feeling any symptoms yet, but she knew that it was only a matter of time before she was having all sorts of difficulties. As far as she knew, Nat hadn't had any children yet, but she might know someone who could give her some advice. Of course, most women had theirs one at a time. Lucy could hardly wait to see the look on Nat's face when she told her she was going to have triplets.

Tarq was leaning over the side of the speeder, reaching into the cargo hold when she returned. His jean-clad buns were aimed right at her, begging to be touched— and those amazing thighs… Then she remembered what they looked like without the jeans and her palms began to itch.

He tossed a grin over his shoulder. "Hungry?"

"Yeah, but I brought my own food."

"Raided the kitchen, didn't you?"

"How'd you know that?"

"Jublansk gave me some food for the road."

Lucy chuckled. "Guess she noticed I took all the bread then, didn't she?"

"Not all of it. You left the rye. She fixed me a couple of corned beef sandwiches with it. Want one?"

Corned beef was one of Lucy's absolute favorite things. Her mouth began to water. "Wish I'd thought of that."

Tarq shrugged. "Hey, it's not like you run away every day. You'll know better next time."

Lucy wasn't sure if he was trying to be funny or not, but when he handed her a sandwich, she realized she didn't give a damn. "Hot?"

He nodded. "This speeder has all kinds of useful features."

"No kidding. It must've cost a fortune." She frowned. "You're really rich, aren't you?"

Tarq shrugged. "Not as rich as Rutger Grekkor. He's the one who tried to kill all of us. His assets were divided among the survivors after his death. We went from having nothing to being well off pretty quickly. Then the guys and I made a killing on Rhylos."

"So I've heard," Lucy said dryly. "According to what Jublansk told me, I got two thousand credits worth of you."

Tarq actually blushed.

"And you paid me fifteen hundred." Lucy took a bite of her sandwich and nearly had an orgasm. She hadn't realized how hungry she was. "Too bad I'm not worth it."

Tarq glared at her. "I didn't *pay* you, Lucy—though I did ask you to call me. You aren't a—" He stopped as though unsure how to continue.

"A what? A whore? A prostitute? A surrogate mother?" Grimacing, she felt suddenly ill, which would have been a terrible waste of perfectly good corned beef. "They're all true."

Tarq's horrified expression surprised her—and was just a little frightening, particularly in light of his glowing catlike eyes and fangs. Get him truly angry and he'd be downright scary. "You don't really believe that, do you?"

Lucy shrugged. "I honestly don't know *what* I believe right now." She gave him a wry smile. "A lot has happened in the past few days."

Tarq nodded as though he understood. He handed her a bottle of water. Cold. *Ice* cold. The thought of how warm her own water would have been after sitting out in the sun all day almost had her kissing him. Almost. She didn't want to give him the wrong idea.

Funny how losing one's virtue was usually the most significant factor associated with being alone with a man. Until now. Her virtue having been already lost, she was in much greater danger of losing her heart. Tarq was nice to her, had made love with her in the most astonishing manner, was the most handsome man she'd ever seen, and was the father of her children. What was not to like?

Stupid question, she reminded herself as she sat down on a nearby rock to eat her lunch. It wasn't a matter of her liking him, but of him having the option to be with practically any woman who tickled his fancy. She wouldn't even make the top ten. Lucy still hadn't figured out why he'd asked her to call him in the first place, though perhaps it was because he thought she'd be a good mother— *and* be able to successfully carry triplets. For once in her life, she was thankful for her relatively wide pelvis.

Just as she should have been thankful he'd found her and offered her a ride. However, one surreptitious glance at him was enough to remind her why she'd been so hesitant. He was only leaning against a rock licking a drop of mayo off his finger, but it was all she could do not to fall at his feet, begging him to toss her a few crumbs of his affection. How was it possible for any man to be so appealing?

Just don't look at him, Lucy. Keep your eyes on the ground. She stared at a fascinating pile of stones until she finished her sandwich.

"Want some pie?"

Despite her best intentions, her eyes flew up to meet his. No, he wasn't tossing her crumbs, he was holding out a piece of her own chocolate pie—on a plate, no less. There was even a fork. His impish smile sent a shock wave through her resolve, destroying it completely.

Lucy was surprised she could even speak. "I probably would've brought some of that myself if I'd had a way to carry it."

"Well, I'm glad you left it for me then. But I'm willing to share." His smile widened into a grin, and Lucy blinked, momentarily stunned by the full effect. If he had any idea what he was doing to her, he was being terribly inconsiderate.

She took the plate from him. "Thanks."

"You're welcome."

With the first bite, Lucy had to stifle a moan. She didn't often get to eat the pies she made and had forgotten how delicious they were.

No, she decided, Tarq wouldn't be inconsiderate, not if he was willing to share the pie he liked so much. He was simply unaware of the lethal nature of his appeal, or the danger it posed to susceptible females. Getting to her through her stomach had to be inadvertent too; he couldn't possibly know her favorite foods.

"So, where does this friend of yours live?"

Thankful for a neutral topic, Lucy was able to respond normally. "She and her husband have a farm on this side of Yalka. She always told me it would be the first place I came to after crossing the Malturn."

"Shouldn't be hard to find then." He paused for a moment, savoring a bite of the pie. "What if you get there and she's changed her mind?"

"Nat wouldn't do that," Lucy said with more conviction than she actually felt. She wouldn't admit that she hadn't heard from Nat for a while. A woman with a farm and animals to care for was bound to be too busy to write. Or call. Or visit.

"Let's say she does. What would you do then?"

"I'll go into town, get a room, and look for a job. Thanks to you, I'm not dependent on charity."

"Glad I could help."

He didn't seem glad. He seemed… irritated. Lucy was about to ask if he wanted his money back, but knowing how important it was to her children's welfare, as well as her own, she kept silent.

Tarq finished his pie and put the plate into a compartment in the speeder. "Are those your only options?"

"Well, yeah, I guess so. I mean, what else is there?"

"I just think you're limiting yourself. You're pretty smart—a lot smarter than I am. You could do lots of things."

"I'm not that smart. All I've ever really done is clean houses, cook, wait tables—stuff like that."

"Bet you could run your own café." His irritation was gone, replaced by a warm smile. "Best chocolate pie in the galaxy. You could put that on a sign. You'd have more customers than you knew what to do with."

Lucy felt herself blushing. "I could probably steal Jublansk from my father. Then I'd have the best pie *and* the best salads—not to mention the best bread. Not sure about the fish, though I *have* watched him make it a million times."

"You could do it."

"Maybe, but getting a restaurant going takes time and

money—and energy. Not sure a pregnant girl would be up to it."

Tarq frowned. "What if I—" He stopped; his frown deepened, his already slanted brows becoming almost vertical.

"Helped me? No, Tarq. You've already helped me enough."

"I could be a partner—you know, put up the money and reap all the benefits?"

The gleam in his eye told her he was teasing, but the words "partner" and "benefits" had Lucy's thoughts headed in a direction they shouldn't be taking. "Sounds like you'd be taking advantage of a poor, pregnant girl."

His attempt at suppressing a smile failed miserably. "Ah, Lucy. I'd never do that."

Lucy suspected he already had—though probably not the way he thought. He'd taken advantage of her aloneness, her vulnerability, and the fact that somewhere along the line she'd fallen head over heels in love with him.

Tarq watched the subtle changes in Lucy's expression with interest. Her wince served as proof that she didn't like his partnership suggestion; either that or she was in some sort of pain. "The offer still stands. Promise me you'll at least think about it. Okay?"

She nodded, but the way she bit her lower lip didn't bode well for the outcome. He wanted another night with her so very badly. Just one more—maybe two, if he was lucky. It wasn't too much to ask, especially if that was all he would ever get. He longed to scoop her up in his arms right now, to kiss away her pain and fears and any doubts she had. He would give her anything. If only she would let him.

"We should get going." He took her empty plate and put it in the cleaning compartment. The sequence began as soon as he pushed the top closed.

"This thing has a *dishwasher*?"

Tarq nodded. Too bad she wasn't the type to be won over by a guy with a cool speeder. Seducing her would be much easier—that is, if seduction was his only goal. "It does a lot of things. I've practically lived out of it for almost two years."

"I never knew they could do all that."

"Most are made for short-distance travel. This is one of the more recreational types. I've even got a tent."

"I saw that." She glanced at the harsh landscape around her and shuddered. "Don't suppose it's big enough to share, is it?"

The thought of sharing a tent with Lucy made his cock twitch. It was already hard—and had been ever since he found her. "What's the matter? Afraid of the dark?"

"It was… a little spooky last night when I was awake and walking. I hadn't realized how different it would be sleeping out here alone."

"Never camped out before?"

Lucy rolled her eyes. "I've never done *anything* before."

Tarq could think of at least one rather significant "thing" she'd done recently. Something entirely new. Even so, this was overshadowed by the realization that he would be able to hold her in his arms again. *For the entire night*. He couldn't stop smiling.

"It isn't funny," she said, glaring at him.

Not wanting to seem like an insensitive idiot, Tarq sobered instantly. "That's not why I'm smiling."

"Oh?"

"I'm remembering *something* you did for the first time—three nights ago."

Her blush jacked Tarq's temperature up a few degrees. How was he ever going to wait until dark?

"Yeah, well, that was different."

Tarq was intrigued. "How so?"

She gazed up at him with those soft brown eyes he was beginning to realize he couldn't live without. "I wasn't afraid of *you*."

A lump formed in his throat, which might have kept him from speaking—if he'd had any idea what to say.

"Nervous, perhaps. But not afraid."

Tarq held his breath.

"I mean, you knew what you were doing. You weren't some creep or a bumbling teenager."

"Oh." Her steady gaze never wavered from his. "And that's a good thing?"

"Well, yeah," she replied. "Why wouldn't it be?"

"Just checking."

So she wasn't afraid of him and he wasn't a creep or a bumbling teenager. It was a start.

Tarq's jeans weren't what you'd call tight, but he couldn't believe Lucy hadn't noticed the lump hiding beneath the zipper. Then again, maybe she was purposely ignoring it. Tarq wished he could do the same, but as the day went on and the kilometers flew by, he was beginning to think he wouldn't survive the night, whether he held her in his arms or not.

She'd dozed off again—either that or she was pretending to sleep so he wouldn't talk to her. He wasn't sure why she would do something like that, but the niggling fear persisted.

Late in the day, they came upon a stream bisecting the trail and Tarq didn't bother to wake her. He aimed the speeder along the banks until he found a relatively smooth spot where a few small trees grew. Even with the water source nearby, the trees were still stunted and gnarled, as though they'd been there for centuries, growing only millimeters at a time.

As the speeder settled on its wheels, Lucy began to stir.

"Good place to camp," Tarq said in response to her curious expression. Getting out of the speeder, he uncovered the cargo hold and pulled out the tent. "This'll just take a second."

Unrolling the tent, he pressed the erect button and the tent slowly unfolded and rose from the ground. He had only to press the same button again to lower it, but he found himself wishing he had a button like that on his dick. It would have made things simpler. At least he could've disguised his reaction to her—and her scent.

Even with the speeder's canopy open, he'd still caught enough occasional whiffs of her to keep him aroused all day. Being together in the tent would be torture if she didn't take pity on him.

"That's pretty neat," she remarked.

Tarq shrugged. "It's come in handy a few times." He was feeling irritated. Maybe taking a little walk by himself would help. At least he'd lose his erection when he couldn't smell her. He'd never been around a pregnant woman for any length of time and wasn't sure if this effect would last throughout the entire pregnancy or if a fuck a day would keep the hard-on away. Maybe after a few months…

"Hungry?"

"Um, yeah. I'll be right back."

She went behind a nearby rock, presumably to pee. Tarq was about to follow her just to catch her with her pants down but decided that wouldn't be very romantic, or considerate. Her absence did, however, ease his cock a little bit, which was a relief. If he'd had any idea how he was going to feel, he might not have tried to find her.

No. That simply wasn't true. He'd gone looking for her, hoping she'd want him. Obviously she didn't. Her pregnant scent was fooling him into thinking she did. Not a creep or a bumbling teenager. Oh yes, and she wasn't afraid of him. She should have been. He was feeling about as surly as a vrelnot.

He pulled her blankets out of the back of the speeder and pitched them into the tent. His own stuff was already in there. His and hers. It wasn't like they'd actually share.

His dick might have felt better while she was gone, but his irritation level increased. She'd been gone much too long. He was about to go looking for her when she finally returned. "What do you want to eat?"

"I've got some bread and cheese," she began.

"You need better food than that," he snapped. "More nutritious stuff. Like vegetables and fruit."

"I've got some grapes."

"Fine. Eat them too."

He glanced up to find her staring at him as though he'd grown another arm. "Tarq, are you mad at me?"

"No." But the way he said it sounded like a snarl. "Want a campfire?"

"Not unless you do."

Tarq did. He needed to set something on fire, either that or kill something. Anything. He toyed with the idea of going hunting for a vrelnot. With his bare hands. He began gathering up dead branches, tossing them into a pile.

Lucy stood there for a long moment, frowning. "Did you, um, visit a client last night?"

"No, I didn't." He whirled around to face her. "And why would you care if I did?"

She put up a placating hand. "Just asking. Do you always get this mean when you haven't had sex?"

Tarq growled at her. Actually growled.

"I guess that answers my question."

"No, it's not that."

"Well, what is it, then? Or are you just tired and hungry?"

"I-I don't know." He picked up one of the larger limbs and slammed it onto the pile.

"What would make you feel better?"

"Huh?"

"Food, sex, or sleep?"

"Oh. Maybe."

"Which one?"

"Aw, I don't know, Lucy. I'm just feeling…"

"Crabby?"

Tarq shrugged. He didn't know what to say. He wanted to fuck her brains out, eat a gargantuan meal, and sleep for a week—in that order—but saying so would probably make him a creep.

"You're probably just tired from driving all day. Why

don't you get that fire started and then we'll eat something and get some sleep?"

Obviously sex wasn't going to be on the agenda. He stomped over to the speeder and snatched up the firestarter. One shot and the collection of sticks went up in flames.

She shooed him away. "Now go sit down by the fire and I'll bring you something."

"There are all kinds of—"

"I'll find it," she said. "Just sit down."

No, he wasn't a creep. He was a jerk, which was just about as bad. He did what she told him, though. The warmth of the fire felt good and watching the flames was soothing. The smoke had an interesting aroma to it. *Rulbnach bark.* He'd smelled it before. Somewhere. His breathing steadied and the pain in his groin began to subside. He was going about this all wrong. He knew that.

He was a little surprised when Lucy handed him a plate of hot food. "How did you know how to work all that stuff?"

"I read the directions."

"Oh." He'd forgotten she could read and figure things out on her own. Not like him. Waroun had shown him how to work every feature of the speeder. Tarq could remember it all, but figure it out on his own? Probably not. "I knew you were smart."

"Not really." She sat down a little apart from him, thankfully upwind. Maybe she understood more about what was bothering him than he realized.

"Sorry I was being so crabby."

"Don't worry about it. If I could put up with my father all these years, I can take a little guff from you."

Tarq hated the idea that she would think of him in the same light as her hateful parent. "I'm not usually like that." He might as well tell her. "It's your scent."

"My scent?"

He nodded. "You smelled incredible the first day we met. And now that you're pregnant, I—" *want to fuck you so bad I can't stand it*. And not merely fuck. He wanted to make sweet, delirious love to her for hours on end. "Pregnant women smell really good to Zetithian men. I've never hung around any of my clients long enough to know that until now. I've been told about it, of course, but never…"

"I see," she said slowly. "And my pregnant scent affects you… how?"

"Can't you guess?"

She sighed, nodding. "You want sex, don't you?"

Tarq gave up trying to be subtle. "In the worst possible way."

Chapter 10

No doubt about it. Lucy was not going to survive this adventure with Tarq—at least not with her heart intact. She reminded herself that their next parting would be every bit as painful as the last, whether they did anything about Tarq's problem or not. Ultimately, from her perspective, it didn't matter what they did, though it obviously meant a great deal to him.

Yeah, right. Who am I kidding? Of course it matters.

Memories. She would have more of them to cherish long after he was gone.

In the end, it was easy. All she had to say was "Okay."

Tarq's pent-up breath went out with a whoosh. "Thank God." He started to put down his plate.

"Eat your dinner first," she said firmly. "I don't know about you, but I'm starving."

"Can you come over here and sit beside me?"

"Not if I intend to get anything to eat." Then another problem occurred to her. "Besides, I haven't had a shower since yesterday morning and I was on the road all night. Not sure you want to get that close to me."

"Believe me, Lucy, that is *not* a problem."

"Maybe not to you, but it is to me." She glanced at the stream. "It's probably too cold to take a bath in that."

"I have some *scrail* cloths. You can use those."

"*Scrail* cloths?"

"From Darconia—desert planet, no water to speak

of. That's all they use there. I prefer taking a shower myself, but they work very well."

Lucy chuckled. "How do you wash them? Does your speeder have a washing machine too?"

"No, it doesn't have a washing machine," he said with a withering glance. "*Scrail* cloths pick up dirt and oils from your body. Direct sunlight makes them repel it. You don't have to wash them."

"Very handy on a camping trip."

Tarq nodded and began wolfing down his dinner.

"Might as well slow down enough to taste that," she suggested. "You'll have to wait until I'm finished anyway."

He was growling again but took her advice.

Lucy wasn't surprised he'd been so affected because her "pregnant" scent wasn't the only one he'd been picking up. Obviously trying to sleep to keep from thinking about him hadn't helped a bit. *Poor Tarq*. He had no more control over his reactions than she did.

Thinking back, Lucy realized that this decision, like so many others, had been made for her. She'd been intending to take Nat up on her offer forever, but she had never had a good enough reason until this one landed in her lap. And now she'd been handed the best excuse imaginable to jump Tarq's bones. She could feel all the desire for him she liked and he would think it was just because she was pregnant. In essence, she would be giving him a pity fuck. *Unbelievable. A Zetithian getting a pity fuck*? It was all she could do to keep from laughing out loud.

But that would've been tacky. She couldn't very well make fun of him, not when he was about to fulfill her fondest wish. Well, maybe not her *fondest* wish, because he hadn't said anything about falling in love with her. He only wanted her because of the way she smelled. *Fine. I can handle that. Maybe.*

Having finished her meal, she put her plate in the cleaning compartment. "How does this dishwasher thing work, anyway?"

"No idea," Tarq replied. "I just put the dishes in, close the lid, and when the light goes off, they come out clean."

"Cool." She leaned over the side of the speeder and flipped the lid off another compartment. "So, where are these *scrail* thingies?"

She'd forgotten he was a cat—didn't hear a sound until he began purring in her ear. "Please, don't do that now, Lucy. I like your scent just the way it is."

"Yeah, well, maybe it wouldn't drive you so crazy if I was a little cleaner."

He was still purring, running his fingers up and down her spine in the most tantalizing way. "But now that I know you don't mind, I *want* you to drive me crazy."

Don't mind? That was putting it mildly.

Tarq pulled her out of the speeder and into his arms. Hot kisses rained down on her lips, cheeks, neck… Oh, no. This wasn't something she put up with out of pity. This was heaven itself.

A long, wet lick began where her neck met her shoulder and didn't stop until he reached her cheekbone. Lucy couldn't tell if he was purring or growling. His hands slid up the back of her shirt, releasing her bra before yanking it all off over her head. Capturing her breasts, he pressed them together and buried his face between them, again licking her like she was made of candy.

Bunching his own shirt up in her hands, she pulled it up around his neck, rubbing her palms over his hot skin, tangling her fingers in his hair. When his tongue found her nipples, she let out a moan. Mingling feathery touches with hard sucks, he drove her absolutely insane.

Wanting to see his naked body before they lost the light, she reached for the button on his jeans. His snarl had her hesitating, but Tarq grabbed her hand and pressed it against his cock. His jeans were soaked and his cock felt like an iron rod.

"This is what you're doing to me, Lucy. I've been like that all day."

He must've been keeping his shirt pulled down over his groin; otherwise she'd never have missed it. "I'm sorry," she whispered. "You should have told me sooner."

With one last lick, Tarq backed away and kicked off his sandals. His shirt and jeans were gone in an instant.

Lucy put up a hand as he began to lunge toward her. "Wait. I want to look at you—I never really had the chance before."

The setting sun was behind her, illuminating every plane and valley of his body while the evening breeze toyed with his hair. Muscles rippled across his chest, and veins stood out on his arms. A line of blond curls led from his navel to the larger nest of crisp hair surrounding his cock—that fabulous cock Lucy had thought she'd never see again. Thick and long, it curved toward her like a snake about to strike, the scalloped head aimed right at her, orgasmic syrup dripping like venom from the points. His meaty balls hung low against those incredible thighs, thick with powerful muscles and lightly dusted with more blond curls.

"P-put your hands behind your head."

The muscles in his arms bunched and his chest and belly stretched upward, accentuating the oblique line where his torso met his hips. More hair curled from the V-shaped indentations beneath his arms, and his strong neck flexed as he swallowed.

He glanced at her arms crossed tightly over her chest. "You're going to have to do the same thing for me, Lucy." His voice sounded strained, barely controlled.

"Not sure I can," she said, shaking her head. "I could never look *that* good. No way."

"That's purely a matter of opinion, and in this case, mine is the only one that counts." He smiled, revealing sharp white fangs, his smoky blue eyes glowing with need. Lowering his arms, his gaze lingered briefly on her breasts, then slid down below her waist. "Please."

Lucy didn't want to uncover her breasts, let alone remove more clothing. Even though she'd been with him before, she still felt shy. But since he was begging...

As soon as she moved her hands away, Lucy knew she was making the right choice. Tarq's cock pulsed, sending more fluid gushing from the head. Though she thought it was a shame to waste it, she also knew there was plenty more where that came from. Stepping out of her moccasins, she untied the drawstring at her waist, letting her baggy khakis fall to the ground. His purring grew louder as he stared pointedly at her panties.

Deciding that there was no point in making a sensual show of it, Lucy simply took them off the way she always did. She was on the point of running to him when she realized that this whole thing was her call. He might have been miserable, but he wouldn't have touched her if she hadn't agreed—heady thoughts for a girl who'd never had a boyfriend. Holding out her hand, she beckoned to him.

Tarq was on her in seconds, pushing her back against the speeder, his lips fastened on her own. The speeder never budged, which was fortunate because he wasn't being the least bit gentle. The moment she looped her arms around his neck, he pulled her legs up on his hips and thrust into her.

For the first time in her life, Lucy felt sexy, alluring. This incredible man had been in torment for the entire day because of her, and she didn't give a damn if it was her scent or the color of her hair that drove him wild. It simply didn't matter. Tarq was in her arms, his stiff shaft buried in her core, and she was taking everything he had to give. Within seconds the first orgasm struck with an impact that shocked every nerve cell in her body. And then another and another...

The last rays of the day turned his hair a fiery reddish gold. As the sky darkened, his glowing pupils waxed brighter, drawing her eyes to his face. His blissful expression still visible in the ensuing twilight, she touched his cheek, tracing the upward curve of his ear to its point. At that moment, in her eyes he was the most beautiful soul in existence, if, indeed, he hadn't always been.

Her touch slowed him as though she truly did have control. Rocking slow and deep, he pressed his forehead against hers, his hair forming a curtain that separated them both from the world. Sighing, he tilted his head back, tears glittering on his upturned cheeks as he gazed up at the sky. Whether they were tears of relief, frustration, or joy didn't matter to Lucy. Even if she had been doing this out of pity, she would have abandoned that motivation to replace it with the truer emotion: love.

Pure, deep, and everlasting.

Tarq could already see stars twinkling overhead, and he wished on every single one of them that Lucy would be his mate. He knew he could ask her to *make* love with him, but he couldn't find the courage to ask her to *love* him. Asking her wouldn't make it happen. Love wasn't something you could decide to do because it was the right thing or because someone begged you to. Either you did or you didn't. You could grow to love someone in time—but time was something he didn't have.

He opened his mouth, but the words didn't come; only a purr escaped his lips. Could she tell what he meant? Probably not. He felt the chill of the night air descend on his shoulders. Lucy would be cold, especially against the side of the speeder. *How inconsiderate of me.* Reaching for her hips, he held her tightly against him as he backed away from the speeder. The rocks hurt his feet, but he ignored the pain as he carried her to the tent. Ducking under the flap, he found the pile of bedding and sank to his knees. Still holding her warmth against his chest, he leaned over to lay her on the pallet. It was fully dark inside and he glanced at the glowstone suspended from the roof of the tent. As he wished for more light, it slowly illuminated, but only enough to enable him to see her. She gazed up at him with such tenderness Tarq could hardly bear to part from her, but he knew he had to. "I'll be right back."

Stepping outside, he checked the fire, which had already burned down to a few glowing embers and posed no danger. Then he gathered up their clothing and a few items he thought she might need and locked down the speeder.

Lucy was right where he'd left her, staring up at the glowstone with awe. "I've heard of these things," she said, pointing to the stone. "They're very rare."

"Not on Darconia," Tarq said. "Which is where I got it."

Lucy nodded. "Must be nice to be able to travel around like that. How do you get from planet to planet?"

"My friend Dax has a ship. He takes me anywhere I want to go, drops me off, and then picks me up when I'm ready to leave." Tarq folded their clothes and stacked them in the corner before securing the tent flap. "I've been lots of places. Some were beautiful, and some not so nice."

"What do you think of Talus?"

"I liked Reltan. It was… peaceful, and the beach was better than most."

"Yeah."

Her voice sounded lost. "Do you miss it already?"

"Sort of. I've never been anywhere else."

Tarq took a deep breath. "It's not too late to go back."

"No," she said firmly. "No. I'm not going back. At least not for a while."

Tarq gathered up more blankets and spread them out next to Lucy. Stretching out, he lay down beside her. "Are you cold?"

"No. I'm fine." She hesitated. "Are you okay now?"

Tarq shook his head. "I'm just getting started."

Rolling onto his stomach, he began again, kissing her and delighting in the feel of her hair between his fingers. Having her there, naked inside the tent, intensified her unique fragrance, sending waves of desire coursing through his blood. This time he didn't fight it but let it flow, guiding his moves. His lips roamed over her body, tasting, feeling, enjoying... Lucy's fingers threaded through his hair, combing it back behind his ears, massaging his scalp. He purred, rather than voiced, his appreciation as she stroked the tips of his ears. Most of his clients never bothered with that particular erogenous zone, but Lucy read his response exactly right. Soothing, stimulating, enticing—her touch was perfect. Nuzzling her breast, he took the nipple into his mouth, laving it with his tongue, teasing it until it was fully erect and Lucy was moaning beneath him. Then he moved on to the other one.

His hands couldn't get enough of her; the soft globes of her breasts, her hair, her satiny skin... every part of her beckoned. Lucy fisted her hands in his hair, pulling him up for a kiss. There was nothing shy about the way she kissed him, her mouth opening to his, delving inside as she welcomed him in. She still tasted like the grapes he'd insisted she eat. How could she be so warm and loving when he'd snapped at her like that? He had no answer other than that she was Lucy, the most kind, giving, and, yes, loving woman he'd ever known. He loved everything she did to him—from pulling his hair to the way she let her fingertips run along the middle of his back.

He worked his way down her body again, this time venturing further, parting her thighs to inhale her scent and taste her sweetness. Intoxicated, he felt like he was drowning in her essence, but he didn't care. One taste and his pulse began to pound in his ears and in his cock. Nothing could keep him from her now.

Moving up over her again, he eased into her wet heat. Slowly, with short, gentle strokes, he reached the limit, his balls resting against her skin, his cockhead pressing on the hard nub of her cervix. He felt her shudder and hug his shaft with her tight vaginal muscles and knew that another orgasm had taken her in its grasp. He pulled back, letting her hold on him fan the coronal ridge back toward the glans. Few things felt better than that, and he rocked in quickly, only to withdraw again with excruciating slowness. He teetered on the brink of ecstasy, stopping only when he knew one more pull would signal the point of no return. He wasn't ready for that. Not yet.

Pushing against the anterior wall, he found her sweet spot. He'd heard it called other things, but in his mind, this was its rightful name. Raking the jagged edge of his penis over it made Lucy tighten up even more, squeezing him so hard he could barely move. "Relax," he whispered. "Give me some room."

"And you will give me joy unlike any I have ever known?"

Tarq smiled. "Something like that."

"I'll try." Her breathing became slow and deep as he felt her body gradually surrender to him.

His cock played back and forth across that small area, teasing, stroking. Her tiny gasps of ecstasy drove him on, sweeping circles inside her, taking pleasure even as he gave it. His fluid elicited a climax from her at regular intervals, but he waited them out, knowing that she would soon melt around him again—a feeling he liked even better than the clenching orgasms. Then her breathing altered, and her scent underwent a subtle change. He could feel it coming; he was close himself. *Not yet... not yet...*

Suddenly, her breath went out with a hiss and he felt the rhythmic contractions begin. Only then did he let his own need take over, pumping into her with short, hard thrusts. Tarq held his breath as his body erupted, spilling his *snard* over her sensitive flesh as she cried out his name.

He cradled her in his arms as the sweeping motion of his coronal ridge began. Not ever wanting to move away from her again, he gazed down at her face; the light dusting of freckles, the gentle arch of her brow, the way her lashes lay against her cheek... she was so beautiful, so sweet... Leaning closer, he kissed her softly parted lips as a tear slid from the corner of his eye. Raising his head, he let it flow down his cheek. No woman had ever made him cry before. Lucy had done it twice.

Unfortunately, women wanted mates who were strong, and Lucy would probably see this as a sign of weakness. Too kind to tell him straight out, she would simply insist on following her original plan. Tarq would never be able to talk her out of it—even if he tried, he was sure to say the wrong thing—and he probably couldn't fuck her out of it, either. Stashing her in the speeder and heading straight for the Noklar spaceport was his best bet, but Dax wouldn't be there to pick him up for another month.

Tarq had money, though. He could keep Lucy in a hotel while he wined and dined her and tried to convince her to come with him. No, that wouldn't work. She was smart. The more time she spent with him, the more she would realize he was nothing but a big dumb stud. Without her family's repression, she would truly shine, and other men would flock to her.

She only let him make love to her because she took pity on him in his misery. Unfortunately, his dick wasn't the only thing making him miserable. A lifetime of insecurities ganged up on him, telling him he was a fool, that no intelligent woman would ever consider him as more than a passing fancy.

Tarq did his best to ignore the warnings of his mind, trying to focus on Lucy and her scent, but he couldn't turn off his unwanted thoughts. Women could get hooked on the effects of Zetithian *snard*. Knowing that, he should have kept his distance. He knew they both needed to rest too, but he wanted to keep her up all night. If only he could fall asleep inside her.

Lucy's sigh interrupted his thoughts, bringing him back to the present. She was smiling up at him with joy shining forth from her eyes. He had given her that joy, which should have been enough for him.

But it wasn't.

It didn't even come close.

Chapter 11

Lucy awoke warm and snug with... She opened one eye the merest slit. Yes, Tarq was still there. Her sigh of relief should have awakened him, but he slept on, as relaxed and contented as a house cat. She could even hear the whisper of a purr as he breathed.

Well, that's one wish granted. Now what do I do? Propping herself up on her elbow, Lucy gazed at his sleeping form. He was even curled up like a cat, his back pressed up against her.

Or was she pressed up against him? Which one of them was responsible for the contact? Since she couldn't remember falling asleep, she had to assume it was his choice. While she found this comforting, she was also intrigued. Did it help him sleep? Did it keep his "needs" at bay, or would he wake up wanting sex again?

While the idea didn't bother her a bit, she thought it might be helpful if she at least attempted to erase some of the scent that was apparently driving him nuts. Figuring that a round with a *scrail* cloth might help, she moved slowly, inching her way out from beneath the blankets. After a quick trip outside to relieve herself, she crept over to the stack of things Tarq had brought in the night before. The odd texture of the *scrail* cloth was immediately obvious. Picking one up, she rubbed it against her arm, feeling a subtle magnetic pull on her skin, almost as though the dirt and skin oils were being vacuumed off. Her hair was the worst; it had a tendency to be oily anyway, and missing a shampoo or two had turned it into a greasy, stringy mess. Not knowing whether she needed to scrub her head with it or if a quick pass over her hair would do the trick, she tried both and was amazed with the results. Soft, clean, and silkier than usual, she shook her head, enjoying the feel as it brushed her bare shoulders. After a quick pass over the rest of her body, she rummaged through her duffel bag and found her toothbrush, thankful that Tarq had also brought in a few bottles of water.

The sound of her brushing her teeth must have awakened him, for his purring grew louder. After a few moments, he sat up and sniffed the air.

"It's no use, Lucy. I can still smell you."

"Sorry. Guess I ought to get dressed and go outside."

Chuckling softly, he crawled toward her. "That's not what I meant." Grabbing her around the waist, he pulled her down and, pinning her beneath his body, kissed her thoroughly. He didn't even have morning breath. *Is there no end to his perfection?*

A tongue delving inside his mouth revealed the reason. He tasted like mint. He'd already been up and had come back to bed, which meant that he'd been the one to curl up against her. This revelation gave Lucy a warm, fuzzy sensation inside, somewhat akin to the feeling she got when a stray animal took a shine to her, which they typically did. This might have been due to the fact that she tended to hand out leftover food to any who hung around the back door to the café, but she'd managed to tame some of the most skittish that way. Even the wild trelinks would eat out of her hand, though most people couldn't stand the ratlike creatures. Lucy saw them as being more like squirrels than rats, but she also knew that her attitude toward them was uncommon.

Tarq, however, was no stray cat. Granted, he had a tendency to roam, but he was in no need of a handout— whether it was food or sex. He could get as much as he liked of either of those things from almost anyone. It didn't have to be from her. And it usually wasn't. She wasn't the first woman he'd awakened beside; he'd probably gotten up early to brush his teeth through force of habit. Lucy tried not to think about that.

Still, no matter how many women he'd been with, at this moment, Lucy was the one meeting his needs, and it made her feel useful, needed, and above all, special. She wanted to give him everything and spoil him rotten. He would probably never come to rely upon her, but the thought that he might was one she couldn't quite shake. She wished she was as beautiful and beguiling as he was irresistibly handsome; then she could make it as hard for him to leave her as it was for her to leave him.

Which she still intended to do. A blissful existence with Tarq at her side forever simply wasn't possible. Still, though she might have dismissed the idea as nonsense, she could dream. The house she'd imagined came back to her again as she kissed him, the way it could be, the way she wished it would be. Putting every ounce of emotion she felt into that intimacy, she was rewarded with his passionate response and silently vowed to return every kindness he showed her tenfold.

Releasing her inhibitions, she kissed him with wild abandon, tasting every part of him her mouth could reach. Fisting her hands in his hair, she forced his head back, exposing his neck to her caressing tongue while he purred his approval. With her lips pressed against his throat, she let the vibrations penetrate her flesh, seeping into her mind and body, soothing and enticing her soul. Tarq hissed as she took his skin between her teeth, biting it gently.

"Oh, Lucy," he sighed. "What you do to me…"

In another moment, he was inside her, his hot shaft melting her from within, moving first with long, steady thrusts, then softening to a slow dance as though he had all the time in the world to make her feel how much he wanted her, needed her…

She wouldn't allow herself the next thought. No, he didn't love her. Her own family didn't even love her. The best she'd ever managed to receive in the love department was in the soft-eyed gaze of a trelink when she fed it stale bread.

Don't think. Just feel. Her spirits lifted instantly as those words took over, letting her become aware of nuances of sensation: his breath on her skin, his fingers threading through her hair, his cock delving deeply, discovering sensitive spots whose existence she'd been unaware of until now. The sound of his purr, his soft growls, the quiet sucking sounds his cock made as it moved within her wet folds—all these things combined to bring her to a high she'd never experienced, even with Tarq. When his slick fluid triggered her climax, she felt separated from her own body, all the while becoming more intimately acquainted with his. As the surge of pleasure began to ebb, her hands found his back, drifting aimlessly over his skin, absorbing every peak and hollow, every muscle as it moved. The beat of his heart, the steady expansion of his chest, the glow in his eyes, the flash of light on the tip of a fang—all these things poured into her, deepening her awareness of him. So much so that when he reached his climax, it felt as though it originated in her own mind.

The powerful burst of exhilaration swept through her before sliding quietly down into the blissful serenity of *laetralance*. Tarq was right about it being the best way to describe the feeling. No other word even came close.

This time, when she felt the sweeping motions inside her, she knew them for what they were. Sadly, she also understood the reason for the downfall of his species. No other man could even begin to approach the levels of joy a Zetithian could take a woman to, no matter how hard he might try. It simply couldn't be done. Regret filled her then. Finding another man was no longer an option. Not when she'd already been with the best man she would ever know.

Tarq watched the joy blossoming in her eyes and, as before, knew it wasn't enough. He had to quit doing that—looking for something he would never find. Not in her. Not in anyone. It was pointless to keep trying when the result was always the same. He couldn't blame her, though. She couldn't help how she felt, how she responded, any more than she could help how her scent affected him.

Sighing, he slid off to lie beside her but couldn't bring himself to let go just yet, leaving a hand splayed out on her stomach. Yalka itself was less than a day away, and this friend's home was even closer. He had one more day—not even another night unless he was lucky and something occurred to delay them. Too bad there wasn't anything interesting enough along the way to make them linger. Until they'd come across this stream, the terrain hadn't changed a bit since he'd left Reltan.

Breakfast could take a long time if he made a point of it. Leisurely. That was the word he was looking for. No hurry. No worry. No fuss. Fix it, eat it, clean up. Pack up the tent... Oh, yeah, he could stretch that out into a good hour and a half, maybe even longer. They could even wash their clothes in the stream and hang around waiting for them to dry, which would take at least until lunchtime. He'd been in too much of a hurry the day before. It was stupid of him not to go slowly when she was asleep. Today, she would be awake and would probably fuss at him for puttering along like a man whose speeder could barely fly.

If her father could be believed, he wouldn't be coming after her so there was no need for haste, and the best he could tell, this friend of hers wasn't expecting her. Tarq smiled to himself. This could turn into a real vacation if he took his time. He could stop every half hour if necessary. He could invent speeder trouble, spot some interesting birds—though he hadn't seen very many—or feign a cramp in his legs from sitting in the speeder for so long. He could make sure she drank plenty of water so she'd have to pee a lot. He would be stalling for time, but she didn't have to know that. Then he realized he wouldn't have to lie if he just flat-out asked her.

"Are you in a hurry to get to Yalka?"

She seemed to hesitate. "Well, sort of. Why?"

"We aren't far from the sea. We could take a side trip if you like."

There it was again—that moment of hesitation that

made his heart drop a beat. She was staring up at the glowstone suspended above them, a blank expression on her face. "That's up to you, Tarq. It's your speeder. I'm just along for the ride."

It was all he could do not to wince. She was so much more than that. "I'd like to go for a run on the beach if it's not too rocky, and then maybe we could go for a swim. Would you like that?"

The same shadow of reluctance played across her face he'd seen when he'd asked—no, begged—her to let him take her to Yalka. It was painful to watch; he glanced away, but it was even more painful to note that her arms lay at her sides, making no attempt to touch him, even though he still had a hand on her belly. *If I only knew what she was thinking!* A second later, he revised that wish when he realized it might not be a good thing—especially if she was trying to come up with a reason to refuse. Tarq didn't think he could stand that. Better not to know…

"We could have a picnic on the beach." He stole another glimpse at her face. She was biting her lip. "Come on, Lucy. It would be fun." Reaching up, he turned her head toward him with a finger on her chin. "When's the last time you did anything fun?"

She stared at him, round-eyed, for a long moment before her incredulous expression gave way to a burst of laughter. "About… oh, let me think… fifteen minutes ago?"

Well, at least she thought it was fun… "I mean a different kind of fun, like a vacation." He traced the outline of her cheek with a fingertip. "Ever done that?"

"No," she replied, her eyes growing misty. "I'm not sure I'd know what to do with myself on a vacation."

Tarq smiled. "That's just it. You don't have to know. You do whatever you want whenever you feel like it." He gestured at the tent. "Plenty of people would say we were already on a vacation. You know, a camping trip in the wilderness?"

"Well, we're certainly in the wilderness, and I guess we *are* camping." She let out a short, rueful laugh. "I'm already on vacation and didn't even realize it, which proves how much I know."

Tarq nodded his agreement. "It's pretty bad when you need me to explain it to you—sad, even." He paused, taking a deep breath. "I don't want you to be sad, Lucy. I want you to be happy."

"I'm working on it," she said. "Leaving home was the first step. Nat and the money you gave me will take care of the rest."

With a firm nod, Lucy rolled away from him and sat up, not seeing the way his hand reached for her, or the stricken look on his face.

All she needed to be happy was money? Tarq knew better. He had more money than he knew what to do with, but he wasn't happy. Maybe it was different with women.

She was already pulling on her clothes. "Want some breakfast?"

Tarq had intended to cook for her, but didn't think he could stand up, let alone fix breakfast. He felt like he was dying. His chest constricted with an ache that not only halted his breathing but probably his heart. With an effort, he drew in a breath.

He was still alive. His next breath proved it. "Sure."

"I've got some bread and cheese we could have. Might be good toasted over the fire."

Tarq managed a smile. "I can do better than that, Lucy. Let me make it."

She was in the process of pulling on her khakis but missed the second leg hole and nearly fell over. "You're kidding me, right?"

"No. Why would you think I'm kidding? I cook for myself all the time."

"Not one of those precooked meals you ate last night?"

"Nope. Real food."

She was still gaping at him like a fish that had been hooked and landed. Tarq, on the other hand, was breathing much easier. Obviously this was something she hadn't expected. His confidence grew. "I'm thinking an omelet with cheese, pesto, and grilled mushrooms."

"Sounds great… Sure you don't want me to fix it?"

Tarq shook his head. "No, Lucy. You're on vacation. Remember?"

She blinked and went back to putting on her pants. "I keep forgetting…"

He understood her now. He could give her every credit he possessed and take her on a trip from one side of the galaxy to the other, but it wouldn't mean anywhere near as much to her as fixing breakfast. *I should have known. She's been working her butt off serving her family all her life. Now it's my turn to serve her…*

Lucy was at a loss to explain why Tarq was grinning at her like the cat that got the cream, but he looked so darn cute she didn't care.

"Are those the same clothes you wore yesterday?"

"Yeah, why?"

"Got any others?"

Lucy nodded. "Yes, but I'm saving them for when these are really—"

"Put on the clean ones."

She gaped at him. "Excuse me?"

"Put on the clean ones. We'll wash those."

"I thought you said your speeder didn't have a washing machine."

"It doesn't, but we can still wash them in the creek."

"Sounds rather primitive."

"Camping is like that," Tarq said. "Look, you couldn't possibly have much in the way of clothes with you, so you might as well wash them while we've got water handy."

"You make it sound like we'll be on the road for a month."

Tarq shrugged. "You never know."

"I don't have enough food for that long."

"Don't worry. I've got plenty."

He seemed to have an answer for everything. "I'll... pay you."

"With what? The money I gave you?" He snickered, holding out his hand for her clothes. Obviously he wasn't going to take no for an answer. "Seems kinda pointless, doesn't it?"

Lucy couldn't argue with that.

He snapped his fingers. "Clothes, Lucy. Now."

"Oh, all right! You can be awfully pushy sometimes."

"Yep."

Glowering at him, she skimmed off her khakis and tossed them at him, hitting him in the face. A second later, she realized why he wanted to wash her clothes. His cock snapped up like a balloon being filled with compressed air. Obviously he wanted to get through the day without needing sex again, and washing her clothes to remove her scent would probably help with that. "Sorry."

He didn't seem the slightest bit upset, but gave her trousers another sniff and began purring. His lips curled into a devilish smile. "The shirt, too."

Eyeing his erection, she blurted out, "But we just did that!"

He licked his lips as though about to devour her. "Yes, we did. And it was fun, remember?"

"Yes, but—"

"Don't worry, Lucy. I'm not going to nail you again—"

"I didn't mean—"

"Until after we've had breakfast." He untied the flap on the tent and pitched her clothes outside. Even after saying that, she watched him walk toward her with some trepidation, but he simply picked up his jeans and pulled them on.

Lucy watched, fascinated, as his cock folded up against his belly just ahead of his zipper. "That is so cool."

Tarq grinned. "Yet another difference between humans and Zetithians."

"Human men can't do that?"

He shook his head. "Not the way we can."

Not having any way to make a comparison, she shrugged. "Guess I'll have to take your word for it."

"I usually tell the truth." His mischievous grin led her to believe otherwise, but if he'd ever lied to her, she hadn't realized it. He nodded toward her sack of belongings. "Go ahead and get dressed. Breakfast won't take long."

After he left the tent, Lucy found another *scrail* cloth

and cleaned herself again. She didn't want him to be as miserable—or crabby—as he'd been the day before, and obviously once was not enough if he could get an erection like that just from sniffing her clothes.

Lucy took her time getting dressed and then spent several minutes combing out her hair and twisting it up into a knot on the back of her head. Finally she couldn't take the suspense any longer and went out.

He really was cooking an omelet over an open fire. The broken shells and bowl he'd mixed the eggs in were sitting beside the fire as proof that it hadn't come out of a box. Smiling up at her, he flipped it over in the skillet with a flick of his wrist, then sprinkled in the mushrooms and added the cheese. Another quick toss and it folded neatly in half.

"I'm impressed."

He cut the omelet into two equal portions and slid them each onto a plate, along with a slice of buttered bread that had been grilling in another pan. "You haven't tasted it yet."

"I was referring to your technique. That's not easy to do."

He seemed pleased but handed her a plate and a fork without comment. There were two cushions lying on the ground behind him, and he motioned for her to sit down. Water was already boiling in a pan set on a trivet over the fire. "Tea or coffee?"

"Tea, please."

Tarq dropped tea bags into two mugs, filled them with water, and set one down beside her. She waited for him to get situated on the other cushion before taking a bite of the omelet.

On another day, she would have described the flavor as orgasmic, but having had a Zetithian-induced orgasm so recently, she knew better and just said, "Mmm…"

"I used to order these all the time in a restaurant on Rhylos. I've been making my own ever since I started traveling."

"Did they give you the recipe?"

"No. But I could taste what was in them."

As a rule, omelets were simple to prepare, but this one had a flavor Lucy couldn't quite place. "I can taste the pesto in with the eggs, but there's something else there."

"It's a Friotian spice called *hyrud*."

Lucy snorted. "Which is something that *everyone* has in their spice rack."

"It's pretty rare, actually," he said, smiling at her sarcasm. "I forget where I first noticed it. Someone told me the name."

"And that's all it takes for you to be able to pick it out? One taste and someone telling you the name of it?"

"Pretty much."

"So you're saying you can taste anything and know what went into it?"

"As long as I'm familiar with the ingredients—and I know what most things are. On Rhylos they had food from all over the galaxy."

"And that's how you knew about Jublansk's secret salad dressing ingredient?"

"Oh, yeah. There were lots of Twilanans on Rhylos. Nobody can make bread as well as they can either."

"And do you know *that* secret?"

Tarq nodded. "It's the yeast they use. I'm guessing it's a strain that only grows on their homeworld."

"No one ever told you about it?"

"No. I can identify everything else, but the yeast flavor is different."

"So you can duplicate any recipe just by tasting it?"

"I can tell you what's in it but not necessarily how it's prepared." He took a bite of his toast and chewed it thoughtfully. "Although, come to think of it, I've never messed up anything I've tried—but I only make the stuff I like. I don't like everything."

"Amazing." This was almost as cool as having a dick that could—no. It wasn't *that* cool. Nothing was. "Ever eat any original recipe chicken from KFC?"

"Yes, but I promised Colonel Sanders I'd never divulge his secret."

Lucy giggled. "Colonel Sanders has been dead for at least a thousand years."

"Must've been his ghost then, which would explain why he said he'd come back and haunt me forever if I didn't keep my mouth shut." If his expression was any indication, Tarq was perfectly serious.

"Really? You *actually* spoke to Colonel Sanders?"

Tarq nodded and took a sip of his tea. "White hair, white suit, white mustache, black tie and glasses... Yeah. Colonel Sanders."

Lucy was stunned. "Well, I'll be damned."

Tarq took another sip of his tea and gazed off into the distance. Lucy was still staring at him as his eyes slid toward her. "Gotcha."

Chapter 12

HER BURST OF LAUGHTER WARMED TARQ ALL THE WAY to his toes. His only regret was that she might choke on her breakfast. Of course, if she did, he'd have an excellent excuse to save her. Then she'd be eternally grateful and swear her undying love for him.

Yeah, right…

At least she was laughing. Not every woman could take having their leg pulled without getting mad.

Still chuckling, she wiped tears from her eyes. "You really had me going there for a minute."

"Sorry. Couldn't resist."

"Yes, but you know, you really could make a killing in the restaurant business with that little talent of yours."

Tarq snorted. "If someone didn't kill me first. You know, most chefs don't like it when you steal their best recipes. Besides, I already made a killing in the sex business. If I had a restaurant of my own, I'd only be doing it for fun."

"True," she conceded. "You could write a cookbook and call it *Recipes and Reminiscences of a Zetithian Stud*. It would sell millions!"

Tarq grinned. "That would be fun too." Until his editor realized he couldn't read worth shit. He'd have to dictate it. Lucy could write it, but he was reluctant to tell her all of his "reminiscences." Some of them were wild enough to make *him* blush.

Lucy was smiling at him. All he really wanted to do was plant babies in her belly and watch them grow, teach them things, and love them and Lucy for the rest of his life. Too bad he couldn't find the courage to tell her that.

"And just in case you weren't paying attention to my reaction, this omelet is really good, Tarq. Thank you."

"You're welcome." It was all Tarq could do not to start purring. But he'd already promised not to nail her until after breakfast, and she'd only eaten about half of it.

Leisurely, he reminded himself. Take it slow. No rushing things. He'd already gotten a little carried away with the early morning sex, but after her scent had been in his head all night and he'd seen her standing there brushing her teeth, naked... Well, a man could only take so much.

Tarq finished his breakfast and brewed more tea, figuring he might as well increase his fluid intake right from the start if he intended to make frequent rest stops. If they ever got started, that is. By the time he got her clothes washed and dried, it would be time for lunch. They probably wouldn't get very far that day. Surely not all the way to Yalka.

"So, Lucy. Have you ever done this kind of thing before?"

"What, you mean having breakfast on the bank of a creek while watching the water flow by? Don't make me laugh," she said with a sardonic snicker. "When would I ever have the time to do that?"

"You've got it right now. This is a nice, quiet spot and it's a beautiful day. We should relax and enjoy it."

She stared at him as though he'd just asked her to commit murder. "Relax and enjoy it?"

"Yeah—and leave those dishes alone. I'll get them." He poured her another cup of tea. Might as well get her well hydrated too… He handed her the cup. "Natalie isn't expecting you, so enjoy the trip."

"That's Natasha," she corrected him. "And I know she isn't expecting me, but isn't someone expecting *you*?"

Tarq had three clients waiting in Yalka. Three clients he was probably going to have to disappoint if that last one was any indication. Spending this much time with Lucy was probably going to make it impossible to move on to another woman—at least not anytime soon. The whole only-being-able-to-get-it-up-for-your-mate thing wore off after a while—or so he'd been told. What no one had ever said was how long it would take. "I think I need a little time off too."

Lucy laughed. "Time off from what? Seems like you're still working."

"Not really. You're already pregnant. This is just for fun."

"And to keep you from getting crabby."

"Yeah, that too." It took Tarq a moment to realize he'd said the wrong thing. He wasn't with her just for fun. There was a whole lot more to it than that. But how to say it? "And it's… comfortable being with you."

Lucy chuckled. "Like an old pair of shoes, huh?"

It was all he could do not to growl at her. "You are *not* like an old pair of shoes."

"I was only kidding—but I know what you mean. It must be hard to be intimate with different women all the time. You just get to know someone and then it's on to the next one."

So she did understand that much.

"But it would also be easier in some ways," she went on. "Like waiting on different customers at the café. Some you like and some you don't, but either way, you don't have to put up with them for long." She paused, grimacing. "Though some of them keep coming back."

"I thought repeat business was what a restaurant depended on."

"Yes, but some are more trouble than they're worth."

Tarq's temper flared. "Who's been giving you trouble?"

"Oh, just some guys that come in once in a while. They didn't seem to like you at all. It made me mad enough to put hair in their soup."

"You didn't!"

"No, but I sure thought about it. Those nasty, dirty creeps had the nerve to call *you* filthy! I wanted to slap the snot out of them." With a regretful sigh, she added, "But that would have been bad for business."

"Maybe so, but it sure would've kept me coming back."

"Too bad you don't eat as much as they do." Lucy stabbed the last bit of her omelet with unnecessary force. "The stupid pigs. Lousy tippers, too."

Tarq hid a smile behind his cup. His own tips would make any others seem paltry, but he was still pleased by her attitude. "Does it feel good to get away from all that?"

Nodding, she set down her plate. "I'll probably run into more of the same in Yalka, but what can you do about it? There are stupid jerks everywhere you go." Frowning, she added, "At least in Yalka they won't be my family."

Tarq wanted nothing more than to protect her from all the jerks and creeps in the galaxy. Well, maybe he wanted a little more than that, but it would do for a start. He wanted to *be* her family. The thought of losing her the way he'd lost his own relations sent a pain ripping through him so hard he winced.

Lucy must have guessed the reason for his reaction, for, after a moment's hesitation, she said gently, "Your whole family is gone, aren't they?"

Tarq nodded. "I was up in a tree when the advancing army killed every last one of them."

"How awful!"

Tarq gazed off across the wilderness toward the mountains. "Yes, it was."

"Sorry. I didn't mean to remind you of that."

"It might be easier to remember if they hadn't loved me, but they did." Turning his gaze on Lucy, he went on, "Which is why I can't understand the way your family behaves toward you. If they only knew how precious…" He took her hand and squeezed it gently. "Don't cut them off completely, Lucy. Let them know where you are and that you're okay. Don't make them wonder what happened to you."

"I'll contact them eventually. But not right away. I want to be in a position where they can't make me come back or interfere with me or my babies."

"You're a free woman, Lucy. No one can *make* you do anything." *If I could, I'd make you love me every bit as much as I love you.*

"Yeah, right. Although how you could say that after meeting my father…" She shuddered and then shook her head as though trying to erase the memories. "Hey, I thought we were supposed to be having fun."

"You're absolutely right. Here, have some more tea

and sit back and relax." He refilled her cup and got to his feet. "I'll throw these dishes in the washer and be right back."

Lucy watched him as he walked over to the speeder. *So much for being able to spoil him rotten.* Thus far, he hadn't given her the chance.

He was right about the importance of family, though, no matter how much of a pain in the neck they were. Even so, she remained firm in her decision to let them stew for a while. Let them miss having her at their beck and call and see how they liked it.

No, that would be punishing them, and Lucy didn't feel the need to punish anyone. She only wanted her freedom, and she had that now. She felt no residual animosity toward them at all. Funny how removing yourself from a situation could make you view it with new eyes.

Eyes that were still riveted to Tarq. He was simply leaning over the side of the speeder to put away the dishes, but it was all she could do not to jump up and run after him. She'd never breakfasted with a man she'd spent the night with, and if she ever had, she was sure he wouldn't have looked even half as good wearing nothing but sandals and a pair of jeans.

Tearing her eyes away from him, she got up, finding it difficult to sit still while he took care of the chores. Aside from that, all the tea she'd drunk was going straight through her. After initially attributing this symptom to her pregnancy, she realized she'd never lingered over breakfast long enough to drink that much before.

Upon her return from a brief trip behind the tent, she

found Tarq in the creek, washing her clothes. He must've also been washing his jeans because he wasn't wearing a single stitch. She was about to ask if that was his only pair of pants when she remembered the bit about getting nailed after breakfast. If he was trying to lure her into jumping his bones, he was doing a damn fine job of it.

Not that she needed any encouragement. The unfortunate truth was that she was afraid she was getting hooked on him. She already suspected that she'd fallen in love with him, but knew that love could be fickle, could turn to hatred on a whim, and could be found in many places. However, the bond between a Zetithian man and his mate seemed to be stronger than love. It was physical, chemical, and undeniable. The more she mated with him the stronger the bond would become. No wonder he seldom stayed as long with other women. If he did, they would never have let him go. He'd said he felt comfortable being with her, but in actual truth, he was playing with fire.

What would a woman do to hang onto him? Throw herself at his feet? Lock him in her bedroom? Stow away in his speeder? Lucy wasn't sure, but giving in to him, even out of pity—convenient though it was—couldn't end up causing her anything but heartache, or withdrawal symptoms, or whatever it was a woman went through when she lost her Zetithian mate.

Surely it wouldn't kill her. She might feel like someone had ripped her heart out, but she wouldn't die. Anything short of that, she could endure. People didn't die of broken hearts, no matter how much they might want to.

"Aren't you cold?"

"Actually, it feels pretty good. The water isn't as cold as you might think, and the sun's already getting hot." A slow, seductive smile touched his lips. "Care to join me?"

"I probably shouldn't," she replied. "In fact, I should probably stay as far away from you as possible. I wouldn't want you to get all crabby again—although a dip in the creek might make me smell better."

He stared at her, aghast. "Would you wash a rose to get rid of its scent?"

"Well, no…"

"Lucy, right now you smell better to me than anything. Better than any flower or any food. It draws me to you like a magnet and makes me feel like I'm drowning in…" He paused as though searching for the right word. "Chocolate."

"Oh." Lucy nearly choked on the word.

He smiled again. "But fortunately nothing can wash it away completely. Don't even bother to try."

"Then I don't need to help you wash the clothes?"

He shook his head. "Not if you don't want to."

"It isn't a matter of whether I want to or not. It's a matter of feeling like I should."

His eyes narrowed. "You know something? You aren't a bit good at letting someone else do stuff for you."

"That's not too surprising. I'm used to doing chores all by myself most of the time."

"Well, if it's such a hardship for you, would you do me a favor and pull my bedroll out of the tent and spread it out there on the bank? I could use a towel, too. There are some in one of the rear compartments in the speeder. The one with a white sticker on it."

Lucy nodded and did as he asked, thankful for the opportunity to do something other than simply stand there and watch him while he worked—even if he did appear to be enjoying himself. The fact that he was naked made her feel even more strange—sort of voyeuristic in a way.

She pulled out the bedroll and then went to get a towel. The compartment was easy to find. Not only did it have a white sticker on the handle, but it was also clearly labeled "Bed and Bath Linens." It was even written in the Standard Tongue.

Did he think she couldn't read? She would have found the towels as soon as she checked the cargo space, whether he'd told her where to look or not. Examining the other storage lockers, she noticed that they were all labeled the same way—the original printed labels along with a different colored sticker on each handle. Everything else in the speeder was a pictograph, some of them hand painted.

The truth slapped her in the face with a force that left her stunned. It wasn't *her* ability to read that he questioned; it was his own. He probably had to rely on the color coding because he had no idea what the labels meant. She thought back to the first day they'd met. He hadn't ordered off the menu; he'd asked her what she recommended. While this wasn't an uncommon thing for a new customer to do, the fact that he'd done it a second time should have made her wonder. Then what he'd said about not being very smart and saying stupid things all the time. And his comment about how smart she was when all she'd done was read the directions on how to heat up his dinner.

But he functioned so well otherwise. He was traveling

all over the planet—and this wasn't the first place he'd done it. He'd known that it was a two-day trip in a speeder to Yalka. Lucy wasn't familiar with the controls on the speeder, but she was beginning to suspect that the navigation system was not only voice activated, but gave voice commands and directions. He hadn't needed it after he'd picked her up because the way to Yalka was perfectly obvious to anyone.

Closing the compartment, she took the towel back to Tarq. He was still in the creek wringing out her clothes. "Here," he said, tossing her the shirt. "Hang that up on those rulbnach trees."

Lucy was on the alert, or she probably wouldn't have registered the fact that he knew the trees by name. "You must've been here a while to know the names of the trees."

"Not really. The bark is exported. It's used to smoke meats on several planets. I forget where I first heard about it."

"Yet another of those culinary herbs and spices you can identify?"

"Yes, but I wouldn't have known what kind of trees they were if I hadn't used some deadwood on the fire last night. The smoke has a very unique aroma."

It was on the tip of her tongue to ask him to spell rulbn-ach, just to test her theory, but she stopped herself in time. If he couldn't read—and hadn't told her himself—he was probably a little touchy about it, maybe even embarrassed. "I didn't know the bark was exported. But then, there are a lot of things I don't know about this part of the world."

Smiling, he wrung out her khakis and tossed them to her. "You need to get out more."

"No kidding." She draped her pants over a low branch.

Even in full sun they would need several hours to dry. Tarq was taking this vacation thing further than she'd thought. "Couldn't we tie our clothes to the speeder and let them blow dry on the way to Yalka?"

The way his face fell at this suggestion made her wish she'd stopped herself from saying that as well. He opened his mouth to speak, but hesitated a few seconds before he replied. "They'd pick up too much dust and end up dirtier than they were to begin with."

"I didn't think speeders kicked up any dust."

"Maybe none that you can see, but I've tried drying clothes that way before. It doesn't work."

His subsequent smile contained a trace of relief—but why would he be relieved? Was he deliberately trying to delay her, thinking her father would catch up with them? Lucy certainly hoped not, but what Tarq had said about not cutting herself off from her family made her wonder—though insisting that she'd come home when she got hungry enough was exactly the sort of thing Uther Force would say. She comforted herself with the assumption that camping out along the trail for a day or two was the sort of thing Tarq did all the time. If that were the case, her presence wouldn't have made any difference—though if he'd intended to take time off from his procreative duties, that plan had fallen through.

Tarq gave his jeans a few quick twists, but they were still dripping when he climbed up the bank. Lucy handed him the towel and hung his pants up beside hers, thinking how domestic this whole scenario would appear to the casual observer—as though she and Tarq had been together for five years instead of going on five days.

Tarq finished drying himself and lay down on his

bedroll, stretching out on his back with his hands behind his head, his hair spread out on the pillow. His cock was standing straight up and he was purring. "You said you aren't in any hurry to get to Yalka, right?"

"Well, no, I'm not…"

"Good, because I just want to stay here and take it easy for a while. It's been a wonderful day so far—great sex, a delicious breakfast, a nice dip in the creek—but if you'd care to take your clothes off and sit on my face, my morning would be complete."

The sight of Tarq's nude body lying on the bank already had Lucy's thoughts headed in a decidedly carnal direction, but his request sent a gush of warmth running down her thighs from her aching core.

Tarq inhaled deeply and his cock quivered, its color instantly changing from deep pink to bluish purple. "Got to you with that one, didn't I?"

"B-but that's not fair!" she sputtered. "I can't help it if you can smell every little emotion I feel!"

With a snicker, he ran his fingers down the length of his penis. "Like you can't see exactly what I'm feeling?"

She wanted to snap at him for touching what she was beginning to think of as her own personal property, but she bit back her retort as he used his whole hand to spread his slick fluid all up and down the shaft. Tarq might not be able to read worth a darn, but when it came to driving women wild, he was a freakin' genius.

"Come on, Lucy. I've had breakfast. Now I'm ready for dessert."

"Um… there's some chocolate pie left."

"I don't want pie," he growled. "I want *you*. I want you to sit on my face while I eat your sweet wet pussy."

He'd never talked like that to her before. No one had. It wasn't what anyone would call romantic, but it certainly had the desired effect. Without another moment's hesitation, she stripped off her clothes and went to him.

Tarq took her hand and pulled her down beside him. Guiding her with his hands on her hips, he soon had her on her knees, her weeping body hovering just above his mouth. "Now, sit."

His hot tongue slid deeply into her core, its tip teasing her mercilessly while he lapped up her juice. "Oh, Lucy. You taste like love."

Lucy reached down and grabbed handfuls of his hair, using it to pull him in deeper as she rose up and down on his tongue. Tarq made an indescribable sound and, a moment later, Lucy felt his warm semen hit her in the back. With a snarl, Tarq sucked her clitoris into his mouth, rubbing it hard with his rough tongue. Lucy couldn't take any more. Falling forward onto her hands, she felt her clit pulsating in his mouth and heard herself making sounds that were more animal than human.

Tarq gave her another deep lick and lifted her from his lips. "Now, do me another favor and turn around and suck my dick."

Closing his eyes, he let out a gasp as her warm mouth closed over him. While she sucked, he pulled her down, lightly nipping her luscious ass. His *snard* lay in a glistening stripe down the middle of her back, which he smoothed toward him until it trickled over her anus. Circling her tight hole with a fingertip, he felt her lurch forward to avoid the contact, letting go of his cock.

"Don't worry, Lucy. This will feel very good."

Using his semen as a lubricant, he teased her gently, gradually probing to the full depth his finger could reach. Her pussy lips still dripped enticingly, and he leaned in for another delicious taste. Smiling as she sighed and went down on him again, he found her sweet spot, caressing it carefully at first, and then bearing down harder as he felt her respond. The orgasms from his cock syrup came and went, but he could tell the difference between those and the kind he was hoping to give her. *Just a little longer…*

Lucy let out a cry as her body crashed down on him, her hot core bathing his face with its amazing essence.

"I need to get inside you, Lucy… Please…"

He wasn't sure she could move without help, but Lucy somehow managed to crawl down his body and impale herself with his shaft. Tarq groaned as the blunt head penetrated and she settled down on him, taking his full length inside her. She not only smelled like heaven, but she fit like she'd been made for him—in every possible way, from her head to her toes and everything in between.

As he gazed up at her, she pulled the clip out of her dark hair, letting it cascade down her back as her body arched backward, driving him in even deeper. He rocked upward, his cock sweeping through her slick core in a slow, deliberate circle. As he moved, his thrusts became more frantic, his body urging him onward—seeking, reaching, grasping—until the moment finally came when infinity opened up and sucked him in.

Tarq pulled her into his arms, kissing her with a ferocity that astonished him. If he'd had any doubts before, they evaporated as her lips melted into his. No other woman had ever affected him the way Lucy did. She was his mate, the one he'd been searching for all his life.

Tarq was about to blurt out everything he was feeling when Lucy rolled away from him. Feeling more bereft than if he'd lost an arm, he stole a glance at her. She was gazing up at the sky with an expression that didn't bode well. She was thinking about something. Hard.

Chapter 13

TARQ TRULY HAD NO IDEA WHAT HE COULD DO TO A woman. None. Otherwise he would have known better than to keep tempting her with words guaranteed to make her give in to her own desires—desires that could only result in more suffering in the end. She reminded herself that sex was a job to him, one that he obviously enjoyed, but a job nonetheless. Even so, Lucy didn't understand how he could keep going from planet to planet spreading his *snard* the way Johnny Appleseed had planted trees without having some regrets about some of those he left behind.

Lucy wondered if he'd ever heard that old legend. It seemed unlikely, but she wouldn't have thought that your average Zetithian would have been able to describe Colonel Sanders, either. Tarq was something of a mystery. Culturally, he could have been born on Earth or one of its colonies, as his speech patterns and style of dress would suggest, and yet in other ways, he was so very alien.

All she knew about his past was that his family had all been killed and he'd "inherited" a large sum of money from the nut who'd tried to destroy the Zetithian race. The *snard* spreading she could understand from the perspective of an endangered species, but she had no idea why he couldn't read or why he'd decided to sell the use of his dick to any woman with a thousand credits to spare. Maybe it was simply to earn enough money so that he could do what he was doing now.

"What are you thinking about?"

She frowned slightly. It was difficult to put into words. "About how I'm camping out in the middle of the Malturn Wilderness with someone I don't really know."

"Is that a problem?"

"Yes—no... Well, it should be, but maybe it isn't. I don't know." She paused, scratching her head. Only a few minutes before, she'd done some really kinky stuff with him. She shouldn't feel so odd asking him about his life.

Then again, perhaps it was best if she *didn't* get to know him. Learning all about him might make him that much harder to give up.

"What would you like to know?"

"Nothing. I don't mean to pry. Forget I asked."

"You wouldn't be prying, but there really isn't much to tell. After my family was killed, I was picked up by a refugee ship and spent the next twenty-five years in space."

"Just flying around?"

Tarq nodded. "We didn't dare to stop on any world or even leave the ship. Amelyana would go down to the surface in a shuttle, bringing back enough supplies to see us through until we came to another inhabited planet."

"Amelyana?"

"She was the wife of Rutger Grekkor, the man who tried to destroy us after she took a Zetithian lover."

"I heard something about that. He must've been really crazy." *And she must've felt terribly guilty...*

"That's putting it mildly. Amelyana was afraid to

even let us establish a colony somewhere. She knew Grekkor would find us and try again, so she kept us aboard her ship until she heard he was dead."

"On a ship for twenty-five years?" Lucy shook her head, unable to comprehend what kind of life that must have been. "Geez, how many of you were there?"

"About a hundred," he replied. "All of us orphans and most of us boys. I was twelve at the time. My friend Dax—he's the one who got Grekkor's personal ship and gives me a ride from planet to planet—was only two."

"So you still remember Zetith?"

"Better than most." His eyes grew wistful. "Our planet was beautiful. Thick forests, deep rivers, open plains, oceans—a lot like Earth, actually—and this planet too—but greener."

"So how come you seem more Terran than Zetithian? I mean, you *look* Zetithian—and I know you are—but you wear jeans and know about Colonel Sanders."

"That's Amelyana's influence," he said, chuckling. "She was Terran and taught us her culture as well as our own. There was a huge database in the ship's computer. Dax was—" He stopped abruptly.

"Dax was what?"

"The smart one," he said with a wince. "I was more interested in girls."

Lucy giggled. "Why does that not surprise me?"

Tarq grinned sheepishly. "It's what I'm best at—and believe me, you had to be good because there were a whole lot more guys than girls. Looking back, I think Amelyana collected mostly male orphans on purpose. Our women could care less about sex and won't cross with any other species."

"You mean it takes a Zetithian guy for a Zetithian girl?"

"Oh, yeah. And you wouldn't *believe* what you have to go through to mate with one of them. *Very* picky."

Having experienced the full force of Zetithian male sexuality, Lucy should have suspected that, but with nothing to use for comparison, she hadn't considered the need for it. She could have been happy with a human male—and would have been, if it hadn't been for Tarq— but had a feeling that nothing less than a Zetithian—no, nothing less than *Tarq*—would do from now on. Not that she'd ever have that option. "And you boys aren't so choosy?"

"More so than you might think. If a woman doesn't smell right, nothing happens."

"Nothing? You mean you can't even…?"

Tarq grinned. "I mean *nothing*."

"Not even if you're, um, by yourself?"

"Not even then."

"Hmm… Definitely different from human males, then—or so I've heard. I figured the whole scent thing was just the icing on the cake, but you're saying you can't do *anything* without it?"

"That's right."

She was looking at his face, but a quick glance out of the corner of her eye was enough to assure her that the damn thing was already standing straight up again. "You probably need a break. How far away do I have to be for it to stop doing that?"

"Depends on which way the wind is blowing."

"Guess I ought to at least be downwind from you then."

"Who said I wanted it to stop?"

Rolling her eyes, she got to her feet. "Don't you ever get tired of it?"

"The sex or the erection?"

"Either one."

"Sometimes," he admitted. "But not today. I—I'll leave you alone, though. I'm sorry for bothering you so much."

Lucy stared at him for a few seconds, not quite sure what she was hearing. He'd apologized the first time for being a little rough, but—

Oh, yeah, right. Pity fuck. She'd forgotten. He even seemed a little embarrassed. "I don't mind. But you did say even you get tired of it sometimes."

Tarq sighed. "Yeah, I did, but that was mostly when I was on Rhylos. We were turning four or five tricks a day, and the last year or so it started getting old. Since I've been traveling, it's been easier."

"The last year or so? How long were you there?"

"A little over four years. It took us a while to get the place going, but our appointments booked up really fast once the word got out."

Lucy did some quick mental math. Not only had he been earning up to five thousand credits a day, he was older than she'd previously supposed. "That makes you what? Forty-five?"

Tarq grimaced. "Oh, so now you think I'm old."

"I didn't say that. I'm only trying to understand—"

"Zetithians age more slowly than humans do, and we have a longer lifespan."

"So, a forty-five-year-old Zetithian is comparable to a human in their thirties?"

"That's about right." Cocking his head, he studied her closely. "I'm guessing you're in your twenties."

It was Lucy's turn to grimace. "Not for long. I'll be thirty in a couple of months."

The terms *spinster* and *old maid* might have been outmoded for centuries, but Lucy felt like they still applied—to her, anyway. However, there was some consolation in knowing that she wouldn't wind up as a *childless* old maid; plus, she'd had some sexual experiences that most married women would envy.

And she owed all of that to Tarq. The need to spoil him rotten came hurtling back. "Can I get you anything? Some tea, maybe?"

He opened his mouth to speak but hesitated. "Uh, yeah. Sure. Tea would be nice."

She tossed a few more pieces of wood onto the fire and then refilled the pan with water from the creek. Setting the pan on the trivet to boil, it occurred to her that she'd done all of that without putting on so much as a pair of shoes. *You've come a long way, baby.*

Tarq must've noticed her bemused smile but misinterpreted it. "I'm not so old that you have to wait on me."

The most logical explanation was much easier to admit than the real one. "Force of habit," she said with a dismissive gesture. "I've been a waitress all my life."

Tarq frowned. "And I've been a stud all my life." He smiled ruefully. "We make quite a pair, don't we?"

Except that they *weren't* a pair and never would be. The twinge she felt near her heart didn't bode well. With a brief nod, she gathered up her clothes. "I'm going to get dressed. I'll be right back."

She headed toward the tent, fighting back tears. Once inside, she let them flow while she wiped away every trace of him with a *scrail* cloth. If only she could wipe him out of her mind as easily.

Tarq went over to the speeder for another pair of jeans and put them on, unable to figure out why his erection wouldn't go down now that she was—

She was sitting on your face, dumb-butt. Opening a bottle of water, he doused his face before wiping away her essence with a clean *scrail*.

Spreading the cloth out on the speeder's canopy, he let the sun do its job. Within minutes, the cloth was clean and dry again. Tarq let out a snicker. If only *his* task was that easy. Getting to know a woman was a lot more difficult than simply fucking her. His body was primed and ready for sex, but the right things to say to Lucy eluded him. For a while there it seemed like things were going fairly well, but something upset her; he could smell it and knew the emotion, but the root cause was a puzzle.

His other plan wasn't working very well either. She didn't know how to accept what he was trying to do for her any more than he knew how to talk about anything other than sex. His whole life had revolved around it, and yet the workings of the female mind still weren't clear to him. He might know how to press the buttons on the female libido, but everything else...

He glanced back at the tent. Lucy was still inside with the flap closed. She obviously didn't want him to see her in the nude anymore. Perhaps she thought she was being kind to him, keeping herself out of his sight and out of the range of his nose, giving him a break, as she'd suggested. Unfortunately, all she was doing was making him doubt himself even more. Either that or she didn't want him at all and was letting her actions speak for her.

The fact that she'd let him fuck her didn't mean a damn thing. Tarq knew very well that human females found Zetithian men irresistible. Too bad their response was less of a choice and more of an instinct.

With the heat of the day, the wind from the sea began to pick up, blowing steadily from the west. Between the sun and the breeze, Lucy's clothes were probably almost dry, and if she was intending to hide out in the tent until lunchtime, there wasn't any reason to prolong the agony. They might as well pack up and get back on the road. Tarq was running out of ideas anyway.

As he'd suspected, his jeans were still wet, while hers were merely damp. He should have jumped at the chance to dunk them in the creek again while she wasn't watching, but turned them around so the sun and wind would dry them faster instead. He'd been stupid to wash them to begin with. Stupid to try to make her stay with him and maybe have a little fun. *Stupid, stupid, stupid…*

He sat back down on his pallet, realizing that this was the way the sleeping arrangements should have been the night before. If he'd been behaving like a gentleman, that is. But he was no gentleman; it had never occurred to him to let her sleep alone in the tent. Acting like a stag in rut, he hadn't considered her feelings at all. He'd tricked her, coerced her—probably even made her feel sorry for him—but he hadn't given her much of a choice.

Tarq didn't know how long he sat there, staring off into the distance, but when Lucy came out of the tent carrying her duffel bag, the first thing she did was to verify what he already knew.

"Your jeans are dry now. Guess we should get going

again." She set the bag down and stuffed her clean clothes into it. "Sorry I took so long. I-I fell asleep."

Tarq thought her eyes looked a little puffy, but didn't comment. "That's okay. You need your rest." He got up and shook out his bedroll and then tossed it into the tent. With a touch of the auto-erect button, the tent slowly folded itself up into a neat bundle.

Lucy held up the *scrails* she'd used. "What do I do with these?"

Taking them from her, Tarq spread them out on a nearby shrub, stifling the urge to sniff them. "They'll be clean in a few minutes." The fire had all but gone out and the pan of water had boiled dry. He kicked some dirt over the few remaining embers and gathered up the dishes.

"I never did make that tea for you. Not much of a waitress, am I?"

She was staring at the smoking remains of their campfire, not even looking him in the eye. He'd blown it, all right. He just wished he understood why. "You're a fine waitress. Don't worry about it."

After dumping the dishes into the cleaner, he went back for the tent and tossed it into the back of the speeder. Lucy was right behind him and pitched in her duffel bag, along with his jeans. She was obviously anxious to get started again. After a brief deliberation, Tarq pulled out a clean shirt and put it on. *Not much point in trying to entice her now…*

Tarq glanced back at their campsite. No, he hadn't forgotten anything. There was no reason to linger. He opened the door for Lucy and helped her climb into the speeder. Despite her apparent lack of interest, his dick was already getting hard.

Might as well enjoy it while I can, he thought as he settled himself in the driver's seat. He'd started the engine and was about to slide the accelerator up when he realized it might be the last erection he'd ever get. *Depressing thought.* "Ready?"

Lucy nodded. "How far away are we now?"

Tarq tapped the navigation control. "We might make it there before dark."

"Good. I wouldn't want to barge in on Nat in the middle of the night."

"We could camp out again tonight if we get there too late."

She bit her lip and took a deep breath. "Hopefully we won't have to. I don't like putting you to so much trouble."

"It's no trouble, Lucy. Really."

She shook her head. "You've done enough for me already."

There was no point in taking it slow now. Tarq hit the control bar and the speeder shot forward like a rocket.

They stopped once for lunch and again for dinner. Lucy barely said a word either time, and the conversation as they traveled was nonexistent. Tarq kept the speeder at full throttle the whole way.

He kept checking the navigation system, wishing that the town of Yalka was getting farther away instead of closer with each passing moment. The tiny arrow crept inexorably closer to the grid of streets on the map. Tarq was staring at it so hard that he would have missed the turnoff to Natasha's place if Lucy hadn't been watching for it.

"Slow down," she said. "I think this is it."

Tarq could see it now. Having kept his eyes fixed on

the track in front of him or on the navscreen, he hadn't noticed the change in the terrain. Trees were no longer stunted and the rocky, barren wasteland had risen up and given way to fields of green. Despite this, it still looked like the road to nowhere.

"Are you sure?"

Lucy nodded. "Five olive trees growing in a cluster next to a big rock. You can let me out here."

"I'll take you all the way to the house."

"No," she said firmly. "I don't want anyone to see us together, and if anyone asks, you haven't seen me. I don't want you to be blamed for any of this."

Tarq almost snarled in frustration. "I'm not letting you go by yourself. What if your friend doesn't live here anymore?"

"She would have told me if she was moving, and there'd be no reason for that. She said she was happy and that their farm was doing well. No, she's still here. Don't worry about it."

"I can't do that, Lucy."

"Oh, yes, you can. If you hadn't found me, I'd have been going down this road alone anyway. I can't see that it would make any difference."

Tarq thought it made all the difference in the world, but then he remembered he'd already promised not to tell her what to do. And if she didn't want to be with him, there was no more to be said. He couldn't force her to love him.

Bringing the speeder to a halt, he watched her tap the door release icon, still not quite comprehending that she was actually leaving him.

"Don't get out. I can manage it from here." Climbing

out of the speeder, she reached into the cargo space for her bag and slung it over her shoulder. "Thanks for everything, Tarq. Take care of yourself."

"I will. You do the same." Tarq was amazed that he could speak at all. "Be sure to register the babies with the Zetithian Birth Registry when they're born. It's... important."

"I won't forget."

Something had to happen. Some miracle or some force of nature would intervene and make her see how wrong it was for her to simply walk away from him.

But nothing did.

With a firm nod, Lucy turned and headed off down the trail, and all Tarq could do was watch her go. She never even looked back. Tarq knew that because he waited until she was out of sight.

And then he waited some more.

Chapter 14

Lucy could barely see through the tears in her eyes as she walked down the lane that wound through the hills to Nat's house. She'd known it was a long way off the main road, but after about an hour, she began to wonder if this was the right place after all. By the time she reached the house, however, her tears had dried enough that she could see quite clearly.

Except there wasn't a house. Each and every building on the place had burned to the ground.

Walking through the ruins and still not quite comprehending the scope of the disaster, she was sure that farther on there would be a snug new house and her friend would be there to welcome her.

There was nothing. Not even a fence post was left standing. The silence was profound, broken only by the relentless wind whistling through tall unmown grass. In Nat's garden, weeds had sprouted among the remains of the last season's vegetables, obscuring the tangle of vines and dried stalks. To the east, the hill she stood upon sloped downward to a smooth hollow, only to rise up again where it met the distant foothills of the Eradic Mountains. Lucy knew it had once been sown with wheat and corn, but nature was already reclaiming it, turning it into a vast meadow of grasses and wildflowers.

She blinked and turned around slowly. If the house had simply been empty, she might have stayed there, but a feeling of malicious intent pervaded the area, warning her that this was no longer the safe haven she imagined. Whatever had happened here hadn't been an accident, and she was terrified that Nat and her husband had perished in the fire.

Lucy realized then just how much she had counted on Nat being there for her. Somehow, knowing that this refuge existed had made her life more tolerable. Now that crutch was gone, leaving her feeling bereft, unsupported, and frighteningly vulnerable.

Normally unflappable, Lucy was unable to suppress a scream when a bird fluttered up from the ground nearby. Heart pounding, she ran to the shelter of a shade tree. Pressing her back against the wide trunk, she was momentarily reassured that at least nothing could grab her from behind, but as she gazed at the western sky, she was stricken with a new fear. The sun was already nearing the horizon. It would be dark soon, and this was the very last place she wanted to spend the night.

Fear spurred her into action, and Lucy hurried back down the lane, covering the distance to the main road much faster than she had before. If she kept moving, she might make it to the outskirts of Yalka before dark.

More than ever, she missed the security Tarq's presence had given her. If only she hadn't been so determined to escape from him, he would have brought her here in the speeder, and then they would have gone on to Yalka. He would have been much more difficult to walk away from then. He wouldn't have left her to fend for herself in the new town; he would have helped her find a place to stay, would have assured himself of her safety before he went on his way again.

But she would never see him again. Given the speed he normally traveled, the odds of catching up with him were slim to none.

Still, this was no different than it would have been if she'd been on foot, as she'd pointed out to him. She would have arrived in Yalka exhausted and with no one to help her. At least she still had the money he'd given her. Without that, she truly would have been lost—a destitute pregnant girl roaming the streets of an unfamiliar town, she would have been at the mercy of anyone who happened to find her.

Shuddering, she realized then how foolish she'd been to leave her home, even with money in hand. What if she were robbed?

"Don't make it any worse than it is, Lucy," she said aloud, needing the comfort of a voice, even her own. "You'll get through this, just like you've gotten through everything else. It will be a little harder, that's all."

Good words, perhaps, but they didn't do a thing for her courage. Then she remembered her pistol. Reaching into her pocket, she pulled it out and checked the settings. Fully charged, it was set on heavy stun.

Gripping the handle, she walked on toward Yalka. As she approached the wooded area to the north, Lucy spotted a flash of metallic green nestled among the trees. Tarq's speeder. He must've decided to camp there for the night instead of going on into the town. With a sigh of relief, she quickened her pace.

When she heard angry shouts, she started running.

—∿∿—

Lucy might have walked away from him, but a couple

of hours spent without her made Tarq more determined than ever. He wasn't giving up and going on his merry way. She was his mate; the raw, empty feeling inside him was proof of that.

Though she would know he was lying through his teeth, he fully intended to show up at the house the next morning asking for directions to Yalka. She would assume that he was making sure she was safe without letting on that they'd been traveling together, but he would also meet this friend of hers, perhaps enabling him to drop in for the occasional visit while he was in town.

While this would have been the most reasonable approach, the longer he sat staring into his lonely campfire, the more the idea of flying back to Natasha's farm and kidnapping Lucy began to appeal to him. This preoccupation left him unwary, which might explain why five human males were able to sneak up on a Zetithian. By the time he spotted them—and their knives—it was too late to run.

Armed only with a mug of hot tea, Tarq did manage to get one of them across the face with the scalding brew, but all it did was make him mad.

Tea dripped from an unkempt beard as the man wiped his eyes. "Fuckin' Zetithian! You'll pay for that."

Tarq shrugged. "Pay? I've got money and a speeder. Take them. I don't really give a damn."

"Oh, we'll take whatever we like," another man said. "But we aren't gonna let a stinkin' fuckwad like you set foot in our town."

"*Your* town?"

"Yeah, *our* town—now that we've gotten rid of all the damned aliens. We aren't about to let another one of you weird fuckers come around planting babies in our women."

Knowing that he was probably incapable of planting babies in anyone but Lucy made this a moot point, but Tarq was suddenly seized with an overwhelming desire to beat the shit out of a gang of thugs, deeming it an excellent way to pass the evening. "I don't think I'd enjoy fucking your women anyway."

"Why? What's wrong with our women?"

"Nothing, really," Tarq replied. "But they probably don't smell very good."

"Are you saying they stink?"

With an insolent smirk, Tarq shook his head. "Your words, not mine."

Tarq's last thought as the man lunged toward him was that he'd been far too easy to provoke. Blocking his knife hand, Tarq smashed the mug in the guy's face. Though it would never hold tea again, the mug still had a handle and was now a much better weapon, having acquired some very sharp edges.

Blood mixed with the tea in his beard as, howling with pain and anger, the man came at Tarq again, his knife held high. Tarq waited until the last second and ducked sideways, landing a kick that sent his opponent sprawling in the dirt.

"Come on, Fred!" another man urged. "Get off your ass and kill that sonofabitch." This was seconded by the others, except for the one opportunist who was now engaged in stealing the speeder. *One down, four to go...*

Like most bullies, Fred didn't have much in the way of physical courage, but he must've had some small measure of pride, for he got to his feet just in time for Tarq to kick him in the teeth.

Which was an unfortunate choice of attack for a man wearing sandals. His toes now bleeding, Tarq hopped backwards, stepping aside just in time to allow a totally pissed Fred to charge past him and run headlong into a tree.

Fred shook off the blow like a pesky insect bite.

"Are you sure you're human?" Tarq taunted. "Anyone with a head as hard as yours must have a little Herpatronian in him."

Out of the corner of his eye, Tarq saw his tent begin to collapse. Sidestepping another mad rush from Fred, he wished the others hadn't taken him quite so literally. He was rather fond of that speeder and the tent had been very useful. Still, being left without money or transportation would give him an excellent excuse to go back to Natasha's house. If she was as kind as he suspected, she wouldn't turn him away, which would allow him to spend more time with Lucy.

The tent was tossed in the back of the speeder and two men jumped in and took off. *Two down, three to go…*

Fred, apparently deciding to fight dirty—as if he hadn't been all along—began another charge, launching himself at Tarq like a missile.

Tarq dodged him easily, but for the first time in his life, he regretted having waist-length hair. To cut it would have been to deny his manhood, but in a fight, it was a liability. Fred snatched at it as he careened past, pulling Tarq down with him.

As if they'd been waiting for a signal, Fred's buddies pounced, pinning Tarq to the ground with the sheer weight of their bodies. One landed on his chest, knocking the wind out of him.

Gasping for breath, Tarq tried to wrestle his way out from under them, but to no avail. Fred cackled with glee as he got to his feet. "About time you two decided to help." He then kicked Tarq in the ribs, which had two effects. One, it hurt like hell, and two, it jolted some air back into his lungs. Unfortunately Fred was wearing boots rather than sandals. After several more well-placed kicks—some of them to his head—Tarq could barely see through the haze of pain and blood and was beginning to welcome death, or at least unconsciousness.

Fred gave him a kick to the ribs that nearly did the job. "We're gonna make sure you leave our women alone, pretty boy. You've fathered enough kids." Brandishing his knife, he knelt beside Tarq. "I don't think you need those balls."

Lucy didn't hesitate. Her first shot missed, but the second hit the big thug squarely in the ass. Unwilling to risk hitting Tarq, she fired a couple more pulse blasts over the heads of the two who were sitting on him— which at least got them to move. Realizing that her shots were coming out of the dark kept her quiet; they couldn't have known that Tarq's rescuer was a lone female, and she wanted to keep it that way. As the two men tried to make a run for it, she actually hit one of them, dropping him in a heap next to the campfire. His buddy made a run for the trees, but Lucy switched to a wider beam and sent several shots after him.

She was rewarded by a loud thud just inside the woods and hoped he'd hit his head on a tree. Running to Tarq, she had to roll his heavy assailant off of him before she could tell if he was still breathing.

Even in the dim light from the campfire, she could see that his injuries were severe, if not life threatening. His face was already bruised and swollen, and blood from a long cut near his temple soaked his hair. He was still breathing, but his respirations sounded coarse and shallow.

Lucy sat back on her heels and looked around her. She was out in the middle of nowhere with four unconscious men, three of whom she was beginning to wish were dead. She had no idea how to help the fourth. Dealing with the demands of a counterfeit invalid mother had in no way prepared her to care for anyone suffering from such extensive trauma. Leaving him to get help was out of the question; as soon as his attackers came around, they would probably finish what they'd started. Then a solution occurred to her that had her laughing out loud.

"Lucy." Tarq's voice was the merest whisper, but that one word contained a sigh of relief.

"How bad are you hurt? I've seen this bunch of creeps before, and believe me, we've got to get out of here before they wake up."

"Hard to tell," Tarq rasped. "Haven't tried to move yet."

"Well, then, don't—at least not until I've made sure they won't come after us."

"Don't kill, Lucy… Not worth it."

"Oh, I won't kill them," she said cheerfully. "But by the time I get finished with them, they'll probably wish I had."

She picked up the knife that had fallen from Fred's

hand. She knew him all right—had waited on him and his little circle of friends enough that she knew most of their names and even their favorite foods. Not that she had any intention of ever feeding them again. She turned the knife over in her hand. Though it had almost been used in a heinous crime, it would still be useful.

Not knowing how long the stun would last, she worked quickly. She cut Fred's shirt up, wishing she had something just a little cleaner to use for bandages. Infection was the very last thing Tarq needed. Wiping the blood from his face, she examined the wound on his temple; it was clean enough, but still bleeding sluggishly. She made a pad of the fabric to apply pressure to the wound, and wrapped a bandage around his head.

Then she went to work on Fred.

Slicing through his belt loops, she yanked off his belt, rolled him onto his belly, and lashed his wrists together. Grinning wickedly, she cut his pants to ribbons and used them to tie his feet, being very creative with the knots. Wadding up his underwear, she stuffed it in his mouth and tied it in place. She saved one last strip for a very special cause. Turning him onto his side, she tied a slipknot in the fabric and, looping it around his genitals, pulled it tight.

"There you go, Fred. I hope your fuckin' dick rots off."

After relieving the other two men of their knives, she trussed them up in a similar fashion—minus the improvised cock strap—and then gathered up what little remained of Tarq's camping equipment. The trivet and the pan he used to boil water were heavy, but she wasn't about to leave anything that useful behind.

She went back to Tarq. He looked terrible, but she

knew that falling apart at a time like this would be no help to him at all. "Can you sit up?"

Tarq's nod was barely perceptible. He was already pale, but the way the color drained out of his face when she pulled him up by the hand had Lucy fearing that he would pass out. He didn't, however, and after seeing Fred's predicament, he even tried to smile. "Remind me not to piss you off."

"I don't think you could ever make me *that* mad," she said bluntly. "Listen, we really need to get out of here in case the guys who took your speeder come back looking for these three. Think you can walk?"

"Dunno, but I'll try."

Thankful that she'd filled her water bottles before setting out to Nat's in the speeder, she got one out of her bag and gave Tarq a drink. Taking a sip for herself, she settled the bottle in her pocket where she could reach it easily.

Getting Tarq on his feet was hard enough, but helping him walk while keeping her bag from slipping off her shoulder and dragging on the ground, leaving behind an obvious trail, was even tougher. Having seen the speeder take off as she approached, she knew her supplies were all they had left; therefore, leaving them behind wasn't an option. Nor was returning to Reltan. Out on the open road, they would be easy prey for any of Fred's cronies, should they be followed. Lucy straightened up and shifted Tarq's arm around her shoulder, wishing she'd been a little taller, a lot stronger, and more of the kick-ass heroine type—especially since something told her that going on to Yalka was a very bad idea. "We'll have to try to reach the mountains."

"Not Natasha's house?"

"No. The whole place is burned to the ground—and it looks like it was deliberate."

"Those men said they'd gotten rid of all the non-humans in Yalka."

Lucy nodded. "It fits. Natasha's husband is a Mordrial. After what these creeps did to you, I'm guessing they're the ones who burned them out—maybe even killed them—which would explain why I haven't heard from Nat in a while." Lucy shuddered at the thought of her friend dying such a horrific death. "Nothing like this has ever happened around here before. There must be some really weird shit going on in Yalka for them to get away with it." She paused, biting her lip. "And you can say 'I told you so' all you like. If I'd let you take me up to the house in the speeder, none of this would have happened."

"Don't blame yourself. If you'd been with me when those guys showed up, they'd have caught us both."

If she'd been with Tarq, they'd have been in the tent right in the middle of—no, after barely talking to one another all afternoon, sex probably wouldn't have been on the agenda. "Yeah, you're right."

They trudged on in silence. Lucy was thankful that they'd left the rocky wastelands behind and that there was still enough of a moon to light the way, otherwise one of them would have turned an ankle at the very least. The woods stretched on toward the foothills of the mountains, and she used the tree line as a guide, noting that the turf along the edge of the woods was closely cropped but not entirely smooth, as though grazed by cattle. It was treacherous in places, but it still made for easier going than trying to keep to the cover of the trees.

And speed was necessary. If the men who'd stolen the speeder should wonder what became of their cohorts and return, catching up to Tarq and Lucy would be simple. They had to keep moving. Lucy didn't know how Tarq managed to keep walking, and when she stole a glance at him, she saw that his eyes were now swollen shut. Lost in a blind labyrinth of pain, he was relying on her to lead him. She did her best to pick the clearest path, but he stumbled occasionally and nearly fell more than once.

Never having been in that part of the world before, Lucy was amazed at how quickly the mountains loomed before her. "Foothills" was a misnomer; there was only one, and it was no higher than the hill Natasha's house had sat upon. Lucy gave no thought to what they would do once they reached the mountains; it was a goal, nothing more, and was probably every bit as dangerous as the open road. They would be prey there too, but at least it would make any human pursuit more difficult. In her mind, all she needed was to reach a place where Tarq could rest in relative safety and she could tend to his injuries. Then they would decide on the best course of action.

If there *was* one.

Chapter 15

AGONY NUMBED HIS MIND TO THE POINT THAT ABOUT the only voluntary function Tarq had left was the ability to put one foot in front of the other. Pain and exhaustion had pushed everything else into the background. Lucy would have a hard enough time staying alive in the mountains without him slowing her down, and he cursed his weakness. The fact that without him and his current predicament she wouldn't have *needed* to take refuge in the mountains made him feel even worse.

No matter how he looked at it, Lucy would have been much better off had the two of them never met. He had never made the first move on a woman. If they requested his services, he was more than willing to comply, but actively solicit them? No. Lucy had been the exception to that rule. In her case, he'd let his nose—and therefore his dick—overrule his better judgment. That mistake had nearly gotten him killed and Lucy... What would happen to a pregnant girl wandering through the mountains, burdened by an injured man? Vrelnots probably weren't the only danger they would face. The mountains themselves would be treacherous, and food, water, and shelter would be hard to come by.

Even taking everything one step at a time was tough when danger lurked in every direction. He was thankful that Lucy had taken his attackers' knives. At least they were armed to a degree, and she still had her pulse pistol. Even so, aside from vrelnots—and he'd only seen the head of the one mounted on the wall at the café—he had no idea what to expect, and he doubted that Lucy did either.

Of course, his being able to see would improve their chances of survival enormously. At the moment, Tarq could only tell they'd reached the mountains from the way the ground beneath his feet had gone from smooth and grassy to steep and rocky.

Lucy had to be as exhausted as he was. Granted, she hadn't been kicked in the ribs, but Tarq could hear her labored breathing and when she finally stopped to rest, he sank gratefully to the ground. "Where are we?"

"About halfway up the side of a valley underneath an overhanging slab of rock. There's a sort of shallow cave here with bushes growing around it. If anyone who knows the area is following us, this'll probably be the first place they look, but I don't think I can go any farther tonight, let alone climb those mountains. We'll have to risk staying here for a while."

Tarq nodded. "We might be here longer than you think. Once I go to sleep, you may not be able to wake me up for a couple of days."

A sharp intake of breath revealed her dismay even before she spoke. "A couple of days? Tarq, we *really* have to keep moving."

"I won't be able to help you. When Zetithians are sick or injured, we sort of shut down while our bodies heal themselves. The only reason it hasn't happened before now is that you kept me awake and moving. I'm surprised I didn't conk out while you were tying up those men."

"Maybe it means you aren't hurt all that bad. I don't suppose you have your scanner, do you?"

Tarq could hear the hope in her voice, but he knew that broken ribs and swollen eyes might not be the most serious of his injuries. He shook his head. "It's in the speeder. All I've got in my pocket are the firestarter and a tea bag."

"Too bad you don't have *two* tea bags," she said ruefully. "I could really use a cup of tea right now."

Tarq couldn't help but laugh. "It's all yours. Anyway, it'd be wasted on me." He didn't want to alarm her, but he might be out longer than the two days he'd mentioned. Being able to heal yourself while you slept was a useful means of survival when no medical care was available, but he'd be pretty much defenseless until he woke up and certainly no help to Lucy. "You drink it."

Lucy sighed. "I would, but we probably shouldn't risk a fire at this point—too easy to spot if we're followed—but I'm glad we've got the capability."

"I'm sorry for getting you into this mess, Lucy," he began, but she cut him off.

"It's not your fault, and I'm not going to let you blame yourself, either. It's Fred's fault and no one else's. You forget about that and focus on getting well." She didn't say anything else, but Tarq could hear her moving about. He tried to stay alert, but his consciousness was slipping…

The last thing he remembered was being rolled over onto a blanket.

—◠◠◠—

Lucy tucked Tarq in and went in search of water, figuring she'd better get it now while it was still dark enough that she wouldn't be seen. She had three water bottles, two of which were now empty. She'd followed a creek into the mountains but had climbed higher up in the valley to find shelter. Thankful for the moonlight, she glanced up at the sky and noted that the moon was past its zenith, but it would be nearly morning before it set, if then. She dug into her duffel bag and found Tarq's pan, then began her descent to the creek. Going downhill was easier but more treacherous than their climb had been. She slipped more than once, for the valley was deeper here, its slope studded with loose rock, stunted growth, and the occasional boulder.

Upon reaching the stream, she scooped up a pan full of water and drank as much as she could hold. The sound of flowing water reminded her of the previous night, having dinner with a very testy Tarq, followed by a night in the tent she wouldn't forget even if she lived long enough to see her great-grandchildren grow up. Of course, if Fred and his buddies ever caught up with them and they figured out why she and Tarq were together, she might not live long enough to see her *own* children born.

Gazing back toward Yalka, Lucy saw no movement in the valley at all, with the exception of a few birds. She had always heard that a trek through the Eradic range was tantamount to committing suicide if you weren't well equipped, but so far, so good. Still, given that reputation, once Fred realized that they'd ventured into the mountains, he might decide to let the vrelnots get them and save himself the trouble.

Refilling the pan and the water bottles, she began to climb, revising her original assessment that the trip down was more difficult. The route they had taken before had been a gentle rise; as they went farther up the valley, she had simply aimed for higher ground. What she was climbing now wasn't precisely vertical but it might as well have been. She'd be lucky if she had any water left in the pan by the time she reached the place she'd left Tarq.

If she could find it. She hadn't been looking for shelter when she stumbled onto it; she'd skirted around some bushes and there it was. Unfortunately, anyone familiar with the region might also know it was there, and Fred had often bragged about going hunting in the Eradics…

Brushing that disturbing thought aside, she continued on, thinking that if what Tarq had said was true, this spot would be home for a few days. She smiled to herself, thinking that if nothing else, she would develop some strong leg muscles, but still wished they'd had a little more food. The stream was deep enough that it might have some fish in it, but Lucy had never been fishing in her life. How did one catch a fish without bait, line, or even a hook?

Occupied with these thoughts, Lucy stumbled upon their den before she realized it. Tarq was lying exactly the way she'd left him, but if he was breathing, she certainly couldn't tell it. Stifling a scream, she nearly dropped the water, but her practical nature quickly reasserted itself. Her heart in her throat, she set the water down and knelt at his side, laying her shaking hands on him, searching for signs of life.

He wasn't cold—in fact, he felt warmer than normal, which was reassuring. Placing her fingertips on the side of his neck, she finally found a pulse—very faint and slow, but steady. Perhaps this was what he'd meant when he'd said his body would shut down to heal itself. On the other hand, he'd said he would sleep for a couple of days, not appear to be dead. *Trust a man to leave out the most pertinent detail…*

After making sure that her pistol was right where she could get to it in a hurry, Lucy settled in beside Tarq. She received no response when she kissed him goodnight and certainly none of the joy she knew he was capable of giving her.

But they were both alive.

Whether they would remain so was anyone's guess.

Lucy awoke with a start. Her back was pressed up against Tarq, but her arms were wrapped around something else. Something warm and furry. Something that smelled like… *a dog?*

She opened her eyes a slit. Yes, it was a dog. A huge black and white long-haired dog that seemed very happy to have found a human to snuggle up with. Raising its head, the dog gazed at her with dark worshipful eyes, and then licked her nose.

Lucy sat up and looked around. She didn't see anyone else but remained wary. "Please tell me you aren't Fred's dog."

Yawning, the dog stretched and stood up, tail wagging.

"No, you couldn't belong to Fred—unless you ran away from him. He'd never have such a nice dog." She gave the dog a tentative pat on the head and turned to check on Tarq.

At first glance he appeared even worse than he had the night before, but then Lucy remembered that she'd only seen him in moonlight. In the harsh light of day, he looked… well… like three guys had kicked the shit out of him.

"Which isn't surprising," she muttered. After assuring herself that he was still warm and his heart was beating, she pushed back the blanket and got up. Rolling him onto his side, she reached into his pocket and found the tea bag and the firestarter. A fire during the night would have drawn anyone—or any*thing*—to their location, but during the day, she deemed it worth the risk. The dog trotted off while she was gathering dead wood for the fire but soon returned with a stout stick in its mouth.

"If you're going to be *that* helpful, you need a name." A quick check under the thick hair showed the dog to be male and collarless. "Hmm… I think your name needs to be… Rufus."

Rufus cocked his head and dropped the stick.

"You want to play, don't you? Sorry, but I have to take care of Tarq first."

She aimed the firestarter at the pile of wood and pressed the button. Rufus let out a yelp as the wood ignited and bounded away. "Hmm… helpful, but not terribly brave."

Thankful that the dry wood gave off very little smoke, she rummaged through her bag, found the trivet, and set it over the fire. After placing the pan of water on the trivet, she took stock of their provisions: two round loaves of bread, a sizeable wedge of cheese, six apples, a bag of olives, three oranges, and a big roll of salami. It had seemed like a lot when she was only planning for a few days on the road by herself, but for an unknown period of time in the mountains with Tarq, it was rather pathetic. Feeding Rufus was out of the question; he'd have to continue fending for himself.

When the water boiled, she poured some of it on a pair of her clean panties to wash Tarq's face. After dropping the tea bag into the remaining water to brew, she got to work. His face was still so swollen that if it hadn't been for his square jaw and pointed ears, she might not have recognized him. Unwinding the bandage from his head, she pulled off the pad. The bleeding had stopped and the wound seemed clean enough, but she washed it anyway. She replaced the bandage and wiped his face. *If only he wasn't so pale…*

Gingerly pulling up his shirt, she surveyed the damage. He was black and blue on both sides and when she pressed her hand to his ribs, one section on his left side crunched beneath her fingers. Broken ribs could mean internal injuries, but there wasn't a thing she could do about it except worry. Having cared for her mother during some of her more helpless periods, she knew that lying flat on his back for extended periods could cause even more problems, and though she was afraid to turn Tarq all the way over on his side, she tilted him slightly to the right and bunched the blanket up behind him to keep him there.

She breakfasted on tea with a little of the bread and cheese, thinking what a waste it would be if morning sickness were to suddenly strike her. After that, she scouted out the surrounding area and gathered up more firewood. Rufus apparently hadn't gone far, for he soon returned, trying to interest her in a game of fetch. She obliged him for a short while but avoided talking to him as much as possible, knowing how her voice would carry.

The valley was quiet, almost desolate. Lucy was beginning to believe they were the only beings anywhere around until a few birds flew overhead and settled to the ground farther to the east. That the birds were able to go about the business of foraging without being disturbed was heartening. If Fred and his buddies were on their trail, the birds wouldn't have been quite so nonchalant.

Taking the longer, less precipitous route to the stream, she carried more water up to their campsite. In her absence, Tarq hadn't moved, so she turned him to his back. Though he remained unconscious, he appeared to have improved slightly. His color was better and the swelling in his face had lessened, but his ribs were still a bit crunchy. Rufus sniffed at Tarq, licking his cheek before stretching out beside him for a nap.

Lucy hadn't had much opportunity to enjoy the peaceful solitude of her journey when she'd first set out from Yalka, but now she found herself doing the sort of thing Tarq had suggested—simply sitting by the fire and watching the day go by.

At first it was nice, but then it began to chafe to the point that she couldn't sit still any longer. It wasn't in her nature to remain idle—though idleness was something her mother and sister had taken to an artistic level—and the lack of available food was bugging her. Tarq would need to eat when he woke up, and if he didn't wake up soon, there might not be anything left.

The idea of fishing returned to her, but there was no way she could think of— "You goonbait! You've got a pistol!"

The fact that she wasn't any good at shooting wouldn't matter; after all, she'd used a wide stun beam to take down the guy in the woods—Tuwain, his name was, if she remembered correctly. If she could do that, the stun would undoubtedly work on fish.

Making yet another trip down into the valley, she searched for a spot in the stream where the water was deep and, after traipsing along its length, finally found a likely fishing hole. There was enough of a charge left on the pistol to allow for a few experimental shots, but it wouldn't pay to use it indiscriminately. With her luck, right about the time Fred found them or they were attacked by vrelnots, the uncharged pistol would have been reduced to a useless bit of metal.

Not wanting to kill or stun every fish in the stream, she chose a fairly deep pool where she could see a few fish moving about beneath the surface. Narrowing the beam, she set the intensity to its lowest setting, took aim, and fired. The shock wave rippled across the surface of the water and she stood waiting patiently.

Four tiny fish floated to the surface.

So much for that idea. If nothing else, she figured they would make a nice snack for Rufus, but as she watched, a much larger fish swam up from the bottom and gobbled down two of them. Lucy stood on the bank, momentarily stunned until it occurred to her to up the intensity and fire again. The fish rolled slowly onto its side. Repeating the sequence, she soon had four nice-sized fish. All she had to do was retrieve them.

Unfortunately, shooting fish in a barrel was much easier than getting them *out* of the barrel. There was a reason the water was deeper there; the banks were steep and rocky and there was a significant drop on the upstream end—almost a waterfall. The approach would be difficult from any direction. Lucy eyed her catch grimly. The rocks below made it too dangerous to simply jump, and climbing down there would be foolhardy without a rope. If she wanted those fish, she was going to have to swim upstream to get them.

Grumbling to herself, Lucy walked farther downstream and stripped to her underwear. She'd heard that pulse pistols could fire underwater, but didn't want to risk losing it, so she left it on a slab of rock near the bank along with her clothes and moccasins. She hadn't gone far when she discovered that her decision to go barefoot had been a mistake. The rocks were sharp and her feet were bleeding by the time she reached the pool.

Lucy had hoped that the current would be strong enough to send the fish drifting downstream, but they hadn't moved at all and were still right out in the middle. She knew how to swim, but also knew that there could be anything at the bottom of that pool—things she couldn't see and could only guess at. Normally she dismissed stories of monsters lurking in the depths, but now that she was actually faced with such a scenario, she wasn't so sure. She picked her way through the rocks to the shore looking for a stick to sweep the fish toward her, but found nothing that was long enough.

Swallowing her fear, Lucy waded through the shallows and swam out gingerly, fully expecting to have her bleeding feet grabbed at any moment by some nasty creature. She corralled the fish, pushing them to the shallow end of the pool, and had almost reached the edge when she happened to glance up at the bank above her.

A vicious beast hung over the edge, jaws agape, just waiting to pounce. She let out a terrified scream before she recognized Rufus. "Where were you when I needed you?"

Rufus barked his encouragement—or his excuse. Lucy wasn't sure which.

Tossing the fish out onto a large flat rock, she was now faced with a new dilemma. She had no way to carry them. "And I am *not* stuffing them in my underwear."

She was about to consider stringing them on her bra straps when she spotted a vine growing near the water's edge. Making another painful trek across the rocks, she tried, unsuccessfully, to pull it loose, learning yet another rule of living in the wilderness: Always carry a knife.

In the end, she used a sharp rock to cut the vine and returned to find Rufus sniffing at the fish. "Don't you *dare*…"

Rufus may not have understood the words, but he clearly understood her tone of voice and backed off.

"That's better. If you had any idea how hard it was to get those fish, you'd understand. I promise to give you some later, but right now I need to get them back up the hill."

By the time she'd made her way back to where she'd left her clothes, her feet were in even worse shape and her empty stomach was protesting loudly. Still, she had gotten four fish, and her bra and panties were dry enough that they felt like clothing again as opposed to a second skin. Sitting on the edge of the rock where she'd left her things, she rinsed her feet and inspected the damage. It could have been worse, she decided; a few scrapes but no deep cuts. She dried her feet with her shirt and then dressed quickly and headed uphill to Tarq.

She wouldn't have wanted him to wake up alone, but was forced to admit that returning to find him sitting up and smiling at her would have done wonders for her peace of mind.

Finally, panting and sweaty from her climb, she reached their hiding place. The fire had long since gone out, and though he looked better, Tarq still hadn't moved. She rested for a few minutes while she attempted to banish her disappointment. He'd said a couple of days, she reminded herself, and a full day and night had yet to elapse. There was still time, and she had fish to clean.

Thankful that Fred had been one to carry a sharp knife, she gutted and filleted the fish, thinking of the last time she'd done it in the relative comfort of the café's kitchen. Jublansk had been nearby, shaping bread dough into loaves when old Jamis had brought in his catch of the day. If only she'd thought to ask him for some tips on how to catch the big ones! Their situations were different—she was fishing out of a creek while Jamis caught his from the sea—but she was sure that similar principles applied. Still, even without bait, hooks, line, or nets she'd managed to bag four fish. Too bad she hadn't thought to bring any of those things with her—not that an adventure in the mountains had been on her agenda at the time…

Having only a pan and a little water to cook in, she wound up poaching the fish. Without sauce or seasonings, it wasn't particularly tasty, but after all she'd gone through to get it, Lucy was hungry enough that she didn't care. She gave Rufus the raw scraps—something she didn't think she'd ever be hungry enough to eat.

Her father's words taunted her… "She'll come back when she gets hungry enough." No way was she admitting defeat. She still had the money Tarq had given her. If nothing else, she could go on to Yalka—and would have if it hadn't been for Tarq.

She had no idea what he intended to do, but after what he'd been through at the hands of the locals, he would probably jump on the first ship leaving Talus. The trick would be getting him to the spaceport in Noklar, which was on the other side of the mountains. She would give him back some of the money he'd given her if necessary, though surely all of his money hadn't been in the speeder. He was bound to have more in a bank account somewhere. If he refused to accept money from her, she'd tell him to consider it a loan and he could pay her back when he could access his funds. He had friends too. He just had to meet up with them.

And somewhere in all of that, she'd have to say goodbye to him.

Again.

Chapter 16

TARQ WAS HAVING A LOVELY DREAM. LUCY WAS caressing his face with her tongue—an odd thing for her to be doing, especially considering the condition of his dick. He'd had boners before, but this one topped them all. He'd much rather she licked him there.

Upon opening his eyes, he discovered that Lucy had somehow turned into a dog.

Just my luck. I've gone completely insane and—

"Stop that, Rufus," Lucy said sharply. "Tarq, are you awake?"

"Mmm."

"Thank God! I was beginning to think I'd be giving birth in this cave."

Tarq sat up and glanced at her with alarm. "I haven't been out *that* long, have I?"

"Well, no," Lucy admitted. "It's been a little over two days, actually, but it seems more like two hundred. How do you feel?"

Blinking hard to clear his vision, he took a deep breath. The subsequent cough didn't hurt his ribs too much—not nearly as much as his dick. Why *that* part of him would wake up first… "Okay, I think."

"I'll get you some water."

"Yeah, water." *Then I need you. Badly.*

She handed him a bottle of water and he took a long drink. "Sorry to leave you to fend for yourself like that.

I'll do better now."

Lucy smiled with, he thought, a touch of pride. "I did okay. Caught fish and everything."

Despite her slightly disheveled appearance, she did seem to be glowing a bit—and it wasn't just her pregnancy. Her fair skin had acquired a few more freckles along with a light tan. Tarq had never seen a more beautiful sight in his life.

"Probably lost a few kilos, but it wasn't anything I couldn't afford to lose."

"You look great." Trying to ignore the joy juice trickling from his cock, he nodded at Rufus. "So where'd he come from?"

"Dunno," she replied. "He was here when I woke up that first morning. No collar or anything, but a really nice dog. He goes off to hunt once in a while and I've been giving him fish scraps, so he hasn't gone hungry."

Tarq smiled. From her expression, she had a good story to tell. "You've been fishing, you said?"

"Yeah. I've gotten better at it, but that first time was a real bitch. I wouldn't have thought I'd be any good at living off the land, but so far I haven't done too badly."

"I take it we weren't followed?"

She frowned. "No—not yet anyway. With any luck, Fred's still lying right where we left him. Would serve him right, too." She swallowed, her lips forming a moue of distaste. "When I think of what he would've done if I'd gotten there a few minutes too late…" Shuddering, she sighed deeply. "I wanted to kill him… I mean I *really* wanted to kill him. To do something like that to a man who'd done him no harm at all…"

"If he comes after us, you might have to," Tarq said soberly. "Kill him, I mean."

Rubbing her eyes, she nodded. "You were right, though. He's not worth it, but if it comes to defending ourselves, yeah, we might have to."

Tarq tried not to think about what might have happened if they'd been discovered in their cave. Lucy would have had to defend herself alone; Tarq would have been no help to her at all. But that was about to change. He was responsible for everything that had happened to her, and it was up to him to get them through this.

"We should get going soon," she went on. "I've been thinking about where we should go from here. We could follow the mountains back to Reltan, avoiding the road. You could contact your friends from there, and I could"—she paused, heaving a sigh—"go home."

"Is that what you really want to do?"

"No, but I'm not sure we have much choice. We need to get you somewhere safe, and I guess my going to Nat's wasn't such a good idea after all. I *would* like to find out what happened to her, though. It's hard not knowing."

Tarq knew exactly how she felt. He'd felt the same way when the refugee ship left Zetith behind. "Once we get back to Reltan, we can make some inquiries and maybe get to the bottom of what's been happening in Yalka."

"Too bad the spaceport is in Noklar, but it's on the other side of the mountains."

Tarq eyed her curiously. "Why the spaceport?"

"I figure you'd want to leave this planet as quickly

as possible." Her head drooped as she looked down at her hands. "You're probably wishing you'd never come here in the first place."

In a way, she was right. Tarq *did* wish he'd never come to Talus, but not for the reasons she suspected. When he left this world, he'd be leaving more than his unborn children behind. He'd be leaving Lucy—and his heart.

"What about you? Would you rather go to Noklar? You could live there and not have to go home—unless that's what you really want."

She shook her head. "No, I don't want to go home. Noklar would be a good place to live and work—people are certainly much more liberal there, it being the space-port city and all. But to get there, we'd have to either go through the Eradics or around them."

From her tone, she didn't relish taking either path. "Then we'll go back to Reltan. I can access my funds from there and buy another speeder to take us both to Noklar. We wouldn't have to see your family at all."

"That sounds like the best plan to me. I—"

Tarq put up a hand to silence her. He heard something in the distance: the high-pitched whine of a speeder engine. "Someone's coming," he whispered. He crawled from his blankets and moved toward the sound. Peering through the bushes that shrouded the cave entrance, he spotted them. Two men standing by a speeder. *His* speeder. A long way down the valley, but... "How far are we from the crest of this hill?"

"Not far," Lucy replied. "Maybe twenty meters."

"Open ground or trees?"

"Shrubs, mostly," she replied. "Like these around the

cave. I haven't been up there. I've only been down in the valley to the creek."

Tarq gathered up the blanket and handed it to Lucy. "Get your stuff together." Thankful that the fire had burned down to ashes, he collected the few utensils they had.

Rufus padded over to the edge of the cave. Growling, he shot through the shrubs, racing down the hillside.

"Oh, no!" Lucy exclaimed. "He'll lead them right to us!"

Tarq stood up, fully expecting to fall down again, but despite a brief bout of dizziness, he was able to remain on his feet. "Might be a good thing if he did. Then we could stun them again and steal my speeder back. But let's not chance it. There's a pistol in my speeder, and if they've found it…"

"Yeah. I see your point." Lucy stuffed the blanket into her bag and then snatched two fish down from the roof of the cave. "No way am I leaving these behind. They were too hard to catch."

Tarq would've loved to hear how she'd done it, but figured that was a topic best left for a more opportune time. Shouldering the bag, Tarq motioned for her to lead the way. "You know what's out there better than I do."

Nodding, she ducked under a bough on the eastern side of the cave and Tarq followed close behind her.

Closely-spaced, low bushes provided excellent cover, and with a minimum of stealth, they were able to pass from clump to clump unseen by their pursuers. Even so, the going wasn't easy and Tarq didn't dare stand up to take a look around. All he could tell was that they were headed uphill.

Lucy didn't falter but kept on at a steady pace. She was currently in much better shape than he was, and it wasn't long before Tarq wished he'd had time to eat lunch before they had to head for the hills. Soon, however, the ground began a downward slope and Lucy stopped.

"We're over the top of the hill now," she whispered. "I'm gonna take a peek." She raised her head to peer over the tops of the branches. "I don't see anything." She took the bag from Tarq's shoulder as he stood up, and though he would've loved to protest, he felt too much relief to mention it. Rummaging through the bag, she pulled out an apple and handed it to him. "You can eat that while we're on the move." Settling the strap of her duffel bag onto her shoulder, she started walking. "I'll carry this for a while."

Tarq had never tasted anything more delicious in his life—unless it was Lucy—and he was down to the core in no time. He felt much better and could have easily resumed carrying the load, but he had to admire her spunk. For a girl who'd never been outside of Reltan, she was holding her own quite well. Not that he wanted to appear weak, but letting her take charge for a while was probably wise. Lucy had been belittled and made to feel stupid often enough. It was time to let her feel her strength.

Tarq knew all about being made to feel stupid. He'd been teased often enough as a boy, which was one reason he tried to hide his inability to read. Lucy wouldn't make fun of him even if she knew, but he'd prefer that she didn't pity him because of it. He wanted her feelings for him to be clear—if she had any.

The ground grew steadily more steep and rocky and the mountains reared up before them. As Tarq studied the terrain, his vision blurred momentarily. When he blinked to clear it, the image was still in his mind, along with a trail mapped out through the mountains to Noklar. He spoke before he truly understood what he'd seen. "We need to turn south when we get past the notch between those two mountains up ahead."

"We have to go that far into the Eradics? Aren't we going back to Reltan?"

Tarq shook his head. "Not if we're being followed. That's where they'd expect us to go."

"But Noklar is more toward the north—almost due east of Yalka."

"Yes, but the best route is to turn south and then go north. There's a wide valley in the middle of the range that will take us straight to it. The climb down from the valley will be the hard part. Noklar sits on a plateau in the eastern foothills."

She stared at him with frank astonishment. "How in the world could you possibly know that?"

"I—I'm not sure."

Her eyes narrowed in suspicion. "This wouldn't have anything to do with your getting kicked in the head, would it?"

Had he been in her place, Tarq would've probably thought the same thing. He frowned, trying to think of the best way to explain. "Haven't you ever just known something and then later found out you were right?"

She shook her head. "Not like that."

"Well, Zetithians do… No one knows why, but—"

"You're saying this was a vision?"

Tarq grimaced. "I don't know if I'd call it that. Well, maybe it is. I've done it before, but it's not quite like other Zetithian visions. They mostly deal with the future." Taking a deep breath, he added, "I saw the same thing in a dream I had several nights ago. This is also how I found Amelyana's ship when I was a kid. I just knew it was the right path to follow."

"Well, seeing as how you made it here alive, I can't really argue with that logic, can I?"

"I wish I could say I'd seen a map, but I haven't."

"Those mountains have been mapped from space, but given the dangers, not many people have actually traveled through them—and lived to tell about it."

"My, how encouraging," he said dryly. "Vrelnots?"

"And other things. Storms, rock slides, you name it. Even hunters don't go very deep into the range. That valley you were talking about… it's there, all right, but it has a really bad reputation. It may be the best route as far as the mountains themselves are concerned, but otherwise, we may wind up wishing we'd stuck around for a showdown with Fred."

"If it's all the same to you, I think I'd rather go up against vrelnots. At least they wouldn't be gunning for us specifically."

Lucy chuckled. "True. They just want to kill us on general principles."

Tarq grinned. She was a plucky little woman for sure. "Well, hang onto your pistol and maybe we can take out a few of them first."

"I hope so. I should probably give it to you. I'd be willing to bet you're a better shot than I am."

Tarq would protect her to the best of his ability, but

he'd feel much better knowing she was armed. "I'm not an expert, if that's what you mean. You keep it."

"Well, here," she said, handing him a sheathed knife. "We've got three of these."

He snapped the sheath onto his belt and they traveled on in silence for a while, Tarq stopping periodically to reassure himself that they weren't being followed. He hoped their attackers would give up if they thought they'd driven him into the mountains, though he couldn't be sure they didn't know Lucy was the one who'd come to his rescue. She hadn't stunned them all at once. One of them might have seen her. If her father offered some sort of reward for her return, it might be worth their while to find her.

Tarq hadn't taken note of the time of day when he'd first awakened, but it must have been late afternoon because it was already beginning to get dark. He didn't relish the idea of running into a vrelnot in the daytime, let alone at night. Unfortunately, the moon that had lit their way a few nights before was already on the wane and rising later. Clouds drifted in, obscuring the stars. Tarq had yet to see it rain since he'd been on Talus. He was hoping it would hold off a while longer.

Lucy finally stopped when she couldn't see to put one foot in front of the other. Tarq's night vision was much better than a human's but he was exhausted, hungry, and had been breathing in Lucy's scent all day. The erection he'd awakened with had never really left him.

"I don't suppose your vision included where the next source of water will be, did it?"

"There's a river running through the valley, but before that, we'll have to be frugal."

She nodded grimly. "Wish I'd had a chance to fill the bottles again before we had to bug out of there. We've only got three bottles as it is, and one of them is empty."

Tarq stared up at the sky. He could see stars again, peeking through the clouds. "We'll make it through. Don't worry."

"Faith in your vision?"

"Something like that. We just have to follow the right path and everything will work out."

Lucy burst out laughing. "I sure hope you're right."

"Me too."

"You're just trying to make me feel better, aren't you?"

"Maybe. Is it working?"

"Not sure. Did your vision include a good place to camp tonight?"

"No, but this place is as good as any." He was kidding, of course. They were standing right out in plain sight. He gestured toward a stand of trees. "Let's camp over there."

They found a relatively smooth spot beneath a tree and Lucy spread out the blanket. "How's your dick?"

"Hard."

She sighed deeply. "I was afraid of that."

"I'll be okay. Don't worry about it."

"Will you be able to sleep?"

"Next to you without getting any relief? Probably not. Um, are we ever going to eat those fish?"

"What? Oh, yeah. The fish. They're already cooked— well, smoked, anyway. I experimented a bit. It's not half bad."

"I'm hungry enough to eat them raw."

"You won't have to. You just peel back the scales

and the skin comes right off. Watch out for the bones, though."

She was right. The fish was only half bad. Tarq would've given a lot for the Colonel's eleven different herbs and spices, but that would have to wait until they reached Noklar. Unfortunately, his dick wasn't as patient as his palate.

If asked, Lucy would've said she was too tired for sex, but with one touch from Tarq, her exhaustion vanished, and when he kissed her, she forgot it entirely. She'd withdrawn from him for most of that last day together, knowing how painful their parting would be. Now that they were back together for a time, it was almost as though that episode had never taken place. But it had. He seemed to have forgotten it, however—either that or it didn't matter to him. Lucy was hoping for the former; the idea that he didn't care was too awful to consider.

There was no denying that she'd longed for this during the hours she'd sat beside Tarq, keeping watch over him and letting him get the rest he needed. She was amazed at the transformation he'd made from the beaten, bedraggled man she'd half carried, half dragged up the valley to the cave. There had been times when she feared he would never wake up and speak to her, let alone make love with her.

He was purring as he kissed her, the vibrations in his throat triggering an autonomic response in her—almost as if she'd been Zetithian herself. Desire washed over her like a wave, and she melted like butter in the sun.

She was distracted momentarily by a soft whine as Rufus approached and settled down nearby. If anyone was following him it wasn't readily apparent, but it was frightening to think how easily he'd found them without making a sound. Still, she was glad he'd returned. If nothing else, he could keep watch while she and Tarq were… busy.

"Better make it a quick one," she suggested. "One of us needs to stand guard in case we were followed."

"I'll take the first watch," Tarq said, his purr never ceasing. "You'll need to sleep."

"You should be the one to sleep first," Lucy said firmly. "You're the one who was hurt."

"Yes, but you're pregnant and you know what *snard* does to you."

Snard. Yet another thing she thought she'd never experience again. "We'll wait and see how you feel when you're, um… done."

"You don't have to make it sound like such a chore," Tarq grumbled.

Lucy rolled her eyes. "That's not what I meant and you know it. I'm just worried about being followed, that's all." This wasn't the only thing bothering her, but it was easier to explain.

"If it makes you feel any better, I heard Rufus coming and knew he was alone."

"You might have mentioned it."

He nuzzled her neck, purring louder. "Sorry, I had other things on my mind."

She pushed him away for a moment, taking a deep breath while attempting to control the reactions of her wayward body. "I really don't want those guys to catch us in the act—or naked. Especially after what I did to them."

"Then we'll only get half naked." She heard the

sound of his zipper being undone and waited while he kicked off his jeans. "There. How's that?"

Lucy giggled. "Should I keep my shirt on too?"

"I'd rather you didn't, but if it makes you feel better, go right ahead."

He helped her out of her khakis and inhaled deeply. "Ah, Lucy. If you only knew what you do to me."

Whatever she did to him had an obvious effect—he was rock hard and dripping—but she suspected his effect on her was stronger. Nudging her legs apart, he pressed himself into her, and she marveled at the way he was able to arouse her despite the fact that she was tired, nervous, and expected Fred's gang to pounce on them at any moment.

As he rocked into her, she forgot about all that and simply gazed into his glowing eyes and let him take her to paradise. What would it be like to have him forever, to not have fears that they would be discovered, and to truly belong to him? To be married to him and do this all the time? To feel no fears, only contentment, and to sleep safe and warm afterward?

Nothing to fear... Everything simply... *wonderful*. Her first orgasm struck and she tightened around him. He felt so hot, so hard, so right... giving joy even before he filled her with his *snard*. He was lying on her now, pinning her to the ground, his weight barely supported by his elbows and knees as he made love to her slowly, deeply, and with such sweet tenderness...

At first only his hips were moving, and then only his cock. He filled her, stretched her, made her feel... *"Ohhh..."* He swept her inner walls, coating them with the elixir of his love.

Love? Was it only her imagination, or did she truly feel loved? Tarq was kissing her, purring against her lips, his tongue sliding deep into the recesses of her mouth to sample her essence. His cock drifted back and forth inside her, sending waves of delight coursing through her body, but there was more. A mental element she'd never detected before. Too overwhelmed to even attempt to analyze it, she simply allowed herself to bask in its glow.

Tarq shifted his weight and began to isolate the movement of his pelvis rather than his penis, and every thrust sent shock waves resonating through her, compounded by the orgasms incited by his coronal secretions. If she'd been wondering why any man would be jealous enough to castrate him, she understood it now. Even if she'd been in love with someone else, she wouldn't have been able to resist Tarq, and once she'd had a taste of the joy, there would be no going back. Having experienced nirvana, just plain sex—even great sex—would lose a large part of its appeal, perhaps all of it.

She'd been relatively passive, but now desire spurred her into action. Spearing her fingers into his hair, she gathered fistfuls of it and pulled while she took control of her inner musculature, squeezing him with all her might.

"Oh, Lucy, please," he groaned. *"Harder."*

Lucy wasn't sure which action he was referring to, so she did both. His response was a deep-throated growl that had Rufus stirring, but the dog relaxed when Tarq stiffened in release. As her euphoria began, he whispered melodious words in her ear—words she didn't understand but made her feel as though he'd told her he loved her. She might ask him to explain later, if she

remembered to do it. Right now she was flying—and
Tarq was right there with her.

Chapter 17

TARQ WAS RIGHT; LUCY FELL ASLEEP EVEN BEFORE HIS softening cock slid from her body. Poor girl, she'd certainly had a time of it while he lay helpless. He tried not to see his involvement as having ruined her life, but that was about the only spin he could put on it. If she loved him, he could make her life easier than she ever dreamed possible, but if she didn't love him, well…

He searched her pockets for the pistol and then moved to a better vantage point, a little away from her so her scent wouldn't distract him. The dog lay beside her. He was thankful she'd at least had Rufus for company; otherwise she'd have been awfully lonely.

He toyed with the idea of retracing their steps in an attempt to get the drop on their pursuers and steal his speeder back. That would make everything much easier in the long run, but it would also diminish the amount of time he'd have left with Lucy. With the speeder, he'd simply take her wherever she wanted to go and then head on to Noklar. Talus hadn't proven to be the best world for him to visit, considering what he had to offer, and even if he could never work in the brothel again, perhaps it was time to return to Rhylos. Or he could buy land on Terra Minor and retire. Either way, he would at least be among friends.

Only one problem with that: He was too young to retire. He had a long life ahead of him, but without love—without Lucy—it would be a very empty, meaningless existence.

The silence surrounded him, filling him with loneliness. Glancing over at where Lucy lay sleeping, he knew everything he ever wanted was right there.

Why didn't he ask her? He'd never considered himself a cowardly man, but knowing that she could rip his heart in two with one word kept him silent. He wasn't ready for that yet. As long as he didn't ask, she couldn't refuse him. She was allowing him to use her body to ease his needs, but that didn't mean anything. Women had been doing that for eons and, often as not, were paid for their trouble. Sex for money was something Tarq understood all too well, though female hookers rarely got rich. Funny how women were willing to pay so much more for it than men.

He pondered this oddity for a time, eventually coming to the conclusion that while men merely sought physical release, women were searching for love—a far more rare and valuable commodity.

The sky began to clear as the waning moon rose over the mountains, but if anything was abroad that night, it was harmless. Tarq waited until the moon hung directly overhead and then woke Lucy.

She crawled out from under the blanket and dressed quickly. "See anything?"

Tarq shook his head. "No, but take the pistol and keep Rufus with you, just to be sure."

He pointed out where he'd been keeping watch and as she turned to go, Tarq took her hand and pulled her into his arms. Maybe he couldn't tell her he loved her and ask her to be his mate, but he could do everything else.

She fit perfectly in his embrace, her enticing aroma and the soft sweetness of her lips luring him toward an end he couldn't see yet.

"Be careful out there," he whispered. "The pistol is set on heavy stun. Don't be afraid to shoot first and ask questions later."

"I won't be." She hesitated for a long moment. "What was the kiss for?"

"I-I just wanted to… thank you for looking after me. I'd like to return the favor and rescue you sometime, but I'd much rather you didn't need rescuing."

"Me too."

Her gaze sought his, but he turned away, afraid she'd see too much even in the pale moonlight. He responded with a nod, knowing if he said anything at all, it would probably be a mistake.

"Get some sleep," she said gently. "I'll wake you at dawn."

He watched her go. Assuring himself that she wasn't visible even to his keen night eyes, he settled down and pulled the blanket over himself. The noise in his mind had kept him awake while on watch, but now it fell silent. With one last prayer that someday he'd be able to spend every night holding her, loving her endlessly, he drifted off to sleep.

Lucy settled down with Rufus, absently stroking his head while he lay beside her. She half wished that Tarq had remained unconscious so she could do the same thing to him. Again. Without his knowing, she'd sat beside him for hours, wiping his face, washing the blood from his hair, kissing him whenever she felt the need. She'd never loved anyone the way she loved Tarq.

That's only because there was never anyone for me to love. This realization hurt more than she would've thought, but she couldn't deny the inherent truth. Perhaps that was why she'd fallen so hard for him. First love and all that.

No. That wasn't true. He wasn't her first love, only her first lover. She'd had crushes on boys in school, but her feelings were never returned, and the attraction had faded quickly. What she felt for Tarq wouldn't diminish with time. The memory of days and nights spent with him would endure.

The night seemed interminable, but Lucy had no trouble remaining alert. The birds were the first to awaken, chirping their morning greetings as the eastern sky slowly brightened. Time to wake Tarq and move on.

Rufus went off on business of his own, and Lucy rose quietly, taking advantage of the natural cover as she made her way back to Tarq. Even knowing that they needed to get on their way, she didn't wake him immediately but stood gazing at him, trying to memorize what she saw—the line of his jaw, the way his ear curved to a point, the soft steady rhythm of his breathing, the way the morning breeze ruffled his hair. Blinking back tears, she was busy gathering up fallen branches when he began to stir.

He yawned and stretched, his deep sigh containing a hint of a purr. Lucy placed the wood in a neat pile, fighting the urge to run to him and kiss him the way he'd kissed her during the night. Pasting on a bright smile, she drew herself upright and turned to him. "Feeling better today?"

Tarq nodded. "Much better. Almost normal, in fact."

"That's good." She glanced toward the mountain pass above them. "I'm not looking forward to climbing that, and nobody tried to kick *me* to death." Unlike her other experiences with Tarq, that was one memory she'd just as soon erase. She still couldn't help feeling it was her fault he'd been caught alone. If she'd been with him, she might have at least been able to talk some sense into Fred. Or not.

"I've been over some pretty rough ground before, but not mountains." He stood and took her hand. "We'll make it, though. I'm sure of it."

Lucy eyed him doubtfully. She was somewhat reassured by the warmth of his grasp, but anything could happen in those mountains. Anything.

"By the way, what do we need a fire for?"

"Well, I—" She broke off there, suddenly realizing that unless they wanted toast, there really wasn't anything left that needed cooking. Not even tea.

"Oh, yeah. Right."

"Guess we need to do a little hunting and gathering," Tarq said. "Hard to do when you're being followed—if we *are* being followed. Seems like they would've come after us last night."

"Maybe they're not any good at tracking people."

"Possibly," Tarq agreed. "But let's put some distance between us anyway. Then we can see about finding more food."

Lucy shook her head. "I've never heard of anyone eating a vrelnot."

"Yes, but vrelnots aren't the only thing living in these mountains, and even they have to eat *something*. There's smaller game around. We'll find it."

Rufus came bounding up, tail wagging. Lucy knelt down to pet him. "And where have you been?"

"Hunting," Tarq replied for him. "See the blood on his cheek? Yeah. There's stuff here to eat. You just can't be too choosy."

Lucy wasn't sure being choosy would be the problem. "If hunting takes as much time as catching fish, we'll probably end up getting caught ourselves."

"Sitting and waiting for it to come to you is what takes time. When you're on the move, you tend to flush out game as you go. You have to be ready for it."

"With what? My pistol?"

"If that's all we've got, but it isn't. We've got knives—"

"To throw at things? I dunno about that…"

"No, Lucy. We've got knives and with those knives we can make other weapons. All it takes is finding the right kind of wood."

Lucy glanced around. The valley had been mostly covered in low bushes, but the mountainside was studded with taller trees. "Well, I certainly hope you know what you're looking for because I haven't got a clue."

Tarq grinned. "I do."

His words echoed through Lucy's mind, reminding her of marriage vows. She put the thought firmly aside for more practical matters. "Even here on Talus?"

He nodded. "The name of the tree doesn't matter as much as the characteristics of the wood. Don't worry. I'll find it."

"Wish I had your confidence," she said with a shudder. "I felt a lot better before we saw that speeder."

"Yes, but the fact that we haven't seen them again is encouraging, and I can hear a speeder a long way off."

"Do you hear it now?"

"No, but that doesn't mean we're safe." He picked up the blanket and shook it out. "Have you eaten yet?"

"I was waiting for you."

"No need for that. I'm okay for now."

Lucy's eyes narrowed and her lips thinned. "You need to eat something, even if it's only half an apple."

Tarq smiled. "I will. But not right now."

Lucy held her tongue, though her thoughts were anything but silent. She dug into her bag and got out some bread and cheese and an apple. Once he'd stowed the blanket away, she tossed the apple at him. "Cut me a piece of that, will you?"

He caught it on the fly and whipped out his knife. Her eyes were drawn to his hands as he slid the sharp blade effortlessly through the fruit, carving out the seeds with a deftness that spoke of years of practice, though whether with apples or other things, she wasn't sure. Either way, he seemed to know how to handle a knife.

When he gave the apple back to her, it was neatly carved into quarters, but her ploy hadn't worked. With a look that said he knew exactly what she was thinking, he sheathed the knife and shouldered the bag. "Let's go. You can eat while we walk."

~~

The mountain pass was more distant than it appeared, and they still hadn't reached it when they stopped to rest at midday. Tarq had rarely spoken during their climb, but had led them doggedly over the rough terrain as though he truly knew where they were headed. Though it was difficult for Lucy to put much stock in a vision, if he'd found his way to safety by following his nose before, well, she had little choice but to be grateful for any clear path to follow.

She was still miffed at Tarq for skipping breakfast but was pleased when he finally broke down and ate something. They had enough food for the time being; it was their meager water supply that concerned her, and she was glad she'd thought to pack oranges. They split one but limited themselves to a few bites of the other foods and a couple of sips of water.

Tarq might have been carrying the heaviest load, but Lucy's feet were killing her. Despite her moccasins' relatively thick sole, she half expected to find that her feet had been reduced to a mass of bleeding blisters. However, upon removing her moccasins, though the cuts she'd sustained while wading through the creek hadn't yet healed, there were no new wounds. Eyes closed, she was absently rubbing her heel when Tarq took her foot in his hands.

His touch was nearly as orgasmic as his cock syrup, and her involuntary gasp drew a smile from him as he began a gentle massage. Lucy lay back and gazed up at the sky while he worked a different kind of magic on her.

"Better?" he asked as he lifted her other foot.

"Much. That feels *wonderful*. Don't stop."

He chuckled softly and continued. Her mind drifting blissfully, she didn't even notice he was purring until his hands slid farther up her leg. "You know, there's nothing like a little taste of joy juice to take your mind off your feet."

"Joy juice? You mean that syrupy stuff your dick secretes? Good name for it. Says it all."

He nodded. "Yes, and nothing will make you feel better than a good, hard orgasm."

Lucy sighed. "True. I don't suppose you could do that and still massage my feet?"

"You just watch me." He lay down beside her, his groin near her head, his hands still on her feet.

Lucy turned on her side and unzipped his jeans. His thick cock sprang through the opening and she scooted closer, taking it in her mouth. As ever, he tasted like forbidden fruit: succulent yet firm, and intoxicatingly delicious. Then an unsettling thought occurred to her and she backed off. "I'd really hate to get caught like this. We should probably make it quick."

"If you use your hands while you suck me, I'll come faster."

"Gotcha." Spreading his glistening fluid from head to root, she sucked the head while her hands worked the shaft. This time, he wasn't holding anything back, thrusting through the tunnel she created with her hands with surprising vigor.

Her sore feet became a distant memory with her first orgasm, and when his semen flooded her mouth, she forgot she had feet altogether.

Groaning, she rolled over onto her back. "Great. My feet feel fine, but now I need a nap."

"No time for that," he said, zipping up his pants. "But I can give you a little pick-me-up anytime you like."

Lucy giggled. "Never a dull moment with you around, is there?"

"I certainly hope not."

"What about you? Do you feel better now?"

Tarq sat up and reached for her moccasins. "It wasn't about me this time, Lucy. That one was strictly for you."

As hard as his dick had been, Lucy had her doubts about that. "But you needed it too. Didn't you?"

His eyes were focused on her moccasins as he put them on her feet. "That goes without saying. If you're within ten meters of me, I need you, want you—"

Tarq froze for a brief moment before surging to his feet, knife in hand. Lucy's heart leapt into her throat as she heard a footstep behind her.

"Well, well, well… What have we here?"

Chapter 18

LUCY STARED UP AT THE MAN WHO STOOD BEFORE Tarq, a mocking expression on his handsome though rather harsh-featured face. Of medium height with broad, powerful shoulders and a coppery tint to his skin, he appeared to be human, but his eyes were the electric blue of a Davordian. His jet-black hair was straight and long, pulled back in a single braid, and he wore a belted tunic that reached his knees under a coarsely woven robe, both olive green in color. Dusty brown boots and pants made from animal hide encased his legs. She'd never seen him before. "Who *are* you?"

"I should be asking you that question, since you have trespassed on my land."

"*Your* land?" Lucy echoed. "I didn't think *anyone* owned these mountains."

"Squatter's rights, then," the man conceded with a nod. "Nevertheless, this is my home."

"You live here… alone?" Tarq asked.

Ignoring this query, the man narrowed his eyes at Tarq and asked a question of his own. "Why are you here?"

"We were… attacked," Tarq replied. "And then escaped to these mountains for safety."

The man's brow rose. "Safety? In the Eradics?" He laughed mirthlessly. "You've obviously been misinformed."

"We knew the mountains were dangerous, but the men who attacked me posed a more immediate danger."

"Ah. So, only *you* were attacked. That explains a great deal. And how did you manage to escape?"

Tarq gestured behind him. "She has a pulse pistol."

"I stunned them."

His smile was grim as his disturbing blue eyes raked Lucy's body. "Pity you didn't kill them."

Lucy shrugged. "Well, I *did* tie them up. But we think they've gotten loose and are looking for us."

The man shook his head. "They don't dare venture into this region. They know better—at least, they do now."

"So you know them?" Tarq asked.

"Yes, I know them, and if we ever find a safe path out of these mountains, they will pay for their crimes."

"We?" Tarq prompted.

"To answer your previous question, no, I am not alone. There are… others."

Rufus trotted up and sat down beside Lucy, his tail thumping. The man stared at the dog for a long moment and then nodded. "Akeir speaks highly of you."

Lucy's eyes darted back and forth between man and dog. "Akeir? You mean Rufus?"

"You may call him Rufus if you like—he does not object—but his name is Akeir."

Lucy suddenly realized who this man might be. "Your name wouldn't happen to be Traldeck, would it?"

"No, I am called Vertigan. Traldeck is my brother."

"Half brother, actually," said another man who was now approaching. The resemblance between the two men was striking, but unlike his brother, this man had flashing black eyes. "We share the same mother but have different fathers."

"Then you must be—"

"Lucy!"

Natasha came flying up behind Traldeck, followed by an assortment of alien beings. As she got to her feet to receive Nat's exuberant hug, Lucy spotted a Norludian, a Zebtan, two Vetlas, a Sympaticon, and one other creature she couldn't identify.

"—Nat's husband." Lucy hugged her friend fiercely. "Oh, Nat, when I saw what was left of your house, I was afraid you'd been killed!" Taking a step back, she held Natasha at arm's length, running her eyes up and down her form, searching for signs of injury. "You weren't hurt, were you?"

"I'm okay now," Nat replied. She held up her right arm, displaying a puckered scar. "I had some burns, but they've healed. What are you *doing* here?"

Best not to tell her everything at once... "I finally decided to take you up on your offer and come for a visit."

"Meaning you ran away from home," Natasha said with a knowing smile. "Thank God." She nodded toward Tarq. "And who's this guy?"

"Tarq? He's—"

"She is my mate."

Lucy had never heard Tarq use that tone of voice before—abrupt and stern, as though issuing a challenge. She gaped at him in dismay, half expecting him to smile or laugh or at least retract his statement. He didn't do any of those things. He simply sheathed his knife and then stood there—feet apart, arms folded, and jaw set— looking her straight in the eye.

Natasha let out a squeal and hugged her again, bouncing with excitement. "You got *married*? That's wonderful! Why didn't you say so?"

Lucy was speechless, so it was Tarq who replied. "She wanted to surprise you."

"I'm certainly surprised, though I shouldn't be. I've always said someone would find Lucy eventually. She's the sweetest, most patient, most giving woman I've ever met. I'm sure you love her very much."

Tarq nodded—a bit smugly, Lucy thought. "And she carries my young."

Nat squealed again. "You're pregnant?"

Lucy came out of her stupor with a bit of a stammer. "W-with triplets."

"You're frickin' kidding me!" Nat exclaimed. "Triplets? How will you *ever* manage that?" Lucy never got the chance to reply because Nat answered her own question. "Never mind. You always *could* do ten things at once. But triplets? Wow… just… wow."

Lucy stole a glance at Tarq who was having his hand vigorously shaken by Traldeck. "So you're a Zetithian? Glad you're already taken. I've heard about you guys."

"What have you heard?" Natasha demanded. "Oh, don't bother to tell me. I'll ask Lucy. She'll tell me all about him. Won't you?"

"Um, yeah, I guess…" *Just as soon as I figure out what in the world he's doing.*

Tarq knew it was a gamble, but he'd seen the frankly assessing gleam in Vertigan's eyes and known it for what it was. He was familiar with Davordians and Mordrials both, but had never run across the combination before. Mordrials tended to be lady-killers and most

Davordians were confirmed sluts—males *and* females. Not that he had any room to talk, but a cross of those two species was bound to be a sweet-talking horn dog. He was taking no chances of losing Lucy to him.

The look on her face had him a bit nervous, though. He couldn't tell what she was thinking. She was shocked—which was expected—but if she was happy, it certainly didn't show. Her friend Nat, on the other hand, seemed properly thrilled. Perhaps some of her enthusiasm would rub off on Lucy. Still, with the other men knowing she wasn't available, he could relax.

Until he was alone with Lucy again. The gods only knew what she'd say to him then.

Vertigan was already setting off and the others were following. Tarq helped Lucy gather up their belongings while Nat chattered away about their life as refugees in the Eradics. "The vrelnots are really scary. None of us has been eaten by one yet, but it's bound to happen eventually. Vertigan is able to communicate telepathically with most other animals, but vrelnots either won't listen or they're too vicious to care what he might have to say to them."

Lucy shuddered. "How do you avoid them?"

"We hide out in caves, mostly," Nat replied. "Vrelnots won't go underground for some reason—which is fortunate. It's tough to hunt for food with them around, though. They go after the same prey that we do. Needless to say, they're better hunters."

Tarq frowned. "Why don't you kill *them*?"

Traldeck snorted. "What? Kill vrelnots? Without a laser weapon? Impossible. Pulse weapons just make them mad."

"What about projectiles?"

Traldeck regarded Tarq as though he were a child who asked too many questions. "Totally useless. Hide's too tough."

Having seen the head of one mounted on the wall in the café, Tarq had to assume that to kill one required using a laser to cut off its head. Unfortunately, as potentially lethal weapons, laser pistols were heavily regulated on most worlds and were therefore scarce. Pulse weaponry was much safer, allowing you to stun your opponent without having to commit murder or cause serious injury—unless you turned up the intensity—and most, like the one Lucy carried, didn't have the "kill" setting on them at all.

Tarq let the subject drop, looping Lucy's bag over his shoulder as he set off down the mountainside with the others. He really hoped that wherever they were going had a decent water supply. Lucy's pregnancy concerned him. How many things had she been doing that she shouldn't? This early, there wasn't much that could harm the babies, but still, he hated to take the chance. He needed to get her to a place where she would be safe and receive the best of care—soon. Tarq didn't have a home of his own—he'd been living at The Palace and then out of his speeder or in hotels along the way—but his mind drifted to Lucy and a house where their children could grow and thrive. He had enough money to give her anything she wanted, short of her own planet, and he was aching for the opportunity to do it.

But none of his wealth mattered if she didn't love him.

—◊◊◊—

The shallow cave where he and Lucy had holed up was nothing compared to the one this band of refugees had been living in. The entrance was small and inconspicuous, but once inside, the place was vast, with a high ceiling and gleaming rock formations. The air was fresh—leading Tarq to suspect there was an opening higher up on the mountain—and he could hear the sound of falling water from deep inside the cave, undoubtedly melting snow from the higher elevations. Tarq wondered how many other creatures had been evicted when Vertigan's little band moved in, but at least they were safe from vrelnots. He didn't relish the idea of waking up to find one staring him in the face—a possibility that had worried him while they were out in the open.

Though these people must've been living there for some time, they seemed to have escaped with very little in the way of equipment. An open fireplace had been built of rock presumably gathered from the cave floor, which was swept clean and smooth. Drying animal skins hung from ledges, and there were sleeping pallets made of dried grasses and leaves, some near the fire and some closer to the outer walls. There was a spit over the fire for the roasting of meat, but no pots that he could see. His own pan and trivet would be welcome additions.

Upon closer inspection, he saw that the spit was made of a long slender bone—its shape suggesting it had once been a rib. If so, the animal it came from had to be at least the size of a horse, perhaps even larger. Tarq hoped it wasn't a predator. The spit was held above the fire by a pair of long forked antlers.

He put Lucy's bag down in an empty spot along a

wall that wasn't overly far from the fire but would allow for some degree of privacy.

Lucy was still deep in conversation with Nat—a pretty woman with shoulder-length blond hair and a rather stunning figure—no doubt catching up on all that had occurred since they'd last spoken to one another. She obviously trusted these people, but Tarq was more wary. He tried to convince himself that it wasn't because Vertigan was an unattached male who viewed Lucy as a potential conquest, but it was difficult. The others he dismissed as harmless, though if the Norludian was anything like the others of his kind, he was bound to be entertaining.

The best Tarq could tell, Vertigan was the leader of the group, though whether self-appointed or elected by the majority was something he'd yet to determine. As Natasha's husband, he wasn't too worried about Traldeck, and the others were obviously willing to be quiet followers.

Vertigan stood gazing at the fire, his eyes nearly as bright as the smoldering embers. Finally he spoke. "Each one of us was persecuted and driven into the mountains—presumably to die—our only crime that of being nonhuman. This has been a trend in Yalka for the past year or more, though not everyone in that city was against us. How many others are living—or have died—in these mountains is unknown.

"We tend to share everything here—for the good of all." He gestured toward Lucy's duffel bag. "You seem to have been more prepared than we were."

"I was… on the road alone for a while," Lucy said. "So I've got quite a few things. Tarq had a speeder that had all kinds of stuff in it, but it was stolen."

Tarq nodded his agreement but eyed Lucy warily. Her real reason for leaving Reltan would make claiming her as his mate seem unlikely. He hoped she wouldn't tell them too much.

"Oh, I get it," Natasha said. "You had to run away from your family first and meet up with him later, didn't you?"

Lucy nodded. "That's pretty much how it happened. I was coming to find him when he was attacked. That's how I got the drop on them."

Tarq let out a pent-up breath—an action that Traldeck seemed to notice.

Natasha nodded her approval. "Good for you, Lucy! Did you know the men?"

"Oh, yeah," Lucy replied. "Three of them, anyway: Fred Crytle, Lenny Mavtis, and another guy named Tuwain. They come in the café all the time. I didn't see the two who stole the speeder, but Fred seemed to be in charge of things." She frowned. "He always did strike me as being a bit of an asshole."

"Did they see you?"

"They might have, but it was dark, so I don't think they did. We saw them in the valley yesterday—with Tarq's speeder. Guess we know now why they didn't follow us up here."

Vertigan grinned for the first time. "We have made it... *unpleasant* for those who do."

Aside from catching people in compromising positions, Tarq hadn't seen much in the way of a show of force. "And how do you do that without weapons?"

Natasha giggled. "He sics the birds on them. It's like something out of a horror movie."

"I'll bet it is," Lucy agreed. "Makes me glad you only sent the dog out after us."

Vertigan nodded. "Akeir is a very astute judge of character."

"And he can tell humans from other species by their scent, which is useful," Traldeck said. "He must like you a great deal. We were surprised at how much time he spent with you."

"What do you mean, how much time?" Lucy glared at them, her eyes shooting daggers and her fists planted firmly on her hips. "Just how long have you known we were out there?"

"A day or two," Vertigan said with a shrug. "We were waiting for Akeir's report."

"Great." Lucy snorted a laugh. "I'm out there trying to catch fish and fend for myself with a badly injured, unconscious man while you guys sat here waiting for the dog to report in. Thanks a whole big bunch."

Tarq perked up at this. If she was angry with Vertigan, perhaps he had nothing to fear from that quarter. "You were very brave and resourceful, Lucy."

"Thanks, Tarq, but if it wasn't necessary—"

"Told you she'd be pissed," the Norludian said. "I was a bit miffed myself. Out there alone with nothing but bugs and berries to eat…"

"But you *like* bugs and berries," Natasha pointed out.

"Okay, so it's the lack of company that bothers me the most." He looked up at Lucy with his bulbous eyes—rather adoringly, Tarq thought. "*She* wouldn't have left me out there all alone. Would you?"

"No, I probably wouldn't have, but—"

The Norludian smiled and held out his hand, waggling

his sucker-tipped fingers at Lucy. "My name is Terufen. Pleased to meet you."

"Um, I'm Loucinda Force," she said, extending her hand in greeting. "But everyone calls me Lucy."

"Charming name," Terufen said. Taking her hand, he wrapped his fingers around it, applying his suckers to her palm. His smile widened into a grin, his tongue protruding between his fishlike lips. "Your essenth ith delithous."

With all that had happened, Tarq had forgotten about Norludians. Taking Lucy by the arm, he pulled her out of Terufen's grasp. "Lucy is *my* mate. Remember?"

Terufen giggled. "Maybe."

The pale-skinned Sympaticon's laugh sounded like metal creaking under stress. Currently in its resting state, its beady black eyes looked out of a gray face that was blurred, like a bad copy of an original. A few wisps of hair sprouted from its flat round ears, and long yellow nails tipped its reedlike fingers. Its thin body was draped with a swath of drab threadbare fabric that was belted at the waist. "I can turn myself into a Norludian female anytime you like, Terufen. You don't need to bother her."

The Norludian's mouth formed a moue of distaste. "Yes, but your essence stays the same, Kotcamp. You taste like a male."

"But I'm *genderless*," Kotcamp protested. "I shouldn't taste like either one!"

"That's the problem," Terufen said, slapping a flipper-like foot on the stone floor for emphasis. "As far as I'm concerned, your essence is about as stimulating as these rocks."

The female Vetla made an odd cackling sound and nudged the male standing beside her. "Good thing we've got each other."

The male coughed and shifted from one foot to the other, rubbing his long nose with a bony forefinger. "'S a matter of opinion."

The female sniffed and her droopy eyelids rose slightly. "I'm all you've got, so you might as well make the best of it. You're not getting any younger, you know."

"I'm counting heavily on science." The male shuffled toward Lucy, his attempt at a bow accentuating the hunched back that was typical of his kind. "My name is Faletok." With a nod toward the female, he added, "And this is my... *wife*, Crilla."

Crilla shook her long stringy hair back from her face and settled her multilayered robes more becomingly around her shoulders—at least Tarq assumed it was meant to be more becoming. It was his considered opinion that nothing *ever* made Vetlas look any better.

The Zebtan was, thankfully, female. Males of that species reportedly had two penises—and a wife for each of them—and were generally thought to be rather cocky bastards, which wasn't too surprising, considering their anatomy. Relatively young and quite lovely—if you liked women with orange eyes, green skin, and snake-like hair—she introduced herself as Walkuta, but otherwise said very little.

The last of the refugees stepped forward. Tarq thought he might have seen one of this species somewhere before, but he'd certainly never spoken with one of them. Less than a meter in height with a head that was too big for its body, its fragile-looking skin was a translucent white. It had spindly arms and legs, huge teardrop-shaped glowing red eyes and, like the Norludian, wore no clothing whatsoever.

"I am Bratol, a male of the planet Zerka," he said, bowing to Lucy. "May I say that you are even lovelier than our beauteous Natasha."

Lucy stared at Bratol as though he'd lost his mind. "Have trouble focusing with those red eyes of yours?"

Bratol wheezed with laughter, revealing a snake-like tongue. "No, my vision is quite good, I assure you. In fact, I can see many things that others cannot."

Lucy's eyes narrowed with suspicion. "And that's a *good* thing?"

"Beyond all doubt," Bratol replied. "I can see the aura emanating from within you. It is truly beautiful."

"Hmm." Lucy seemed skeptical. Tarq couldn't decide if Bratol was serious or not.

Natasha's laughter broke the tension. "He's always saying things like that. You'll get used to him eventually."

Lucy continued to eye him askance. "I'm wondering what else he can see that he's not telling us about."

Bratol blinked, his eyelids closing horizontally rather than vertically, sweeping in from the outer side of his eye toward his nose—if the slit between his eyes was indeed his nose. Tarq wasn't completely sure.

"I see many things," the Zerkan said mysteriously. "Some I mention, some I keep to myself… for a time."

Tarq glared at Bratol, wondering if one of those things he could "see" was that he and Lucy were not truly mates. Or perhaps he could see that Tarq believed it but Lucy didn't. Unfortunately, it wasn't a question Tarq could ask. He'd seen a lot of charlatans on

Rhylos—people who would tell you what you wanted to hear and call it your fortune—but had never put any stock in anything they'd had to say. As far as he knew, Zetithians were the only species that could predict the future with any degree of accuracy—and even their visions weren't available on demand—but this Zerkan was new to him.

Lucy took a step toward Tarq and away from Bratol. Deciding that a show of his affection—or protection—was in order, he enfolded her in his arms and eased her back against his chest. Pleased that she didn't resist, he nuzzled her ear, never taking his eyes off Bratol.

Bratol smiled, displaying glittering crystalline teeth. "Your auras blend well together."

Somewhat encouraged by this comment, Tarq began purring and kissed Lucy on the neck.

Bratol laughed aloud. "Oh, yes. Quite well indeed. A perfect pair."

Abandoning his initial distrust, Tarq decided that this guy was worth listening to after all.

Chapter 19

LUCY STILL HADN'T FIGURED OUT WHAT WAS GOING on, and Tarq purring in her ear was about to drive her to distraction. Surely he wouldn't keep on like that while others were watching, and she was relieved when he stopped purring and released her.

Her head cleared quickly. The best explanation she could arrive at was that her pregnancy was what made her aura so beautiful, and the fact that it blended well with Tarq's was because he was the father. That is, if she could believe a word Bratol was saying.

She gave Bratol a halfhearted smile and a brief "thanks" and went over to where Tarq had laid her bag, motioning for Nat to follow. "I've got some things—apples, salami, olives, and a couple of bottles of water. Not much bread and cheese left, though. But Tarq had this."

The sight of the pan and trivet elicited a collective sigh from the entire company, but it was Natasha who spoke. "Oh, my frickin' God! We can actually boil water and stew the meat! I'm sick to death of roasted rock rat!"

Lucy thought it was funny that a common saucepan would turn out to be such a prize, but she knew how useful it had been. "Too bad it's not bigger, but it *has* come in handy. Wish we had more of his supplies. Tarq's speeder had *everything*—including a stasis unit. He even had herbs."

"We've found lots of edible plants and herbs growing

wild," Nat said. "But you can sprinkle on all the seasonings you like a rock rat and they still taste pretty much
the same."

Lucy chuckled. "So how do you catch rock rats, anyway? Does Vertigan tell them there's free food here and
then clobber them?"

"Pretty much," Nat replied. "The larger animals are
too smart to fall for it—and way too fast to catch—so
we're stuck with the rock rats. Fortunately there are lots
of them."

"Larger animals?" Tarq echoed. "You mean the ones
with antlers?"

Nat nodded. "They call them draniks around here, but
they're a lot like deer. They feed on the shrubs growing
farther down the eastern side of the mountain. We don't
often see them up this high."

"Maybe we could stun them with my pistol," Lucy
suggested.

"We should probably save that for when we're shooting at people," Tarq said. "I used to be pretty good with
a bow when I was a kid. I might be able to get one."

Nat looked at him curiously. "A bow or a dranik?"

Tarq gave her a wink. "Both. Be back in a bit."

Lucy watched him go, feeling an immediate sense
of loss.

Nat tapped her shoulder. "Where's he going?"

Lucy shrugged. "To get a bow and a dranik, I guess."

"He can do that?"

"He can do lots of things—always full of surprises."

"C'mon, then," Nat said. "Let's fix you two a place
to sleep."

She led Lucy over to their stockpile of bedding and

they each gathered up a big armful and took it over to
the spot Tarq had chosen. He'd certainly made sure that
no one would question the two of them bedding down
together, though the reason for his assertion that she was
his mate was obvious. If he was going to be around her,
inhaling her pregnant scent, his need for sex would drive
him crazy without release. Unfortunately, this ruined her
chances with anyone else—not that most of the others
appealed to her in any way—but Vertigan was unattached and more human in appearance than Tarq was.
Too bad she wasn't attracted to him.

She couldn't explain why that was. There was nothing wrong with him; he was handsome and appeared to
be a strong and capable leader. All in all he was a decent
sort of man, if a bit domineering, but she didn't feel one
scrap of interest in him.

That was Tarq's fault. He'd spoiled her completely. In
fact, he'd spoiled her to the point that she wouldn't even
take him to task for telling such a big fat lie, though she
knew she probably should. She still couldn't believe he'd
said it. The one thing she'd wanted to hear more than anything, and he'd sprung it on her out of the blue. For one
brief shining moment, she'd thought he truly meant it, but
then reality set in. Knowing it to be a lie, she couldn't even
enjoy the fact that no one else had any reason to dispute
his claim. Among these people, they could live together
as husband and wife. The tough part would be explaining
why Tarq would eventually leave Talus without her—
assuming they ever made it to Noklar. After that, Vertigan
might start to look better to Lucy—particularly when she
had triplets to care for. A good provider would be a definite plus, provided he would be kind to Tarq's children.

Lucy spread the dried grasses out on the cave floor. "So, Nat, if you could get through these mountains to Noklar, would you go?"

"Any place is better than this," Nat said as she added more of the bedding. "In fact, Traldeck would like to leave Talus altogether and go somewhere with a more liberal attitude toward nonhumans." She shook her head sadly. "You'd think that in this day and age prejudice would be a thing of the past, wouldn't you? But it's alive and well in Yalka. Wasn't always like that, though—not openly, anyway." She nodded toward the two Vetlas. "They were run out of town in the middle of the night, chased with whips and stones. At their age, it's a wonder they survived."

Lucy was horrified. "How awful!"

"Vertigan has a house in Madric, but he was staying with us the night they burned us out. Otherwise he might have been spared all of this. Walkuta won't say what happened to her. In fact she hardly speaks at all. Bratol and Terufen were having a drink at a local bar when someone must've stunned them. They don't remember anything until they woke up out here, so they weren't in too bad a shape. Kotcamp saw what was happening and changed into human form and followed them, hoping to help. Knowing he was probably next, he decided to stay here too."

Lucy pulled a blanket out of her bag. "He? I thought he was an 'it.'"

Nat took the other end of the blanket and they placed it over the pile of bedding. "I've picked that up from Terufen. He always uses the male pronoun when referring to Kotcamp, and 'he' sounds much nicer than 'it.'"

"True. We had a Tryosian named Neris working at the café. I've always thought of her as a 'she.' Gets confusing sometimes, doesn't it?"

"Yeah. But that Tarq is very definitely a 'he,' even with all that pretty hair."

Lucy smiled. "It *is* nice, isn't it? And yes, he's *definitely* a male."

Her next question was one Lucy had already prepared an answer for. "So, how'd you meet him?"

"He came into the café for lunch one day, and we sort of hit it off."

"I'll say you did! And I'm so glad you finally left home. I always figured when you decided to rebel it would be in a big way. I guess I was right."

Lucy snickered. "Yeah, my father didn't like him at all. Wouldn't surprise me if he—" She stopped there, staring down at the makeshift bed openmouthed. "Oh, my *God*…"

"What is it, Lucy? What's wrong?"

"Oh, surely not…" She felt faint, as if all of the blood had drained out of her head.

"Lucy!" Nat's eyes were as round as saucers.

"I think my father told Fred to be on the lookout for Tarq. In fact I'd bet money on it! I can't believe it!"

"You don't know that for sure," Nat said. "Your father doesn't hate aliens, does he?"

"Not in general—after all, Jublansk and Neris aren't human and they've worked at the café for years—but he took an instant dislike to Tarq. Didn't want him talking to me—even as a customer. When Tarq went there for breakfast the morning after I left, he accused him of having something to do with my disappearance."

"Well, he did, didn't he?"

"N—yes." Lucy almost swallowed her tongue, realizing how close she'd come to spilling the beans. "But he only did that to, um, throw everyone off my trail. Maybe Father told Fred about Tarq and figured that was all he needed to do to get rid of him."

"But if you were already gone, why would he do that?"

Lucy shrugged. "Who knows? Like I said, he didn't like Tarq, and Tarq said my father was very angry."

"It's a wonder he didn't come after you himself."

Lucy shook her head. "Tarq heard him say that he wouldn't waste time on hunting me down. Said I'd come home when I got hungry enough—but that doesn't mean he wouldn't casually mention to Fred that a Zetithian was in the area—though Fred might have seen one of Tarq's advertisements."

"Advertisements?"

Lucy grimaced. She was digging herself in deeper with every word she spoke. "It has to do with the kind of… work he does."

Nat nodded and Lucy prayed she would let the subject drop. She didn't. "What kind of—" Nat stopped, listening closely.

Lucy heard it too—a loud hammering noise coming from outside the cave. They weren't the only ones. Everyone scurried toward the entrance and exited the cave. Lucy spotted Tarq up in a tree a little farther down the mountainside. Using Fred's hunting knife as a chisel, he was chipping away at a stout limb, hammering the knife with a club-shaped piece of wood. Moments later, the limb gave way with a loud crack and fell to the ground. With the knife in his teeth when he wasn't using it as a piton, Tarq climbed down from the tree, making it look much too easy.

When he turned and saw everyone staring at him, he laughed. "When I said I was going out to get a bow, you didn't think I was going to the store, did you?"

"Um, no, we didn't," Lucy said. "Guess you found the right kind of wood, huh?"

"That's right." Shouldering the limb, he carried it back up the rocky slope to the cave. Dropping it on the ground, he sat down and began stripping off the bark. "The inner layer of the bark has long fibers that can be used to make the bowstring, which is actually the hardest part."

Once all the bark had been removed, he hacked off the smaller branches until he was left with a pole about a meter and a half in length. Using the side of the knife blade as a chisel while he pounded on the blunt edge with the wooden club, he began splitting the wood. Lucy watched him with interest. His movements were fluid and precise—and totally sexy. After a few moments, she stole a glance at the others. Vertigan and Traldeck were clearly fascinated, while Nat and the others viewed him with frank admiration.

He'd been at work for twenty minutes or so when he stopped to test the bow's flexibility and looked questioningly at his audience. "Don't you all have anything better to do?"

Traldeck shook his head and Vertigan cleared his throat rather self-consciously. "No, this is far more interesting than skinning rock rats."

Tarq shrugged and went back to work. When he'd finished shaping the bow, he cut notches in both ends.

Then he sat down and began stripping the fibers out of the bark. When he had accumulated a large pile, he twisted them into long strands which he then knotted together and tied to a tree branch. Inserting a small stick in the free ends, he used it to twist the separate strands into one long piece of string. Taking it down from the tree, he tied a loop in one end and then tested the bow for length and made another knot in the string and strung the bow.

Terufen immediately began applauding and the others joined in with enthusiasm.

"Very impressive," Vertigan said. "What about arrows?"

Tarq nodded toward some of the smaller trees. "The water sprouts that grow straight up from tree limbs make great arrows. Of course, arrows will be a lot easier to make if you can get some of your bird friends to donate a few feathers."

Vertigan grinned. "I believe that can be arranged."

"What about you, Traldeck?" Lucy asked as a new thought struck her. "You're a full-blooded Mordrial. Can you talk to animals too?"

Traldeck shook his head. "No, Lucy. My talent is reading people."

Tarq's heart nearly stopped beating. As it was, he dropped the knife. He wasn't about to ask Traldeck to explain further; however, Lucy wasn't quite as reticent.

"You can read minds?"

"Not exactly," Traldeck replied. "I can't read actual thoughts the way Vertigan does with the animals. I sense emotions."

Tarq breathed a little easier upon hearing this, and he stooped to pick up the knife. You could tell what emotions most people were experiencing just by looking at them. Being able to read them wasn't that neat a trick.

"I also control fire," Traldeck went on. "Vertigan is a master of the wind."

"What about the fire that burned down your house?" Lucy asked. "Couldn't you put it out?"

"I can only *start* fires, Lucy," Traldeck said sadly. "I'm no better than anyone else at putting them out."

"I did try," Vertigan said. "But there's a limit to how hard I can make the wind blow." He smiled his apology. "Mordrial powers vary in strength from person to person. Some can call up a hurricane, while others, like myself, must content themselves with the lesser winds."

As much as Tarq was sweating, he wished Vertigan would send a breeze in his direction, but the air was surprisingly still. He left the group of onlookers to their conversation and went to cut wood for the arrows. Making arrowheads wouldn't be difficult; there were plenty of rocks lying about, some of the sort that would chip and flake easily. The wood fiber string could be used to tie them to the arrows, though once he brought down a dranik, he could use the sinews that attached muscle to bone for the job. More antlers would be a definite plus. He could make all sorts of tools—and weapons—with them, and the bones could be used for a lot more than spits for roasting meat.

Though he doubted the others would believe it, Tarq was actually enjoying himself. He'd loved the freedom of the outdoors as a child; unfortunately, the war and his subsequent life aboard the refugee ship had put an end to that. After the liberation, they'd landed on Terra Minor, which was a nice enough planet, but he hadn't felt like he belonged there and had never really understood why. As a result, he didn't have to think long before agreeing to go to Rhylos to work in the brothel with his friends. His work there had given him more than sexual satisfaction; it was a useful occupation—at least, according to his clients—but making his own tools and living off the land also appealed to him. He felt more at home and confident out in the wild perhaps because, as with his work in the brothel, he was seldom called upon to read anything.

Gathering up his arrows and several of the stones, he went back to the cave. Vertigan was sitting outside skinning rock rats, Natasha and Crilla were gathering berries, and everyone else, including Lucy, must've been out collecting firewood.

"We have to get all this done before dusk," Traldeck said as he approached, carrying a load of wood. "After that, the vrelnots come out and it isn't safe."

"Is that why you haven't gone any farther?"

Traldeck nodded. "We've scouted out a few more caves, but this is such a nice one—much bigger than the others we've found—and not knowing if there are any we could reach in a day has kept us here." He smiled. "But of course that was before the gods sent us you."

"Me?"

"Oh, yes. You know the way through these mountains, don't you?"

Tarq frowned at him. "I thought you couldn't read minds."

"It's true, I can't. But you *do* know the way, don't you?"

"I believe I do, but—"

Traldeck dropped the wood onto a pile near the cave.

"We will follow where you lead, Tarq. I can promise you that."

Tarq had no idea where all this was coming from. "What did Lucy tell you about me?"

"Nothing," Traldeck replied. "She didn't have to. I can feel her faith in you."

Tarq didn't give a damn about her faith; he wanted her love. "It was a vision I had. Zetithians have them sometimes. I could see the path through the mountains to Noklar."

"A safe path?"

"I have no idea, but I had a vision like this once before and arrived safely."

Traldeck nodded and glanced at the sky. "It will be dark soon. We should get inside. Have you found everything you need?"

"Yes," Tarq replied. "I should be able to go hunting tomorrow—can't promise I'll actually get anything, but I'll do my best."

With a deep sigh, Traldeck put a hand on Tarq's shoulder, ushering him toward the cave entrance. "I can scarcely imagine the possibility of having something besides rock rat for dinner tomorrow. If for no other reason, this gang will be kneeling at your feet."

"I find that hard to believe."

"You've obviously never had to live on rock rats before." He paused for a moment as they entered the cave. "My brother has kept us well-fed with his ability to lure the rats, and he has worked hard to keep us safe. Your arrival is opportune, but he may be… resentful of you in some ways." Traldeck nodded toward Lucy, who was gathering wood farther down the slope. "He is already setting his sights on your mate."

"Lucy is mine." It felt good to say it aloud again. Tarq thought if he said it enough, he might actually believe it. Eventually. Of course, the trick would be to convince *her*.

Traldeck nodded. "Yes, but Mordrial women sometimes take more than one mate. My brother may not see your claim on her as being exclusive. Do not be surprised to find yourself in competition with him. He has shown an interest in Natasha, but fortunately she does not see him as a potential lover."

Tarq frowned. "I didn't know that about Mordrials." *Yet another thing I don't know.*

"It isn't a widespread practice, but it does exist. Mordrial males accept the idea, but men of other species may not."

Tarq shook his head. "I've never heard of Zetithian women doing that."

"It is also rare among humans, but still, it may become an… issue."

"Thanks for the warning," Tarq said. He gave Traldeck a brief nod before taking a seat on a slab of rock near where he'd placed Lucy's belongings and began work on the arrows immediately. The way he saw it, the less time spent preparing for the journey to Noklar, the better. Giving Vertigan the time to persuade Lucy that she needed two husbands wasn't a risk he was willing to take.

Lucy watched Tarq and Traldeck enter the cave together as she trudged back up the mountainside. It wasn't terribly steep there—Nat had commented that she could've planted a garden just below the cave entrance if she'd only had some seeds—but carrying a load of fallen branches made the climb more difficult. She'd had to venture fairly far from the cave to find anything. Having lived there for some time, their little band of refugees had picked the immediate area clean.

She had mixed feelings about joining up with this group. True, she was ecstatic to find Nat and her husband both safe and sound, and being alone with Tarq was, in her opinion, heavenly no matter where they were. Unfortunately, she had misgivings about the sleeping arrangements. The cave was bound to be pretty quiet at night, and the sort of orgasms Tarq gave her tended to be a bit noisy. Everyone would be able to hear him purring too. There might even be an echo.

On the other hand, there *were* two other couples, and if the men were anything like Tarq…

No. They were *nothing* like Tarq. Couldn't possibly be. No way!

This last thought had Lucy smiling as she ducked under the boughs of shrubbery that obscured the cave entrance. Kotcamp was putting wood on the fire while Walkuta threaded the rock rats onto the spit. The skinned rats did nothing to enhance her appetite and Lucy had a feeling that before long, their new friends would be fighting over the salami she'd brought from the café. She hoped Tarq was as good at hunting with a bow as he was at making one.

Tarq was sitting off to one side of the cave, intent on his task. He had a pad of what she assumed was rock rat hide to protect his palm and was popping off flakes from a small piece of rock with the tip of an antler.

She stood watching him for a few moments before she spoke. "Making an arrowhead?"

Tarq replied with a nod.

"I had no idea antlers were that hard."

He glanced up briefly but didn't meet her eyes. "They make very good tools. The trick is finding something to cut them with. You can break them if you apply enough force, but they don't always break where you want them to."

Lucy nodded. "That's true about lots of things." She continued to stand there, watching him work, but couldn't think of anything else to say. Nothing at all. This puzzled her somewhat, until she recalled that this was their first private conversation since he'd claimed her as his mate. Being tongue-tied was understandable, but there were certain things that needed to be said.

"Um, Tarq," she said, lowering her voice. "I know why you told them I was your wife or mate or whatever you want to call it, but since we're in a group of other people now, you may not have the same problem as you did when it was just the two of us."

Tarq studied the rock he held in his hand for a moment, and then began chipping at it again. "What makes you think that?"

"Well, today I was out gathering firewood while you were making arrows, and you said you would go hunting tomorrow." She paused there, shrugging her shoulders. "You won't be close enough for my scent to bother you."

The antler made a crunching sound as he popped more flakes from the stone. "So you're saying you don't want to sleep with me anymore?"

"No, not that I don't *want* to… just that you may not *need* to." Lucy swallowed against the lump in her throat. "We could say you only said what you did to, oh, I don't know… protect my reputation or something."

"But you *are* pregnant," Tarq reminded her. "And I *am* the father."

"Yes, but—"

"And we've already told everyone that. What do you suggest we tell them now?"

Lucy grimaced. "The truth?"

"What *is* the truth, Lucy? Tell me. I'm not… clear on it."

Lucy wasn't sure either. And she certainly couldn't tell *him* everything.

"Look, we won't be here forever," Tarq said. "Traldeck has already figured out that I know the way to Noklar— although I'm not sure how he knows it. If you didn't tell him, he must be better at mind reading than he claims. Anyway, I think we'll be on the move again soon."

"I didn't say anything to him at all—at least not about that." She stared at his hands, still moving constantly as he shaped the stone. "So you're saying you want to continue this… charade for the time being?"

"Do you have a better idea?" He turned the rock over in his hand. It was already beginning to look like an arrowhead.

"Well, no…"

"Do you want to be free in case Vertigan is interested in you? He is, you know. I could see it in his eyes the first time he looked at you."

Lucy rolled her eyes. "Yeah, right. Like I'm *so* irresistible."

"You are to me."

"That's only because of the way I smell. It's got nothing to do with who I am or what I look like or anything else. And even if Vertigan *was* interested in me at first—which I seriously doubt—he won't be now that he knows I'm pregnant. Guys don't like raising other men's children."

"Hey, Lucy," Nat called out as she entered the cave. "Didn't you say you had some apples? Not many of the berries were ripe today. I thought maybe we could chop up some apples and make a fruit salad—we haven't had that kind of variety in ages."

"I'm sure you haven't," Lucy called back. "I'll get them." Thankful for the interruption, she slipped past Tarq and went to retrieve the apples.

To her chagrin, her hands were shaking as she reached into her duffel bag. She hadn't wanted to avoid sharing a bed with Tarq; she'd only intended to give him an out if he wanted one. Odd that he didn't take it. She was among friends now—not all alone like she'd been while on the road to Yalka—and had less need of his protection. And he certainly didn't need her anymore. He was as healthy as he'd been before he ever met up with Fred's gang.

Still, the others seemed to need him. If they were truly searching for a way out of these mountains—and she had no reason to dispute their word—Tarq could lead them to Noklar. They could report to the authorities there and maybe something could be done to protect the nonhumans in Yalka. She'd been a witness and could identify at least three of the culprits. Once they were brought to justice, perhaps she and the rest of the group could go back to Yalka—they to their homes, and she to find one of her own. Vertigan could return to Madric, and Nat and Traldeck could rebuild their house. Everything would be as it was—as it should have been. They could go on with their lives. She would have her babies and all would be well.

Except for one thing: Tarq wouldn't be there. And that was one part of the happily ever after that Lucy could do without.

Chapter 20

IN TARQ'S OPINION, ROASTED ROCK RAT WASN'T BAD AT all. More seasoning would've improved it, but the meat was tender, mildly sweet, and didn't taste the least bit gamey. He had an idea that the others had simply grown tired of it. Like Traldeck, they were all very excited about the possibility of having dranik for dinner and Tarq hoped they wouldn't be disappointed.

Despite the difficulties they faced, Tarq found living in a cave and sitting around the fire after dinner to be quite pleasant. Staying here for a few more days while they built up a store of dried meat for the journey to Noklar would be no problem, unless Vertigan used that time to get closer to Lucy. Still, having a good supply of food would be best for keeping on the move. Having to stop and hunt along the way would slow them down considerably.

Water was another factor. Lucy had carried enough for herself, but her meager supply of water bottles wouldn't be sufficient for all of them. Reaching the river in the valley below would solve that problem, but with the vrelnots hunting them, they might not be able to stay close to the water all the time. If the river current was flowing toward Noklar—which, considering that the water originated high in the mountains, it probably did—they could travel much more quickly if they only had a boat…

But boats were time-consuming to build. A log raft would be best, but cutting the wood, lashing the logs together with only knives? That would take a very long time. Unless…

Tarq tossed the rat bones into the fire and wiped his mouth with the back of his hand. Leaning back against the rock formation behind him, he stretched his legs toward the fire, dropping a casual arm around Lucy's shoulders. When he gave her a little squeeze, she scooted closer to rest her head on his chest. Bratol sat on the opposite side of the fire, gazing at them as though their blended auras pleased him. This was the sort of behavior the others would expect from a recently mated couple, and though Lucy might have only been pretending, Tarq was enjoying every minute of it.

But to make it last, they needed to reach Noklar. "So, Traldeck, you say you can control fire. Tell me, how does that work?"

"Oh, you should see him," said Terufen. "He sets things on fire just by looking at them." His own bulbous eyes danced with mischief. "Don't ever turn your back on him."

Traldeck glanced sideways at the Norludian. "I have *never* set anyone on fire."

"Well, maybe not," Terufen said with a sniff. "But you can't say you've never been tempted."

Traldeck chuckled softly. "So true."

"Could you cut down a tree?"

"To be perfectly honest, I've never tried," Traldeck replied. "I can warm up objects and start campfires—even ripen some kinds of fruit. But a tree—a really large tree—might be beyond my ability."

Kotcamp turned to Tarq. "Some of them can shoot fireballs out of their eyes. I've seen them do it."

"If I could do that, taking down vrelnots and draniks would be easy." Traldeck shook his head. "No. I could start a fire at the base of a tree, but after that…" He shrugged.

Tarq nodded toward Vertigan. "What about blowing them down? Could you do that if the tree were weakened at the root?"

"Possibly," Vertigan replied. "But what do we need to fell trees for?"

Tarq glanced at Traldeck. "I take it you haven't told everyone what you… suspect."

Traldeck shook his head. "No, I thought it best if you told them."

Tarq took a deep breath. "I know the way through the mountains to Noklar."

Despite Traldeck's assurance that they would follow wherever he led them, Tarq didn't expect everyone to be thrilled, and they weren't. Bratol didn't seem at all surprised, merely smiling as his red eyes swept over their companions, most of whom seemed somewhat unsettled by this pronouncement. Vertigan's eyes flashed as the two Vetlas began muttering to one another, and Kotcamp actually changed color. Tarq couldn't blame them. Even with a clear path to follow, it would still be a long, dangerous trip over rough terrain. Of course, none of them had to come with him if they didn't want to. "I know of a pass through the mountains, and beyond that there's a broad valley with a river running through it that leads east to Noklar. I was thinking about building a log raft to float down it, which would shorten the journey by several days."

"And make it a lot easier," Terufen said with a vigorous nod. "I *like* this idea."

"It will depend on what kind of trees we find growing there," Tarq said. "Something lightweight and buoyant would be best."

Lucy raised her head. "What would we tie them together with?"

"Don't know," said Tarq. "That also depends on what we find. Just something to think about."

Nat shuddered. "I'm more worried about the vrelnots. They *are* the main reason we're stuck here. Otherwise, we could've gone on to Reltan and bypassed Yalka altogether."

"How long have you been here?" Lucy asked.

"About three months," Nat replied. "But there was trouble even before that. We probably aren't the only ones hiding out in these mountains."

"Though we may be among the few survivors," Vertigan said. "Without this cave, we would have been picked off one by one."

"But things are different now," Traldeck said with a firm nod.

Kotcamp made an odd buzzing sound. "Nothing is different except that there are two more of us. The vrelnots won't be impressed with our numbers."

Bratol let out a wheezy chuckle and waved a hand, his translucent skin glowing in the firelight. "But we have Tarq among us now. I have a feeling that the vrelnots are about to meet their match."

Tarq laughed nervously. "I wouldn't count on that if I were you. My vision only showed me the route to Noklar, not how to kill vrelnots."

Bratol's eyes grew sly as his eyelids swept inward.

His nasal slit dilated briefly and he nodded. "This is true, but not entirely. A safe path to Noklar includes dealing with any dangers along the way. There is more to you than you know."

"Oh, here we go again," Terufen grumbled. "He says shit like that every time anyone opens their mouth."

"But he is usually correct," Walkuta said quietly.

Everyone else turned to stare at the Zebtan woman as though she'd shouted. Tarq hadn't heard her say much of anything before. Apparently no one else had, either.

"That's because he always says something really vague," Terufen argued. "It could end up meaning anything."

"No, it doesn't," Walkuta said. "I believe him." Flames reflected in her slightly protuberant orange eyes as she fixed her gaze on Tarq. "In your strength we place our faith, in your hands we place our lives, and our feet will follow the path of your making."

Tarq gaped at her, openmouthed. Though he'd seen a few of them on Rhylos, he'd never spoken with a Zebtan before and had no idea whether this sort of thing was typical of her kind or not.

"Wow," Nat whispered. "That's more than you've ever said in all the time you've been with us."

"One is silent while one waits for deliverance." Walkuta closed her eyes and raised her arms. Pressing her palms together, she slowly lowered her hands to her chest. The tangled strands of her hair then began to move, rising up from her shoulders to twist into a neat knot at the nape of her neck, and she bowed her head as though in prayer.

"Well, now," Terufen said with a smirk. "*That* was different."

Tarq didn't think so. It was very similar to what Traldeck and Bratol had said, which was more than a little disturbing. He wasn't used to having people depending on him for much of anything. He enjoyed that relationship with Lucy—though as independent as she was, she didn't lean on him nearly as much as she could have, or as much as he would've liked—but to have so many looking to him for guidance was a new experience for Tarq. Waroun would have laughed his head off if he'd been there. Dax probably wouldn't have derided him, but then Dax had been the one he'd rescued on Zetith. That journey had been uneventful for the most part. He didn't think he'd be as lucky this time.

Having witnessed what appeared to be a religious experience—at least for Walkuta—Lucy was starting to freak out a little. She was beginning to understand how Moses's wife must have felt when he undertook the task of delivering the Hebrews to the Promised Land. Not that she could have put a label on the feeling. It was… odd.

Traldeck grinned at Tarq. "Told you so."

Tarq shifted uncomfortably. This may have only meant that his butt was getting numb from sitting on the stone floor, but Lucy suspected there was more to it than that. He was probably feeling as peculiar as she was. As she snuggled closer to him, he relaxed almost immediately and Lucy sighed with contentment. Moses's wife had probably done the same thing when the burden weighed heavy on her man. Lucy would support Tarq in any way she could, even though helping him through this particular endeavor would ultimately shorten her time with him.

I'm not going to think about that. He told them I was

his mate, and I'm going to play the part the best I can. Which wouldn't be difficult, and if he didn't like her acting like a wife, well, that was his problem—one he'd brought upon himself.

The day had been long and eventful, and with the warmth of the fire, a full stomach, and Tarq's comforting presence, Lucy's eyelids were soon drooping. More plans were being discussed, but she wasn't listening. Her mind focused instead on the rhythmic beating of his heart, the steady in and out of his breathing, the vibrations in his chest as he spoke the occasional word.

She was already dreaming when Tarq gathered her up in his arms and carried her to bed. As her body sank into the softest thing she'd slept on in several days, she opened her eyes, her gaze falling upon Tarq. Backlit by the fire, his hair shone like a cloud with the sun hiding behind it. He settled in beside her, purring softly as he cradled her against his chest. She slipped her hands beneath his shirt, pushing it up to bare his chest.

"You're not too tired?" he whispered.

"No. I've been looking forward to this all day. Just needed a little nap."

Tarq purred his reply, pushing the clothing from her body. "Not *all* day," he chided. "As I recall, we were doing something like this when Vertigan found us."

"Yes, but this is different. Warm, cozy, safe… Almost like when we were in your tent—maybe better."

"I can't argue with that. Too bad we aren't somewhere more… private."

"Mmm… don't care…"

Tarq pulled away for a moment to rid himself of his shirt and jeans. When he returned, Lucy wrapped her arms around his waist. His skin was warm and smooth beneath her hands, and she stroked every part of him she could reach. Easing onto her back, she took him with her, pulling his hair to bring his face down for a kiss.

His purr roughened into a growl as his head descended. "Mmm… Lucy. Love that."

Her core released its moisture, and one nudge of his knee between her thighs had her welcoming him inside. The rustling of the dried grasses beneath the blanket filled her ears as it cocooned her head and body, and she sank deeper into the pile as Tarq filled her with his cock, gliding in the full length and then out again, gently, rhythmically.

Her body contracted in orgasm as he worked to give her joy far beyond any she could have imagined before he came into her life. Hard but smooth, he moved like a wave inside her, reaching and caressing, seeming to know exactly what she craved. She'd already gone past caring about where he'd honed his technique and the countless women he'd been with. His experience made him what he was—uniquely wonderful and completely unforgettable. He'd claimed her as his mate before witnesses—in many cultures, that was as binding as any document or ceremony—but whether he kept that promise to her didn't matter. He was hers for the moment, and for now that was enough.

She slid her hands up his arms to rest on his shoulders, thankful that she could hold him one more time. Had anyone ever touched him like that before? She thought not. Relishing his heat and strength, she held him, caressing his body and delving into his hair. She looked up at his face to find his glowing cat eyes watching her.

Not caring what he might see in her eyes, her own gaze never wavered. She cupped his cheek in her palm and he leaned into it, purring like a cat seeking a caress.

I love you.

She couldn't say the words aloud, but she could feel them, express them in so many other ways. Her heart ached and tears slid from the corners of her eyes. *I love you, Tarq. Can you hear what I'm thinking? I love you so much. Don't leave me. Don't forget me. You're mine. I'm yours. Always.*

Tarq leaned down and kissed her. If only he could read minds like a Mordrial, he would know what she was thinking and she would have no secrets from him. But then he would know too much, know the power he had over her and perhaps take advantage of it.

No, not Tarq. He wasn't the sort of man to use a woman, and yet that was exactly what she'd let him think he was doing—using her body to assuage the need that her scent created in him. Did it bother him to think that? He'd been used by women as a breeding stallion for years, only seeing himself as good for the pleasure he could give them and the children he could sire.

But Bratol was right: There was so much more to Tarq than he knew. Walkuta and Traldeck had made him uncomfortable, putting their faith and trust in his ability to lead them out of the wilderness, but Lucy also had faith in him. Tarq would give all a second chance just by being there to show them the way.

Lucy had reached a point where she simply couldn't stand it anymore. Choking back a sob, she wrapped her arms and legs around him, hugging him close as another orgasm ripped through her body.

Tarq buried his face in her hair, drowning in her scent as she pulled him down. He let himself believe it was emotion and not simply her climax that was responsible for her hungry embrace, and he held on to that belief with both hands. She could have offered him a thousand ways out of their predicament and he wouldn't have taken a single one of them, regardless of the reward. *She* was what he wanted. Nothing more, nothing less. He was taking no chances that Vertigan or anyone else might claim her—not the way he claimed her now with his body. Lucy was his mate. At some point she would accept the fact that they belonged together. Forever.

Tarq knew countless ways to please a woman, but expressing love was something he'd never done. He rocked into her with slow, deliberate thrusts, letting his body speak for him. *This is how much I love you, Lucy. Can you feel it? Do you understand what I'm trying to say?* Kissing her neck, he tasted her skin, savoring her warm, salty essence while his purring grew softer and his hands lost themselves in her hair. Every part of her beckoned to him, urging him onward, and he kissed her deeply, his tongue penetrating her sweet warmth.

The rush of blood through his ears blocked out everything but her soft sighs of pleasure as his passion went spiraling out of control. He drove himself in, sweeping her succulent core with his cock, exploring every surface, plumbing every depth. When Lucy's teeth sank into his shoulder, a searing heat engulfed him, triggering an eruption that ripped away part of his soul and sent it hurtling into her along with his *snard*.

Tarq opened his eyes. The fire had died down until the darkness within the cave was nearly complete, but he could see the glow from his own eyes reflected in hers—could see teardrops glittering on dark lashes rimming eyes grown round with wonder. Dropping his head, he rained kisses on her face, sipping her salty tears and whispering words of love in a language she couldn't possibly understand.

For now, he only wanted to say the words and see the joy in her eyes. Time was on his side. He would have her beside him as his mate for the length of this journey. During that time, he would do everything in his power to ensure that when they reached Noklar, he wouldn't need to translate the words for her. She would already know.

Chapter 21

TARQ WAITED UNTIL AN HOUR OR SO AFTER DAWN TO go hunting for draniks. On any other world, he would've gone out earlier since prey animals were typically more active during the twilight hours, but he felt sure that the draniks would have figured out that it was best to remain hidden until the vrelnots were gone for the day.

Lucy was still sleeping peacefully, and while he dressed, he fought the urge to linger, to hold her while she slept, and be the first thing she saw when she opened her eyes.

But there would be other mornings for that. He had to get moving. Before, he had wished that they might never reach Noklar. But now the need to arrive in that city was more urgent than ever. Just as soon as the spaceport was in sight, he would tell her he loved her. That way, he could steal her right out from beneath Vertigan's nose before she had a chance to change her mind, and she couldn't back out because she'd already be there with all the others believing her to be his mate. She couldn't say no then. Not after all he'd done to get her there safely.

Well, yes, she could. She could leave him standing in the spaceport with his heart ripped out while she took the first transport to any place she chose. She might even leave on Vertigan's arm. She still had the credits Tarq had given her and would no longer need his money or his protection. The only reason she would leave this world with him would be if she loved him. Unless Dax were to offer her a free ride on the *Valorcry*. Then Tarq would have even more time to spend with her. Hmm...

With that cheery thought in mind, Tarq tested his bow. A few practice shots proved that it was powerful, if not terribly accurate. Still, with a large enough target, he doubted he would miss. It felt good to handle a bow again, and with a bit more practice, his aim improved.

After tying the arrows to his belt with a braided cord he'd made from bark fibers, he slung the bow over his shoulder and set out. The mountainside was shrouded in mist, the dew lying heavy on the grass and dripping from the trees. Farther down the slope, the fog thickened until sight and sound were both obscured. Knowing that he might come upon the dranik herd at any moment, he walked softly, for if they were to flee, he wouldn't get off a single shot before they disappeared into the mist. Ordinarily he would have scouted the area to discover their feeding grounds and then come back even earlier and wait for them to arrive, but he felt certain that his natural stealth would be enough to overcome this handicap.

He paused from time to time to listen. Hardly a sound penetrated the fog. A few birds called out high overhead, but he heard nothing that sounded like a particularly large animal moving about. He had gone a few meters when he stopped again. A snapping twig. The soft munching sound of a grazing animal chewing on plants.

Then he heard it: a wing beat just above him as a shadow passed over. Whatever it was, it was huge—either a bird of prey or a carrion eater. Slowly, carefully, Tarq readied his bow and crept silently onward.

The fog began to lift. There was nothing in sight. Tarq realized that what he'd heard must have seemed closer due to the dense fog. Then he heard the rushing beat of wings and the clattering of small hooves over rough ground. Moments later he found what had caused it.

He was right about one thing: It was huge. An enormous bird of prey with leathery bat-like wings and a slender scaly body—and the head of a vrelnot—had made its kill and was already feeding on the fallen dranik, ripping strips of meat from its bones with its razor-sharp beak.

"Holy shit." Obviously the vrelnot's nocturnal habits also included the occasional hunting trip in the early morning fog. And why he hadn't put the whole "prehistoric bird" thing together when he'd seen the head mounted on the wall was beyond him. *I never was very smart, though.*

For the moment the vrelnot was occupied with its kill and ignored him. But then it turned its large glassy eyes on Tarq as though trying to decide whether he would be better eating than the dranik buck it was currently devouring.

Apparently Tarq looked tasty.

With a flap of its reptilian wings, the vrelnot began to advance. Tarq nocked an arrow and raised the bow, staring the beast straight in the eyes. Outrunning it wasn't an option; by standing his ground Tarq already had it slightly confused, but if he missed the shot, he was dead. Another step of a clawed foot, and then another. The vrelnot opened its beak and hissed. Tarq didn't move a muscle.

After taking another step, the beast paused. Tarq held his breath, waiting.

The vrelnot took another step, stopped again—and blinked.

Tarq loosed the arrow, hitting the monster in the center of its left eye.

The vrelnot's screech of rage and pain nearly split Tarq's eardrums, and it swung its wings wildly, thrashing about as it attempted to dislodge the arrow. A swipe of a talon-tipped wing knocked Tarq to the ground and sliced through his pant leg, opening a long gash in his thigh. Tarq rolled away and leaped to his feet just as the vrelnot took another wild swing. Tarq could feel blood running down his leg and knew he had to finish this quickly. Spotting the bow, he ran toward it, snatching it up as he passed.

Never dreaming he'd be fighting for his life, Tarq had made only three arrows, one of which was now being cast aside by the vrelnot. Though wounded in one eye, the beast could apparently still see, its head following Tarq's movements as he scrambled toward the vrelnot's blind side. *Only two arrows left.*

Reaching down for another arrow, he discovered that one of them must have broken when he fell. As the vrelnot lunged at him again, Tarq ran sideways, back into the beast's blind spot. Once there, he nocked his last arrow and waited for a clear shot. As the vrelnot swung its head to the side to focus its remaining eye on him, Tarq fired.

And missed. The arrow glanced off the side of its head.

His only hope now was to lure the beast out of the way so he could retrieve the arrow, either that or find the one he'd shot first—if it hadn't already been trampled into bits. Tarq was beginning to wish he'd brought along Lucy's pistol. Granted, it might have only made the thing angrier than it already was, but it was still better than nothing. He didn't relish the idea of being close enough to try to kill it with his knife.

With no other ideas coming to mind, Tarq resorted to throwing rocks. There were plenty of these lying about, and he hit the vrelnot with a few of them, one even striking the creature in its wounded eye. There was no way he could kill it with a rock, even if he'd had a slingshot—which he made a mental note to make if he managed to get out of his current predicament alive—but it did serve to distract the animal while Tarq tried to think of another tactic.

Finally deciding to use himself as bait, Tarq circled around and made a run for the fallen dranik. "Better come and get me before I steal your breakfast," he taunted.

If the thing had been pissed before, it was livid now. Extending its wings to their fullest extent, the vrelnot flapped them once and rose into the air. Tarq waited until it was almost upon him and then dashed beneath it. Making a dive for the arrow, he rolled away and was back on his feet in seconds.

The arrow was undamaged. Tarq readied his bow.

Still airborne, the vrelnot made a loop back toward Tarq, its wings almost skimming the ground. At the last second before the bird swooped in for the kill, Tarq darted sideways into its blind spot. The vrelnot struck, getting nothing but talons full of dirt and rocks. It turned again, sweeping the area with its one remaining eye.

Tarq waited for a clear shot, but this time when the

vrelnot spotted him, it lunged toward him with its beak open wide, hissing like a steaming kettle. Tarq let it get almost within striking distance and fired.

This time, the arrow found its mark, hitting the vrelnot squarely in the other eye.

Now completely blinded, the vrelnot was more dangerous than ever before, shrieking and flapping its wings madly as it plunged toward Tarq's last position, the arrow still embedded in its eye. Snatching up a rock, Tarq darted in between the huge wings to slam it against the end of the arrow, driving it deeply into the monster's brain. With a final screech, the vrelnot fell dead.

Panting hard, Tarq glanced around him. The only dranik in sight was the one the vrelnot had killed. He had no desire to try to butcher the vrelnot—the hide was probably too tough for his knife to slice through and the meat was bound to taste terrible anyway—so he salvaged his stray arrows and heaved the dead dranik over his shoulders. Fortunately the buck wasn't very large and the vrelnot hadn't had time to eat much of it. The climb up the steep slope to the cave was difficult, but at least he didn't have to be quiet this time, and he *was* bringing home his kill. Sort of.

"If I don't bleed to death before I get there." Tarq glanced down at his leg periodically, noting that though the bleeding was now sluggish, he'd already lost a fair amount of blood. Still, he was grateful that the talon hadn't caught him a little more to the left. Dranik meat was sure to be a tasty treat, but no matter how good it was, it certainly wasn't worth losing his dick.

Having heard the horrific sounds coming from below, Lucy and the others were already headed down the mountainside when she spotted Tarq and let out a scream. He had blood all over him and at least some of it appeared to be his. "Tarq! You're bleeding! What happened?"

Terufen scurried over to Tarq, hopping up and down and cackling with glee. "Ha ha! You got a dranik! We are gonna eat tonight!"

Tarq glared at him. "No. The *vrelnot* got the dranik. *I* got the vrelnot." He leaned over, dropping the bloody carcass to the ground. "Someone might have at least *mentioned* that the damned things could fly!"

"Sorry about that," Vertigan said sheepishly as Rufus sniffed at the dead animal. "I guess we figured you knew that."

Nat, at least, was properly impressed. "You killed a *vrelnot*? Wow!"

Traldeck scratched his head. "Never seen one out this time of day. Must be the fog."

"You *think*?"

Lucy had never seen Tarq quite so angry before, but Bratol was laughing his creepy oversized head off. There were tears streaming from his eerie red eyes and he was wheezing so hard Lucy thought he would choke—and half wished he would. She felt like slapping him—or at least stunning him with the pistol she held in her hand. *No, not worth wasting a shot on him...*

Bratol waved a hand as he regained control of himself. "As I said, there is more to you than you know. This is how you will deliver us."

"What? Deliver you how? As a bleeding carcass slung over my shoulder?" Tarq appeared to consider this and seemed to like the idea—if it were Bratol's carcass, that is.

"No, by proving that the obstacles we face are not insurmountable." As Bratol approached Tarq, his eyes began to change color. "Allow me to help you."

Lucy watched in horrified fascination as the little alien's eyes changed from red to purple, then blue, followed by a deep aquamarine. Tarq's expression went blank as he leaned down, allowing Bratol to take his face in his hands. The Zerkan's snake-like tongue slipped out of his mouth, growing in length until it reached Tarq's wounded leg. A ball formed at the base of Bratol's tongue and slid slowly down the length of it until it was expelled onto the wound with a quick gush of aquamarine slime. Bratol bowed slightly and released Tarq as his tongue whipped back into his mouth.

Lucy cleared her throat. "Okay. Now *that* was weird."

"We Zerkans are known for our healing powers," Bratol said. "The fluid will help him heal more quickly."

"He heals pretty well on his own," Lucy said. "You just have to let him sort of… sleep it off."

Tarq staggered for a few steps and sat down heavily on the ground. "I'm all right. I think." He swallowed hard and gave his head a quick shake. "Weird is right, though." Blinking hard, he leaned forward, pressing the heels of his hands against his forehead.

Lucy wasn't sure what to do. Slapping Bratol was pointless now, even if she *was* still mad at him for laughing at Tarq like that. Well, maybe not laughing *at* him exactly, but it still struck her as being a rather tacky thing to do, whether he'd "healed" Tarq or not. All she knew was that she wanted everyone else to go away and leave her alone with Tarq.

"That's a good-sized dranik you got there," Kotcamp

said. "Thank you. You have done what no one else has been able to do since we got here."

Walkuta nodded in agreement. Pressing her palms together, she bowed as though about to bestow a blessing on Tarq—or the dranik. Lucy wasn't sure which. Either way, she was losing patience with them. "Look, why don't you all take that dranik back to the cave and get it ready to cook. Walkuta can bless it or whatever and I'll stay here with Tarq until he can walk."

Vertigan and Traldeck nodded and picked up the dranik. Terufen danced alongside them as they carried it up the slope, clearly tickled to death at the prospect of such a rare culinary delight. The others followed. Rufus, however, elected to remain.

As soon as they were out of earshot, Lucy helped Tarq to lie down so she could get a look at his leg. Whatever had cut him had been very sharp, slicing through his pants, leaving a straight cut through the flesh of his upper thigh. The edges were clean and the wound was already beginning to close, though whether from Tarq's ability to self heal or from Bratol's blue-green spit, she couldn't have said. However, she had few doubts that Bratol was responsible for his current state.

As he lay there stretched out on the ground beside her with Rufus curled up against him, Lucy was reminded of the time she'd spent in the little cave in the valley, keeping watch over him and wondering if he'd ever awaken. She consoled herself with the fact that he wasn't injured anywhere near as badly this time—he was only resting, rather than comatose—but nevertheless she found herself combing her fingers through his hair the way she'd done back then.

She sat there for some time, waiting for him to regain his strength. Gazing out at the mountains to the east, she was wondering how in the world they would ever get through them when Tarq's stomach let out a loud, persistent growl. Lucy pressed her lips together, trying not to smile. "That's what you get for going out hunting before breakfast."

Tarq sighed and rolled onto his back, giving Rufus a pat on the head. "Yeah, well, you know how it is when you've got a new bow. You just have to go out and see how well it works."

"And?"

"Killed a vrelnot with it, so I'd have to say it works pretty well." He grimaced, rubbing his head again. "Need a slingshot, though—or something like it. With all these rocks lying around everywhere, there's plenty of ammunition. Don't suppose you've got anything stretchy in that bag of yours, do you?"

Lucy thought for a moment. "Um, the elastic in my underwear, maybe? It's pretty stretchy."

Tarq began chuckling uncontrollably. "I can hardly wait to tell Dax I killed a vrelnot—or anything else, for that matter—with a pair of ladies panties."

"Actually, an elastic bra strap would probably work better, but you haven't done it yet, you know," she chided. Though somehow she suspected he would, even if he only used the slingshot to kill a rock rat.

"Got a spare bra?"

Lucy nodded. "Two of 'em."

"Gonna let me have them?"

"Nope."

"Hmm… Guess I'll have to think of something else."

"I guess you will. Feeling better?"

"Yeah. The effect is wearing off a bit." Tarq sat up. "Remind me not to go out hunting too early next time."

"I would have done that this morning if I'd been awake."

Tarq gave her a conciliatory smile and then sat for a moment, his brow furrowed as though wrestling with a problem. "I've been thinking. If I can get more draniks, I can use the hide to make a bola. Might even be able to use vrelnot hide if we can cut through it. A bola will bring down a dranik without any problem—and if I make one that's big enough, it might even take down a vrelnot."

Lucy giggled. "Okay. I'll bite. What's a bola?"

"Another primitive weapon. Basically, it's three heavy balls tied to three pieces of rope and you tie the ends of the rope together. You hold one ball and swing it around over your head and then let go of it. They're used to trip animals by tangling up their legs, but I'll bet you could tangle up a vrelnot, too—knock them right out of the air."

"Maybe Bratol was right. Maybe vrelnots aren't such insurmountable obstacles after all."

"Maybe not. Let's hope so, anyway." He took a deep breath. "I think I can walk now." He cocked his head and gave her a sly smile. "Want to see one up close?"

"A vrelnot? Sure. After you've had something to eat, we'll go back down and take a look."

"Nah, let's go now. There's something I'd like to check out, now that I've had time to think about it."

"You're sure you can walk okay?"

"Yeah. That slimy stuff actually makes you feel pretty good after a while." He got to his feet and held out his hand.

"You *must* be feeling better," she commented as he helped her to stand.

"Good as new," he insisted.

He set off down the mountain, never releasing her hand. Obviously not requiring any support himself, Lucy was about to mention that he didn't need to pretend to be her mate while they were alone, but the feel of his hand was so comforting, she opted not to mention it.

Lucy had seen a few pictures of vrelnots—and was mentally kicking herself for not mentioning the wings to Tarq—but seeing the real thing up close was even more terrifying than she'd anticipated. It was lying on its belly, its dull brown wings stretched out on either side. Based on the size of the trophy at the café she would never have guessed it would have such a wide wingspan, but it had to have measured at least five meters across, and its talons were as long as her forearm and hand combined. She didn't have to ask Tarq how he'd been injured, either; the barbs on the wingtips and whiplike tail told the tale.

Tarq pulled out his knife and stabbed the hide. There was some resistance, but he *was* able to cut through it. "Huh. Wonder where Traldeck got his information. Granted, this thing has been dead a little while, but still... Well, I'm sure I can defend against them with a bow. Just have to make more arrows. Sharper, heavier points would probably help too." He wiped the blade on the vrelnot's skin and slipped it back into the sheath on his belt.

Lucy frowned. "But if they only come out at night, will you be able to see them?"

Tarq chuckled and gestured toward his eyes. "If I can find you in a dark cave in the middle of the night…"

"Point made. But you have to sleep sometime."

Tarq shrugged. "We'll post a guard in shifts. Trust me, those things make enough noise that we would hear them coming." He glanced up at the sky. "The moon is waxing again too. I won't be the only one able to see in the dark."

Lucy wasn't completely convinced, but his confidence was contagious, especially when he pulled the arrow out of the vrelnot's eye socket. "It went in that far? How close *were* you?"

Tarq laughed. "About this close. It wasn't in that deep to begin with. I fired from a few meters away and then rammed the arrow on through with a rock."

Lucy felt the blood drain out of her face. "You mean you were standing right *there* while that thing was still alive?"

He walked away with a wink and a nod, nocking an arrow as he went. When he had gone about twenty paces, he turned and loosed the arrow, which sank into the vrelnot's side with a good solid thunk. "Hmm. Obviously no one has ever tried shooting them with arrows before."

Lucy still hadn't quite recovered from the shock of Tarq being so close to that lethal beak and was surprised at how normal her voice sounded. "Or they shot at them from too far away. Once word got around that pulse weapons were useless and that they could only be killed with a laser, everyone else must've simply taken it on faith. I know I wouldn't want to go up against one with nothing but a bow and arrow—though I'm a little surprised that some macho guy hasn't seen it as a challenge and come up here to kill one with his bare hands or something equally ridiculous. There are always a few in every crowd."

Tarq grinned. "Hey, at least I did it with an arrow and a rock."

"If you *had* come out here to fight it with your bare hands, I'd—" Lucy caught herself before finishing that sentence, deciding that threatening to smack his butt might not be the best thing to say in this instance—made her sound too much like a wife.

He yanked the arrow from the vrelnot's hide and then stood smirking at her with his head cocked to one side. "You'd… what?"

"Um, nothing," Lucy replied. She glanced around nervously. "Didn't you want to skin this thing or something?"

The smirk became even more pronounced. "Maybe." He thrust the arrow through the loop that hung from his belt. "Or maybe I just wanted to bring you here to show you what a tough macho man I can be."

"Why would you want to do that?" Her voice was much higher pitched than normal, something Tarq was bound to notice. Clearing her throat, she took it down a notch. "Anyway, I've never been impressed by that sort of thing."

"So you think I'm trying to impress you?"

Feeling more flustered by the second, she brushed a stray wisp of hair away from her eyes. "Isn't that what you just said?"

He shook his head, smiling at her in the strangest way. "I never said I wanted you to be impressed."

"Well, what you did *is* impressive," she said firmly. "Very impressive." Nodding toward the cave, she added, "None of those other guys could've done it."

Tarq shouldered his bow. "Why, thank you, Lucy. That means a lot to me."

He took her hand and together they headed back to the cave with Rufus trotting along ahead of them. Tarq didn't tease her anymore, and though Lucy was grateful for the respite, she had a sneaking suspicion that the game wasn't over—not by a long shot. He'd simply let her off the hook. For now.

Chapter 22

GRANTED, IT WAS ONLY A SHAM, BUT LUCY MADE A damn good wife. Upon their return to the cave, she made sure Tarq got something to eat and then led him to a little niche at the rear of the cavern where water trickled down from above like a miniature waterfall. The water's incessant dripping had carved a pool in the rocky floor over time which measured roughly a meter and a half from rim to rim, the overflow disappearing through another crack in the mountain's heart. Shielded from the rest of the cave by a large stone slab that evidently had fallen from the ceiling, it was relatively private.

The water was icy cold, but when Lucy helped Tarq strip off his clothes in order to rinse the blood from them, he was surprised there wasn't steam rising off him. Just her nearness made his temperature rise, not to mention what it did to his cock.

Bratol had told him to leave the healing fluid on his wounded leg until the sticky residue dried and flaked off. Tarq was doing his best to keep it dry and still get the blood off his leg, but it was difficult.

"Here, I'll do that," Lucy said. Leaving his clothes to soak in the pool at the foot of the waterfall, she handed him a wad of crushed leaves. "I'd never heard of it myself, but Crilla calls this stuff soapweed. It grows wild here in the mountains and sort of lathers up when you get it wet and mush it up with your hands."

Without the benefit of soap or scrail cloths, Tarq had been a little concerned that Lucy might not be able to stand the stench of him before long and was pleased to find that the soapweed actually worked. It even had a fresh herbal scent.

Kneeling down in front of him, Lucy began soaping up his leg with the leaves, seeming not to notice his massive erection. "Believe it or not, I brought a needle and thread with me in case I had to repair the duffel bag, so I can probably sew up that split in your jeans—if the needle hasn't gotten lost. It might've poked through the bag somewhere along the way."

Her tone was merely conversational, but Tarq sucked in a breath when she slid her hand up his leg— more due to how close she came to his groin than her proximity to the wound. "What would you use in place of the needle?"

"I thought maybe I could use a thorn. There are some bushes just down the hill that have really sharp ones."

"Good idea. And if that doesn't work, I'm sure we can figure out another way." He gasped again as her knuckles grazed his balls.

"Kinda touchy there, aren't you?"

Since his cock was as hard as the rock he was standing on, Tarq would've thought the reason for his reaction was perfectly obvious. Then again, whenever he was near her, he was almost always hard. She might have been getting used to it, but *he* certainly wasn't. "The water is making your hands cold."

She nodded complacently. "Traldeck can heat up the water as it comes through the crack in the rocks up above just by staring at it, but he has to be standing here while someone else takes their shower. He said he didn't mind—I washed my hair this morning while he did it; couldn't stand that cold water on my head—but if you want any privacy at all... well, you'll just have to tolerate the cold."

Tarq made a mental note to make sure Lucy was well out of range of his nose anytime Traldeck was acting as water heater for him. Otherwise things could get a little embarrassing.

"No, wait!" Lucy jumped to her feet. "Hold on. Got an idea." As she scurried off, Tarq could hear her calling out for Traldeck. Fearing the worst, Tarq retrieved his jeans and was at least holding them in front of his stiff penis when Lucy returned, waving the saucepan. Traldeck followed close behind her.

"Now, Traldeck, if you'll just stare at that pool of water and get it really, really hot, the water coming down will cool it off some, and then I can dip it out with the pan and use it to rinse him off."

Traldeck grinned at Tarq. "She takes good care of you, doesn't she?"

This was so much in keeping with his own thoughts, Tarq forgot himself to the point that he started purring. Clearing his throat before making his reply, he smiled in agreement. "Yes, she does."

"I'm just trying to get him clean without washing off that"—Lucy paused as though at a loss for what to call the nasty, sticky goo Bratol had spit on his leg—"stuff."

"Wish you'd been around to think of this sooner," Traldeck said. "We could've saved each other a great deal of embarrassment. Of course we didn't have the pan to scoop up the water, but it would still be easier."

Tarq nodded. "Lucy is very smart." He almost added, "She can read and everything," but he managed to stop himself in time. He saw no point in making it obvious that he was somewhat envious of that skill. After all, nearly everyone could read.

Traldeck fixed his gaze on the water until it began to steam. "Want me to make it boil?" he asked Lucy.

Tarq didn't wait for Lucy's reply. "No."

Lucy sent Tarq a quelling glance. "Yeah. Boiling would be great. And don't worry, Tarq; I'll cool it down before I pour it on you."

The water was soon boiling vigorously and Traldeck left them, a knowing smirk on his lips.

Tarq gave up trying to be subtle and began purring. Loudly.

"None of that now," Lucy said firmly. "Traldeck's already got enough ideas about what we're doing over here."

Tarq laid his jeans down on another slab of fallen rock nearby. "I'm sure it's because he and Natasha have done the same thing."

"Yes, but they're married."

"So are we—at least everyone here believes that we are."

Lucy brushed the hair back from her face with a hand that was visibly shaking. He was making her nervous again. "True. Guess I'm not quite used to the idea yet." Sighing, she nodded toward the steaming pool. "Better get this done before the water gets cold. We need to wash your hair, too. It's got blood in it."

Tarq reached out and raised her head with a finger beneath her chin. "Traldeck is right. You take *very* good care of me, Lucy. Whether you're my wife or not." Leaning down, he kissed her soft, warm lips.

The pan made a loud splash as it fell from her hand and her arms encircled his neck. Needing no further encouragement, Tarq deepened the kiss, his tongue as anxious to explore her mouth as his cock was to plunge into her body.

The corner of his mouth lifted in a smile as Lucy returned his kiss with as much enthusiasm as he could have wished. "How about we take your clothes off too?" he whispered against her parted lips. "We don't want them to get wet, do we?" He nodded toward the slab of rock where he'd laid his pants. It was nearly flat and lay at a slight angle to the floor. "I'll bet Traldeck and Natasha have used that same spot."

"Probably." The soft breathiness of her voice sent a quiver through his cock.

Grasping the hem of her shirt, Tarq pulled it off over her head before unhooking her bra to free her breasts. In the dimly lit cave, her skin seemed to glow as he bent down to suckle her nipples. He loved the way they became tight and swollen as he teased them with his tongue, alternating a gentle massage with firm thrusts of the tip. Together with her heady scent, the soft sounds she made acted like a catalyst, intensifying his need for her and multiplying his desire.

His hands slid to her waist, caressing every luscious surface they encountered. There wasn't a single part of her he didn't love, didn't cherish with all his heart and soul. Pushing past the waistband, he sent her pants gliding down her legs to puddle around her feet. Lifting her into his embrace, he carried her to the slanted rock. As he lay her down upon it with her head near the apex of the gentle incline, he discovered that it was even more perfect than he'd thought: the perfect height, the perfect angle. His cock slid into her with an ease that made it clear just how much she wanted him.

Tarq knew he wouldn't last long. The setting, the sight of her lying there before him, her eyes already grown misty with desire, plus the exhilaration he'd felt following a successful hunt—and possibly even Bratol's healant—all combined to sharpen not only his need but the urgency to give her joy.

He squeezed the pelvic muscle that acted as a pump for his lubricating fluid, knowing that the more his cock poured into her, the greater her pleasure and the greater the strength of her climaxes. Her own muscles rippled around his shaft, gripping it firmly as he rocked into her. Sighing deeply, he whispered, "Do you have any idea how good it feels to be inside you?"

"Mmm… I dunno… maybe about half as good as it feels to me?"

Tarq smiled. Sucking his lower lip between his teeth, he shook his head slowly. "A lot better than that."

Raising her feet to rest on his shoulders, he arched his back, letting his cock reach into her until his balls brushed against her bottom. Then he let it dance while he watched her face, loving what he saw there even more than his own pleasure—the soft curve of her lips, her blissful smile, her heavy-lidded eyes gazing at him through a sensual haze. Each deep-throated cry of rapture sent him rocketing ever higher. There was only one sensation he was missing.

Withdrawing slowly, he knelt until her legs draped over his shoulders and her succulent entrance was right in front of his face. Swiping his tongue over her soft folds, he paused to savor a flavor more intense than the strongest aphrodisiac, a flavor that made his balls tighten, threatening release. He waited a moment before diving in again, this time driving his tongue deep into the hidden recesses of her core.

Backing off to tease her clitoris, he heard her moan, felt her legs pressing tightly against his back, and delighted in the way her tight bud throbbed as he stroked it with his tongue. She fell silent for a moment, and then Tarq was treated to his favorite sound of all: her sharp cry of ecstasy, followed by gasping moans as her body quivered in orgasm. He prolonged both her climax and his own pleasure, pressing hard against the firm nub and slowly licking upward, pausing as he reached the point, then letting it pop from beneath the tip of his tongue. Her clitoris surged against his lower lip, doubling his joy each time until her body lost the ability to respond.

As he attempted to rise to his feet, she stopped him.

"Tarq," she said in a breathless whisper. "Turn me around. I want to do that to you."

Though the rock she was lying on was cool and hard, wherever Tarq's body touched hers tingled with a heat that threatened to consume her. Lucy hadn't exaggerated when she'd suggested that her level of enjoyment was twice that of his. They might have been equal, but no way could hers be surpassed. And it was about to get even better...

Tarq did as she asked and the altered position put her at exactly the right height to view his stiff, dripping cock and meaty balls hanging just above her eyes—a sight so erotically stimulating that her core contracted once again.

His skin was slightly damp and petal soft beneath her tongue, and she pulled him down, urging him to widen his stance until his one rested on her lips. As her body reacted with another jolt, her mouth opened wide, allowing one of his testicles to drop into her mouth. She savored the warm feel of it, realizing how much she adored this level of intimacy she had with him. She'd never even begun to experience anything like it before and couldn't imagine sharing it with anyone but Tarq. The mere idea of being with any other man was abhorrent.

Tarq's gasps of pleasure were like music to her ears, his flavor a delicacy on her tongue, and his body, his smile, his entire self appealed to her in a way that was somehow symbiotic. The more time she spent loving him, the stronger she became, the bolder her demonstrations of that love. If only she could say it. If only she could *hear* it…

His nuts were delectable, but his cock was surely the tastiest part of all. Releasing his scrotum, she pulled the scalloped head down to her lips, licking it with long, steady strokes, doing her best to continue despite the fireworks igniting within her own body.

She reached up and grasped his thick shaft, squeezing firmly as she slid her fist up and down its length. He was wondrously hard and the scalloped points tickled her tongue as she devoured him. With the addition of her other hand to massage his balls, she brought him quickly to climax. His slick *snard* coated her tongue, filling her mouth with creamy sweetness.

The effect hit her with the power of a meteor, making her forget that she was lying on a pair of wet jeans on a very hard rock. Any discomfort, any reservations, any fears of discovery faded away with the power of her *laetralance* delight. Soon, Lucy knew she would regret suggesting this position, which normally would have sent blood rushing to her head, but right now her blood was busy elsewhere, heating and relaxing every muscle in her body.

Fortunately, Tarq wasn't feeling quite the same effects and kept his wits about him enough to gather her up into his arms and carry her to the pool. She had to assume he'd at least tested the temperature with his toe, for he waded in and set her down gently in the warm water. Lucy wanted to roll over and finish washing him, but at the moment she simply didn't have the strength. As he sat down beside her, she gazed up at him, loving everything she saw—except for one tiny little detail…

Chuckling softly, she reached out, pushing up the bandage that he still wore tied around his head to cover the wound Fred had inflicted. With all the excitement of the previous days, she'd gotten so used to seeing him in it, she hadn't even considered that he might not need it anymore. "I think we could probably get rid of this."

"I like it. Keeps the sweat from dripping into my eyes."

"Needs washing, though." She tossed the bandage aside and briefly examined the wound, which was now completely healed, before threading her fingers through his blond locks. "There's still blood in your hair from the *last* time something tried to kill you. What *is* it about you that makes others feel so murderous?"

"It's 'cause I'm so tasty," he said with a wicked grin. "Fred was afraid I'd steal all the women in Yalka right out from under his nose—"

"Yeah, right," Lucy snickered. "Like any of them would be under *his* nose anyway."

"—and the vrelnot seemed to think I'd taste better than a dranik."

"Well, I certainly can't argue with the vrelnot on that one." She breathed a sigh of pure delight. "You're absolutely delicious."

"I'm glad you think so." He pulled her close and kissed her. "Mmm… You taste pretty good yourself." Retrieving the pan, which was floating beside him, he filled it with water. "Now, where were we?"

"Don't get your leg wet," she cautioned.

"I won't," he replied. "See? I'm lying on the other side. That green slime isn't anywhere near the water. Besides that, I'm going to wash you first."

"But I've already had a bath today."

"Doesn't matter," he said and began pouring the contents of the pan onto her mound. "I sort of messed up part of you—and I always try to clean up my messes."

Lucy bit back a moan as he dropped the pan and slipped his hand between her thighs. Pushing her legs apart, he caressed her sensitive folds, and she gave in to the sensuous wonder of the combination of Tarq's talented fingers and the luxury of hot water. He kept it up long enough that she was quite certain she'd never been so clean in her life, and then he leaned down and kissed her with the same degree of thoroughness.

She could've lain like that forever, but the water was already beginning to cool. Breaking off the kiss, she pushed him away with a hand in the center of his chest. "At least let me rinse you off and get the blood out of your hair before the water gets too cold."

Tarq was purring as he leaned back against the side of the pool. Lifting his injured leg, he rested it on the dry rock at the water's edge, exposing his groin. "I think we've already washed everything but my hair and my dick. Go for it."

Lucy didn't really want to move, but she wanted to yell for Traldeck to come and reheat the water even less. Getting to her feet, she found the clump of soapweed lying forgotten on the cave floor and dipped it into the water. Heat seemed to improve the foaming action, and she was able to work up a good lather with surprisingly little effort.

Tarq's eyes were glowing and his lips curled into a seductive smile as she stepped back into the pool and knelt down at his side. Judging from his expression and the way he was purring, Lucy had an idea she was about to get nailed again.

"Don't look at me like that or we'll never get this done."

Tarq chuckled wickedly. "It's not a chore for you, is it, Lucy?"

"Well, no, but we've been in here long enough. Someone else might be waiting to use the, um"— she glanced about, trying to decide whether or not this area warranted being called a bathroom or a shower—"facilities."

"Okay. I'll be good." He lay back with his hands behind his head, his hair trailing in the water. He might have looked angelic, but his cock was getting stiff again. Not only that, it was pointing right at her.

"You already *are* good, but you probably knew that."

As Tarq roared with laughter, Lucy retaliated by grabbing his dick and proceeding to give it the scrubbing of its life. By the time she was finished, tears of mirth were streaming from his big blue kitty-cat eyes.

"Okay, now turn around so I can do your hair."

Tarq was still chuckling when he sat up, pivoting on his butt before lying down on his back with his legs up over the side of the pool. Lucy settled in behind him, half wishing the water was deep enough to dunk him, but unfortunately it wasn't even deep enough to get his ears wet. Lathering up his long curls, she had to wash and rinse it twice before she was satisfied that she'd removed all of the blood.

"All done," she said sweetly and got to her feet. She stepped out of the pool and picked up her towel— another of those goodies she'd stashed in her bag that would probably prove to be as popular an item as the salami—and dried off quickly, donning her clothes before Tarq even got out of the water.

Snatching up Tarq's shirt and jeans, she rounded the slab of stone that shielded the shower area from the rest of the cave, calling back over her shoulder, "I'll get Traldeck to dry these real quick."

It wasn't until Tarq stood up that he realized she hadn't left him the towel. He stepped out of the water and slipped on his sandals.

And waited.

And waited some more.

By the time she returned, he was getting rather chilly; his skin had nearly air-dried and his erection was a thing of the past. "Couldn't you have at least left me the towel?"

"It was wet," she explained as she handed it to him. "Traldeck had to dry it, too. It's pretty neat the way he does it. I wasn't watching him that closely when he heated the water, but his eyes look really strange."

"I'll bet they do." Tarq shivered as he wrapped the towel around him. "At least it's warm. You know, I wouldn't have minded using the towel the way it was. I was about to freeze my nuts off waiting for you."

Lucy gazed at him with round, overly innocent eyes. "I couldn't leave you with a damp towel." Tarq watched as the corner of her mouth twitched into a mischievous smile. "Even if it *was* your fault for getting me all wet." She bit her lip, obviously doing her best not to laugh.

She'd done it on purpose! "Why, you little—"

Lucy squealed and darted around the stone slab and out into the cave with Tarq hot on her heels. What he'd do when he caught her, he had no idea, but chasing her seemed like the thing to do at the time. They'd already run past Crilla and Faletok, who stared at them open-mouthed, when Tarq remembered he wasn't wearing anything but a towel.

Heading toward the mouth of the cave, they streaked past Traldeck, who shook his head knowingly. *"Newlyweds."*

Chapter 23

TARQ HAD INITIALLY WANTED TO GET TO NOKLAR AS quickly as possible, but after a few days of life in the cave—hunting draniks by day and making love with Lucy by night—he considered telling Vertigan the way and letting the others go on without them. At least then he wouldn't have to worry about Vertigan trying to become Lucy's second husband. Unfortunately, without Traldeck around to heat the water, bath time in the cave wouldn't have been anywhere near as much fun.

Along with being a good source of food, bringing down draniks had an additional perk. Their fur was just about the softest Tarq could imagine, and Lucy had gotten very creative with it. Traldeck could cure the hides just by gazing at them for a short while, and Lucy had used her precious thread to stitch together a few items, among them a proper quiver for his arrows and a mitt for handling hot items around the fire. She also cut a long strip of hide and pounded it repeatedly with a rock, making the leather soft and pliable, not explaining to anyone what it was to be used for.

Tarq found out later that evening. He wouldn't have thought that anything in the entire galaxy could feel as good as any part of Lucy you'd care to name, but dranik fur in Lucy's hand? *Fabulous*. She'd wrapped half of it around his cock, using the other end to tease his balls. Relaxing completely as she stroked him, his climax had come as a bit of a surprise—to both of them.

One other thing that came as a surprise, once he realized it, was the fact that, unlike so many of the women he'd been with, Lucy was constantly finding new and different ways to not only please him but to drive him absolutely wild.

All his life Tarq had been the one to hone his technique for the benefit of his clients. He was, after all, a professional; it was his business to know what women liked, and relying solely on the fact that he was Zetithian would only get him so far. He couldn't have his repeat customers viewing what he had to offer as mundane; if nothing else, it was a matter of pride. Still, though the idea that Lucy might be getting pointers from Natasha did occur to him, he preferred to believe that she was inventing them on her own—just for him—which in his eyes made her truly unique and made him love her that much more.

It took several days of hunting and drying the meat before everyone agreed that there was enough for the journey to Noklar. Crilla and Faletok held out the longest, though Tarq suspected their reluctance was due more to the daunting aspects of the journey for two aging Vetlas than it was for a lack of sufficient food. Still, he'd had the opportunity to observe them and felt that they were hardier than they gave themselves credit for.

Carrying an adequate supply of water was the factor that concerned Tarq the most; game was plentiful in the mountains, but water would be scarce until they reached the river valley. Kotcamp had heard that vrelnot hide was waterproof, so, armed with knives, Tarq, Vertigan, and Traldeck had set about skinning the carcass. The meat was tough and barely edible—though the dog seemed to enjoy it—and the hide even tougher, but they managed to get enough of it to give Lucy something to work with.

After the first painful attempt at piercing the hide with her one and only needle, Lucy resorted to using thorns and bark fiber to stitch together vrelnotskin water bags. As if this task wasn't difficult enough, ensuring that they were watertight required a double row of stitches. Lucy had still been afraid they would leak, but she discovered that, once filled with water, both the hide and the wood fibers swelled slightly, sealing the tiny holes.

Each day when he was out hunting, Tarq gazed out over the mountains, the route to Noklar etched so clearly in his mind he could even see it with his eyes closed. How to protect everyone from the nightly vrelnot raids continued to concern him, even though he knew his bow was capable of at least wounding them. Terufen had proved adept at making arrowheads, and each evening he and Tarq made as many arrows as they could. He also made several more bows with the intention of arming each of the party, whether they could shoot straight or not, and a spear, which he thought might be useful if he ever had to engage a vrelnot in close combat again.

Bratol had told Tarq about another ancient weapon called the atlatl, a sort of throwing handle used to launch much longer arrows or darts, as he called them. Tarq was able to make one from Bratol's description, and though he wasn't as accurate with it as the bow, he had to admit it would probably be useful if he ever had to bring a vrelnot down out of the sky. Once he understood the theory, Kotcamp had been making and practicing with bolas night and day. Traldeck and Vertigan worked on felling trees and got to the point that they could drop one in a reasonable amount of time. The wood came in handy, supplying fuel to smoke the dranik meat as well as bark fibers for making rope.

They were as well prepared as they could possibly be, given the circumstances. The hardest part would be taking the final plunge.

———

After dinner, Lucy sat next to Tarq as she worked on reinforcing her moccasins with vrelnot hide. The discussion around the fire centered on everyone's plans for the following day, which was typical. Tarq and Kotcamp would go hunting, several of the others would practice with their bows, Crilla would gather more soapweed… The decision everyone was dreading was the one thing that wasn't discussed. No one seemed to have the courage to come out and say it.

Walkuta had been sitting quietly—so quietly, in fact, that when the Zebtan woman's high, clear voice cut through the general chatter, Lucy missed her stitch, stabbing her thumb with the needle. "We should leave tomorrow. There is a disturbance in the heavens."

Lucy dropped her moccasin to suck her bleeding thumb. No one spoke. Everyone stared at Walkuta as though her green skin had suddenly turned red. "A disturbance in the heavens?" Lucy echoed. "You're kidding us, right?"

Walkuta shook her head, the thick tendrils of her hair

swaying as though they were submerged in water. "The rains are coming. I can feel their approach."

Lucy had heard enough tales of the fierce storms in the Eradic range to know that she had no desire to experience one firsthand—and hadn't thought she ever would. "But the rainy season doesn't start for at least another month. With any luck, we'll be in Noklar long before it hits."

Walkuta turned her sepulchral gaze on Lucy from her rocky perch on the opposite side of the fire, the reflection of glowing embers in her huge orange eyes intensifying her bizarre appearance. The nape of Lucy's neck prickled. Walkuta was either completely nuts or a legitimate prophetess—Lucy hadn't decided which— but whatever the case, she was still… unsettling. "The rains will be here soon. We must make haste."

Some of the others murmured their dissent, but Tarq spoke up. "She's right. We should go."

Faletok stirred the dying fire with a long stick. "Is this part of your vision?"

Crilla sat beside her husband, nodding vigorously. "His vision is a true one. I'm sure of it."

Faletok shot a withering glance at his wife from beneath his droopy lids. "No one ever said it wasn't." Fixing his gaze on Tarq, he repeated the question.

"No," Tarq replied. "But we *are* ready. Putting it off won't help us."

"We need more practice with our bows," Vertigan said. "I don't relish the idea of a bunch of novice archers trying to take down a vrelnot."

Bratol was smiling slyly, as though he knew a secret that no one else was privy to. "He will lead and we will follow."

Traldeck nodded his agreement, but Vertigan's blue eyes flashed with annoyance. Lucy had suspected that Vertigan—as the unofficial leader of the pack—would want to be the one to decide, and apparently she was correct. "We are not ready," he said bluntly. "Starting out now would be suicidal."

Bratol smiled benignly in the face of Vertigan's anger. "Oh, I doubt that. There will be risks, of course, but nothing in this life is without risk—nothing worthwhile, that is."

Vertigan's attitude did not improve. "If the rainy season is indeed upon us, what better reason to remain where we are?"

Terufen snorted. "And stay here for another year waiting for better weather? I don't think so. I'm willing to take the risk. And for your information, the rest of us aren't so bad with our weapons. We may not be able to shoot a vrelnot in the eye, but Crilla can hit a rock rat at ten meters and Kotcamp throws a mean bola. I vote we go now."

The thought of waiting until the next dry season rolled around sent a spasm through Lucy's heart when she realized what else that might mean. "And I'm pregnant. I may not be having much in the way of symptoms now, but I have absolutely no desire to make the trip when I'm about to deliver or have three babies to carry. Not gonna do it, Vertigan. No way."

Vertigan obviously hadn't considered this or what was more likely—particularly in light of his sheepish expression—he'd simply forgotten. "That's a pretty good reason, Lucy." He sighed with apparent misgivings. "I guess we should go then."

Lucy nodded and swept her gaze over the entire company, all of whom were nodding in agreement. They might never be in complete accord again, she thought grimly. It was now or never.

———✺———

The next morning the mountainside was again enveloped in dense fog, and given Tarq's vrelnot experience, everyone voted to stay put until it lifted. Lucy busied herself making sure everything was packed securely. Though her skill in stitching hides together with sinew and bark fibers had grown considerably, how they would hold up during the journey was unknown. After a check of their gear, she smiled to herself thinking that they pretty much *had* to move on. Between Tarq and his bow and Kotcamp and the bolas, the dranik population had thinned considerably.

Lucy hated to admit it, but she was going to miss the cave, and not only because it had a shower. She and Tarq had lived there as a married couple among people who believed the lie. Not that she'd given anyone reason to doubt it. Playing the part of Tarq's mate had been all too easy.

When the fog lifted at last, she took a final look around, noting that her eyes grew misty when her gaze landed on the pile of grasses that had been the bed she'd shared with Tarq. With a wistful sigh, she shouldered her duffel bag and the bow and arrows he had made for her. More than anything she wished she would never have to use them, but doubted that her luck would hold. When she'd considered how much luck had been involved in everything that had occurred since she first laid eyes on

Tarq, she had a feeling she'd used up her allotment for the year—perhaps for her entire lifetime.

They set off at mid-morning, Tarq leading the way as though he truly did know exactly where he was going. He never faltered, seeming to know the best path around every obstacle they passed. Vertigan questioned his choice a few times but was never able to convince anyone else that Tarq had taken a wrong turn. Lucy tried not to walk too close to him. Distracting him with her scent seemed like a bad idea since moving quickly was necessary for their collective safety. There would be no stopping for sexual needs, either; in fact they barely stopped long enough to eat lunch. Lucy suspected that Tarq would have preferred to keep moving even then— possibly in light of their late start—but he never said so.

Reinforcing her moccasins turned out to be her best accomplishment yet—aside from the water bags they each carried. Lucy was doing her best not to drink until she absolutely had to, marching on when she would have preferred to stop and rest. Tarq would undoubt- edly have moved more quickly alone; Bratol and the two Vetlas were rather slow, and though some of the reason lay with their age, the rest was explained by their comparatively short legs.

Rufus—Lucy still couldn't think of him as Akeir— trotted along with them, occasionally running on ahead and then returning to check up on each member of the party. Lucy suspected he was reporting back to Vertigan, but as Vertigan himself seemed rather quiet, she couldn't be sure.

Nat and Traldeck tended to stick together, as did Kotcamp and Terufen, and after a bit Walkuta fell in alongside Lucy. The Zebtan's frequent glances at Tarq didn't surprise Lucy overmuch; she'd have been doing the same thing herself had she not been posing as his mate.

When Walkuta spoke at last, Lucy wasn't terribly surprised at the topic she chose. "You made a fortunate choice in him."

"You mean Tarq?"

Walkuta nodded toward the Zetithian, a worshipful gleam in her orange eyes. "He is a fine man. An aura of greatness surrounds him."

Lucy would have agreed wholeheartedly if that aura denoted his greatness as a lover, but somehow she didn't think that was what Walkuta had in mind. "Greatness? How?"

Walkuta's eyes became shuttered and mysterious. "In many ways," she replied. "But perhaps the greatest is his humility."

Lucy couldn't argue with that. Tarq was secure in his sexuality but never boastful or aggressive. If he hadn't had a vision, he probably would have been content to let Vertigan take the lead.

"He is a practical man and doesn't let his ego rule him," Walkuta went on. "I find that trait to be… admirable, and so unlike the males of my species." She shook her head sadly. "I left my own world in search of just such a man. I consider it most unfortunate that now that one has finally come my way, he is already mated with another."

Lucy shouldn't have been surprised to find that other women might be envious of her, but never having been the envy of anyone before, the notion hadn't occurred to her. Still, had Tarq kept his mouth shut about being

Lucy's mate, Walkuta would undoubtedly have volunteered to satisfy his needs.

The instantaneous sense of possessive ire that this thought inspired came as a bit of a shock to Lucy, and she had to fight to keep from telling Walkuta to keep her greedy little green Zebtan hands off him.

She glanced up just in time to see Traldeck toss a knowing smile over his shoulder. Thus far, his ability to manipulate fire had eclipsed his talents as an empath, but Lucy would do well to remember it if she intended to keep her secret. She turned to find Walkuta regarding her as though expecting a reply. "Sorry I found him first."

Walkuta laughed—something Lucy had yet to hear her do. "There is no need to apologize. I am simply stating a fact. And unlike the majority of females on my world, I have no desire to share my mate with another woman."

Lucy grinned, her previous emotional reaction already forgotten. "Prefer monogamy, do you?"

"Oh, yes," Walkuta replied. "Whether a man is equipped for two or not." She glanced at Vertigan. "But perhaps you would not object to being shared by two men?"

Lucy's eyes widened.

Walkuta smiled knowingly. "Oh, yes. The possibility exists. Vertigan is a Mordrial. Since they cannot always reproduce with the one they love, their women often have two husbands. Strange species…"

Lucy certainly couldn't argue with that, though Walkuta's species was even stranger. "I… I've never heard that before." That Vertigan was interested in

Lucy, even Tarq had seen, but Lucy still didn't believe it. Vertigan had given her no clues that his feelings lay in that direction. "Are you saying that Vertigan wants to—"

"Be your husband? Yes, I believe he does. He is watching you, but seems uncertain. From what I've been able to observe, Zetithians are fiercely monogamous. I doubt that Tarq would be willing to share."

"Probably not." The fact that Tarq had claimed Lucy as his mate moments after he'd first noticed Vertigan's interest made it obvious that he wanted no part of a polygamous relationship, whether he'd known about this Mordrial tendency or not. However, her connection with Tarq was anything but typical. Once they reached Noklar, their ways would part. If Mordrials were indeed accustomed to their wives giving birth to a second husband's children, perhaps Vertigan wouldn't see Tarq as a rival and therefore would not be averse to helping to support and raise his offspring. Still, her situation was already complicated enough. "I don't believe I want another husband." Not that she truly had one now.

Walkuta nodded. "It *is* a strange custom, though not unheard of. Many worlds have practices that are quite fascinating." Her expression clouded, becoming unreadable. "Then there are others I wish I'd never seen. Perhaps I should have stayed home."

"I know what you mean," Lucy said, thankful for a new topic. "Things haven't turned out quite the way I expected since I left Reltan, but there are parts of this little adventure that I wouldn't have missed for the world."

Crilla spoke up from the back of the pack. "Me too. I would never have guessed I'd be so good with a bow."

Faletok made a rude noise, which Crilla ignored.

"Of course, I'm only able to kill rock rats because I pretend they're my husband," Crilla added. "Improves my aim."

Lucy laughed along with the others but was of the opinion that the only way to improve her own aim would be to imagine that her target was something trying to kill Tarq—which might turn out to be the case eventually. Then she remembered how murderous she'd felt when dealing with Fred and knew that she would defend Tarq against any foe in a heartbeat, whether she was armed or not. Even though she might die trying to save him.

She found herself staring at him. Never mind how great he looked—broad shouldered and tall, his long blond hair tucked beneath the bow and quiver slung across his back, the knife at his hip, the load of provisions he carried—what she saw went much deeper. She loved him. Completely and utterly loved him. But what about when he was gone? Could she ever feel that way about Vertigan?

The force of this emotion was such that Traldeck turned and smiled at her again. With a nod toward Tarq, he asked, "How come you two aren't walking together?"

Lucy's face flushed hot with embarrassment. "I, um, distract him too much. It's because of my scent."

"Ah," said Traldeck. "I see."

He probably didn't—at least not entirely. Lucy caught a glimpse of Tarq's sly smile as he glanced back at her, but he never slowed his pace. He understood the problem—and was probably grateful for her consideration—even if no one else did. Though the mere thought was like a knife through her heart, Lucy knew she should probably stay well away from Tarq throughout the entire journey. She had no desire to re-live the awkward moment they'd had when Vertigan found them.

Vertigan—whom she'd had to remind of her expect-ant state. She'd spent a good bit of the previous night lying awake wishing she hadn't put this argument into words. While Tarq slept beside her, thoughts of how her pregnancy would progress, how she would endure the labor and delivery of his three children, how she would care for them and watch them grow—but most of all, how she would go through all of this without him—kept her mind in turmoil. Vertigan might have been the answer to the practical aspects of this, but what about love?

Pain ripped through her heart once again, bringing tears to her eyes and causing her to stumble.

Walkuta steadied her with a hand on her arm. "Are you unwell?"

"N-no. Just… hurt my foot on a rock. I'm okay." It was a lie, but Lucy doubted anyone would realize it—until Traldeck glanced at her again. His movement caught her eye, and she looked up to see concern mixed with puzzlement written on his face, followed by the shock of comprehension.

He knew.

Chapter 24

ALTHOUGH JUST EXACTLY *WHAT* HE KNEW WASN'T clear, Lucy deduced that Traldeck was at least aware that there was something fishy about the relationship between herself and Tarq. She quickly averted her eyes—which probably confirmed his suspicions. Hiding her emotions from him would've been wise, but since he could evidently pick them up from two meters away with his back turned, she had no idea how to do it. She could just as easily have concealed them from herself.

Marching onward, Lucy did her best to focus on her feet and her surroundings instead of her troubling thoughts. A lighthearted conversation or a song would've been helpful, but traveling through a mountain range on foot—no matter how good your guide—was conducive to neither. Everyone was left to their own thoughts, though it was apparent that hers had proven more interesting to Traldeck than anyone else's.

A glance to her right confirmed that the sun was already beginning to set, which did nothing to improve her mood. It would be getting dark soon, and if Tarq knew of a safe place to spend the night, he wasn't telling anyone about it. *Great. Something else to worry about.* She shook her head and repositioned the strap of her duffel bag which, though now padded with dranik hide, had been cutting painfully into her shoulder for the past hour or more. She would have switched it to her other shoulder, but considering everything else she was carrying—her bow, quiver, and a vrelnotskin canteen—she would've had to stop in order to do it. It was easier to keep moving. *Happy thoughts, Lucy. Think happy thoughts…*

The fact that they were currently walking downhill was the happiest thought she could come up with at the time—that and the clear blue sky. The way Walkuta had talked, she'd expected to be caught in a downpour at any moment and prayed that the rains would hold off for a few more days. If the weather got too bad, returning to their cave would still be an option when they were so close. The trick would be to find another one farther on.

—◆◆◆—

Night was falling. Tarq understood why Lucy had been avoiding him all day—his head was clear and his dick quite soft—but his heart ached to have her by his side. She was much safer surrounded by others, as opposed to taking point with him, and though this was comforting, he still didn't like it.

Wanting nothing more than to bed down with her and inhale her glorious scent, he'd been on the lookout for a good campsite for the past hour but had yet to spot one. Unfortunately, his vision hadn't included the where-abouts of any caves along their route, though they were passing through a relatively thick stand of trees, which provided some shelter. The other question was whether or not they should risk having a campfire when they stopped for the night. Wildlife tended to avoid fire as a rule, but the habits of vrelnots were unknown to him. For all he knew, they might be drawn to it like moths.

He'd almost decided to pick a dense tree to camp

beneath when he finally heard what he'd been hoping to hear: the gurgling of water as it trickled over rocks. Following the sound, he discovered a sheltered spot with a rocky overhang above it, not unlike the place where he and Lucy had stayed while he recovered from his injuries. A spring bubbled out from a fissure in the rock, collecting in a small pool at the source before running off down the mountain.

"Great spot," Kotcamp said as he glanced around, nodding with approval. "I absolutely love it!"

"So, did you know this was here?" Terufen asked.

Tarq was nothing if not honest. "Well, no. Not exactly."

"Who cares?" said Terufen. "I was expecting to have to sleep out in the open and get eaten by a vrelnot during the night." He scurried over to a small alcove and set down his pack. "This is much better."

Tarq could only conclude that the Norludian's standards were low. It didn't quite live up to his own hopes, for there was no place for him to be private with Lucy. He might do better to avoid her altogether and take the first watch; otherwise, he was in for a miserable night—in more ways than one. He'd missed her all day and his dick hadn't even been hard. Not being able to hold her through the night would be torture. He was sure her feet would need massaging too—a task he had no intention of shirking.

"Wait!" Walkuta said as she approached. "I must perform the Rite of Domicile."

Tarq glanced at her in surprise.

Natasha rolled her eyes. "She did this to the other cave, too. Not sure exactly what good it does, but—"

"The Rite of Domicile cleanses the area, making

it safe for us to abide here for a time," Walkuta announced. "It cannot be left undone." Standing in the center of the sheltered space, she did an intricate dance with an accompanying chant in each direction, finishing as she had before by pressing her palms together and bowing her head.

The remainder of the company entered and settled in, all obviously weary and anxious to rest. Tarq wasn't sure they would get it, though. The little hollow in the mountainside was camouflaged with coarse shrubs, but that didn't necessarily mean they would be safe from attack—particularly if vrelnots hunted by scent like most nocturnal predators. Masking the scent of so many different species would be difficult, and he wasn't betting on Walkuta's ritual to keep the beasts at bay.

Setting down his gear, he passed through the boughs of pungent shrubbery out onto the open slope to get a feel for their location. He had made a slight detour from the path he'd envisioned, but this campsite was worth it. That route had allowed them to pass between two peaks with comparative ease, yet more mountains loomed ahead of them with no hint of the valley beyond. He reminded himself that they were still heading south, and probably wouldn't see anything but mountains until they turned north and then east again, which might take several days.

Had it not been for the threat from the vrelnots, Tarq would have considered their journey to be relatively pleasant thus far. He couldn't vouch for the others, but he was feeling better than he had for some time; the exercise and the crisp mountain air obviously agreed with him more than living in a cave.

Cave. He turned around and studied the nook carved out of the mountainside. He suspected that vrelnots wouldn't go into the other cave simply because they wouldn't fit through the entrance. This place was much more open and if a vrelnot landed in front of it, they would be pinned against the back wall of the mountain with no way to escape. Disguising their scent would be helpful, but the question was, how to do it?

When he passed back through the shrubs, the answer came to him instantly. Gathering handfuls of the aromatic leaves, he carried them inside. "Does anyone know what these smelly plants are?"

"They're called cripwood," Crilla replied as she sat down heavily on a slab of fallen stone. "When brewed, the leaves make a restorative tea, if you can stand the taste of it. I prefer to use it as a foot soak." Wincing, she twisted sideways, stretching her hunched back until it popped. "I could probably use some on my back, too."

Natasha was frowning. "Well, if you're going to make tea, I think Traldeck should heat the water. A fire might be all it takes to tell the vrelnots to come and get us."

Tarq nodded. "That and our scent. This stuff might be enough to throw them off, though. It's pretty strong."

Lucy came closer and took a whiff. "Whew! Really opens your sinuses, doesn't it? You think we should sprinkle the tea on our clothes?"

Bratol chuckled, indicating himself and Terufen. "Only if you wear clothing. Perhaps we should bathe in it."

"Forgot about you two," Lucy said with a grin. "Though as potent as it is, drinking it might be enough to make you smell weird."

"I think I'll pass," said Terufen, his mouth forming a moue of distaste. "So, Crilla, is it good for the skin?"

Crilla began to reply, but Faletok cut her off. "She had one of those plants growing in our yard and used the tea all the time." He gestured toward his wife. "Does it *look* like it's good for the skin?"

Since Crilla's skin was rather wrinkled and leathery, Tarq had to assume that it wasn't.

"The tea had nothing to do with it," Crilla said irritably. "If I look old, it's because I *am* old—though it could be the result of having to live with you for so many years."

Tarq glanced at Lucy, who was biting her lip to keep from laughing. He'd never seen her look more adorable, though he made himself a promise that he would never make similar comments about her, not even to make her laugh. In his eyes, she would always be beautiful, and he wanted to be there with her when she was as old as Crilla, loving her every bit as much as he did right now.

"I'll brew some up," Traldeck said, taking the leaves from Tarq. "If it keeps the vrelnots away, so much the better, but we've all got sore feet."

Vertigan snorted. "It might make a good liniment, but I've never heard of anything that would repel vrelnots."

"I doubt that it's ever been tested," Bratol said pleasantly. "And though I wouldn't want to take part in a formal experiment to prove it, it's better than nothing."

Natasha shuddered. "If I were a vrelnot, *I* certainly wouldn't want to eat anything that smelled like that. It's disgusting!"

Lucy glanced at Tarq. "Do you think it would help—?"

Tarq had a pretty good idea what she was about to ask and wanted nothing to do with it. If his dick ached all night long from inhaling her scent, well, it would just have to hurt. He didn't even wait for her to finish the question. "No, it won't," he replied. "But then, I've probably got a better nose than the average vrelnot."

Kotcamp shook his head vigorously. "Oh, no, Lucy! We can't have *you* smelling any different. I'd never be able to sleep."

Lucy blinked, gaping at the Sympaticon with total bewilderment. "What in the world are you talking about?"

"I *adore* listening to you!" Kotcamp said. "I've never slept so well in my life!"

It was Tarq's turn to bite his lip to keep from laughing. Lucy still didn't get it.

"Nothing wrong with *my* hearing, either," Terufen commented. "Wish I could make women carry on like that."

Lucy blushed as their meaning finally registered. "I don't make *that* much noise."

Terufen nodded. "I'm sure you'd make a lot more if you weren't trying to be discreet—but you don't have to, you know." Sighing, he waggled his tongue and sucker-tipped fingers at her. "We love it."

"Speak for yourself," Faletok muttered. "It's been giving Crilla *ideas*."

Tarq was beginning to feel a little uneasy. If someone didn't change the subject soon, Lucy might never let him near her again out of sheer embarrassment. A glance at Vertigan revealed that listening to Lucy had given him ideas as well. No, claiming Lucy as his mate hadn't completely eliminated that threat. But was it really a threat? Lucy hadn't said anything about Vertigan attempting to get closer to her. Unfortunately, Tarq wasn't sure if she would tell him or not.

"I'm starving," Bratol said, rubbing his belly. "What do you say we all sit down and have some dinner?"

Tarq smiled gratefully at the little Zerkan. "Great idea. Let's have some of that delicious smoked dranik."

Natasha laughed. "Mmm, yeah. Great stuff. Right up there with roasted rock rat."

"Too bad we don't have any of Lucy's chocolate pie," Tarq said, but immediately wished he hadn't mentioned it. No matter what you did to it, dranik meat couldn't begin to compare.

"Oh, my frickin' God!" Natasha exclaimed. "I haven't had Lucy's pie in ages! Isn't that just the best stuff you've ever tasted in your life?"

Tarq could think of at least one flavor he preferred, but mentioning it would send the discussion right back to where it started. "I asked her to marry me right after taking the first bite."

Lucy giggled. "He was kidding, of course."

"Maybe, maybe not." Reaching around her waist, Tarq pulled Lucy up against his hip and dropped a kiss on the top of her head. "Fell for her at first sight—well, no… actually it was more like first whiff." As soon as the words were out of his mouth, Tarq realized he'd directed the conversation back to her scent again. Not waiting for further comments, he steered Lucy over to the far side of the shelter where he could be relatively private with her. Thankfully, no one followed.

"You were laying it on a little thick there, weren't you?" Lucy said, keeping her voice low. She cleared a spot on the ground with the side of her foot and sat down.

"Maybe," he conceded. "But what did you expect me to say?" He wasn't surprised at her reaction, and even though he'd been telling the absolute truth, he still hadn't told her all of it. He'd fallen in love with *Lucy*, not her face or her aroma—no matter how marvelous they both might be.

She didn't answer, nor did she look up at him.

"I thought you'd be more upset over what Terufen and Kotcamp said."

When she still made no reply, Tarq's spirits began to plummet. "I'm sorry if this embarrasses you, Lucy. I'll leave you alone if you like." It hurt like hell to say it. He held his breath, waiting…

She shrugged and picked at the laces of her moccasins, still not meeting his eyes. "I never thought about us providing entertainment for the others—and it might not be entertaining to everyone. Some of them may find it annoying."

"I don't see that they have anything to complain about. It isn't as though it goes on all night, and they all believe we're newlyweds. I'm sure they don't think any less of you for what we do together." He knelt down beside her. He lifted her head with a hand cupped beneath her chin and gazed into her troubled eyes.

"But we're not *really* newlyweds. I-I guess I'm having trouble getting past that. I mean, sometimes I almost forget it's a lie, but then I remember…" She paused, blinking back tears. "I'm just not sure how to feel about it."

Tarq hesitated. Was this the moment to declare himself or not? "Would it help if I told you I wasn't sure how to feel either?"

"Maybe. But I'm pretty sure Traldeck knows—maybe not exactly what's going on, but I think he's sensed that there's something odd about our… relationship."

"Well, there *is* something odd about it, isn't there? You had to run away from home to be with me—or so everyone believes. That's a little different."

"If that were the only thing he believed, I wouldn't be worried, but—"

"Lucy, there's no need to worry, no matter what he or anyone else thinks. As far as any of these people know, we *are* mates."

"So you think we should just keep on the way we have been?"

"At least for now. There's no point in creating any unnecessary drama. We've got enough of that already."

"True." She took a deep breath and smiled. "I guess I'm just feeling tired and a little grumpy. I'll try not to worry about it anymore."

"That's my girl," he said, planting a quick kiss on her lips. "You just need to eat dinner and get some rest. You'll feel better in the morning."

She nodded and began rummaging through her bag. "I'm fresh out of apples and chocolate pie, but could I interest you in some dranik?"

"Sure." Tarq took the strip of dried meat she offered him, unsure as to whether he'd dodged a bullet or missed a golden opportunity. Time would tell.

Kotcamp volunteered to take the first watch, and Lucy got her first chance to see him transform. Sitting a little apart from the others, his natural shape began to blur until he appeared to be nothing more than a great lump of stone with eyes. The only time he gave himself away was when he blinked or spoke. Traldeck had brewed up several batches of cripwood tea and sprinkled it over each of the company. It's effectiveness as a vrelnot repellent was questionable, but it did wonders for everyone's aching feet. Crilla lamented the fact that she could only use it as a liniment rather than a soak, which led Lucy to conclude that Tarq was much better at foot massages than Faletok.

Lucy was already curled up on her blanket when Tarq spooned up behind her, his lips brushing her neck and his erection pressed up against her bottom. Enveloped in the warmth of his arms, the soothing vibrations of his purring permeated throughout her body. The last thing she heard was Terufen whispering, "Aw, c'mon, Tarq. Make her moan!" as she drifted off to sleep.

If only she could have awakened as pleasantly. Walkuta was right. The rainy season had arrived with a vengeance.

Horrific lightning struck from every direction, splitting the air with deafening crashes of thunder. Torrential rain pounded the dry ground, sending rocks and mud careening down the mountainside. Carrying sufficient water would no longer be a problem. To get a drink, Lucy would simply have to tip her head back and open her mouth—provided she didn't drown. The rain was so loud, Tarq could have been making mad, passionate love to her and even *he* wouldn't have heard her scream.

If he'd been there, that is. Sitting up, she glanced around. Despite the fact that it was still the middle of the night, the frequent flashes of lightning illuminated the little cave quite well. Tarq was nowhere in sight. Then she spotted Kotcamp stretched out snoring on a patch of ground at the rear of the cave and realized that

Tarq must've taken the next watch. Getting to her feet, she picked her way across the stony floor and found him sitting near the edge of the overhang, bow in hand. He glanced up and motioned for her to join him.

"Glad we didn't decide to camp under a tree," Lucy said as she sat down.

He put his arm around her shoulders, giving her a quick hug. "Me too. Any idea how long these storms last?"

"Even in Reltan they're pretty fierce but blow themselves out quickly. I've heard these mountain storms are more violent, though."

Tarq nodded as though this confirmed his suspicions. "Kotcamp says he saw a vrelnot flying down below, but it never came up this high."

"It's probably best that we didn't have a campfire. Would've been nice, though. I really enjoyed sitting around the fire, talking and watching you make arrowheads."

"We'll probably miss a lot of things about that cave before we're through, but everything will be better when we get to Noklar."

Lucy nodded her agreement, but wasn't convinced. Some of the best times of her life had happened while living in that cave with their little band of alien outcasts. Reaching Noklar would put an end to all that, along with several other things she'd miss—like sitting with Tarq's arm around her while the storm raged outside. She closed her eyes, committing to memory every nuance of this moment—Tarq so solid and strong beside her, his chest the perfect resting place for her head, the howl of the wind, the flashes of lightning that lit up the mountainside beyond—storing them up for comfort in the lonely times ahead.

What would he say if she told him how much she loved him? Doubtless he'd heard similar declarations from countless other women—women who, like herself, never wanted to let him go. Did he realize how many broken hearts he'd left behind him along with all of those babies? If so, he evidently deemed it worthwhile in order to perpetuate the Zetithian species, just as he deemed it worthwhile to prostitute himself. Jublansk was probably right when she'd said he enjoyed what he did. Lucy had never doubted that he derived pleasure from mating with her, even though she wasn't as beautiful or shapely as someone like, say, Natasha. Apparently it didn't matter to him. He could pretend to love anyone.

And he did it so well. If Lucy hadn't known better, she would have believed his every word and every loving gesture. Her eyes filled with tears as she wrestled with the pitfalls of falling in love with such an excellent actor. Not only did he have everyone else convinced that he loved her, he'd also gone a long way toward convincing her. If only it were true.

But it couldn't be. Generally speaking, men didn't fall in love with Lucy, no matter how much they liked her chocolate pie, and she couldn't blame it all on her father's irascible behavior. Though both Walkuta and Tarq had said Vertigan was interested, Lucy still hadn't seen any evidence of it and wasn't sure she believed it— and even if he had been, it was only due to a lack of options. Vertigan had been living in the mountains without female companionship for at least three months prior to their arrival. Desperation was undoubtedly a factor, not unlike Tarq's physiological reaction to her pregnancy. It had nothing to do with her as a person.

The storm raged on, but it was nothing compared to the turmoil in her heart. Tears as heavy as rain poured down her cheeks as she asked herself if she loved Tarq as a person and not just for what he was. She would spend the rest of her life pondering this difficult question; her only wish was that she could do it with him by her side, just as he was now.

"Morning will be here before you know it, Lucy. Think you could go back to sleep for a while?"

Of course. Her presence by his side was distracting him from his duties as sentry. It was thoughtless of her to sit there crying, which likely made her scent that much stronger. "Probably not," she said at last. "But I guess I should try. By tomorrow night, I'm sure I'll wish I had."

He gave her another squeeze, brushing her hair with a kiss. "Vertigan has the next watch, so I'll be back with you soon."

"Okay." She got to her feet, forcing herself to keep from drawing attention to her tears by wiping them away. Bless him; he even made it sound as though being with her was the part he looked forward to most. Oh, yes, he played the part of a loving husband all too well. She permitted herself a brief touch on his shoulder when she wanted nothing more than to throw her arms around him and kiss him endlessly. Instead, she pressed the fingers that had touched him to her lips as she walked away.

"Not feeling well?" Vertigan's voice sounded out of the nearby darkness as Lucy settled back down to wait for Tarq. "Or is the storm keeping you awake?"

"The storm mostly," she replied.

"Do you need...?" Vertigan didn't finish his question, but given all she'd heard, Lucy had a sneaking suspicion she knew what he'd been about to say. "Are you afraid?"

It was as good an excuse as any. "Sort of, but I'll be okay. You don't need to worry about me."

"But I do," he said. "Worry about you, that is. I should have thought about what it would be like for you to give birth out here in the wilderness. But I…" He blew out a pent-up breath. "Let's just say I wasn't anxious to leave the cave because the closer we get to Noklar, the closer I'll be to never seeing you again."

"I won't be—" Lucy caught herself just in time, thankful he couldn't see her expression of dismay. "What I mean is, once we get through this, I'll probably visit my family now and then. And I'd like to keep in touch with Nat." Swallowing hard, she tried to think of what else to say. How much easier would it be to simply tell him the truth? "So I'll be around."

"True. But it won't be the same."

"Nothing ever is." Everything would change once they reached the spaceport. Tarq would meet up with his friends and she would never see him again. She would probably see Vertigan though. Forcing a laugh, she added, "Not sure we'd want it to be. Or do you think you'll look back on the time you spent here in the mountains as 'the good old days'?"

"That depends on what happens next."

If her suspicions were correct, Vertigan would probably be pleased with the turn of events. Tarq would break her foolish heart and Vertigan would be there to pick up the pieces. "Guess we'll just have to wait and see."

"I guess we will."

Lucy knew she had to end this conversation before she broke down and told him everything. She wasn't quite ready for that. "Good night then."

"Sleep well. I'll be taking the next watch, and I promise to do my best to keep you safe."

She thanked him but knew that though he might be able to shield her from the weather and the vrelnots, for the heartache that lay ahead, there was no protection.

Chapter 25

THE NEXT SEVERAL DAYS WERE SPENT DODGING STORMS and rockslides. "And to think, we were worried about vrelnots," Terufen grumbled as Kotcamp pulled him to his feet for the fifth time in as many hours. Tarq had assumed that Terufen would have less trouble than the others navigating through loose stones, but his flipper-like feet only gripped the rocks, not the mud beneath them. As a result, he was skidding more than he was standing. Tarq was about to offer to carry him when Kotcamp transformed into an ape-like creature with broad shoulders and long hairy arms.

"The better to carry you," Kotcamp said as he hoisted Terufen onto his back.

Terufen beamed. "Ah ha! He even comes with a Herpatronian feature. I *like* it!"

"You wouldn't like me if I really *was* a Herpatronian," Kotcamp said with a shake of his round, snub-nosed head. "Nasty, hateful creatures as a rule. Not friendly at all."

"None of that, now," Traldeck scolded. "That's the kind of attitude that got us all kicked out of Yalka."

Kotcamp shifted Terufen up onto his shoulders. "If they were kicking out Herpatronians, I probably would've helped them. About got the shit beat out of me by one of them once. Had to turn myself into one just to defend myself."

"And what happened then?" Lucy prompted.

"I beat the shit out of him," Kotcamp replied. "He wasn't much of a pugilist, really. Very erratic with his punches. Longer arms, though. Gave him the advantage until I evened up the odds."

Lucy chuckled along with everyone else and it warmed Tarq's heart to hear her laughter—something he hadn't heard for several days. Granted, there hadn't been much to smile about, but even when they camped for the night, she'd been very subdued. Not having the chance to exchange more than a few words with her during the day didn't help matters, and it left him wondering if he was somehow responsible for her mood. In the evenings, she was understandably tired, and with the others sleeping so closely nearby, sex was out of the question. Mornings were the worst. Silent to the point of surliness, she ate very little and frequently withdrew from the group, going off on her own with only the dog for company. Tarq was worried about her; he just didn't know what to do about it.

They marched on. The day was fine for a change, the sky a clear blue with puffy white clouds and no hint of a storm. Birds—small ones—sang as they soared overhead, and the crisp air was seasoned with the scent of herbs. The terrain had changed slightly, becoming more rocky and open with no trees to speak of; only coarse grasses and a few shrubby plants dotted the mountainside.

That morning they came upon a grazing herd of what Vertigan identified as qualskins, goatlike animals with thick brown pelts and long, flowing tails. The flock scattered quickly, but Kotcamp was able to bring down one of the smaller ones with his bola. Traldeck gutted it, leaving the entrails for Rufus, who wolfed them down with gusto.

Fresh meat was certainly a plus after days of eating dried dranik, but what was more encouraging was that they had finally turned east. Tarq could see open sky out beyond the mountains now, as opposed to the endless peaks they'd seen when traveling north or south, and beneath that open sky lay the river valley.

Later that afternoon, Rufus returned from a scouting mission and reported to Vertigan that he'd found a campsite up ahead that would provide cover in the event of a storm. Upon their arrival, they found an outcropping of rock with a sheltered place beneath it, which, though relatively deep, had a ceiling barely high enough for Tarq to stand upright. Vines covered with large purple blossoms cascaded down from the overhang, forming a curtain that partially blocked the interior from view.

Though not nearly as well protected as their first location had been, it was still better than lying out in the open with nothing but boughs of cripwood to camouflage their sleeping forms, which was how they'd spent the previous night. If a vrelnot was ever going to attack them, that would have been the time, Tarq decided. Even when he was off watch, he had slept fitfully with his bow in one hand, an arrow already nocked, while the other rested on Lucy's hip. The only explanation for their safety was the ritual Walkuta performed each evening.

She was in the process of blessing or protecting or sanctifying—Tarq wasn't sure which applied—their current site when Lucy scampered off once again.

Tarq watched her go, muttering, "What is *wrong* with her?"

Natasha snorted a laugh. "Wake up, birdbrain. She's pregnant."

"So?"

"You know… morning sickness?"

Tarq shook his head. "I don't know what you're talking about."

Natasha gaped at him as though he'd lost what was left of his mind. "She's probably just over the hill there puking her guts out."

Tarq was horrified. "Being pregnant makes her *sick*?"

"I'm guessing he's never had a pregnant wife before, let alone a human one," Bratol said with an air of diplomacy. "I would imagine that Zetithian women do not suffer that misery."

"Not that I've ever heard," Tarq said. He stood facing the direction that Lucy had gone and, sure enough, she was quite pale when she came back into view. "But that explains a lot."

"I was *never* ill when I was expecting," Crilla said smugly. "Had no problems whatsoever."

"No, you didn't," Faletok grumbled. "That distinctive pleasure was left for me to enjoy."

Natasha crowed with laughter. "Are you saying that Vetlan *men* get morning sickness?"

Faletok's droopy-eyed expression was even more dismal than usual. "Every morning and every night. It's a pheromone that pregnant Vetlas produce. Made me swear off sex entirely for a couple of years."

Traldeck was smiling. "Built-in birth control."

"And quite effective," Crilla said with a nod. "But he got over it."

"To my everlasting regret," Faletok mourned. "That last child was a royal pain in the—"

"What'd I miss?" Lucy asked as she rejoined the party.

"A discussion about morning sickness," Tarq snapped. "Why didn't you tell me you felt bad?"

Lucy shrugged. "It's a perfectly normal symptom, and there's nothing you can do about it anyway. I'll be better in a couple of months."

"*A couple of months*!" Tarq was beside himself. "You'll—you'll *die* if you can't keep any food down. How have humans managed to survive?"

Walkuta waved her hands for silence. "I believe I can help."

Lucy shuddered. "If you're going to suggest that I drink cripwood tea, I don't want to hear it. That stuff makes me gag even when I'm *not* nauseated." Addressing Tarq, she went on, "And I won't die. Like I said, it's *normal* for me to feel this way."

"Well, normal or not, you need to let Walkuta do whatever she can for you," Tarq said bluntly. He didn't feel sick himself, but he was beginning to understand why Faletok had sworn off having sex because he was about to do it himself. Getting Lucy with child was one thing. Making her sick was quite another.

"I'm not sure a Zebtan remedy would work on a human," Lucy said. "It might make me feel even worse."

Tarq was about to retort when Walkuta cut him off. "No need to worry," she said calmly. "It is a ritual, not a potion."

"Okay," Lucy said, clearly relieved. "A ritual I can handle, just as long as I don't have to dance or stand on my head or anything weird like that."

Walkuta seemed slightly offended. "You won't have to do anything of the sort. The ritual only requires the blood of the father."

Lucy paled. "All of it?"

"Oh, no," Walkuta said hastily. "Only a few drops."

Tarq didn't hesitate. Whipping out his knife, he pricked his finger with the tip of the blade. "Here, take all you need."

Walkuta nodded her approval. "You have chosen well. The heart finger will provide the greatest protection."

Tarq looked at his hand. He'd cut the third finger on his left hand out of convenience, no more. Then he recalled the human custom of wearing a wedding ring on that finger and questioned whether his choice had truly been random.

Walkuta took Tarq's hand and squeezed more blood from his fingertip. "His blood must make contact with your skin in three places, Lucy. The head, the heart, and the womb."

"This should be interesting," Terufen said from his perch on Kotcamp's shoulders. "Does she need to be naked?"

Kotcamp gave Terufen a bounce. "Hush up. This is serious."

Walkuta ignored them. Pressing her palms together, she began to chant, presumably in the Zebtan tongue. Her hair swept up on its own accord and twisted into a knot as she bowed her head. When she finished her chant, she motioned for Tarq to proceed.

The head part was easy. Tarq pressed his finger to Lucy's forehead, leaving behind a smear of blood. Then he undid the top buttons on her shirt and touched between her breasts. He tried not to think about the last time he'd had his hands on her, but since his body was already responding to her scent, this was difficult—as was figuring out how to discreetly touch her "womb." He glanced at Walkuta, who motioned for him to continue.

The skin of her lower abdomen would have to do in this situation, he reasoned. Pulling up her shirt, he slid his hand down over her stomach, passing beneath her clothing. He stopped when she let out a giggle. "That tickles."

His heart gave a lurch as he gazed into her big brown eyes and saw not only merriment there but also warmth, tenderness, and a deep, abiding trust. He could've held her gaze for hours, but when he pressed his bleeding fingertip to her skin, her eyes squeezed shut and she inhaled sharply. Her knees buckled and she would've fallen if he hadn't been standing close enough to catch her. When she looked up at him, her pupils dilated completely, followed by a constriction so brisk that if he'd blinked, he would've missed it. He gasped as the realization struck him that it was the same effect his semen had—on her eyes, anyway.

Walkuta nodded. "It is as I suspected. Zetithian females do not experience the illness of pregnancy because their mate's semen protects them from it."

"But how does my blood on her skin help?"

"The same substance is contained in your blood and can be passed on to her through her skin." Walkuta's orange gaze fixed on his own. "You have been avoiding this intimacy because you are sleeping in such close proximity with the rest of us, haven't you?"

Tarq grimaced. "Well, yes, but she hasn't felt much like it, either."

Walkuta glanced at Lucy, who was now at least able to stand. Tarq thought her color was a little better, too.

"You didn't become ill until you'd been without him for a day or so, did you?"

Lucy frowned. "I hadn't put the two together, but now that you mention it, that's about when it started."

Tarq found this very encouraging. "So, to keep her from being sick, we have to...?"

Walkuta smiled. "Yes, you have to..."

Terufen was cackling with glee, but Kotcamp took it a step further. Grasping Walkuta's hand in his furry paw, he kissed it. "Bless you, Walkuta. And thank you from the bottom of my heart."

Lucy was blushing. Vertigan and Faletok were grumbling—Faletok for what he was having to do as a result, and Vertigan possibly because he wasn't getting any—but everyone else seemed pleased.

"Well, now that we've got that settled, let's get that qualskin ready to eat," Natasha said. "I'm starving!"

Kotcamp set Terufen on his feet and changed back into his usual colorless, wispy-haired self. "Sure hope it doesn't rain again tonight. I really don't like holding that form for long. All that hair makes me itch."

Lucy had never been so embarrassed in her life. Not that she wasn't delighted to have a good reason for making love with Tarq—if you could call it that—but the lack of privacy was freaking her out a bit. She wasn't sure she could handle knowing that Terufen and Kotcamp were listening. No doubt several of the others would also be listening. At least it would be dark enough that they couldn't watch.

She reminded herself that they had apparently been listening all along, and with that cheery thought in mind, she went to work clearing out the area beneath the rocky overhang. They'd taken to carrying cripwood boughs with them to use as brooms, as well as for their scent and camouflage, and she and Crilla used them to sweep the floor clean of loose rocks. If there was one thing Lucy had learned on this outing, it was to bed down on a smooth spot. The tiniest pebble would seem like a boulder after laying on it for a while.

She glanced at Tarq, who was shaking flakes of stone out of his sandals. Seemed like they were stuck together on this trip no matter what—she giving him pity fucks and he providing her with a remedy for morning sickness. *What a pair...*

He looked up at her and smiled. "Feeling better?"

She almost hated to admit it, but she felt perfectly fine. Her feet didn't even hurt. "Lots," she replied. "Though I wonder if it would have worked without all the chanting."

Tarq nodded. "Walkuta has a theatrical streak in her." He put his sandal back on and stood up. "Half the 'healing' is in the show."

Lucy couldn't argue with that. As rituals went, it had been fairly dramatic. "Speaking of healing, I'm sorry you had to cut your finger, but we couldn't have sex right there in front of God and everybody just to prove she was right."

Tarq grinned wickedly. "Well, we *could* have..."

"You *know* what I mean." Lucy tried to glare at him, but her smile gave her away.

His grin turned to laughter. "It's *so* good to see you smiling again. I've missed that."

"I haven't felt much like smiling lately." She propped her broom against the stony wall. "Didn't realize it was that obvious, though."

"It was to me, but then I'm probably more interested in whether or not you're happy than anyone else is."

Lucy frowned. "And why is that?"

"You're my mate, Lucy. Your happiness is important to me."

"But I'm not really—"

"Whatever," he said with a shrug. "I'd still rather have you happy and healthy than sick."

She knew the feeling. Watching him prick his finger had been almost as painful for her as it must have been for him.

Traldeck started a fire while Natasha and Faletok butchered the qualskin. "Nice to have fresh meat again," Natasha said. "Think we can eat all of this tonight?"

"I *know* we can," said Terufen. "Slice it thin so we can cook it fast and put out that fire before the vrelnots come out."

"They're likely to be thick out here tonight with that herd of qualskins nearby," Vertigan said. "We should double the watch." He glanced at Tarq as though expecting him to disagree.

Tarq ignored the bait. "That works for me," he said. "I can take the first shift."

"And I will join you," Bratol said. "Your skill with a bow and excellent night vision should offset my shortcomings as a sentry."

Lucy smiled to herself. Bratol's chief claim to fame as a guard was his ability to remain alert for hours without any apparent ill effects. Lucy didn't have trouble staying awake herself, but she usually paid for it the next day. Doubling the watch would mean that her turn would come around that much sooner. *Oh, joy...*

Qualskin steaks roasted over an open fire were absolutely delicious. Lucy was thankful she could keep it down and wondered how long the effects of Walkuta's ritual would last. Perhaps every other night would be sufficient...

———⁓———

Tarq woke Lucy with a hand on her shoulder. "Vrelnots," he whispered. "Get your bow."

Lucy sat up. She had no idea what time of night it was; for all she knew, Tarq could've been asleep by her side for hours. Moonlight streamed in through gaps in the leaves to reveal the others, all awake and silently preparing for attack. Even Rufus kept still, which seemed strange until she remembered that Vertigan had probably given him telepathic instructions. She picked up her bow and quiver and took her place in the line of archers.

Peering out from behind the thin shield of brush they'd used to supplement the hanging vines, Lucy could see them in the moonlight—four huge vrelnots circling above the mountainside. She could hear movement below and saw that the herd of qualskins had returned and were grazing near their shelter, apparently unaware that other creatures were sleeping there. Lucy decided they must've been really stupid because they didn't seem to notice the vrelnots either.

Until one of the huge birds swooped down and plucked a young qualskin right out of the herd. *Then* they scattered. Unfortunately, several of the woolly goats headed straight for their campsite, apparently accustomed to taking refuge there themselves.

Tarq shot the first one that came close and the others went galloping off in different directions. A second vrelnot flew in behind the first, not seeming to mind that someone had saved it the trouble of making the kill. However, instead of flying off with its prey, this one landed just outside the little cave. Lucy slowly backed away from the curtain of leaves and watched as the beast began to feed, hoping it would be satisfied with one qualskin and not go looking for anything else. Then she remembered what Tarq had said about the vrelnot he'd killed leaving a dranik to come after him and she felt like throwing up—a feeling that probably had nothing to do with her pregnancy.

She glanced over her shoulder at Tarq. He'd moved farther back and traded his bow for the atlatl, holding the dart at the ready. She knew the atlatl was a highly effective weapon—she'd once seen him launch a dart with enough force that it passed right through the body of a dranik and came out the other side—but its use required an overhand throwing motion. Even crouched down as he was, the low overhang didn't allow much room for that.

Everyone was frozen in place, bows drawn while they waited for the vrelnot to finish its meal and leave. It was nearly finished when Lucy's own dinner of fresh qualskin finally got the best of her. She tried to stifle her belch but only succeeded in turning it into a hiccup.

The vrelnot cocked its ugly head, peering directly at her. Then it began to advance. Slowly. Menacingly.

Holy shit.

Lucy was too petrified to move as arrows sang out from bows all around her. The vrelnot screeched in agony as a few of them found their mark. None were fatal, but instead of fleeing, the beast seemed determined to destroy its attacker and came straight for her—the source of the only sound it had heard—its beak open wide, hissing its rage as it tossed aside the boughs that separated them.

Certain death was less than a meter away when Lucy finally regained control of her muscles. Drawing her bow, she aimed for the eye and fired point blank just as Tarq's dart flew over her head and drove straight down the vrelnot's throat. She'd barely registered the hit when Tarq yanked her back out of the way. Snatching up a rock, he leaped forward, hammering in her arrow as far as it would go. The writhing vrelnot fell dead, the tip of its beak a hairsbreadth from where Lucy had been crouched mere moments before.

Nobody moved, and for a long moment the silence was so complete, Lucy could hear her own blood rushing through her ears. In the next instant she was in Tarq's arms, his hot kisses raining down on her face.

Lucy was stunned. He was kissing her as though her death would've destroyed him. She was about to return those kisses with equal ardor when she realized that he was only doing what a supposed mate would do in such a situation. It didn't mean what she thought it meant. For one split second she hesitated, but emotion overcame her and she threw her arms around his neck, returning his kisses with passionate fervor, spearing her fingers through his hair.

Then she recalled that though it was still dark, every one of the aliens present at least claimed to have better night vision than a human. Breaking off the kiss with a show of embarrassment that wasn't entirely feigned, she leaned into him, her arms wrapped around his waist, her head nestled against his chest. His heart was pounding hard enough to break a rib, but it grew steadier the longer she held him in her embrace.

Lucy glanced up as Terufen parted what was left of the curtain of vines, its lovely purple flowers now limp and tattered, and peered out into the night. "Think there's any of that qualskin left?"

"If there is, we should drag it well away from here. That carcass is nothing but vrelnot bait now." Tarq's voice resonated through her, the mere sound of it providing reassurance and hope.

"Yes, but what about the vrelnot carcass?" Natasha sounded worried. "Won't it draw other vrelnots too?"

"Probably," Vertigan agreed. His voice came from directly behind Lucy, sounding much less self-assured than usual. He'd said very little since their private conversation, but she'd felt his eyes on her, just as she now felt his hand lightly touching her shoulder. *So, he does care...* "Though we might be able to move it if we all got together and pulled."

"It would be much easier to move ourselves," Walkuta pointed out. "Dawn is approaching."

"I don't know about the rest of you, but I'm not sure I could sleep after that," Traldeck admitted. "After all, there's nothing quite like getting an early start." Clearly as shaken as the rest of the group, his attempt at a hearty tone sounded a little forced.

"We've all had at least *some* sleep," Tarq said, which confirmed Lucy's earlier suspicion. "And we'll be traveling downhill from here. We can take a longer lunch break if need be."

"But what if the vrelnots attack us?" Crilla asked.

Bratol chuckled softly. "I believe we have proven to be quite capable of defending ourselves. I vote we move on."

Lucy's eyes searched the semidarkness. Everyone was nodding.

"Then let's get moving," Terufen said with a shudder. "That dead bird is starting to give me the creeps!"

Chapter 26

THE TRIP DOWN FROM THE MOUNTAINS WAS UNEVENTFUL and though reaching the river was a goal of sorts, as far as Lucy was concerned, it was more akin to the fiery pits of hell than the Promised Land. She wouldn't have wanted to wander in the wilderness for forty years the way Moses and the Hebrews had, but their arrival in Noklar would mark the end of her "marriage" to Tarq. She wasn't ready to face that yet and probably never would be.

Vertigan, however, seemed more anxious than ever for them to move on, almost as though he knew that Lucy and Tarq would part ways when they reached the end of their journey. Traldeck might have told his brother of his suspicions about the questionable nature of her relationship with Tarq, but though Vertigan was gradually becoming more attentive to Lucy, at the same time, he was also backing off in his resentment of Tarq. He seemed to be demonstrating the advantages of having two husbands and also proving that he could live in harmony with the existing pair.

Lucy kept these thoughts to herself, not even discussing them with Walkuta, who had first mentioned the Mordrial polyandry custom to her. Since his initial claim that Lucy was his mate, Tarq hadn't acted as though he considered Vertigan a potential rival. Lucy had assumed it was due to Tarq's generally nonaggressive attitude, but could it be that he was aware of what Vertigan was attempting to do? Would he take it a step further and actually welcome Vertigan?

No. His allowing Vertigan to approach Lucy was one thing. *Lucy* would have to be the one to accept a second man. But should she? Right now she had no desire to divide her affections between the two men, and not only because she wanted to savor her last days with Tarq. The difference in the way she felt about each of them was staggering. It would be unfair to Vertigan to see how much more she cared for Tarq than she did for him. She loved Tarq with all her heart, but she felt only friendship toward Vertigan. Would that change once Tarq was gone? Or would his memory lie between her and Vertigan forever? Somehow, Lucy thought it might.

Tarq glanced back over his shoulder. Vertigan was keeping pace with Lucy and had been for the past several days. He knew that she was only staying back in the pack to prevent her scent from distracting him, but it also gave Vertigan the opportunity to score points with her. Thus it was Vertigan who helped her over the more difficult terrain, Vertigan who smiled and attempted to tease her into a better mood. Tarq's only consolation was that she wasn't sleeping with the Mordrial.

Would she compare the two and decide that Vertigan was the better man? Tarq knew that Mordrials didn't have the sexual abilities that Zetithians possessed, but there were other factors to consider. Vertigan was handsome, capable, and *intelligent*—and he hadn't fucked his way across the galaxy. Lucy might see this as a plus.

Tarq's worst fears were realized after dinner that evening. He and Lucy were sitting a little apart from the

others when Vertigan approached with a tight smile that
changed to a frown as he spoke. "There is a... matter I
wish to discuss with you."

Tarq glanced at Lucy. Her eyes were downcast,
avoiding the gaze of either man almost as though she
knew what the "matter" was and didn't want to acknowledge it.

Unfortunately, Tarq had been expecting it as well.

With a brief nod from Tarq, Vertigan sat down
on the ground, facing them both. "I don't know how
much you know about my people, but I must tell you
that it is not uncommon for a Mordrial woman to take
two husbands."

Lucy made a sound that could have been anything
from a gasp of dismay to a protest. Tarq considered telling Vertigan to get lost, but the Mordrial held up a hand.

"Please, hear me out," he said. "I realize that neither
of you are accustomed to this practice, but"—he paused,
glancing at Tarq—"I want you to know that I seek to
join, not to supplant. There are... physiological reasons
for this among Mordrials, and while those reasons do
not apply to humans, a Mordrial male does not see a
woman as truly taken until she has two husbands."

"So you wish to share her?" Tarq was surprised he
could even voice the question.

"I wish for the permission to—"

Lucy interrupted Vertigan with a slight cough.
"—demonstrate your affection?"

Vertigan nodded, but with a sigh of relief at her under-
standing. "I do. However, I realize that this is not your
way. I only ask that you... consider my... offer."

"I'll... think about it." Lucy spoke quietly, only

allowing herself a quick glance at Vertigan. She didn't even look in Tarq's direction.

Tarq's heartbeat slowed to a dull thud. He had no intention of sharing Lucy with anyone. As he saw it, if she accepted another mate, it would be an indication of how little she cared for him. He consoled himself with the fact that she hadn't greeted Vertigan's offer with a big smile and an enthusiastic hug, but her response could mean almost anything. She could be trying not to hurt Vertigan with an outright rejection. Or she could be searching for a way to let Tarq down gently. The hardest part for Tarq to endure was not being able to voice his own opinion. If Lucy had truly been his mate, it would have been different. As it was, he didn't have a leg to stand on.

When they finally reached the valley floor and the source of the river the next day, Tarq was treated to an even greater display of Vertigan's worthiness. He worked tirelessly with his brother to fell trees for use in building the raft, never surly or impatient, always cheerful and willing. Was Lucy seeing this? Would she come to prefer him over Tarq? Their union wasn't real. He'd never asked Lucy to be his mate, and she had never accepted him. He'd forced it on her. What would she do if she had a choice?

―――

Having had plenty of time to work out the details, the building of the raft progressed so quickly—*too* quickly, in Lucy's opinion—that after only two days of intense teamwork, the raft was ready to embark on its maiden voyage. Walkuta performed yet another ritual to ensure their safe passage, but when Lucy climbed aboard and took a seat near the makeshift sail, which had once been her blanket, she was shivering with dread.

To make matters worse, Tarq sat down beside her, leaving the steering of the raft to Kotcamp and Vertigan, both of whom were experienced sailors. "You aren't afraid of boats, are you?"

"N-no," she replied. "At least I didn't think I was."

"Don't worry about a thing, Lucy," Terufen advised. "Compared to what we've already been through, this little boat ride will be a picnic in the park."

Lucy doubted that. She'd heard stories about the settlers who'd tried to establish farms in the Noklar river valley. Those who'd made it out alive told horrific tales of vrelnot attacks and floods from the mountain storms. Given that the rainy season had only just begun and the ground was still dry enough to absorb the water, floods were unlikely, but the vrelnot threat remained.

She turned to gaze at the snowcapped mountains rearing up behind them and then at the peaks that flanked the river all the way to Noklar. Viewing them from her current vantage point, she considered it a miracle they'd made it this far. An excursion down the river couldn't possibly be that easy.

Kotcamp poled the raft away from the shore while Vertigan summoned up a stiff breeze. Once they reached midstream and were cruising along at a brisk speed, Lucy began to understand why people had tried so hard to settle this region. Though the mountains and coastal regions were by no means completely barren, this valley was peaceful and green and teeming with wildlife. The river was broad, with a lazy current that would've made for slow going without a sail and the wind Vertigan provided. Swaying trees along the grassy banks trailed branches in the water, while birds as colorful as the flowers flitted from tree to tree, their calls blending together in harmonic song. If it weren't for the vrelnots, this would've been a genuine paradise.

As the river carved its way through the valley, it was joined by tributaries from other sources high in the mountains and the current grew stronger, increasing their speed. If this kept up, they would reach Noklar in no time. Under any other circumstances this would have been a cheery thought, but as matters stood, Lucy's heart grew heavy with sorrow as she watched the picturesque valley slide past.

With no guarantee they would find a safe place to camp, they decided to continue on even after dark, risking a possible vrelnot attack for greater speed in reaching Noklar. The trick would be stopping the raft before it went over the falls at the valley's end. They would have to rely on the rudder and Vertigan's ability to control the wind to reach the shore, but the current there was bound to be strong.

Since Tarq's night vision was better than anyone else's, he slept that day to enable him to remain alert at night. Not having anything better to do and wanting to spend as much time with him as possible before the end, Lucy opted to doze beside him. The gentle rocking of the raft wasn't making her feel sick—yet—but though they had managed to catch a few moments alone during their descent from the mountains, they'd had none to speak of since. She cherished every second she spent with him and deeply regretted that last silent speeder ride to Traldeck and Natasha's farm. She viewed it now as time wasted, thinking that if they'd tarried on the road for just a little longer, perhaps none of this would have happened.

She reminded herself that if they'd never had to take refuge in the mountains, she would never have known what had become of Natasha, which was an important factor to consider. But even though Natasha meant a lot to her, Tarq was beyond price. She gazed at him as he lay sleeping, taking note of the way the breeze ruffled his hair, smiling at his occasional purr, and hoping that she played at least a small role in his dreams. Surely he wouldn't forget her. Her eyes clouded with tears and her heart ached as she realized how much she longed to keep him there beside her forever—vibrantly alive and loving—rather than the faded, lingering memory of someone long gone.

He must've felt her eyes on him, for he awoke, and with a loud purr, he pulled her closer to rest her head on his arm. He even kissed the top of her head as he wrapped her in his embrace. It was all she could do not to sob, for these were the times she would miss even more than the ecstasies they shared as lovers—the quiet moments spent together, the warmth of his smile, and the sound of his laughter. Closing her eyes, she could still picture him lying there beside her, and the image lasted on into her dreams.

Tarq longed to tell Lucy what was in his heart, but first he had to see her safely to Noklar. *Then* he would tell her. He knew he must've had a good reason for making that decision, but at the moment he couldn't recall what it was. "I love you, Lucy," he whispered.

But she didn't hear him. She was already fast asleep.

—∿∿—

Night fell, leaving only starlight glistening on the waves as the raft drifted onward. Cloaked in an eerie darkness, the valley no longer seemed peaceful and serene but was instead filled with a deep sense of foreboding. Even the bird calls had changed; while the songbirds slept, the air was filled with the menacing cries of predators on the wing.

Tarq sat near the front of the raft scanning the sky, though he doubted that even he would see more than a shadow blotting out the stars if a vrelnot were to approach. The last quarter moon was rising late; it would be midnight before there was enough light to see well, and clouds off to the west heralded another storm. With a steady wind behind them, Vertigan lay sleeping, his services no longer required. He and Kotcamp had agreed to split the night into two shifts at the rudder, while the watch was divided into three. Kotcamp maintained a course down the center of the river with Lucy posted at the stern and Terufen near the mast. The others lay grouped together in the center, sleeping fitfully until the time came for them to take over the watch.

Granted, the raft wasn't large, but Tarq begrudged every millimeter that lay between him and Lucy. Though he understood the need, he had to content himself with glances that occasionally caught her eye. From this he derived at least some comfort, but the words *I love you, Lucy* still reverberated through his mind like one of Walkuta's chants, keeping time with the beat of his heart, even slipping past his lips as a whisper from time to time.

Since most of his experiences with vrelnots had occurred near dawn, Tarq felt reasonably safe at the moment. With any luck, the storm would track to the north
or south, though with the way the wind was filling the
sail he doubted it. Still, the storm was a long way off
and might blow itself out before it reached them. *And
draniks might sprout wings and fly…*

Tarq had good reason for worrying; thus far every
storm the Eradics had conjured up seemed determined
to seek them out, either to destroy them or to make
their journey as arduous as possible. He knew, of
course, that storms didn't have minds of their own, but
that was the trouble with having to keep quiet while
on watch: your mind was free to imagine all sorts of
disturbing things.

He glanced back at Terufen, whose bulbous eyes
gleamed in the starlight. With eyes like that, the Norludian's
field of vision had to be better than anyone's—certainly
better than his or Lucy's—but if he'd seen anything that
Tarq hadn't, he gave no sign.

They hadn't gone much farther when Tarq heard the
ominous flap of leathery wings. Searching the sky, he spotted it off to the southeast, flying west above the riverbank.

"There," he whispered, pointing. "See it?"

"I only see one," Lucy whispered back. "Are there
others?"

"I don't think so. Remember, don't shoot at it
while it's directly overhead. We don't want it landing
on the raft."

"I'll try to keep that in mind."

Tarq heard the sarcasm in her tone and had to admire
her pluck. She might not be able to see well enough to

shoot at anything, but having already come face-to-face with a vrelnot and emerged victorious, she no longer seemed petrified with fear. Granted, it was only gallows humor, but it was humor nonetheless.

"Leave it to a fuckin' vrelnot to ruin an otherwise lovely evening," Terufen grumbled. "Wonder if they ever go after fish."

On the word, the vrelnot turned and circled around to the east, flying straight down the river toward them.

"I don't like the looks of this," Tarq muttered, trading his bow for the atlatl. "Don't waste your arrows. Wait until it's in range and hold your fire until it goes into a dive."

They waited breathlessly, but the vrelnot didn't dive right away. Instead it circled again, this time making a wide loop to come at them from the bow. Tarq could see it clearly now, its talons outstretched, preparing either to land on the raft or to snatch one of them right off it. He heard the twang of bowstrings as Lucy and Terufen both fired arrows into the night.

Regardless of whether they struck the beast or not, the vrelnot kept coming. More arrows were fired and Tarq threw a dart that ripped through the thin skin of the wing. The others were stirring, making a considerable racket as they scrambled for their bows. They could make all the noise they wanted, Tarq thought grimly. Keeping quiet certainly wouldn't help them now.

Tarq launched another dart and immediately threw again. The first one missed, but the second found its mark, hitting the huge bird at the base of the wing. The vrelnot tumbled out of the sky, but its momentum carried it forward, skimming above the sail toward the rudder, plucking Kotcamp off the stern before plunging into the river beyond.

Lucy screamed and rushed to the side, staring down at the water where Kotcamp had fallen. The raft had already sailed onward; all she could see was a swirling vortex where the vrelnot sank. There was no sign of Kotcamp at all. Rescue was next to impossible; even if they took down the sail, there was no way to stop the raft and turn around out in the middle of the river. Unless…

"Vertigan!" Lucy shouted. "Can you make the wind blow us back upstream?"

"I can try," he said. "But the current is really strong here and so is the wind. It may not be enough."

Vertigan focused his eyes on the starlit sky, and moments later the wind shifted, blowing steadily from the east. Lucy scanned the surface and then her eyes darted toward the shore. As dark as it was, it was difficult to tell if they were moving at all. Even so, holding their position might enable Kotcamp to swim toward them—if he were still alive and conscious. Tarq lashed a rope to the mast and tossed it overboard, and Lucy watched for any sign that Kotcamp was trying to reach for it, but saw nothing. The rope trailed behind the raft, floating untouched on the waves.

Vertigan scrambled past the others to take the rudder. "Can you see anything?"

Lucy shook her head as Tarq joined them, his sharp eyes searching the dark water. "Nothing," he said finally. "Not even a ripple."

Vertigan glanced behind him. "We're still drifting. Don't think we can hold this position much longer."

"We've got to give him more time!" Lucy pleaded. "He had to have gone down really deep with that vrel-not. It would take a while for him to surface."

"I'm going in," Terufen said suddenly. It was only this warning that enabled Tarq to seize the Norludian by the scruff of his neck before he made his dive.

"You'll never find him," Tarq said bluntly. "And you'll probably end up drowning yourself."

"I'm a good swimmer," Terufen protested. "I can find him."

"And then what? You might make it to shore and walk the rest of the way to Noklar—or meet up with us wherever we happen to stop—but in the meantime you'd be sitting ducks for any predator that came along."

"But he was the best friend I ever had!" Terufen wailed. "I'll never forgive myself if I don't try."

"And he would never forgive you if you died trying—especially if there's no way to save him. And there isn't. Not unless he saves himself."

Tarq's words were brutal, but they had the desired effect. Tears filled Lucy's eyes as Terufen sagged hopelessly in Tarq's grasp. The night was quiet once again, with only the muted sounds of flowing water, the wind in the rigging, and Terufen's sobs to break the silence.

Walkuta stepped forward and took the Norludian's hand, leading him away from the edge of the raft. "Come. Together we will mourn our friend's passing and send his spirit on to his maker."

Tarq nodded at Vertigan, and the east wind swiftly died. The raft sailed on, leaving Kotcamp behind.

There were no further attacks during the night, but the next day dawned on a very subdued and mournful crew. Vertigan showed his brother how to steer the raft while the rest of the company sat in silence, deep in their own private thoughts. Terufen had finally gone to sleep but was awake now and still seemed stunned. Lucy could scarcely believe it herself. To have come so far through so many dangers and then lose one of their friends in such a way was unthinkable, and yet it had happened.

The storm had passed by to the north, leaving behind a fresh breeze that drove them downriver even faster than the day before. The current was stronger too, and having seen maps of the region, Lucy knew that the river would take a bend to the south not long before reaching the falls. Tarq had said they needed to make for the northern shore, which would allow the best passage down past the falls to Noklar, but thus far no one had said how they were going to do that. Even with Vertigan to control the wind, she was beginning to believe that a watery grave awaited them all.

Lunchtime came and went and Lucy tried to nap, but even with her head pillowed in Tarq's lap, she couldn't relax enough to fall asleep. Finally abandoning the attempt, she sat up, rubbing the stiffness in her shoulder. Glancing upriver in the forlorn hope that she would see Kotcamp waving at them from the water, she spotted a huge fish swimming doggedly behind them, its dorsal fin knifing through the waves. "Look at that!"

Crilla nodded. "I've been watching it for a while now. It doesn't seem to be fast enough to overtake us, and I'd hate to think what it would do if it ever did. It's certainly too big to catch and eat."

"It's probably just waiting for the raft to sink so it can eat *us*," Natasha said nervously.

No one seemed willing to say what they were probably all thinking, which was that it had already eaten Kotcamp and was now following the raft, hoping for more tasty morsels to fall overboard.

"Think we should shoot at it?" Faletok asked.

"We should not kill a fellow creature on suspicion alone," Walkuta said wisely. "Its presence here may have nothing to do with us at all."

Lucy doubted that and so, apparently, did Natasha. "I'm getting sick and tired of everything and everybody trying to do us in. In fact, I'm not even sure I want to go back to Yalka. Seems like the whole damn planet is against us."

"My friend Dax can take you anywhere you want to go," Tarq said. "If all goes well, he may even be waiting at the spaceport."

"Not sure how we'd ever be able to afford space travel now," Natasha said. "It's not as though any of us has any money."

"I do," Lucy said. "I could loan you some."

Tarq shook his head. "No need for that. Dax wouldn't charge you much anyway, and like I said, he's a friend of mine."

Faletok snickered. "Must be a really *good* friend."

Tarq chuckled softly. "Well, I've known him since he was two years old, and he's only alive today because I found him and took him with me to the refugee ship right before Zetith got hit by an asteroid."

Faletok recoiled as though he'd been slapped. "Ah… yes," he conceded. "A *very* good friend."

Lucy cocked her head, listening. Something was different. "What's that sound?"

"The falls," Tarq replied. "We're getting close now." He stood up, directing his gaze downriver. "I can already see where the river bends."

"Guess I'd better steer toward the north shore, then," Traldeck said.

Tarq nodded. "Even if we beach the raft here, we can still walk the rest of the way. The water looks pretty rough up ahead too. There's bound to be a helluva current the closer we get."

Traldeck eased the rudder over and the front of the raft nosed to the left, heading for the shore. Moments later the raft gave a lurch, followed by a loud crack, and then began to spin completely out of control. "I think we hit a rock," he shouted. "The rudder's broken."

"Must be shallower here than we thought," Faletok said. "Look at the turbulence ahead. Rapids."

Natasha let out a scream, waking Vertigan, who scrambled to his feet, heading for the now useless rudder. Walkuta began to chant, Bratol had something akin to a seizure—wheezing to the point that Lucy was sure he would stop breathing altogether—while Terufen moaned and rolled onto his side—the only sound he'd made all day.

"We may have to swim for it," Tarq said.

Lucy gauged the distance between the raft and the shore. She wasn't sure she could swim that far. Not against such a strong current.

Crilla voiced a similar concern. "I don't know how to swim."

"Then we'll move on to Plan B," Tarq said with

unflappable calm. "Vertigan, can you get the wind to blow from the south?"

"I can try," Vertigan replied. "Not sure it'll be enough against this current, though. Guess we should have beached this thing sooner."

"No shit," said Tarq. "These rapids weren't part of my vision."

"Sure would have been nice if they had been," Vertigan said.

It was a testament to the shift in Vertigan's attitude that he hadn't taken the opportunity to make some disparaging remark. Lucy was still waiting for it when she finally realized it wasn't going to come. The wind shifted, presumably due to Vertigan's intervention. If she'd had any doubts that Vertigan's aim was not to sup-plant Tarq, but to join him as Lucy's second husband, they were now put to rest.

Tarq nodded. "That's the trouble with visions. They don't always tell you everything." He stooped down to pick up the long pole they'd used to launch the raft. "Might be able to touch bottom with this and at least keep us off the rocks."

The raft suddenly dipped into a pocket of current so rapid, Lucy thought the whole thing was going to slide right out from under her. Wedging her fingers between the logs, she clung like a leech, riding out the wild bucking of the raft. When she stole a glance at Tarq again, she saw that he already had the pole in the water and prayed that he would hit something with it and not simply follow it over the side, plunging into the turbulent depths.

Her prayers were answered. The pole grated on rock

and Tarq managed to lever the raft a little closer to the shore, which they were racing past at an alarming speed. The falls were in sight now; they'd taken the bend in the river without even noticing it. Terufen was helping Tarq with the pole, his sucker-tipped fingers fusing to the wood with a grip so tight he was dangling from the end. The raft jerked sideways, nearly unseating her again.

"That wasn't a rock," Traldeck yelled. "Something hit us."

Lucy looked for any sign of flotsam that might have been washed through the rapids along with them but only saw a thick gray dorsal fin. The strange fish that had been swimming in their wake all day had finally caught up with them. Rising up from the water like a prehistoric monster, it rammed the side of the raft and then slid back, gathering force as it drove in again, its teeth-studded jaws agape as it bit into the water-softened wood. Lucy had never even seen a picture of such a creature before. It was as though this valley had been cut off from time itself, and a species that had died out in other regions eons ago had lived on in seclusion.

Vertigan snatched up his bow and nocked an arrow, aiming for the blunt-nosed head.

"No!" shouted Tarq. "In trying to kill us, it's actually pushing us toward the shore. Let it be. Just keep that wind blowing."

Tarq was right. Between what he and Terufen were doing with the pole, the fish butting its head against the raft, and the force of the wind in the sail, they truly were getting closer, finally running aground on the rocks near the northern bank.

"We can make it from here," Traldeck said. "Not much current and fairly shallow."

"I am *not* getting in the water with that creepy fish sitting there waiting to eat me," Faletok said with a sniff.

Lucy glanced at the fish, which seemed to have broken off its attack and was now swimming into the shallows. As she watched in speechless horror, its fins stretched to become long fingerlike projections that gripped the rocks to heave its pale body out of the water. What it would do next was anyone's guess, but Lucy had an idea she was about to become dinner.

Chapter 27

Except it wasn't a fish.

It was Kotcamp.

"Sorry about being naked," he said as he stood up, though his smile wasn't the least bit apologetic. "Lost my toga when I transformed."

Terufen let out a whoop and leaped from the raft, splashing through the water to throw his arms around his friend. "We thought you were dead!"

Kotcamp returned the hug with equal gusto. "Yeah, well, I thought I was too, until I finally got my wits together enough to morph into a fish. Almost forgot I could do that, but it was either that or drown. I was trapped under that damn vrelnot for ages. Blasted thing sank like a stone!"

Terufen gave him a quick punch in the arm. "You could've at least changed back long enough to wave at us. Here we've all been so upset—"

"Hey, it was all I could do to keep up with you as it was. Didn't want to risk it. Besides, I sort of came in handy, didn't I?"

"Yes, you did," said Bratol, who had recovered from his wheezing fit. "I've never been fond of boats, but this trip was almost the death of me. And I never even got my feet wet."

"Hold on a sec." Lucy took down her blanket from the mast and tossed it to Kotcamp. "There you go. You can wear that. We wouldn't want you scaring the tourists."

"Tourists?" Tarq echoed.

"Oh, yeah," Lucy replied. "Never been there myself, but the falls are one of Noklar's biggest attractions."

Tarq cut off a length of rope and handed it to Kotcamp for use as a belt. "Must've missed it when I was passing through town."

Kotcamp draped the blanket over his shoulder. "I've been here a couple of times. Nobody ever climbs up this high, though—too dangerous. In fact, it's roped off. We'll probably get arrested."

"Who cares as long as we share a cell?" Terufen said. He gave Kotcamp another hug, smiling broadly. "I'd hate to break up this little band of ours any sooner than we have to." He glanced at Vertigan. "I'll even share a cell with you—that is, if you'll promise not to take potshots at my best friend—especially when he's trying to help us."

Lucy waited for another retort from Vertigan that never came. "Sorry. Stress got to me."

"Which is why Tarqy-poo is a better leader," Terufen said with a sniff. Obviously he wasn't going to let Vertigan off the hook that easily. "Never lets it affect *him*."

Lucy nearly choked on her tongue. *"Tarqy-poo?"*

Terufen waved dismissively. "Term of endearment. Or a nickname. All good leaders have them, you know."

Kotcamp laughed along with the rest as he waded toward the raft. "Let's get you all off that raft and get going. We'll be in Noklar in time for dinner." Morphing into his Herpatronian form, he took Lucy in his arms and carried her to shore.

Tarq gathered up his gear and jumped off the raft. *Dinner in Noklar?* After all they'd been through, the thought was as exhilarating as it was terrifying. But perhaps he didn't have to declare himself right away. It'd be pretty silly to ask Lucy to be his mate when everyone else sitting around the table already thought it was a done deal. Maybe he should wait. Give himself more time to pretend…

Looking back, Tarq realized he'd let the perfect moment slip right past him when he'd saved Lucy from the vrelnot. True, they'd had several close calls since then, but he would have taken on a dozen vrelnots with far more confidence than he felt asking Lucy to spend the rest of her life with him. Would she have him in spite of his past and his inability to read, or would she decide Vertigan was a better choice? He was forced to admit that he truly had no idea what she would do. True, Lucy had done a lot of things that made him feel as though she loved him, but it could just as easily have been an act. She'd never said the words, not in front of the others and certainly not in private.

"I think the first thing we should do is tell the police about Fred and his gang," Lucy was saying. "We need to get the ball rolling right away."

"Even before dinner?" Terufen rubbed his belly. "Couldn't that wait until tomorrow?"

Lucy shook her head. "It would carry more weight if we all arrived at the police station as soon as we hit town—and looking like we'd been trekking through the mountains—rather than after we'd spent the night in a hotel."

Hotel. Tarq could share a room with Lucy. A room where they could be alone. *Together.* No one listening, no one able to barge in on them or interrupt intimate moments. Suddenly restaurants and police stations held no appeal for him whatsoever.

"Okay," said Terufen. "Police station first, restaurant second, and then a hotel."

Natasha's moan bordered on orgasmic. "I can't *wait* to take a real shower—and put on some different clothes! I've been wearing the same outfit for almost four months!"

"No you haven't," Lucy said dryly. "That's one of my shirts you've got on."

"Oh, you know what I mean," Natasha said. "I'm just *so* ready to get back to civilization!"

Tarq wasn't sure he shared this sentiment. There were, after all, many things about civilization that tended to sap his self-confidence. Mentally kicking himself for missing the boat as it were, he settled his bow on his shoulder and threaded his fingers through the handgrip on the atlatl. Just because they hadn't seen any other predators upriver didn't mean there weren't any down here by the falls. Maybe he could rescue Lucy again. *Then* he would ask her. No matter who was listening.

The climb down was treacherous, but their journey through the Eradics had prepared them well—not that it wasn't tricky. Tarq led the way, with Traldeck bringing up the rear. Though Lucy had started off protesting that she would distract him too much, he kept her close beside him. He wasn't about to let her take a tumble just because she made his dick hurt—not without him there to save her, anyway—and giving Vertigan the opportunity for any heroics was out of the question.

Unfortunately, though Tarq did have to catch her twice as she slid past him, nothing was anywhere near dramatic enough to warrant a proposal.

Darkness had already fallen when they reached the base of the falls and ducked under the barrier. No one was there to notice where they'd come from; apparently the falls weren't visited much at night, possibly due to the fear of vrelnot attacks this close to the mountains. Following the river, they walked on into the city, drawing a few stares along the way, though not as many as one might expect. Unlike the picturesque villages of Madric and Reltan, Noklar was a bustling spaceport city, and as such, there wasn't much that the inhabitants hadn't seen before. Tarq had spent some time in Noklar when he first arrived on Talus Five, but not enough to know his way around. "Where do you suppose the police station is?"

"Hel-*lo*," Vertigan said with a touch of sarcasm. "There's a sign right there."

Tarq glanced where Vertigan was pointing and all of his old insecurities came crashing back on him. Though the jumble of letters eventually resolved themselves into words, Tarq knew he'd have to stand there a good five minutes before he figured out exactly what they said. And he'd been looking right at it too. *Here we go again…*

His vision had only shown him the way to Noklar; it was no help at all when it came to navigating the city streets. He might be able to hold his own in the bedroom and out in the wilderness, but without the information in his speeder to guide him, in a city this size, Tarq was flat-out lost.

Natasha snorted a laugh. "If we walk around town carrying bows and spears long enough, they'll probably pick us up and take us there."

"If it's all the same to you, I'd rather not be arrested right off the bat," said Lucy. "We need to get there and make our statement as soon as we can. Then we can get on with our lives."

If Lucy's life didn't include him, Tarq didn't see much reason for that moment to come any sooner than need be. But he had to at least feign enthusiasm—and he had to let someone else take the lead. Not that this had ever been a problem for him before, but he'd been among friends who cared about him then, not with Vertigan whom he still viewed as something of a competitor whether he'd wanted to be Lucy's second husband or not. Sharing a mate was unheard of for a Zetithian. For Tarq, it was all or nothing.

When Tarq didn't make a move, Vertigan was more than happy to lead them on to the station. Upon their arrival Vertigan stalked inside, his commanding demeanor drawing a few appreciative glances from the females present—some law-abiding and some not. He asked a few questions before they were directed to another desk where the officer listened patiently to his statement, everyone else chiming in with their own versions of how they'd been harassed and hounded out of Yalka. Natasha and Traldeck's story seemed to have the most evidence to support it, but Tarq was dumbfounded when the man finally spoke.

"Not that your statements don't fit with quite a few others we've been hearing lately, but there's some proof surrounding *his* story at least," he said with a nod toward Tarq. "Some friends of yours have been looking for you. They picked up the signal from your speeder in Yalka a couple of days ago, and when they didn't find you with it, they reported you missing. We impounded the speeder, asked some questions, and made several arrests, but, generally speaking we don't send search parties into the Eradics, which is why no one has found you before now. Not that they haven't looked."

Relief washed over Tarq knowing that Dax and Waroun had been searching for him, but as he'd said when Kotcamp fell into the river, sometimes you have to save yourself. "Do you know where they are?"

"Probably at the spaceport," the officer replied. "They've done some flyovers but didn't spot anything, which isn't too surprising. It's a wonder you all made it out alive."

"We probably wouldn't have if it hadn't been for Tarq," Lucy said. Tarq's heart warmed as he detected a touch of pride in her voice. There might be hope for him after all.

Natasha nodded her agreement. "Yeah, we'd been holed up in a cave for months until he showed us the way through the mountains."

"He ought to get a medal," Terufen said firmly. "Bravery, resourcefulness, you name it."

Tarq thought this was a ridiculous notion. He'd only done what his vision had told him to do. He didn't want a medal. He only wanted Lucy.

The police contacted Dax and Waroun, who then picked them up at the station. After visiting a bank where everyone was able to access their funds to provide for their trip home, Dax took them all back to his ship to clean up. The *Valorcry* had enough rooms for all, though with the others still around, Tarq knew he could still have an excuse to share one with Lucy. He debated telling Dax the whole story, but there were plenty of other tales to tell. That one could wait.

After what Natasha exclaimed to be "The most wonderful bath I've ever had in my life!" they were provided with new clothes by Kots, the *Valorcry*'s housekeeping droid, and then went to dinner at a local restaurant. Not wanting to risk letting Lucy get away from him any sooner than he could help, Tarq had hoped they would dine aboard the ship. He'd even considered telling Dax the same story he'd told the others. That way, he might have been able to persuade him to take off with Lucy still on board so he could hang onto her a little longer. She couldn't very well avoid him if they were on the same ship.

In the general conversation over dinner, most of the party decided to spend the night in hotels rather than take advantage of Dax's hospitality. This trend seemed to be led by Vertigan, and the others followed suit. The mantle of leadership had passed and Tarq had no desire to take it back. Lucy didn't say a word about where she intended to stay, but it was beginning to look like Tarq wasn't even going to get a last night with her. Not unless he begged. None of their companions mentioned that Lucy was his mate, either. Though it had been news to Natasha, apparently they presumed that Dax and Waroun knew all about it.

Then there was Vertigan's offer to Lucy. She hadn't said a word about it yet and Tarq had no idea whether or not she and Vertigan had discussed it. He hated to be considered selfish, but he didn't think a man should have to share the woman he loved with another mate. And what if she chose Vertigan over him? Tarq sat through the meal, picking at his food, unable to stomach more than a few bites of it. His entire life was on the line, even more so than it had been when he'd battled against vrelnots or during the fight with Fred and his cronies—or even when he'd left his home and found his way to Amelyana's ship. What would his life be like without Lucy by his side, just as she was now? How could he possibly endure the years ahead alone?

He glanced at Lucy's plate. She wasn't eating much either. The protective effect from his semen had probably worn off, for it had been several days since they'd made love.

Made love. It wasn't simply sex anymore—possibly never had been. As far as Tarq was concerned, their time together was all about love, not simply procreation, and the mere thought of not being able to love Lucy forever was almost more than he could stand. She was probably feeling sick again too. And there wasn't a damn thing he could do about it.

———

With arresting hazel eyes and dark hair that curled so tightly it resembled dreadlocks, along with the feline eyes, fangs, and pointed ears that marked him as a Zetithian, Dax was every bit as gorgeous as Tarq but in a completely different way. A single gold hoop dangled from his ear and a flame tattoo curled up one side of his neck to his jaw, which when compared with Tarq's wholesome blond good looks, gave him the appearance of a very bad boy.

But those looks were deceiving. His mate Ava, a petite half-human blonde with huge aquamarine eyes inherited from her Aquerei father, had joined them for dinner, and Dax couldn't have demonstrated his love for her more clearly than if he'd shouted it from the rooftops. Waroun, Dax's business partner and navigator, was a typically irreverent Norludian, and between himself and Terufen, he kept everyone in stitches throughout the meal—everyone, that is, except Lucy.

Though she did her best to chuckle along with the rest of the party, Lucy had never felt less like laughing in her life. Her hands were icy cold and her stomach was twisted into so many knots it was difficult to tell whether what she was feeling had anything to do with her pregnancy or whether it was due to Tarq's imminent departure.

Dax and Waroun waiting for him had probably seemed like a godsend to Tarq, but Lucy felt like she'd been punched in the belly when she'd heard they were already on Talus. Though perhaps it was better this way. No last night to spend with him, no pretending to love him when no amount of pretending was required…

She sat back in her chair, resting her elbow on the arm while blinking back tears, her knuckles pressed tightly against her lips. If anyone noticed, they would probably assume she was only trying to keep her dinner from coming back up, but they'd have been wrong. It was all she could do to keep from screaming out the truth or professing her undying love for Tarq, one or the other—she didn't know which. Either one would have caused acute embarrassment for both herself and Tarq, and she wasn't about to give in to it. She was going to end this with grace and dignity; she wouldn't cry, wouldn't plead with him to take him with her. Then, and only then, would she go find a hotel room somewhere and give her tears the vent they so desperately needed.

She could feel Vertigan's eyes upon her. He was waiting for an answer but she still couldn't give him one. She hated to think that he was Plan B—and he probably wouldn't have liked the idea either—but not knowing what would happen next kept her quiet.

Did she dare hope for a truly happy life together with Tarq? Or would she settle for a so-so existence with Vertigan?

No! She couldn't do that. She didn't love Vertigan. It was that simple. It would be different if she hadn't known what loving Tarq felt like, but now that she did, nothing short of that would do.

Vertigan's weren't the only eyes fixed upon her. Glancing up, she met Traldeck's gaze. Oh, yes, he knew—beyond a shadow of a doubt. The smile he gave her was obviously meant to be reassuring, but Lucy couldn't even smile back, only able to acknowledge him with the slightest lift of her brow. Had Vertigan discussed his offer with his brother? Had Traldeck assured him that she and Tarq were merely pretending to be mates? If so, it would explain Vertigan's silence. He might simply be waiting for Tarq to leave.

Kotcamp and Terufen gave every inclination that they intended to party all night long. However, Faletok and Crilla both looked exhausted, and Bratol, who had been jovial throughout the meal, was also beginning to show signs of fatigue. Lucy would miss them almost as much as she would miss Tarq—almost, but not quite. Vertigan's deepening scowl made it clear that he realized Lucy didn't want another husband. She hadn't said anything but knew she should take him aside and explain the whole mess. But he might assume that she would take him as soon as Tarq left, which was *not* what she wanted.

Vertigan was sitting across the table from her. All she had to do was catch his eye…

Moments later, his electric blue eyes locked with hers. Wistful sadness washed over her as she held his gaze, then slowly she shook her head. His eyes reflected his emotions as they passed from disappointment to anger, and then to acceptance. He became restless, shifting in his chair, clearly demonstrating his desire to be elsewhere. When Traldeck nudged Natasha, undoubtedly murmuring his suggestion that they call it a night, Lucy let out a shuddering sigh. Traldeck probably thought he was doing her a favor—and perhaps he was. Lucy had been tortured long enough. No matter what the outcome, it was time to get it over with.

As the party broke up and good-byes were said and hugs exchanged, Lucy promised to visit Natasha and Traldeck soon. Vertigan shook her hand with a tight-lipped nod. She wanted to apologize, to say she was sorry she couldn't love him, but he turned away before she had the chance.

"And we'll have to have a reunion party next year," Terufen insisted. "This was the best time of my life."

Lucy couldn't argue with that sentiment. With a growing ache in her heart, she waited until the others had departed, steeling herself for the moment she had always known would come eventually. Having had a little practice didn't help at all. The same sinking feeling she'd had when she'd spotted the clump of trees that marked the turnoff to Natasha's farm hit her as she turned to Tarq, only this time that feeling was quadrupled. No, this wouldn't be easy. She'd be lucky to get through it without bursting into tears.

Lucy held out her hand. "Well, Tarq, I guess this is good-bye. I'm sure you want to get on with your... mission or work or whatever you call it."

Tarq stared at her in complete and utter disbelief. She was actually smiling. Surely she wouldn't reject him—wouldn't hold his past against him. Not now. Not after all they'd been through together. He'd witnessed the exchange between Lucy and Vertigan, and it had given him hope. Now he realized his mistake. She was leaving him. As soon as she caught up with Vertigan, she would begin a new life. A life that should have included him.

Waroun giggled. "Hottest damn stud in the galaxy! He's got so many women clamoring for him, he—ooof!"

Dax had silenced his buddy with an elbow in the ribs that would have him hurting for a long, long time.

"You can't possibly mean that." Tarq's heart felt as though it had taken a plunge over the falls. "It's because of Vertigan, isn't it?" Not waiting for a reply, he took her hand. "Look, I know I'm not very smart, and you don't need me because you're already pregnant, which means I've done what I'm best at, but don't you love me just a little?"

Lucy gazed at him with an expression more bleak than any Tarq had ever seen. "Don't make this any harder than it has to be, Tarq."

"But does it have to be good-bye? Lucy, I *love* you. I know I'm not good enough for you, and I know you can take care of yourself perfectly well without my help—or Vertigan's—but please don't walk away from me again."

Lucy let out a sob and there was a tremor in her voice when she spoke. "I tried so hard not to love you. I've been telling myself not to let you get to me because I knew I'd have to give you up. Do you have any idea how that feels?"

Tarq nodded. "Oh, yeah. I know *exactly* how that feels."

She drew in a ragged breath. "But you could have anyone… anywhere…"

He shook his head slowly. "The only one I want is you."

Tears poured from her eyes, forming rivulets that ran down her cheeks. Tarq longed to kiss them away and make absolutely certain that they never came back. "All this time we've been together… You might have at least said *something*."

"I told you I wasn't very smart."

Her eyes flashed with anger and she stomped her foot. "Don't say that!" She all but shouted it at him, her sudden vehemence startling Tarq to the point that he actually took a step backward. "Don't you *ever* say that again! I know damn well you can't read worth a darn. I've known it for ages and I don't care. Do you hear me? *I don't care.* You're the best, smartest, most wonderful man I've ever known. There's nothing wrong with you. Absolutely *nothing*."

"I wasn't smart enough to say anything about how I felt. I've been waiting until now to tell you, but I didn't think you needed me—or *wanted* me."

She stared at him incredulously. "How could you possibly think that?"

"You're very good at pretending, Lucy. You never told me how you felt."

Lucy's eyes widened. "Like I was supposed to tell the most handsome, sexy, desirable man in the galaxy that I loved him with all my heart? You heard what Waroun said, and I'm sure he's right. There are probably hundreds of women who want you—and those are just the ones you've met. There are probably thousands more who'd give their right arm for one of the last Zetithians."

Tarq spread his arms and looked around him. "Then where are they?" He stopped, shaking his head. "They aren't here because they don't want me. I'm nothing but a big dumb stud. Vertigan is a better man than I'll ever be."

"No, he isn't. He's a decent man, but he doesn't have your kindness, your humility, your ingenuity, or any of the other things that make you so special. And you *are* special, Tarq. I'm simply not deluded enough to think that you could ever return the love of an ordinary little waitress like me."

It was Tarq's turn to be angry. "There's nothing ordinary about you, Lucy," he snapped. "You're smart and sweet and wonderful—much too good for the likes of me. I kept telling myself that, but it didn't stop me. I loved you anyway."

Tarq couldn't say another word. All he could do was hold out his arms. Lucy hurled herself into them and Tarq seized her, raining kisses all over her face, tasting the salt of her tears mixed with her own uniquely powerful essence. "Don't ever leave me again, Lucy. You're my mate and have been from the very first moment we met. I'll die without you."

Lucy was still sobbing uncontrollably, her face buried against Tarq's chest when Dax took him by the arm. "Come on. Let's get back to the ship."

Tarq scooped Lucy up in his arms and carried her to Dax's speeder, vowing not to let go of her again until the *Valorcry* was at least ten light years away from Talus Five.

Chapter 28

SOFT LIGHTS, SMOOTH SHEETS, AND THE WOMAN HE adored. Tarq was in heaven as he nuzzled Lucy's neck, purring more contentedly than he ever had before. Surrounded by her scent, her love, and her arms, his body said all the words he'd found so hard to voice before, but no longer. Whispering in her ear as he moved inside her, he spoke them aloud, both in his own language and in the one she understood.

"My dear, sweet Lucy. I love you so."

She smiled up at him, her touch on his face as gentle as her gaze. "You've been telling me that all along, haven't you?"

Nodding, he shifted his weight, his cock seeking a new angle to further demonstrate his feelings. "I can't remember when I didn't love you, but I didn't think you wanted me so I told you in my native tongue and let you wonder. You were too convincing with words, acting as though you were only taking pity on me, but when you were here with me, letting me love your body the way I craved, I could feel it. And your scent was like no other."

"So it's not just because I'm pregnant?"

He shook his head slowly. "No. Not entirely. The aroma of motherhood was there, of course, but I could also smell your desire—and it was there even before I heard your voice or gazed into your beautiful brown eyes." He smiled, dipping his head to scatter kisses on her cheek and down the slope of her neck. "I was lost the moment we met."

"And you never felt that way about anyone else? All those other women?"

"Not a one." Her lips were soft and delicate beneath his own. "That's because out of all the women I've been with, you were the only one I ever truly made love to. Just you, Lucy. Only you."

Lucy gazed up into the deep blue glowing eyes of the only man she had ever loved—and the only man to ever return that love. "You're sure you won't miss the... variety?"

His lips curled into a smile. "Variety is highly over-rated once you've found the perfect mate—in fact, it's practically impossible."

Frowning, she raised her hand, letting his hair brush across her skin, delighting in the feathery touches. "How so?"

"Zetithians mate for life, Lucy. Once that happens, straying from that mate simply won't happen."

"Really? You mean you can't do... *this*... with anyone else now?"

He sighed deeply, his purr caressing her soul. "Can't, won't, and don't want to. I tried. I had another client in Reltan. Couldn't do it. Her scent was all wrong. Everything about her was wrong. And do you know why?"

Lucy shook her head.

"She wasn't you."

His kiss drowned any words she would have spoken, his tongue tracing her lips, delving inside, letting her feel him, taste him—delicious and delightfully decadent, like a chocolate pie still warm from the oven. If everything about that woman in Reltan had been wrong for Tarq, everything about *him* was right for Lucy.

Sighing, she threaded her fingers through his hair, pulling him closer, loving him with every beat of her heart. "Mmm... I'm so glad you came here looking for women to bear your children. If you hadn't, we never would've met, and I agree with Terufen: The time we spent in the mountains was the best time of my life."

Tarq grinned wickedly. "Lucy, m'dear. Trust me. You ain't seen nothin' yet."

Her eyes widened as he began to dance and plunge inside her—pushing her to the heights of ecstasy and beyond.

He kissed her again. "Feel good?"

"You know it does."

Chuckling softly, he licked the side of her neck. "Amazing how much better it can be in a proper bed."

Lucy gasped as he shifted into another gear. It was all she could do to nod her agreement.

"We've made love in a tent, on a riverbank, in a cave, on a rock, on the ground, and in your tiny little bed—and it was all good—but here I can do things I never did before. Like this..."

In an instant, he'd flipped over onto his back, taking her with him. The few times Lucy had ever been on top, she'd been lying down or facing away from him, with his muscular thighs stretched out beneath her gaze. This time, however, she sat upright, facing him while Tarq lay flat on his back, his hair spread out over the sheets and his hands behind his head, displaying the muscles in his arms. Then there were his glowing cat eyes, gracefully pointed ears, the tips of his fangs, and the way he *smiled*... The view from up there was positively stunning—almost too much for one pair of eyes to process—and when she spoke, her voice was a whisper tinged with awe. "You're the most beautiful thing I've ever seen."

Tarq shook his head slowly, his smile stretching into a broad grin. "That's *my* line."

She snorted a laugh.

"You don't believe me, do you?"

"I guess it's one of those 'eye of the beholder' things."

"You can think that if you like, but I know better." His smile was slow and secretive. "And I can make you even more beautiful."

"Oh yeah? How?"

Flexing his pelvic muscles, he sent a gush of his orgasmic fluid pouring into her core. His curved cock then began to glide back and forth—slowly at first, and then with increasing speed—driving her wild as it stimulated every surface and nerve ending. Lucy's soft sighs became moans that soon transformed into cries of ecstasy.

His lips curled into a satisfied smile as Tarq changed his tactics, thrusting upward, driving his cock deep into her body. The steady push sent more of his juice to mingle with her own, and as it worked its magic, her abdomen contracted and she fell forward, bracing herself with both hands on his chest.

"Getting prettier," Tarq whispered. The relentless motion had Lucy gasping for breath. There was no way he was telling the truth.

Rocking, rotating, and thrusting until at last his hips bucked up from the bed, Tarq signaled his climax with a feral growl. Lucy felt the spurt of his *snard*, bathing her in its creamy warmth while she waited breathlessly for the impact.

A sigh escaped her lips as his *snard* began to stir her blood from within. Moments later, passionate fire raged throughout her bloodstream, flooding every erogenous zone with searing heat while radiating blissful warmth to each muscle, nerve, and fiber of her body. His scalloped corona began its sweeping motions, prolonging the superb sensations as she lapsed into peaceful *laetralance*.

Lucy heard his quiet laugh and opened her eyes.

"Now *that's* beautiful."

Breakfast the next morning was in the dining room on the *Valorcry*, which was fancier than any restaurant Lucy had ever seen. She felt as though she should be wearing a formal gown at the very least.

She liked Tarq's friends, though, and had no trouble feeling comfortable around them—even after telling them the real story behind her "marriage" to Tarq.

"Want a ceremony?" Waroun asked. "Dax is captain of the ship, you know."

"He can do that?" Lucy asked with surprise. "Even when the ship is sitting on the ground?"

Waroun cackled with laughter. "Well, we could always lie about the time, or take off. Whichever you like."

And so, after Dax had put the *Valorcry* into orbit, Lucy and Tarq promised to take one another for better or for worse, in sickness and in health, never to part until death should claim them. Lucy kissed Tarq with all the love she could put into it, caressing the line of his jaw as she tasted the warmth of his lips one more time.

How had she ever convinced herself that she could walk away from him? As it was, she never wanted to let him out of her sight.

Later on that afternoon, the discussion at the lunch table turned to some less than pleasant topics.

"And did you hear? Fred, Tuwain, and Lenny were some of the ones arrested," Lucy said. "I wonder if Fred—"

"Still has his dick?" Tarq chuckled. "I hope so—though he might be a little sore."

"You *hope* so?" Lucy couldn't believe her ears. "Tarq, he deserved everything he got and you know it," she said hotly. "Don't go defending him now."

"I'm not. It's just that I can… sympathize… sort of. I'd hate to think how I'd feel if someone did that to me."

"Someone *did* do that to you—almost. Besides, I didn't truss him up *that* tight—I mean, I managed to show *some* restraint, though I'd never been so angry before in my life. You can't know how I felt."

"No? What about when that vrelnot was coming right at you?"

"That's different. You expect an animal to act that way. It's not expected of a creature with intelligence—though I'm not sure the word 'intelligent' applies to Fred." She glanced at Dax as something else occurred to her. "Speaking of intelligence, mind if I use your comlink?"

"Sure," Dax replied. "Go right ahead."

Tarq frowned. "Who are you calling?"

"My father," Lucy replied. "Figure I ought to let him know what happened to me—though I should probably just talk to Jublansk. Not sure anyone else would care."

Taking a seat at the console, Lucy tapped in the

number for her father's restaurant, knowing full well he'd never be the one to take the call.

"There you are!" Jublansk was beaming as her image popped up on the viewscreen. "I knew we hadn't seen the last of you. You're looking mighty fine, Lucy. Running away from home seems to have agreed with you."

"You could say that," Lucy said. "I, um, well… Tarq and I just got married—and I'm pregnant, too. Thought I should tell somebody."

"Congratulations to you both—but I could've guessed that," Jublansk said with a smirk. "What with you two making eyes at each other all the time."

"Oh, come on, Jublansk. We weren't *that* obvious."

"Yes you were. To me, at least. And I've got an idea your dad saw it too. Could've told him he was driving you away, if he'd ever listen to anybody. But some things never change. So you're married, huh? And expecting too? Where're you headed now?"

"I don't know," Lucy said truthfully. "Tarq says we can go anywhere we want." She paused, glancing at her new husband. "He's filthy rich, you know."

Jublansk snickered. "Told you he made a killing on Rhylos with that fancy cock of his. He's planning to retire, isn't he?"

"Yeah. He sort of quit that job after he met me."

"That's nice to know." Jublansk tapped her tusk contemplatively. "Don't s'pose you two have any plans to open a restaurant somewhere, do you?"

Lucy looked at Tarq, who shrugged and said, "Why not? We could start a Zetithian place on Rhylos, or even Terra Minor—wherever you want."

Lucy smiled. If this kept up, she was going to be *so*

spoiled—not to mention how much he would dote on their children. "Maybe," she said to Jublansk. "Why do you ask?"

"Well if your father gets any meaner, I'm gonna be lookin' to find me a new job. Neris, too. Ever since you left, he's been more of a bear than ever and business has dropped off considerably."

"Well we *do* need to go into Yalka to pick up Tarq's speeder. We'll be there in a day or two. I probably should tell my folks where I've been—not that they'd ever believe it."

Jublansk barked out a laugh. "You've been all over the news, Lucy. Trust me, they know *exactly* where you are and who you're with, which is probably why the old man is so pissed. If I was you, I'd say my good-byes over a comlink."

"I might just do that," Lucy said. "But I'll see you in a few days anyway. Be looking for me."

"I will," said Jublansk. "You take care."

Terminating the link, she turned to Tarq. "So, a restaurant of our own? Really?"

"Hey, between your chocolate pie and Jublansk's bread, we're bound to make a killing."

"And don't forget your knack of being able to tell what's in anything you taste—even Kentucky Fried Chicken."

Tarq laughed. "But Colonel Sanders made me promise I'd never tell anyone the secret recipe."

Lucy smiled wickedly. "Guess that means you'll just have to make the batter yourself. And if we're working together, I'll be able to keep an eye on you."

"Don't worry, Lucy. I won't be looking at any woman but you."

"Who says that's why I want to keep an eye on you?"

Lucy burst out laughing and Ava chuckled right along with her. Ava was pretty sure she knew exactly why Lucy wanted to keep an eye on her husband and it had nothing to do with his attractiveness to other women.

"Hey, wait a minute," Ava said with a frown. "Colonel Sanders has been dead for at least a thousand years. People have been trying to duplicate that recipe ever since. No one's done it yet. You're saying that Tarq knows what's in it?"

Lucy nodded. "Yes, and I'm sure he can make it. Tarq can do anything." Lucy cast a sidelong glance at Tarq, daring him to disagree.

Tarq appeared to give this some thought before he spoke. "You know, as long as I've got you, maybe I *can* do anything. Might even learn to read better."

Lucy grinned. "Right answer."

**Escape to the world of
the Cat Star Chronicles,
by Cheryl Brooks**

OUTCAST

FUGITIVE

HERO

Read on for a sneak peek…

OUTCAST

Every man's dream…
One man's nightmare…

———※———

LYNX WAS ONLY SEVENTEEN WHEN HE WAS TAKEN prisoner in the war that destroyed his planet. Slated to be executed, he and the other members of his unit were instead sold into slavery. Thrown into the hold of a ship with no food and very little water, the new slaves were smuggled halfway across the galaxy to a slave auction on a distant world.

Dragged onto the auction block, the terrified boy almost wished he'd been killed. To be bought and sold like an animal was unheard of on his own planet of Zetith, where the world had been green and beautiful and the people were free. On this planet, whose name he never knew, he was sold to a trader who then sold him to someone else.

Stowed in the hold of yet another ship, exhaustion outweighed his fear, and Lynx fell asleep on the journey, only to be rudely awakened by two men. As one held him down, a flexible tube was painfully injected into the soft skin of the inner side of his left upper arm.

"Take that out, and you die," he was told, then was given a drink and left again in the darkness.

Lynx lay sobbing with fear and pain and hunger.

Even war had not terrified him like this. He had no idea where he was, or where he was going, and he believed that death would have been preferable to the life he now faced. He felt completely and utterly alone. Not knowing if the journey lasted for days or weeks, he lost all track of time and was fed at odd intervals, which served to disorient him that much more.

At last, the ship landed, and the bright glare nearly blinded Lynx as he was pulled into the harsh sunlight by his captors, who marched him down a dusty street and into a large palatial building.

"Pretty, isn't he?" the ugly, harsh-voiced man remarked to his cohort as they stripped Lynx of his bonds and his clothing.

"He'll fit right in!" the other man laughed. Unlocking a large, ornate door, he pushed Lynx inside. "You're their slave now," he said with a nod. "You do whatever they tell you."

The light inside was much brighter than the corridor through which Lynx had been brought, and it took a moment for his eyes to adjust as the scent of perfume wafted forward and curled into his sensitive nose. Green was the first color he saw: lush, tropical plants growing in profusion. Then he saw the women—scores of them, all beautiful, and all as naked as he was himself. They smelled of desire, and, despite his fear, that desire aroused him instantly.

Not knowing what to do, Lynx simply stood by the door but was beginning to feel somewhat relieved by what he saw. Being the slave of women wouldn't be so bad; he was fairly certain they wouldn't beat or torture him. But Lynx had never understood women. Most of the time, he felt intimidated by them—never knowing what to say or do—and had remained alone in the background while his friends found lovers. Granted, he was young, but the concept of enticement was something that Zetithian males generally grasped at an early age; Lynx, however, was mystified.

As he stood there waiting, the women ignored him at first, but his erection eventually elicited a few stares, and soon he was being touched by several soft hands—hands which soon found his hard cock and played in the fluid which had begun to ooze from the scalloped edges of the wide corona on the head. Lynx gasped as they fondled him before pulling him down onto the soft cushions on the floor. He'd never felt such pleasure before in his life. Then one of the women licked him, savoring his fluids until her body contracted in a powerful orgasm. Then another tasted him, and another, and another. He had the same effect on all of them, and they marveled at his attractive feline features and his sexual prowess.

He was the slave of other slaves, and he did whatever they asked, though his own needs were never considered. Not even given food of his own, to survive he had to scavenge what he could from what the women left behind. If they ever felt the need to punish him, they made sure that there was nothing left for him. When they finally gave him permission to eat, they laughed at the way he wolfed down his food.

Still, it was easy at first, for he was young and his sexual desires were at their peak. Day after day he fucked them, fed them, licked them, and massaged them. He catered to their needs and overheard their conversations, but more than anything, they craved his body, for he affected them in a way that no other man had ever done. He was both lover and slave to each of them, who were, in turn, the slaves of a man who owned far more women than he could possibly service.

At first, Lynx didn't understand their language very well, but as he learned, he discovered that the women's greatest fear seemed to be that of bearing his child. Whenever one of them discovered her pregnancy, he saw the terror in her eyes as the others reassured her that Lynx couldn't possibly be the father. This puzzled him greatly, for he could never understand why having his child was such a horrible thing—or why they never did—but he heard it constantly, and his heart grew bitter. They would take what pleasure he could give them but wanted nothing more; not his children, and certainly not his love.

And so, for many years he lived with them, at first only watching as their children were born, then later assisting with the births and caring for the children. He liked the babies and never held it against them that they weren't his own. He could never understand why none of the children ever resembled him, though he'd had intercourse with each and every one of their mothers. After a while, he came to realize that he must have been unable to father children, and this weakened his self-esteem even further.

His sleep was seldom undisturbed, for there was always a woman seeking his attention—whether it was to bring her food or to make love to her—and before long, it all began to seem the same to him. What he had initially considered to be a blessing now became a curse. The sound of female voices began to grate on his nerves,

and the constant bickering among them irritated him
almost to the point of screaming. There was no respite,
no time to himself; they were always there, always
demanding his undivided attention and the sexual
gratification he could give them.

His bitterness grew, and his exhaustion was never-
ending. As time went on, his erections began to diminish,
becoming infrequent before finally ceasing altogether.
Then one day, three men marched into the harem, seized
Lynx, and dragged him out to be resold. He heard some
of the women laughing, and, knowing that they must
have complained about his impotence, any feelings he
might have had for them turned to dust.

Marched naked to the auction block, Lynx was sold
again, but this time, his companions were all male,
which was a welcome change. The men might have
been rough and crude, but they were undemanding, and
Lynx slept well for the first time in many years. His
new owner, a just man who didn't believe in slavery,
told Lynx that after five years of service, he would
be freed. Seeing hope for the first time since he was
enslaved, Lynx put in his time, working hard and learning what the men could teach him, after which he was
freed. He stayed on for several more years, working in
the diamond mines and saving his pay, for he had heard
of a new colony on a planet called Terra Minor where
he could be his own master and live out the remainder
of his days in peaceful solitude.

Peace and quiet were the things he longed for most
of all, but to find that peace, Lynx needed money, so he
saved his own and watched as other men gambled away
their pay or wasted it on the favors of women. As a free

man, Lynx saw women and could smell their desire, but he was never aroused by them, and he avoided them whenever he could, for, having been used and betrayed by women, he now despised them all.

But their voices still haunted his dreams, and he would wake up in a cold sweat with the sound of their laughter echoing through his mind as he was dragged away—not one of them even whispering good-bye.

FUGITIVE

Manx knew she was watching him. The gentle breeze that blew across the deck and sent her erotic scent wafting down toward the lake confirmed it. He stretched upward with his head thrown back, inhaling deeply as he felt his body respond. Within moments, her scent intensified; she was not only aroused, but, judging from the strength of her enticing aroma, she was also naked; there was nothing between them but the cool night air. His mind took that image and savored it—her soft breasts, her hard nipples—and even across the distance that separated them, he could sense the wet heat between her thighs, could almost hear her body calling out to him, and his cock turned to stone.

He closed his eyes and imagined her coming to him, her touch gentle on his skin, her fingers teasing him to a feverish pitch. She was the most intoxicating female he had ever encountered, and he knew that soon, he would mate with her. But for now, he held back, sensing her shyness and knowing just how tenuous his own existence was. He might be captured at any moment and taken from her, though it was easy to ignore that fact when his body was demanding release.

Reaching down, he touched his rigid penis, the orgasm-inducing fluid already beginning to ooze from the starlike coronal points of the head. Pleasuring oneself was almost unheard of among his kind—few Zetithian males were even capable—and though he knew that males of other species engaged in such practices regularly, he'd seldom felt the need for it until encountering her. This woman's scent was particularly potent, and she did things to him no other woman had ever done; made him reckless when he'd been so cautious in the past, made him want to risk everything for the chance to sheathe himself with her and give her joy.

For now, he could only imagine holding her in his arms. As his eyes closed again, he dreamed of her soft lips kissing his stiff shaft, her hot mouth sucking the snard from his testicles, and her entire body crashing into orgasm just from tasting it. He could almost see her deep, auburn hair shimmering in the moonlight, light that was even now caressing her skin as he longed to do himself. He didn't know the color of her eyes—hadn't been close enough yet to discover that secret—but he knew how they would gaze up at him, heavy-lidded with desire, but soft with the expression of her love.

And she *would* love him; he was certain of that. He'd watched her down by the lake while she created her stunning works of art. She imparted the love she felt for those creatures onto the canvas, just as she had with the image she'd painted of him. He'd felt that when he first viewed the portrait; something in the gentle brushstrokes made him feel that she had actually swept her hands over his back, down to his waist and thighs. She had somehow captured not only his image, but her feelings toward him—furtive, tentative, and definitely intrigued.

His cock was slick with his fluid—fluid that he hoped would affect her just as it had affected the women of his world—and his hands tightened around his cock, pumping faster, seeming to pull him forward as though seeking her out. Turning his profile toward her, he let her see what she was doing to him, and he felt a sudden gush of his fluids at the thought of her eyes on him. In his mind, these were no longer his hands, but hers, wrapping him in a firm tunnel, squeezing him hard, tightening so that he had to push even harder to slide through them.

He felt his balls tighten and his breathing grew coarse and ragged as he began purring—whether she could hear him or not. Widening his stance, he let his head fall back, his long, black curls tickling his backside the way hers would as she passed behind him. He wanted to know the feel of her, the taste of her. He knew her eyes were on him, their heated gaze exploring his body—and, knowing that he didn't need to be secretive any longer, he was no longer silent, letting his grunts of effort be as loud as they needed to be, letting her know what she was doing to him.

At last he felt it: the unmistakable signal of impending climax. With an accompanying roar that echoed across the still lake, his balls repeatedly squeezed out his snard in long, powerful arcs. He imagined it hitting her succulent breasts, her beautiful face, and her softly parted lips, and as she tasted it, he could almost see her expression of joy.

As he took in a deep, cleansing breath, he smiled. She had seen him, and he could smell her climax even from where he stood—could even hear her soft sighs of ecstasy. She would be his mate. It was only a matter of time.

HERO

TRAG KNEW IT WAS A MISTAKE TO ATTEND THE WED-
ding. Not that he begrudged Manx and Drusilla their
new state of wedded bliss or that he didn't enjoy seeing
his old friend again, but because he knew he'd be sitting just exactly where he was right now; on Kyra's left
while his brother, Tychar, sat on her right. She was as
warm and lovely as she had been on the day Trag left
Darconia, but just as firmly fixed as his brother's mate
as she had been on the day they met. There was no
getting past fate, destiny, or Zetithian visions, particularly
when they involved a future mate. Tychar had known
Kyra would be his long before he ever saw her; he just
hadn't bothered to mention it to Trag.

Trag was thankful that he was wearing clothing,
which he hadn't done when he and Ty had been slaves
to the Darconian queen, because his reaction to her
scent was the same as always; his cock was so hard he
couldn't think about anything else.

He stared at Jack in a desperate attempt to divert his
thoughts as she performed the wedding ceremony. It
gave Jack great pleasure to be able to have all of the
remaining Zetithians aboard her ship, and gave her even
greater satisfaction to be tying the knot between the last
known Zetithian and his Terran mate.

Finding Manx had been nothing short of a miracle,
and though Trag had prayed to the Great Mother of the

Desert for one more, so far she hadn't been attending to him. He tried turning away from Kyra, but her scent lingered in his head until the shallow breaths he'd been taking finally caught up with him and, inhaling deeply, he succumbed to the memory...

He and Tychar had converged on Kyra immediately. She had said yes, so there had been no point in waiting any longer. He fed her fruit while Tychar wiped the sweat from her body, and Trag tasted her sweetness in every way he could. He licked her lips after each bite until she kissed him, sucking his tongue into her mouth and driving him insane with desire. Her intoxicating kisses soon had him purring like mad as his hands caressed her body. She tasted like hot, wet love and her aroma was like nothing he'd ever imagined, igniting flames of passion that threatened to consume him. When Tychar pulled her thighs apart and urged him to taste the source of her scent, Trag licked her soft, wet lips, thrusting his tongue deep inside her, devouring her until, with a gush of creamy wetness, she came in his face. A triumphant snarl erupted from the depths of his throat, and when Ty pushed her beneath him, Trag didn't hesitate; he buried his stiff shaft in her soft warmth and felt love for the very first time.

Trag lost control after that, fucking her harder than he'd ever fucked anyone in his life. It took a while to regain that control, and when he did, he used every move on her he could think of, purring with delight and enjoying the vision of her lovely eyes and gentle smile.

And then, at his suggestion, she'd sucked Tychar. Trag's balls tightened at the memory of it... He'd never seen a more erotic vision before—or since—and it was

a wonder he hadn't lost it right then, but Ty got there
ahead of him, spraying her face and tongue with his
sweet snard. It was one race Trag didn't mind losing
though, for her orgasm seized his cock and sent him
over the edge. Trag had felt that ejaculation clear down
to his toenails and the double dose of Zetithian semen
had Kyra babbling on about something—just what, he
couldn't recall—but his satisfaction had been complete.
He had given joy to a beautiful woman—a woman he
now loved, but knew he could never call his own.

It was Trag's first, last, and only time with Kyra.
After that, it became clear that she loved Tychar, not
him, and when Queen Scalia's death freed the two men
from slavery, Trag had tried to make the best of it. He
might have withdrawn from Kyra and never tasted her
love again, but he certainly hadn't forgotten it.

He tried to imagine what it would be like to love another woman but it was difficult. Any Terran woman
would remind him too much of Kyra, if for no other reason than her scent. Telling those who urged him to find
a mate that he was holding out for a Zetithian woman
made it easier, first, because it gave him breathing space,
and second, because he knew in his heart he'd never
find one. He was certain they had all perished when
Zetith exploded, and if any had been living offworld,
the Nedwut bounty hunters had surely killed them all by
now. He and his brother had only survived because of
Queen Scalia's protection. What chance would a lone
Zetithian female have against such determined killers?

Though he visited brothels from time to time, he
never recaptured that feeling, and Trag's secret devo-
tion to Kyra never wavered—at least in his waking

moments—but his dreams were confused. Whenever he tried to recall them, the image seemed blurred, as though his own mind was uncertain of whom he should love. Was it Kyra, or was it someone else?

Trag didn't know for sure, but with the marriage of Manx to Drusilla, he was now the last Zetithian without a mate, and he was no closer to finding love than he had been as a slave living among the reptilian Darconians. It shouldn't have been that hard for the pilot of a starship to find the woman he was destined to meet, but, then again, it was a very big galaxy…

—⁓—

Micayla's earliest memory was of a smothering darkness. She could sense her mother's terror as she fled through the crowded spaceport, but wrapped in the folds of Jenall's cloak, she was unable to see the source of it. Nevertheless, she could feel Jenall's sweat and hear her pounding heart and gasping breaths as her mother pushed herself to the limits of her endurance and beyond. Later, Micayla would understand what it meant to be running for one's life, but at the age of two, the concept of fear meant very little.

There were loud noises and the sound of people screaming, but her mother ran on, bumping, jostling, her feet slapping against the smooth floor. Suddenly, Jenall halted and opened her cloak, and Micayla found herself looking up into the face of an odd being—smooth-skinned and dark, with almond-shaped eyes and softly curling ringlets framing her face.

"Take her," Jenall rasped. "Hide her and keep her safe."

The response might have been unintelligible, but

the intent was clear: the woman opened her own cloak and Micayla was thrust into her waiting arms. As they watched, Jenall turned and ran on, but though her brief pause might have saved her daughter's life, it didn't save her own.

Micayla heard her father's roar as Jenall fell into a nerveless heap and saw him whirl around, his long dark hair flowing out behind him as he set his two sons on their feet and ran to his mate's aid. Micayla didn't see any more, for her rescuer turned and hurried away with her precious bundle—leaving the scene as quickly as any prudent bystander would do. Micayla heard three more shots and then silence.

Virgin

by Cheryl Brooks

—◈—

He's never met anyone who made him purr…

Starship pilot Dax never encountered a woman he wanted
badly enough. Until he met Ava Karon…

And he'll never give his body without giving his heart…

Dax is happy to take Ava back to her home planet,
until he finds out she's returning to an old boyfriend…

As their journey together turns into a quest neither expected, Ava
would give herself to Dax in a heartbeat. Except he doesn't know
the first thing about seducing a woman…

—◈—

Praise for The Cat Star Chronicles:

For more Cheryl Brooks, visit:

www.sourcebooks.com

Rogue

by Cheryl Brooks

---

*Tychar crawled toward me on his hands and knees
like a tiger stalking his prey. "I, for one, am glad you came,"
he purred. "And I promise you, Kyra, you
will never want to leave Darconia."*

"Cheryl Brooks knows how to keep the heat on and the
reader turning pages!" —Sydney Croft,
author of *Seduced by the Storm*

Praise for *The Cat Star Chronicles:*

"Wow. Just…wow. The romantic chemistry is as
close to perfect as you'll find." —*BookFetish.org*

"Will make you purr with delight. Cheryl Brooks has a
great talent as a storyteller." —*Cheryl's Book Nook*

For more Cheryl Brooks, visit:

www.sourcebooks.com

Warrior

by Cheryl Brooks

—~~~—

*"He came to me in the dead of winter,
his body burning with fever."*

—~~~—

Even near death, his sensuality is amazing…

Leo arrives on Tisana's doorstep a beaten slave from a near
extinct race with feline genes. As soon as Leo recovers his
strength, he'll use his extraordinary sexual talents to bewitch
Tisana and make a bolt for freedom…

Praise for The Cat Star Chronicles:

"A compelling tale of danger, intrigue, and sizzling
romance!"—Candace Havens, author of *Charmed & Deadly*

"Hot enough to start a fire. Add in a thrilling new world and
my reading experience was complete." *—Romance Junkies*

For more Cheryl Brooks, visit:

www.sourcebooks.com

Slave

by Cheryl Brooks

———∿∿———

"I found him in the slave market on Orpheseus Prime, and even on such a god-forsaken planet as that one, their treatment of him seemed extreme."

———∿∿———

Cat may be the last of a species whose sexual talents were the envy of the galaxy. Even filthy, chained, and beaten, his feline gene gives him a special aura.

Jacinth is on a rescue mission… and she needs a man she can trust with her life.

Praise for Slave:

"A sexy adventure with a hero you can't resist!"— Candace Havens, author of *Charmed & Deadly*

"Fascinating world customs, a bit of mystery, and the relationship between the hero and heroine make this a very sensual romance."—*Romantic Times*

For more Cheryl Brooks, visit:

www.sourcebooks.com

Acknowledgments

Unlike my previous books, in which I relied heavily on my own imagination, the writing of *Stud* required some research. Also, beginning with the writing of *Virgin*, I discovered the joy of working with a critique partner, as well as input from beta readers prior to its publication. With *Stud*, I began using both of those tools much earlier in the process with what I hope are favorable results.

And so, for their assistance in the writing process, I'd like to thank:

"Atlatl" Bob Perkins, who maintains that the atlatl is what put humans at the top of the food chain, for his instructional YouTube videos.

EDGO23 for the videos on how to make arrowheads using the flint knapping technique.

johnjayrambo11111 whose bow-making videos contained only one line of dialogue: "Gonna make a bow using only this knife," and then demonstrated that it could, indeed, be done.

paleoaleo for the videos on the use of deer antlers to make flint knapping tools.

wildernessoutfitters for their videos on how to make bowstrings, arrows and how to fletch them, as well as primitive rope making techniques.

My critique partner, Sandy James, for her invaluable help in writing this book.

My agent, Melissa Jeglinski, for her editing expertise and for putting up with my moods.

Beta readers April Payton, Mary Grzesik, and Shanna Pemberton for their help in smoothing out the manuscript.

My friends, fellow writers, and family whose support and encouragement helped keep me going.

And all the folks at Sourcebooks for believing in me.

I couldn't have done it without you!

About the Author

A native of Louisville, Kentucky, Cheryl Brooks is a critical care nurse by night and a romance writer by day. A lifelong lover of horses and animals in general, she lives with her husband, two sons, two horses, four cats, and two dogs in rural Indiana. She enjoys cooking, gardening, and has played guitar since the age of ten. A member of the RWA and INRWA, her previously published works include The Cat Star Chronicles series: *Slave*, *Warrior*, *Rogue*, *Outcast*, *Fugitive*, *Hero*, and *Virgin*. Utilizing her rich fantasy life and a knack for unobtrusive boy watching, she is currently branching out from paranormal romance into erotic novellas, both contemporary and paranormal, and loving it!